The Captain and The Candles

Life is as a candle's flame;
when one flickers and passes so will the other

By Gary J. Pool

Published by Gary J. Pool

Tabor, Iowa

The Captain and The Candles

This book is a work of fiction. Names, characters, places and incidents are the product of the author's imagination or are used fictitiously. Any resemblance to actual events, locales or persons is coincidental.

Published by Pool Publishing, Tabor, Iowa 51653

Printed in the United States of America
by Instantpublisher.com

ISBN: 978-0-615-56330-5

I would like to extend a special thank you to my wife Jan and to my daughters Andi, Pam, Loretta, and Lorna for their assistance with book preparation, their opinion, support and encouragement that has made this publication possible.

Contents

Prologue

The mid 1850's found the nation's attention focused on the Midwestern states and territories. Slavery, a volatile topic since the days of the Declaration of Independence had been bantered back and forth in congress for over fifty years. The politician's in congress only answer to the problem was to pass the buck in hopes the whole ordeal would magically disappear. The northern states representatives fueled by religious fervor fought for complete abolishment of slavery while the southern contingent, mostly for economic reasons, demanded its preservation in the original states. A second great fight developed over the admittance of new states from the vast western territories carved out of the Louisiana Purchase.

Iowa had achieved statehood in 1846, entering as a free state; however ten years later the southwestern corner along the Missouri River drainage remained a sparsely populated lawless prairie. Small towns and villages struggled to gain a foothold in the wild primitive hills and bluffs that lined the Missouri and Nishnabotna River valleys.

Southwest Iowa lacked roads, communication or building materials. Even in this lush green fertile land, food was often times difficult to come by. The basic daily existence that the immigrants had known in the east often proved difficult to obtain. But strong religious beliefs and a never ending dedication to the work at hand carried the faithful through the most trying of times. A town would be founded, a church built and a school of higher education erected from the native lumber and locally produced red brick from a clay deposit located on the north edge of town.

James Lang, born to southern aristocracy, the son of a wealthy slave owner had been educated in the best colleges and military schools the south had to offer. Nothing was too good for the Lang's; they enjoyed the finest clothes, fastest horses, and gourmet foods. James had served with valor in the Mexican War as a Captain in the American Army. However garrison duty after the war proved too monotonous for the young cavalier leading to his resignation from the military, followed by a few misadventures as a mercenary.

A short trip home and a long conversation with a worried senior James Lang found the handsome young officer riding north with the intention of infiltrating and spying on the now notorious Reverend John Brown and his army of abolitionists. This mission sounded simple enough to the young adventurous man but his lack of experience with the gang of rabid northern abolitionists and the train crews of the Underground Railroad would prove a daunting task.

The south's uneducated runaway slaves knew little of geography but were told in songs and stories to follow the drinking gourd in the sky; which meant looking for the

North Star located at the end of the big dipper handle. Walking at night toward the North Star would invariably lead the runaways into a free state where sanctuary could be found. The runaway slaves were also told to look for a single candle burning in windows of the northern houses which might indicate an abolitionist's home. A towel draped over a front gate or marks left by previous travelers were also signs of possible salvation.

The runaways moved cautiously at night hoping to find a station on the Underground Railroad where conductors would pass them along to another safe house. It was true that no real railroads existed in the far reaches of the midwest at that time but this loosely knit organization did their best to move the contraband goods along at a fast pace.

James Lang knew little of the operation of the Underground Railroad nor the signs of safety. He did however know the fugitive slave laws that made harboring an escaped slave a federal offense. He was also aware of the slave chasers who were well paid to track down, even in Free states, and forcibly return slaves to their southern owners.

On his arrival to Mt. Zion, Captain James Lang would find a new world; a world of lies, deceit and violence; the likes of which he had never experienced. He would have to learn the rules quickly if he hoped to survive the ordeal that lay ahead. The young Captain would face a test of his religion, a trial of physical pain, but the worst experience would be derived from a broken heart that would plague him the rest of his life.

A CANDLE LIGHTING

Bong.... Bong.... Bong.... the reverberations danced through the hot dry air and across the courtyard. The sound flowed through the open door and pane-less windows of the small one room adobe house with its unmended thatched roof which leaked profusely in the wet season. The only closure on the doorway was a thin tattered blanket tinted in alternating red and yellow bands. Smoke stains and cooking spills marked the front of the mud plastered fireplace that engulfed most of east wall. The west wall held two small windows and below them stood the only piece of furniture to be found in the house, a bed. It was poorly hand-made from slender tree limbs and tied together with leather thongs. Its mattress, crude by any standard, was a large canvas sack stuffed with dried wild grass that rustled and clumped up with every movement of the occupant.

Flies and mosquitoes among other pests moved at will through the hut's windows and door to torment whatever creature may be in habitation at the time. The present squatter lay sprawled over the mattress, his profuse sweat mingled unnoticed with the already stained and odorous canvas mattress cover. His pale blue-grey eyes stared off into the deeper blue sky outside the window, as forlorn thoughts and images formed in his fevered brain. Now and then a soft bong, bong from the bell tower of the abandoned Catholic

Church across the empty courtyard would pierce his clouded thoughts.

Destiny or God's punishment for a life of sin, in either case, was a poor end to a life that had started with so much good will and promise. The once healthy athletic body lay gaunt and weak. The wound in his lower abdomen oozed a dark pungent fluid continually now. Fever combined with another bout of malaria, raged unabated through the middle aged man's organs day and night.

What would old Doc Bright back home do to save a patient in these straights? He thought. *Tennessee was a world away now and not just in miles but in time and shape. Besides, old Doc passed away during the "War of Rebellion" as he called it.*

What was his first name, anyway? The exhausted brain quizzed itself. *Seems like it started with a "G", but everyone just called him Doc Bright or Old Doc; everyone except father, who had known him before he set up a practice in town.*

Arsenic, about a pinch in a cup of hot tea and honey to cover the bitter taste administered twice a day would be his prescription. No doubt a double spoonful of castor oil once a day would help purge out the body, at least according to Old Doc's way of thinking. No matter, Doc's gone and there's not a real physician within a hundred miles of this sun burned piece of earth. Gideon, yes, Gideon Newton Bright, that was old Doc's full name; quite a title for man of such small stature and feminine features but a good man and even more dedicated doctor. He remembered now.

"James Lang!" he would scold in his high pitched voice, "you will come to no good with all your devilment." Old Doc's prediction seemed to have come to fulfillment in the passing of time, the pain-ravished brain admitted.

Remorse is a bitter medicine at best and seldom cures anything, yet little else could be done at the moment. Thoughts of harsh words, false accusations, and bitter feuds filtered through the burning brain. Memories of whispered words, sweet perfume, and flattering phrases came to mind only to be overshadowed by the guilt of love lost. Scenes of large green trees and expansive lawns trodden by beautiful young women in long flowing dresses, warm greetings by family and friends were only dreams now; dreams whose time had long since faded into a mental fog of fever and pain. But they did exist once, he was sure of that, somewhere in a time long ago. A time before the brand of traitor preceded his name and a curse succeeded it.

Those family ties were long since broken; in truth, most had passed. His friends had all traveled the same road to oblivion, old friends now long dead and gone as he would shortly be with no one to care or mourn the loss. It seemed a harsh enough death here alone for a brave and honest man; but for no one to be saddened made it doubly so.

A man meets many people in life, both good and

bad, and of all these, there is only one his heart yearned to be informed of the demise of James Lang. After so many years whatever feelings that may have existed were surely gone but still the knowledge of a deception completed should be verified. If only a final message could be sent to the one who still stirs the heart and warms the soul.

Bong, bong, pealed the bell softly, then a pause, bong, bong. Must be birds, his weary mind reasoned for the breeze is far too gentle to affect the bell clapper. The bells mock 'call to services' of a famished parish gave notice that the flame of life still remained in the soldier's ravished body; and where a flicker of fire endured so does hope persist. Not a hope for life but rather a chance to relieve the burden of one so dear.

If only there were paper and pen, a letter could be composed for whoever finds these pitiful remains. Perhaps a peon will pass before the all consuming last breath and will hear the sad story and relay it to his Petron in hopes that they may pass it along. That is the only wish that burns now in a body ragging with heat; not a wish for life, but for solace.

The hot steamy haze of the brain separates once more, and the bell's soft bong, bong drifts through the mist. But there is an accompanying beat this time, one not heard before. Faint though it may be, the rhythm continues even after the bell's final ghostly refrain. *Louder, yes it's more distinct now and growing closer, it must be hoof beats, praise God.* The gaining intensity of the steady clop, clop, clop seemed more beautiful than any musical note from the finest orchestra. *Whether it be friend or foe, a messenger arrives delivering aid or an ending of life, either would be welcomed.*

The hoof beats stopped near the church and faint words passed between two men but the words were quickly evaporated by the scorching dry air. His ears recognized the sound of sandals scrapping slowly across the hard baked ground of the courtyard as they approach the small hut. All sounds from without ceased, no movement can be distinguished so it's now or never. The soldier's feeble body is commanded by an even more distressed brain to summons up all its reserve of strength hoping to make its presence known.

Yell, throw something, or at least move to attract the attention of whoever is standing outside that window in the burning sunlight. Whatever the action taken, it must be done now. Exert all of your will power, all your strength and bring on a signal of some sort. A famous rebel yell, or an Indian war cry, calls the steaming brain had recorded so many times would serve most adequately. Concentrate, strain, take a deep breath and "hello", *yes that was it, faint but certainly effectual.* But the effort was too much for the ravished body, so once again the protective brain shuts down and prevents any outburst.

Slowly and with great difficulty the soldiers thoughts clear; a cool breeze floats through the open window and bathes his body in gentle relief. *I can't be dead,* he thought. *Certainly there are no cooling breezes in hell.* The thoughts are interrupted by the sound of mumbling and then bong, bong. *A sign that life lingers on in my old body,* he thought. *But what is that moaning sound? I must open my eyes and face whatever awaits me, the delirious brain ordered. Open and face the music, for if it is Satan, I'm ready.*

There kneeling beside the crude bed, his partially opened eyes beheld a small man dressed in brown sack cloth, his gray head bowed in prayer. "Who are you?" The soldier managed to whisper.

The mumbling ceased and the small head turned up slowly to reveal a narrow bony face covered with brown leathery looking skin, eyes black as night and a smile that spread across the entire mass. "I'm Father Francis," came the soft reply.

The two vastly different men eyed each other intently, and a quiet fell over the small hut. "You are American?" the Father asked.

"Yes, I'm from the United States," the soldier answered weakly, "name is Captain James Lang."

"Well Captain, we . . . my men and I found you here a few hours ago and have since bathed you and dressed your wound, hoping to give you some relief."

"Thank you and your men, Father, for the kindness but I never expected to see another human this side of the great divide." James said.

"Normally you would not, but we came here to our old mission to remove the bell to replace the cracked one at our new church. God does work in mysterious ways," the Father said in a religious tone, "I only wish we had come sooner to your aid."

"Your timing is perfect Father, for it's now that I really need you. I fear this wound would have proven fatal no matter at what point you may have found me." James Lang said in a matter-of-fact tone.

"I will hear your confession and give you absolution if that is what you desire." The priest said with a reassuring pat of his hand on the wounded man's shoulder.

"No Father, it's not salvation I think of now." James hesitated a moment resting and drawing a long breath. "I must make a death-bed declaration with you as a reliable witness. One who can record it and pass it along to those who need to know of it." James whispered. "If you will do that for me Father, it will lighten my burden so and bring about an end to a life of torment and mistrust of others."

"It would be against my vows to aid in a sin if that's what you are asking my son." The aged priest replied.

"I would never ask any such sacrilege of a holy man but rather I desire only to bare my soul and at the same time erase the trouble and doubt in many people who cared for me." A silent pause passed between the two men as Father Francis searched his heart for guidance and James' mind raced through arguments to persuade this deeply devout man to comply with this simple request.

7

The sweet gentle desert breeze floated in the windows and out the door of the small adobe hut, its soft touch cooled the skin where the good Father had applied a damp cloth.

"Perhaps if I were to tell you the tale, the complete and truthful tale of my descent into purgatory, you would consent to my last wish." The wounded soldier whispered weakly.

The aged priest's dark eyes pierced deeply into James Lang's feverish blue unwavering orbs and quickly divined that they reflected a heart and soul of a good and true man. As the men talked the lengthening evening shadows forced the old priest to light a nub of a candle and place it on the top end of the bedpost. Its flame danced and flickered in the breeze and gave a shadowy appearance to the smooth mud colored walls.

"Yes, I would be most happy to hear your life's story my son, for we have all this long night for the telling." Father Francis said with a smile while touching his wrinkled slender fingers on James' large meaty hand.

"No Father, I must hurry for I fear my life is as that candle's flame; when one flickers and passes so will the other, and the tallow in that candle seems to melt at a rapid rate."

"Very well my son, tell your story in any way you choose, it will be my privilege to hear of your life." The small priest strained to lift the wounded soldiers head and place a wooden cup of red wine to his swollen blistered lips. "Just a few swallows for strength first," he whispered.

"Thank you." Lang replied and lay back as the wine took effect and eased the discomfort raging in his body. Long slow breaths seemed to aid in relaxing the mind as his thoughts drifted back to those days so long ago, a time of great energy and a future bright with prospect for life and love.

"As I stated earlier Father, this is not a confession in the religious sense but you may take it that way if it is comforting to your belief." James started in a flat tone.

PRELUDE TO A CONFESSION

I was born and raised to the affluence of the south, with all the decadence and privilege its wealth could provide. Those innocent days of youth were spent in enjoyable pursuits; riding, hunting, partying in excess, extracted through the wages of sweat and degradation of others. As a boy I never considered where all this lavish existence originated but assumed it was preordained and was my destiny in life. There was always this shield around us children, a sphere of glass that prevented truth and reason from penetrating our hearts and minds. So complete was this ideology that even the black servants who we came in contact with daily reinforced the tenets preached by our elders. It was not until entering the U.S. Military Academy that any exposure to abolitionism ever fell on my naive ears.

Graduation from the academy was followed by service in war down here; garrison duty in the west, chasing savages and long spells of boredom. In the 1850's the tedium of military life on the Great Plains drove many of the younger officers, including myself, to resign in search of more exciting pursuits. With fathers blessing and financial support, I traveled about in search of adventure, much akin to the knights of old looking to right wrongs and protect the helpless. What foolish vain notions filled our empty heads in those days, service to God and country, childish dreams. In truth we were nothing but mercenaries, part of the

11

illness rather than the cure, spreading the disease as we traveled.

In the spring of 1856 a wealthy abolitionist of my acquaintance offered a paid position in the Border States area providing military training to a small band of religious zealots, who had grand plans but no actual military knowledge of war. Father encouraged my taking the placement with these antislavery factions in hopes of infiltrating their ranks for the benefit of his cause, the expansion of slavery in America.

I was visiting friends in Kansas City where it was rumored one might find employment of a military nature due to the conflict raging in that border area. The word of my desire to serve the abolitionist's cause spread and as luck and some treachery would have it; I managed to meet the famous John Brown. He was impressed with my credentials that my friends bolstered by adding a few white lies. In short he offered me the position of training officers for his army. I jumped at the offer and shipped my horse and belongings upriver by steamer, arriving in Nebraska City in late April to find a community ripe with whispered secrets and skullduggery. There were rumors of run-away slaves being hidden near the town and being transported east across the river to awaiting eager curriers. It was reported that the Reverend John Brown had passed through the area the day before my landing. This was the man I was to join in Iowa and whose troops I was to train. Curious as to the man's true nature, my gentle inquires produced very little in the way of useful knowledge, other than personal opinions as to his true intent.

After purchasing a few supplies, I crossed the Missouri River on Col. Hick's steam ferry and rode north by east as directed, stopping in a small town on the river bottom then known as Cutter's Landing. The cordial people of Cutter's Landing who were affiliated with John Brown and his beliefs provided detailed directions on the route best taken by a stranger to arrive safely at my destination.

The country was one of rich bountiful hills and valleys overgrown with lush green vegetation and flowering plants which required only the hand of man to turn into a Garden of Eden. It was easy to see why these people had abandon homes in the settled and secure east to build a new life in this fertile land. The ride across the flat floodplain ended abruptly at the base of high sheer-walled bluffs where I was told the confluence of Wide Creek and the Missouri bottom would be found. I quickly discovered the reported faint trail that led into the wide mouth of the free flowing muddy stream. It was said this creek could be followed all the way to my destination, the small hill top town of Mt. Zion.

The creek was lined with tall hardwood trees while the high bluff tops were barren except for the long narrow bladed native grass which danced to the wind's continual songs. Eagles and hawks soared gracefully in wide circles far above the summits of these strangely formed bluffs. What a solemn place, one a man could dream of passing his life's precious days enjoying, but duty called and I pressed on up the narrowing valley for several miles. The water flow slackened and began to clear as it neared the original spring that rushed from the soil near the top of a grass covered hill. At the crest one could view the small hamlet of Mt. Zion; its white houses and tall church steeple reflecting the bright sun now at my back. The scene held my attention for several moments as the buildings seemed to dance and weave in the heat waves that rose betwixt us. What would this town hold for me, the adventurer; new friends or enemies, life, love, or maybe death? Whatever it was, I felt eager to confront the challenge that lay before me on that hot spring afternoon.

I soon crossed a faint wagon road that led into the south end of a main street where it ascended a long hill past several small log homes of not too affluent appearance. The wide street topped out onto a large flat treeless open area of irregular borders approximately three quarters of a mile north to south and nearly a full mile east to west. Laid out along the north-south street were two blocks of general stores, small shops, livery and harness makers. The one blaring omission was the lack of any tavern or inn where a body might slake ones thirst after a dusty ride or to gain information concerning the community affairs. Not spying any town hall or municipal offices, I stopped at the blacksmith shop to obtain information as to where I should report my presence.

Now, nearly every Ferrier shop that I have ever patronized had its share of loafers and spectators; however this one contained not one except the smithy and his apprentice, both men of few words.

Perhaps a stranger posing in formal dress and speaking with a southern accent might put them on the defensive. I thought. So I quickly moved on to the next establishment, that of a dress maker.

The Iowa soil is rich black fine loam that requires little rain to produce a sticky paste; a little more and the land becomes a miring mass and a quickly passing early morning shower had easily liquefied this rich soil into a rich mud. The small budding settlement had very few civilized improvements. Hard surfaced streets or sidewalks were unheard of except in the form of rough cut slabs of sawmill by-products. These were often laid bark side down into the soft soil to allow some egress about the small commercial area of town. Being of irregular thickness and rounded like the logs they originated from, traversing the rudimentary walks could prove quite treacherous. The proprietor of the dress shop had recently installed just such a convenience for her clientele and treading on the dry but rolling unfamiliar surface quickly proved my undoing. Losing my balance on one particularly long narrow piece, I side-stepped to another that immediately skidded out from under foot depositing me backside first onto the wooden walkway. This most ungraceful fall was observed by the occupants of the dress shop who all raced clatteringly through the narrow doorway to my embarrassing rescue. Three trim young ladies and one heavy set middle-aged matronly woman swarmed about the accident site chattering, unsure as to what course of action propriety would allow in this situation. The impact had cracked the back of my head on one particularly large piece of wood and additionally knocked the wind from my body. I lay covered in thick Iowa mud, head reeling, trying to catch my breath and being subjected to the four women's babbling when a soft warm hand touched my forehead. The caress was tender and ever so gentle, like that of a cooling breeze on a warm summer eve. A beautiful fragrance of unknown name filled my nostrils and though stunned, I determined it emanated from the delicate hand that soothed my suffering.

As my wits slowly returned and my eyes cleared, they focused on the most glorious face this side of heaven's own angels. There, at less than arm's length, hovered the face of a young lady; her natural red lips smiled while mouthing consoling words of pity. She was blessed with the fairest complexion and the most brilliant green eyes that sparkled and danced with a certain amount of mirth. Ringlets of shinning black hair escaped from her bonnet and fell around that mesmerizing face, framing it in a radiant glow. This angel of mercy had knelt down beside me among the wooden slabs and mire to render as much assistance as was possible to a mishappened stranger. The heavy dark mud had already soiled her bright blue dress and hands as she gingerly lifted my bleeding head up and rested it in her waiting lap.

"I tell you, Father, if man had the power to foresee the future and I had known mine that day, I would have crawled on hands and knees to my waiting horse and rode with all speed away from that tiny village. But the human spirit is often lacking in judgment when concerning matters of the heart and I am perhaps the weakest example of that race."

I looked into those green eyes and they into mine and our hearts and souls were forever entwined like the honey suckle vine becomes attached to a garden trellis. At that instant I knew and she knew we were experiencing something that happens only once in the course of a lifetime and then only to the fortunate few. She stopped her consoling banter, her hand ceased to soothe my battered head and both were frozen in time unable to speak or even breathe. Messages flew between our locked eyes with the speed of lighting as if Zeus were the telegrapher tapping out the coded words. Only these words could be received by none other than her and I; all others were deaf to the symbols that filled the air. I lay in the euphoric comfort of her lap being dissolved by the jade colored irises, engulfed into the black holes that served as pupils, my image dissected by her brain. Life could have and mercifully should have ended in that one brief moment of ecstasy but the blessing of death eluded me, substituting in its stead a life of heartache and anguish.

The middle aged matronly woman broke the spell by shaking the green eyed woman's shoulder with growing vigor, calling her name repeatedly. "Jessanne, Jessanne, answer me, are you all right?" The self induced incantation was over and the beautiful slim face and the flashing green eyes turned reluctantly from me in response to the urgent calls from above.

"Yes," she mumbled, "yes, I'm fine, just trying to be a Good Samaritan to this injured soul, Mrs. Pratt."

"You frightened me child," Mrs. Pratt blurted out, "I thought this handsome stranger had put you in a trance that might steal your soul forever."

"Now, Mrs. Pratt you know the Church elders discourage such talk of trances, spells and such. It is blasphemy after all and they will demand penance from those who speak of such things." Jessanne scolded in self-defense.

I managed to right myself and make a more proper introduction to the town's folk who had gathered at the sight of my mishap. All seemed genuinely concerned for my health, especially a Mr. Darius Hunter, husband to the proprietor of the shop in front of which I had fallen. Hunter was a short fat middle aged man dressed in a long black suit coat and pants to match; only the former appeared much newer than the latter. His small bald head was edged with white hair which formed a wreath just above the two nubbins serving as ears which supported the legs of his wire-framed glasses. The other end of the spectacles consisted of two tiny gold wire loops which balanced precariously in the middle of the sharp ridge of a very large nose. Mr. Hunter's voice was high pitched and nasally but he spoke very eloquently as he made introductions of the three ladies and many of the other towns people. However, I was oblivious to all except for the beautiful green-eyed angel who had soiled her gown while administering to my bloody head.

I heard only the name of Mrs. Joshua Gates, wife of the minister to the only church allowed in this small village. *"Jessanne, Jessanne,"* that's what the matronly woman had called her; Jessanne, the name echoed through my head and buzzed in my ears, drowning out all other names and information that Mr. Hunter attempted to bestow on me. I'm sure the onlookers attributed my inattentiveness to the blow to my head and not to the blow to my heart. *How could it be that this woman who had struck a chord so deep in my soul be the wife of another?* I stuttered and stammer for appropriate words when the introductions ceased but my heart was breaking while at the same time my brain whirled with excitement at the very thought of her name, Jessanne. I longed to make my excuses and flee the area and quite possibly the town itself, but something held me as if I were mired knee-deep in that rich Iowa mud and unable to extract myself.

The conversation continued with Mr. Hunter as he suggested possible lodgings and where to locate John Brown at that time of day. During those brief words my eyes uncontrollably fell on those mystical green orbs of angelic Jessanne. We locked vision repeatedly for long seconds at a time, until one or the other was torn away by outside distraction. It was the most powerful seconds of my life up to that time and indeed remains so to this very moment. There are no words that can define what I believe she and I experienced in that first magical meeting on that mud covered hilltop in Iowa.

CANDLELIGHT ACROSS THE COMMON

The matronly lady led Jessanne reluctantly away while Mr. Hunter escorted me down the grass lined impassable street to the house of a Mr. Calvin Vest. The Vest home sat just south of the commercial block on a large treeless lot very nearly devoid of vegetation. The Vest family was made up of eleven children, some hogs, numerous dogs and two small goats that passed the day destroying any and all plant life trying to exist in the house yard. The building itself, one of recent construction, was a four-room one story design with several windows and doors that the brood of children, hogs, dogs and goats scurried in and out of continuously. The congenial Mr. Vest invited me to share his humble lodgings but it took very little thought to decide against any such habitation. I needed a place of quiet and privacy, and I might add one of dignity if I were to serve as training officer to a group of raw recruits.

Mr. Vest recommended that I contact a Mrs. Mills who often took in travelers or others wishing to find lodging of a non-permanent nature. The Mills' house was a small two-story combination log and rough cut frame structure one block west of the main business district. The house sat on the southwest corner opposite of a large treeless park that encompassed one block square and was surrounded by several of the immigrant's recently fabricated log homes. The white church I had seen when first approaching Mt. Zion sat in a very prominent position directly across the street from the north side of the grassy park. I learned this church was the only house of worship in the community and would, I understand, remain so for many years to come. With my head still ringing from the fall at the dressmaker's shop, I timidly approached through the open front yard gate, careful to step around the treacherous wooden slabs employed as a walk-way, and sidled up to the Mills' home front door.

A gentle knock on the open door's frame produced a high pitched feminine squeal from deep inside the buildings shadowy interior. "Is this the Mills residence?" I called in my most winning voice.

"Yes – yes," came a hesitant reply from a round ruddy middle aged face that suddenly peeked around the doorframe of the next room.

"I am Mrs. Mills, what may I do for you?" The woman asked in a curious warm manner.

"My name is James Lang; a Mr. Vest directed me here in search of lodging."

"Oh, Mr. Lang!" Mrs. Mills said excitedly, moving her short round matronly body through the doorway and waddling hurriedly across the parlor floor to greet me. "The whole town has been expecting you for several days now. Won't you please come in?" her offer was filled with warmth and sincerity.

I had no more than cleared the front doorsill when the woman saw the still bleeding wound on my head and demanded she be allowed to dress it properly. She sat me down on a straight backed wooden chair before hurrying off to retrieve a pan of warm water and clean cloth to make a bandage for my head. I protested slightly that all this fuss was not needed but the woman would not hear of it.

Mrs. Mills tenderly attended to the minor cut, all the while interrogating me on how my head was injured and what exactly I would be doing in town. The woman had a pleasant way about her and the friendly conversation after a long lonely trip was indeed quite welcome. With the medical attention complete, Mrs. Mills insisted we share hot tea and cookies as we discussed my need for lodging while in town.

The room she had to offer turned out to be a small one-room out-building probably intended to serve as a cookhouse or washhouse. It consisted of a log-walled cube with a single bed, heat stove, small table and wash stand. While spartan by eastern standards, it would be ideal for my irregular comings and goings required while serving in the capacity of a military training officer. My new lodging, while constructed of native logs was of a sound workmanship, no cracks in the chinking or leaks in the shake-shingled roof. Mrs. Mills would provide meals and laundry service as my needs might require depending on duties call.

The lady and I struck a deal on the spot without any further shopping on my part about this little settlement, as the situation was nearly perfect. The Mills' house was situated close to town, the church, and the park that would be used as parade ground for the men that I was expected to train.

Mrs. Mills also offered a stall in the small shed out back to stable my magnificent stallion and the use of a pasture not far away. It seemed I had happened upon the perfect accommodations for a man of my limited needs. The amiable landlady then led me back to her front gate with the intention of pointing out as many of the important features of the area as could be seen from that vantage point. Proudly, Mrs. Mills directed my attention to the newly erected church that was the center of all community life and one of the reasons for the town's founding in the first place. Her history of the religious movement was followed by a cordial invitation to attend any and all activities at the church including Sunday services, week-night Bible study, dinners and picnics. I thanked her politely but managed to do so without making any commitment to take part in such somber events. Little did I know at that moment how enthusiastic I would become for being exposed to this new religion.

Our visual tour continued as Mrs. Mills pointed out and named the owners of the various houses that were located across the narrow dirt street bordering the large square park. The first, a small log home belonged to a Mr. Kimball who was the town's blacksmith. It was followed by the two story white frame home of Mr. and Mrs. Boyd. Mr. Boyd was one of the town's original founders, surveyor and leading deacon of the church. It was because of Mrs. Boyd's generous donations that the town was able to pay for the materials to be imported for such a fine edifice which also served as the meeting house.

As sinful as it may be, the next house on Mrs. Mills' guided tour was the one that would draw all my attention or perhaps distraction would be a better word, for the remainder of my stay in Mt. Zion. This magical dwelling was the home of Reverend Joshua Gates and his beautiful wife Jessanne, the angel of mercy who so lovingly ministered to my needs after the fall at the dress shop.

Mrs. Mills continued to name those remaining residences surrounding the park but my mind and my eyes drifted back to the small white house where my heart yearned to be at this moment. However it was not to be on this warm pleasant evening for Mrs. Mills insisted I join her and Mr. Mills for supper. These first days' experiences were all quite new to my spartan lifestyle and I had never been one to yield to desire or flirtation as many men who travel about do. And yet I had never been drawn so powerfully to any cause, religion, or person as I was to this dainty enchanting woman. I felt like a drowning man caught in the torrent of a swollen river, powerless to swim and no one attempting to throw a life line. I had just met the most fascinating woman in the world but she was married to one of the most influential men in the area.

"Yes, thank you very much. I would appreciate a good meal and the opportunity to meet Mr. Mills." I answered my new landlady after finally clearing my mind of the enchanted image of the spellbinding Mrs. Gates. And so it was with great reservation that I settled into the community of Mt. Zion, Iowa hundreds of miles from my home and yet only a few rods away from where I really desired to be.

Mrs. Mills set a splendid table; and Mr. Mills was a good-natured man of about fifty years who had been solicited to move to Mt. Zion to establish a general mercantile store. As we dined the couple explained that this was a one-church town, dedicated to bringing Christianity and advanced education to southwest Iowa.

"You won't find any drinking or gambling establishment within the city limits or for that matter within gunshot range of the town's boundaries." Mr. Mills commented.

This was to be expected, but the suspicion which peaked my interest was the fact that the members of this church were hardened abolitionist, committed to the suppression of slavery.

"Certainly," I said, a bit shocked at Mr. Mills' candor to a stranger, "such God fearing people would not break federal law and ignore the fugitive slave act. I can only speak for myself sir, in that I have never knowingly broken any of God's commandments nor I pray any of man's laws."

"I must warn you that Reverend Brown is something of a fanatic when it comes to the topic of slavery in this country." Mills replied.

"Yes, I have heard rumors of this man who calls himself Captain Brown. Do you know where he earned his rank?" I asked inquisitively.

"I asked Reverend Brown that very question;" Mr. Mills smiled coyly, "the good Captain informed me that it was a rank bestowed upon him by God. Captain Brown is an officer of the Lord's Army to liberate the slaves and purge this land of sin and injustice."

"Now, now, Mr. Mills," Mrs. Mills said softly.

"Well Mrs. Mills, that is the very words the man said to me on the front steps of the only church in this town." Mr. Mills retorted before directing his words back at me. "But you may judge for yourself for it is with Captain Brown that you will be working while in our little settlement."

"I thank you for your honesty and I'm sure I will indeed discern the man's true character during my service here in Mt. Zion."

After some pleasant small talk I excused myself for the night with Mrs. Mills promising to call me before breakfast in the morning. I then wandered out the back door into the house yard and the days gathering dusk where I easily found the path leading to my new dwelling. I paused midway of the journey to watch the lamps and candles being lit in an attempt to obliterate the overwhelming darkness that was slowly devouring the hilltop settlement of Mt. Zion.

I stared intently into the blackness at the position across the park where my senses told me the home of Reverend Gates was located. Long torturous minutes of uncertainty passed without so much as a glow of a single match through the nearly two hundred yards of gathering gloom that divided my lonely position and that of Jessanne Gates. Finally when night had enveloped the hilltop and all shapes were indistinguishable, a single flickering candle flame struggled to life in one of the front windows of the Gates house. It was a sad lonely little light compared to the well illuminated houses surrounding the great open parade ground, but it offered complete solace to my empty heart as I stood in total darkness in the midst of the Mills family backyard. That solitary candle flame brought reassurance to me that Jessanne was home in the bosom of her family at a time of day when the lady of the house should be home. This viewing of the single candle flame would become a ritual nearly every evening of my stay at the Mills house. Little did I know it would come to signify different meanings and evoke a wide range of emotions in my tormented soul.

RECONNISSENCE OF MT. ZION

I awoke early suffering stiffness and a headache from the previous day's fall. I limped outside my room to observe the new day being born clear and hot with little air moving and the humidity high enough to cause a body to break a sweat just taking a leisurely breakfast at Mrs. Mills' bountiful table. Mr. Mills had generously consented to show me around the town and perform proper introductions to those I would meet on a day-to-day basis. Immediately after the breakfast meal was finished Mr. Mills ushered me out the door and down the dirt street that led to the small business district only a block away. On arriving at the corner of the wide still muddy thoroughfare intended to be the main street, and what was hoped to become the most important area of the new village, we encountered the Reverend John Brown.

The man was mounted on a feeble boney looking horse covered in sweat and whose head drooped in exhaustion. The Reverend showed many of the same traits as his weary mount, raw boned and unkempt would be an apt description of the person who would later gain such notoriety. Brown's long grey beard and slow difficult movements as he dismounted to greet me said much about the man's age and state of physical condition.

Mr. Mills offered formal greetings and we shook hands in the normal custom between men down through the ages. The Reverend Brown's only acknowledgement of our prior introduction was a nod of his head and the gruff mumbling of my last name.

"Have you been out on another scouting trip on that poor animal?" Mills asked in a reprimanding tone.

"Someone must patrol the surrounding country for there are spies and scoundrels lurking around every corner in this state." Brown replied coolly. I found the man lacked any sense of humor or for that matter, not the least bit of compassion.

"Yes, yes," Mills agreed, "but I have offered you the use of my saddle horse as have several others for these long forays into the wilds. Someday this old horse will give out on you miles from town and you will be forced to employ shanks mare for the return trip."

"This is the animal the Lord provided for my use in his glorious cause so it will suffice until he decides to render unto me a new form of transportation." Brown argued hotly, obviously offended that anyone would question his judgment. This was a lesson I quickly learned and attempted to implement while associating with the famed Reverend Brown.

The hour neared seven o'clock and Brown directed me to meet him at the Mills home at nine o'clock so that he might acquaint me with duties of my new position. He then led the plodding horse around the corner in the direction of the Mills home.

"Where does the good Reverend live?" I asked.

"Reverend Brown stays first with one then another or sometimes he completely disappears for long periods without warning or any explanation of his absences upon returning. The man distrusts everyone so he keeps no set routine in fear that someone may wish him harm." Mr. Mills explained, his voice reflected a trace of doubt as to the Reverend's competency.

Mr. Mills hurried up the now awaking main street calling out greetings to those who moved about readying their establishments for the start of a new day of business.

"That is Alfonso Knapp." Mills announced, pointing to a tall gaunt man in the process of unlocking the front door of a small one room frame building. "He is the barber and dentist in town, if you have a need for either." A few more paces and Mr. Mills called out to a dainty appearing young man dressed in a fashionable, but unpressed suit who was ambling along as if he had nowhere to go. "Morning Doctor Rutledge." The small man spun around quickly as if he were caught by complete surprise or half asleep.

"Oh, good morning, Buck." Doctor Rutledge called out with a wave of his tiny hand. This was the first I had heard Mr. Mills' first name or nickname, but he seemed to readily accept the title.

"That building is a combination boarding house and restaurant." Buck Mills indicated a narrow two story building with a deep covered front porch that sat

31

several feet above the level of the street. "The room added on the back is Doc's office and home, so if you need any medical help you will know where to find it." Buck reported in a not so reassuring voice.

"I try to avoid the need for a Doctor or a dentist," I stated agreeably, "but then one never knows," I added quickly.

"I think you will find Mrs. Mills a suitable barber unless you are unusually particular and she has done more doctoring than most when it comes to setting broken bones of tending to fevers. Please feel free to call on her for either service." Buck Mills offered earnestly.

"Thank you sir, I will remember that when the time comes that I might need her talents."

"Good," Buck smiled, "this is my store." He announced with some pride walking slowly to a large log structure situated on the west side of the main street. "It may not look like much but if you can't find it in my store it most likely does not exist in Mt. Zion." Buck laughed out loud. "Come in and I will show you around so you will know what I have in stock just in case you might need anything."

"Thank you sir, there are a few items I require but was unable to transport by horseback on the trip here."

"It's time you dropped the sir, young fella," Mills said warmly. "Everyone calls me Buck except the Misses and Reverend Brown. I'm not much of a person for formalities and titles, so please just call me Buck."

"I will do so if you will call me Captain Lang," I said laughingly, "my name is James and I wish the folks around here would use that name; you see I'm not much of one for putting on airs myself."

"Sounds fine to me James but if you accompany us to church tonight I will most certainly introduce you to the congregation as Captain James Lang."

"That will be just fine Buck, but I hope these good people realize the title is quite unnecessary." A large ornate mantle clock perched high on the shelf behind the counter struck eight o'clock and I realized it was time for Buck Mills to open the door to his mercantile store, so I excused myself saying I must make preparations to meet with Reverend Brown.

"Have a good day and don't let Brown brow-beat you, I'm sure you know far more about military life than the good Reverend has ever heard of." Buck advised seriously.

THE TEMPEST

The nine o'clock meeting with Reverend Brown went well. He explained that my duties as training officer would be to school his army in the manual of arms, close order drill and marksmanship. This fell easily within my scope of experience and would still allow for some free time to ride and explore the countryside. Brown informed me that I was to use the level block square park as the parade ground where he also intended to bivouac the troops who were expected to start arriving any day. A rudimentary rifle range had been laid out about a quarter mile away from the park on land owned by Mr. Boyd.

After the tour I had several questions for the Reverend; how were the men to be fed and where they were to wash or do laundry. His only answer was "the Lord would provide." It may seem strange now but I think the man truly believed God would perform a miracle and these problems would be dealt with. In truth this burden fell to the good Christian citizens of the newly founded settlement who supported the abolitionist views of Brown and were too compassionate to turn away a soul in need. Fortunately Brown's optimistic army of one hundred or more men never materialized; in fact the normal compliment usually totaled fewer than twenty recruits.

The remainder of my day was committed to getting settled in at the Mills house and a leisure familiarization ride about the general area of Mt. Zion. I had no intention of straying far from town and take a chance of missing the evening church meeting where I was to be formally introduced to the congregation but, more importantly, it would provide a proper sanctified meeting with the fair Jessanne Gates. The very thought of seeing that divine being thrilled me to the quick. I felt like a school boy with a crush on the new schoolmarm. I knew it was sinful and improper, and yet, I could not shake that tingle, the soaring feeling that lifts one above and transcends all propriety.

A good, intelligent, God-fearing man would have dismissed the matter from his mind or removed himself from the temptation but my common sense failed when it came to this particular woman. Perhaps consulting a priest or minister would have been in order, or laying my soul bare to a close friend might have resulted in a round of wise counseling that could have alleviated my torment. The only problem lay in the fact that the only man of the cloth nearby was married to the subject of my affections and none of my new associates could be trusted with such a delicate situation. This was a battle which must be waged in solemn silence or all would be lost to the tune of great embarrassment, hurt feelings and broken hearts.

The evening meals at the Mills house were always held at exactly six thirty as Mr. Mills regularly closed his mercantile at six o'clock, the half hour difference was to allow for a late customer and for Mr. Mills' short walk home. This night the ritual of locking up was accompanied by six evenly metered beats of the churches tower bell. The tolling bell was to inform the citizens of Mt. Zion a church meeting would be held that night. The night church meetings began sharply a seven o'clock which did not allot enough time for supper and the one block long walk to the church. But Reverend Gates ran a taut ship and demanded punctuality from those who wished to attend services. This night was no different as 'hurry' was the watchword as the food flew from plate to mouth without frivolous conversation about the table. The dirty dishes were merely cleared from the dinner table and remained unwashed contrary to Mrs. Mills' house rules as we rushed out the kitchen door, for none wished to call down the wrath of Reverend Gates by arriving late. Although the summer sun normally had many hours before sunset it disappeared behind an enormous black cloudbank just as the three of us turned north on the hard packed dirt street that led to the small white church.

"We should have brought an umbrella Mr. Mills." His distaff side admonished just after a brilliant bolt of lightning exploded across the dark western sky. The flash was quickly accompanied by a horrendously loud clap of thunder.

"It's too late now." Mr. Mills replied earnestly, the lightening caused him to quicken his pace and lengthen his stride.

"That was very close," Mrs. Mills said in a nervous tone, "in fact the storm may be upon us before we can reach the safety of the church."

"Indeed," I agreed, "that front is moving very fast and will most likely be here in the next few minutes."

We had no more than reached the buildings front door before a large powerful gust of wind could be seen rolling across the open grass prairie just to our west. The raw natural force of the advancing wind held us transfixed, unable to move through the open church door as the boiling line of dust and debris slammed into the three of us with all the violence of a run-away team of horses. The blast from the wall of fast moving air blinded us with flying dust and we were forced to turn away from the howling torment. Mr. Mills and my hats were ripped from our heads and disappeared into the gathering gloom. The initial shock wave was quickly followed by a sudden drop in temperature as cold air swept over the hilltop, chilling everyone to the core.

The Mills and I regained our senses and cleared our eyes, turning back to gaze into the teeth of the impending storm. The wind fell silent and the sky had in that short few seconds transformed from black to a deep green. We exchanged glances as a faint distant roar rapidly increased to a deafening roar, a sound that can only be described as that of a thousand horses racing straight for you.

"Hail!" I yelled grabbing both Mr. and Mrs. Mills by the arms and forcing them through the open church door in hopes of avoiding the merciless pounding one receives if caught out in the open by a deluge of frozen ice balls. Those first small white pellets which impacted the grass where we had stood only seconds before were quickly replaced by a torrent of goose egg size hail stones. The incessant pounding of hail on the vaulted church roof grew steadily from plainly audible to a wild nerve-racking crescendo. Through the open door we could watch the falling stones blast deep craters in the soft black Iowa soil. It was a blessing to be inside any structure protecting one from the punishment being metered out by the storm's raging furry.

The Honorable Reverend Gates, ever the efficient straight-laced individual, demanded we find pews and that the meeting come to order through the din of the hailstorm intensifying all around us. The wind rattled the windows and doors with extreme violence while debris consisting of tree limbs, dirt, and nearly any object not fastened down collided with the board siding of the small church. The noise produced by the gale winds and hail that battered the exterior of our sanctuary induced a state of great anxiousness in many of the congregation; especially the women and children present. I willingly admit, through it all my sinful eyes searched the gathering for Jessanne who was located at the piano with her slim back to the pews.

"Please close the door Mr. Wells!" Reverend Gates roared. "And ring the bell to indicate everyone is present." Wells was a small elderly man who followed the church leaders bidding without question or hesitation except this night the bell was struck only three times. The three even beats were a futile effort in the face of the gale wind screaming through the bell tower, for we seated just below the bell were able to hear only the faintest of sounds.

Reverend Gates solemnly opened the evening's proceedings with a long impassionate prayer dealing with subjects completely unrelated to the threatening tempest without, nor was there any connection to life on the Iowa prairie. He droned on and on offering little to calm the fears of those who were so unsettled that night and in need of reassurance from persons of authority. But no encouraging words were forth coming; only harsh demands that every soul follow the letter of biblical law without exception. After what seemed an eternity, Reverend Gates pronounced a loud "Amen" which the congregation echoed in a less than enthusiastic response.

The blessed Amen ended with great relief to all the long minutes of boring drudgery and gave Deacon Boyd the opportunity to spring to his feet and thank the good Reverend for what he termed a stirring and beneficial prayer. As the storm slackened slightly and voices were more easily heard, the Deacon opened the meeting officially and thanked everyone for their attendance on such a bleak night. Then Mr. Boyd asked for any new business. Mr. Mills rose slowly to his feet in order to be recognized formally by the Deacon.

"Yes, Mr. Mills." Deacon Boyd said sternly.

"Thank you Mr. Boyd," Mills began, "it is my privilege to introduce to the congregation a new boarder at our house." He gestured for me to rise beside him before continuing. "This, ladies and gentlemen, is Captain James Lang, late of the United States Military, who has so graciously agreed to use his expertise in the training of any recruits whom might rally to our midst." A small round of applause served as the congregation's greeting.

"Thank you, Deacon Boyd, Mr. Mills and the citizens of Mt. Zion. It is an honor to be of service to this fine Christian congregation. I am delighted to be in such a beautiful, industrious town filled with warm kind hearted souls who hold the future in such high regard."

I had just finished my small flattering acceptance speech when the front door to the church flew open with a deafening bang. The congregation was simultaneously startled by the sound and turned in unison to stare back over the rows of pews at the offending door. All assumed the storm had forced the door's weak latch to release allowing the heavy wooden slab to swing freely and mightily against the interior wall. The lamp which normally lights the vestibule was extinguished by the wind gust leaving the entryway in total blackness. A sudden massive bolt of lightning illuminated the outside world equal to the brightest sunlit day. There in the doorway stood a small lone figure of a man soaked with rain and muddied to the knees.

The only sounds were those of the tempest raging outside the church, for none of its parishioners extended an invitation to this pitiful looking man who silently withstood the onslaught of nature's wrath. A few more explosions of blinding light drove the man to remove his rain soaked hat and step through the open door.

"What do you want"? Gates demanded in a stern voice.

"Please pardon the interruption," the small man with a meek voice began, "my name is Rockwood Honeyman. My family and I are camped down near the Missouri River bottom nearly straight west of here. I have come here on the gravest of business this dark night." The man paused to look around the group of staring faces. "I have a beautiful five year old daughter who disappeared from camp in mid-afternoon and I have been searching ever since," he stated, "I stopped in Mills Mercantile yesterday as we passed through and knew of nowhere else to solicit help. I pray some of you men will aid me in my quest to find my precious baby Ada." Honeyman fell quiet; his eyes examined every face in the building for any sign of compassion for his cause.

"Which religious faith do you follow Mr. Honeyman?" Reverend Gates demanded.

"I am a disciple of the teachings of Joseph Smith." The man answered with great conviction.

"Then you are Mormon!" Gates voice roared in a volume equal to the storm without.

42

"Yes sir, we subscribe to that faith."

"Then sir you have made a futile journey, for we do not associate with people of your ilk." Gates stated flatly without any discussion with his flock. "We solicit neither your fellowship nor your business."

"I know how you people feel about my religion but I am not asking for myself but for my poor little baby who is lost on such a terrible night." Honeyman pleaded with a soft cry in his high pitched voice.

"No!" Reverend Brown exclaimed forcefully jumping to his feet. "We will not aid the cause of heretics or adulterers!"

"Thank you for your time." The small man said dejectedly turning to exit through the still open door. His pitiful rain-soaked body slumped from fatigue and the desperation of knowing he must continue the search for his loved-one unaided. Rockwell Honeyman shuffled his heavy boots on the rough wooden flooring and tripped slightly on one of the irregular cracks between two boards. The misstep threw Honeyman against the door frame with a heavy thud that could be easily heard over the storms thunderous furry.

"Wait a moment sir." I called out to the man as he struggled to regain his footing on the now slick muddy floor. "I will be glad to assist in your search."

"NO, you will not!" Reverend John Brown cried out as if in pain.

"I just need a few minutes to saddle my horse and retrieve my rain slicker." I continued while ignoring Brown.

"I said NO Mr. Lang and speaking as your superior that is a direct order!" Brown's tone and body gestures indicated just how agitated this strange person had become.

"If, sir, I had felt the need for men to feel superior to me I would never have resigned my commission in the United States military. I believe every man my equal and there is no delineation among any human created in God's image."

"You have been given a directive Mr. Lang and if you wish to consort with these people then you will do well to remain in their company." Gates bellowed, shaking a long white boney finger in my direction.

"I cannot believe what I am hearing from people who claim to be God fearing followers of Christ. This is a helpless little girl who is wandering those bleak hills in a dark violent stormy night. She must be cold, hungry and terrified in a strange world not knowing where her parents and loved ones are. You will find I am a bit headstrong and tend to do the right rather than the popular thing." I replied. "Now if that is not what you are looking for in a military training officer, then you decide while I am gone. But whatever your verdict, I am going to search for Ada Honeyman until the child is found!" The last sentence saw my temper flare and my self-control vanish as my voice became louder and my movements more animated.

"But you don't know the country," Mills argued, "these hills are very tricky to travel through in the dark. Why, there are some 40 foot drop offs and the soil is fine and turns very slick when it rains, and that's not to mention the fast moving run-off water that can wash a horse and rider away in just seconds."

"Yes sir, and as we stand here talking that little one is out there in those rough hills facing those very hazards!" I snapped back before considering Mr. Mills' good intentions. "I do appreciate your concern but I am use to traversing such land and I have a very competent horse. We shall make out just fine, please do not be worried for us."

"We shall pray for you Mr. Lang." Mrs. Mills interjected.

"Thank you but do your praying for little Ada, she is the one who is in trouble." I replied as calmly as possible.

Turning my attention back to the girl's father, I moved to where the distraught man leaned against the doorway, and promised "We will find your daughter, Mr. Honeyman. Now, I think it best if you wait out front while I fetch my horse and slicker." I ushered the exhausted man outside the church's dry, lighted interior and into the cold pelleting rain and blackness, turning back long enough to issue an ultimatum to the congregation. "As I said, you make up your minds as to my future here while I search for this child." With that said, I swung the heavy wooden door closed with excess authority.

THE SEARCH

"Where is your mount sir?" I called through the driving rain.

"I haven't one, I walked here." Honeyman replied with the most volume he could muster.

"Then we will ride double back to the area you think we should search. Please wait here, I will return in just a few minutes." I promised in a confident tone, hoping to bolster the man's spirits. Honeyman nodded his head feebly causing a large cascade of rain water to pour from the wide brim of his battered old hat.

I raced to the Mills house, grabbed my rifle, spare hat, and slicker before saddling my horse and returning to the church yard. Mr. Honeyman stood head bowed beside the dark muddy street awaiting my splashing return. He groaned wearily as he swung his short legs behind my saddle and settled in for the greatly appreciated ride back to the Honeyman camp. I followed his directions out of town and down a long slippery hill towards the high western bluffs and the mighty Missouri river that lay just beyond. As we rode, Mr. Honeyman attempted to relate, between heavy claps of thunder, the circumstance surrounding little Ada's disappearance. The story sounded a bit questionable but still plausible if given the benefit of the doubt. The heartsick man recounted how little Ada and her twelve year old sister had gone to fetch the milk cow that had wandered off up the creek into the hills.

Soon the older girl Cora returned leading the lost animal screaming at the top of her lungs that a wild savage had attacked the two girls. Honeyman immediately retraced the girl's steps by following the tracks of the cloven hoofed cow but the thunder storm overtook him before being able to trail the little girl farther than some tall bushes. He then wandered amidst the steep bluffs, through the high wind and blinding rain while calling little Ada's name in a futile attempt to locate his loving daughter.

The trip to the river bottom became very difficult as we were forced to navigate several rain swollen streams and treacherous, slippery hillsides but my strong fearless mount never faltered in his mission and we covered the five or so miles in about an hour. Once at the river bottom camp, Mr. Honeyman introduced me to his distraught wife who forced a cup of cold rain water diluted coffee into my hand. One quick gulp of the thin brew and I excused myself from the family in order to resume the search for the lost little one. I suggested that Mr. Honeyman remain in camp to rest until sunrise as a little light would greatly facilitate a man searching on foot. I rode off now unencumbered by the passenger on behind and began a wide circle of the hill area to the east of the Honeyman camp. I reasoned to myself that such a small child would not travel very far and would in all likelihood be hiding fearfully in some type of cover. I rode slowly calling out the child's name as loud as possible through the din of the ragging storm but felt certain neither my voice nor that of the child's would be audible for any distance in this tempest. I moved carefully from cover to cover just as a good hunting dog would do in an attempt to flush game from its hiding place. This was a slow methodical process, first calling the child's name repeatedly before inspecting each bush and patch of weeds along the sweeping semi-circle bounded on the east by the nearly perpendicular bluffs.

I had covered half of the hillside when a deep wash came into view that needed to be closely inspected; so I guided my horse through the narrow opening and preceded up the incline toward the ridge. Seconds after entering the wash I rode near a small bush from which some animal flushed and ran excitedly up the ever narrowing ravine. The distant lighting flashes revealed very little of the fleeing creatures identity but allowed me to track its rapid movements. I saw no reason to pursue the animal for even in the dim light it was obvious the escapee was larger than a five year old child. I watched intently as the animal struggled to reach the hill's razorback ridge lying just at the top of my point of view. Mother Nature had perfectly synchronized a powerful lightning bolt to strike at the very place and time the desperate thing managed to surmount the crest.

The explosion was overpowering, at a distance of 30 feet my ears ached from the sound and my eyes were blinded by the intensely brilliant light. The muscles in my mount became as hard as stone and every hair on his hide stood straight up like a bristle brush. But it was in that split second of light that I realized the stricken animal was indeed a human in full flight, suddenly frozen in place by the electricity coursing through its body. That image of a human form being impaled by a jagged blade of fire was burned into my momentarily blinded eyes and seared into my memory forever.

When my horse and my senses slowly returned we moved cautiously up the rain slickened draw to investigate the unbelievable event that had unfolded before our very eyes. I was unable to accept that a human had actually been struck by that lightning bolt and felt sure the whole matter was a trick played on my weary senses by a brain relieved to have survived such a spectacular phenomenon. I prayed as my horse struggled up the incline, I would not find the body of little Ada Honeyman on that barren hill top.

Once at the hill's summit, I dismounted in order to search more closely for a body, if a body did in fact exist and to prevent my horse from accidentally stepping on the victim if it miraculously still held any life. There, at my feet lay the object I had dreaded to find, a small lifeless body. It had been the target of one of nature's most powerful agents of destruction; that of instantaneous death by electrocution.

I knelt on the wet muddy slope reluctant to gaze upon the slight pitiful figure lying prostrate before me. A sudden flash of lightning streaked across the ebony sky illuminating the world below and exposing to my great surprise the remains of a slight built Negro boy. I shuddered in response at the violent loss of the black youth's life on such a mournful night in such a lonely spot. Still, I was elated this was not little Ada Honeyman lying so forlornly on the soggy ground and, thank God, I would be spared the painful task of notifying her parents of their child's tragic demise.

I, an experienced combat veteran, sat in the dark on that desolate windswept ridge engulfed by shock and remorse at the needless death of this young Negro boy. A deep sense of guilt swirled through my brain, for I felt directly responsible for driving the dead youth from his place of sanctuary into the path of the lightning bolt. I had never intended him any harm, and the fact that he even existed was a complete surprise to me. Many questions flashed through my troubled head; who was this youth, where did he come from and what was he doing hiding on the lonely hillside in a thunder storm of near biblical proportions? Perhaps the Honeyman's could provide answers to the troubling questions but for the moment the search for little Ada Honeyman must take priority. The child must be presumed alive and it might be possible to rescue her. As for the dead Negro boy, I had done all I could do for him in this earthly world. I stood up and gazed around through the storm in an effort to find my bearings in order to later retrieve the boy's body for burial.

Mounting the rain soaked saddle I rode on, doing my utmost to resume the urgent search for the missing child but found it difficult to keep my mind focused on the task at hand. Returning to the pattern of calling the child's name and inspecting any and all cover was very time consuming but I knew of no other way to proceed. Traveling only a few rods farther, my mount stopped. Suddenly his ears flew upright and his nostrils flared to their fullest opening. I studied the animal's strange reactions knowing full well something had caught his attention. The animal's head turned continually to the right as if drawn by some unseen magnetic force further up the steep hillside. I gently urged him to move on but all four feet remained firmly planted where they had originally stopped in the soft muddy bluffs. I had long ago come to realize while man is the most intelligent of all animals, often times his senses are lacking the development of the other creatures that also inhabit this world.

I dismounted and began to move slowly up the hill, calling the Honeyman girl's name in as congenial voice as I could muster under the trying circumstances. The first clump of bushes contained nothing except briars but as I neared the second patch a faint sound rose to greet my alert ears.

"Ada?" I called out tenderly. "Are you in there?" A low faint whimper was the encouraging reply which drove me to eagerly paw through the sticker incrusted plants and vines to finally discover one tiny bare foot. That foot led to a leg and the leg to the mud-covered torso, the object of my search this retched night. The girl's calico dress was entangled in the foliage that had so successfully concealed the child from human searchers but not from the senses of one of mans most loyal companions, his horse.

I struggled to free the shivering, nearly unconscious child from the bonds of encircling thorns but little could be done to prevent inflicting more scratches on the already bleeding tike's body. Once I pulled the limp doll-sized girl free, I wrapped her in my rain slicker and mounted my still weary horse for a hurried trip to the Honeyman camp.

On hearing my approach, Mr. and Mrs. Honeyman rushed to meet me and joyously received their lost lamb back into the fold. The cold wet rain could not diminish the warm glow I felt at facilitating the loving reunion of such a happy family, regardless of their religious belief.

Once little Ada was safe and warm in her parents embrace I broached the subject of the dead Negro boy, but they professed no knowledge of such a person being in the area. I, having passed just recently through Nebraska City, knew some slaves were in residence there and many more were to be found in northern Missouri and along the Iowa state line. Still, we were several miles from those locations and the boy showed no signs of a master or reason for being in the area.

Mrs. Honeyman suggested the boy's presence here could be the work of abolitionists who were known to operate an Underground Railroad in this area.

"Hush mother," Mr. Honeyman warned sternly, "attend to your child; we have enough trouble without inciting the locals with wild accusation."

I would have liked to inquire deeper into what actual knowledge these people had of the law breaking activities of the locals but seeing Mr. Honeyman's nervous response, it seemed best not to pursue the subject further. Still, Mrs. Honeyman's suspicion about the Underground Railroad having a hand in the dead boy's appearance might be the real answer to my questions.

CAPTAIN & MY LADY

By sunrise, dark and ominous as it was, little Ada Honeyman was resting peacefully so I took my leave of the situation saying it was time to retrieve the boy's body and take it to town for proper internment. The parting was filled with the warmest of thank yous and promises to pray for my soul and I realized these Mormon folks were good people. I rode slowly back up to the crest of the bluff and was surprised at how easily relocating the body turned out to be. I had feared wild beasts would find the boys remains during the hours before dawn and desecrate it before my return. It was a great relief to find the youth's body lying unmolested just where the stroke of death had deposited him the night before.

Thick clouds filtered the morning sun down to a faint glow but it's steady light made a closer inspection of the deceased more practical. The youth's clothes were nothing but rags consisting of tattered knee length pants and a cheap shirt that was shredded to small strips. Without touching the body it was easy to see partially healed bloody whip marks on the small boney back. His bare feet were covered with calluses and were heavily scared. Deep groves were visible around each ankle indicating the boy had worn shackles sometime in the not too distant past. His head had short cropped black hair with some old jagged scars which appeared to be made by a knife or other sharp instrument to form a particular pattern. I guessed the remains at weighing less than a hundred pounds and decided it best if the body was loaded onto my weary mount causing me to walk the long soggy miles back to Mt. Zion. Both my horse and I stumbled and slipped many times on the trek through the steep hills and across the still flooded creeks.

By late afternoon just as the sun broke clear from the eastwardly moving clouds we wandered into the tiny hilltop hamlet. I was plastered head to foot with thick brown paste from the bluff and my poor mount had not faired any better. This strange mire, having combined with the hair of his silky coat caused it to stand up like a bristle. I fear we were a terrible sight; man, horse, and dead boy slung over the saddle so soiled that no one seemed to recognize us. We walked slowly down Main Street under the eyes of local citizens without anyone coming forth to offer assistance or to even inquire about the lost child or the body tied to my saddle.

I halted in front of Mr. Mills mercantile, looked all about before hitching my exhausted horse to a porch pillar then stepped to the stores doorway. "Mr. Mills." I called through the open doorway.

Buck Mills hurried to investigate my urgent call and the look on his face told me just how pitiful I appeared to those who had witnessed my arrival. "What has happened?" he asked excitedly steering me to a split log bench on the stores front porch.

Jessanne Gates, unbeknown to me was shopping at Mr. Mills store and overheard my words as I hailed him for assistance. She followed on Mills' heels and was shocked at my disheveled appearance and the cargo stretched across my mud-splattered saddle. I began to rise but she placed her hand on my shoulder and gently pushed me down onto the bench.

"What new misfortune has befallen you, sir?" She asked kneeling beside the bench where I sat. Her words were filled with genuine concern and her sparkling green eyes flashed with unspoken worry. The lady swiftly retrieved a white lace handkerchief from her handbag and began to tenderly wipe the grime from my haggard face. Though exhausted, her slightest touch rejuvenated me in both body and spirit.

"Are you injured Captain Lang?" Her words were kind and tender while her eyes looked deep into mine.

"Only my pride, but thank you for asking." I stuttered out wearily.

"Please do tell us what happened last night." Jessanne asked sweetly. "I think it very gallant of you to undertake such a dangerous search for that lost child." She whispered softly while Buck Mills scurried off to locate a pan of water and some towels to further clean my person. Ours eyes locked together and we remained so in complete silence until Mr. Mills' boisterous return.

"Now tell us the tale from beginning to end." Mills demanded.

I gave them a quick sketch of the night's events and that I had brought the Negro boy back to town in hopes of learning his true identity.

"I fear you have wasted your time Captain." Mills replied. "I know of no slaves or blacks in the general vicinity."

"He must have come from somewhere." I countered weakly.

"We do not believe in trafficking other men or the use of humans, black or white, as animals to do our bidding sir." Mr. Mills stated firmly.

"Be that as it may." I heaved a long discussed sigh. "Someone must reach a decision as to the proper disposal of this young man's remains."

"I do not understand Captain." Mills said, as if he had never heard of interring the dead.

"Do you people have a cemetery for this town?" I asked a bit put off by what seemed to be Mills' reluctance to face the situation.

"Yes, of course it lies just north of town but we only have two graves in it as of now." Mills stated nervously, fearing that I would suggest the Negro boy be buried there.

"Then may we bury the boy there?" I asked, my patience wearing thin from the long night.

"That would have to be taken up with the Reverend Gates and the church deacons." Mills informed me politely.

"Then I must find them directly for the weather is quite warm and this boy must be interned very soon." I insisted.

"That cannot be, for all three are out of town for a few days." Mills disclosed reluctantly.

"Out of town!" I said in surprise. "Out of town where?"

"Just moments after you departed to look for the missing Mormon child a courier arrived calling for help from a black man being held in jail illegally in Oregon, Missouri. All three loaded up and left hoping to secure the man's freedom before he could be shipped down river." Mr. Mills explained rather sheepishly.

"Let me get this straight." I said, my voice trembling with anger. "Those three men who objected to assisting in the search for a lost child because of her religion undertook a lengthy trip out of state to defend a black man sitting safely in jail?"

"Well," Mills began to stammer, "it seemed the right thing to do."

"Not in my book sir." I growled. "Not in my book." A strange silence fell over the three of us as I looked hard into the face of my landlord as he shuffled about like a nervous child.

"Then I should not look to anyone around here for assistance in the disposition of this poor unfortunate boy?" I asked in disgust. Mr. Mills merely turned from my icy stare and Jessanne hung her beautiful head in shame as I waited for a reply.

"Fine!" I exclaimed forcefully. "Then bring me a good shovel and charge it to my bill."

"What are your intentions, Captain Lang?" Jessanne asked affectionately, touching my hand tenderly with hers while Mills scurried from my sight to fetch the shovel.

"I will do the only thing I can Mrs. Gates, I will transport the body back to where God called him home and make a proper grave there for his mortal remains."

"Thank you sir, you are indeed a good and true Christian gentleman." Jessanne whispered gently, giving my large rough hand a squeeze. The sensation passing through my body at that moment defies mortal description but electrifying is as close as my limited vocabulary can equate. Her hand was the softest most angelic thing I had ever felt and I knew I had been blessed to have this woman show such tender affection to the likes of a poor lowly soldier.

"I fear sir, that both you and your animal are too exhausted to safely complete such a difficult task." Jessanne uttered in her compassionate sweet voice.

"I have no choice, for the boy must be buried and it seems no one around here is willing to help, so I must handle the chore myself." I said bitterly, beginning to have serious doubts as to what form of Christianity this church adhered to.

"I will pray for you sir." Jessanne whispered, and then paused as Mr. Mills returned with shovel in hand intending to tie the tool to my saddle. "I shall pray for you and of course for the soul of the young boy who will lay forgotten on some forlorn hilltop grave until resurrection time."

"Thank you Mrs. Gates that will make my load much easier to bear." I said in a low voice to prevent Mr. Mills from over hearing. "Now I must take my leave of your kindness and make my way back to the bluffs to enter my new occupation of undertaker." I said with a weak smile.

"But you cannot go without something to eat." Jessanne said urgently.

"I would not think of entering anyone's home in such a condition and there is no reason to clean up for I shall be additionally soiled upon my return." I explained politely not wishing to expend the time required to bathe, change cloths and sit down to eat.

"I have bread baked fresh this morning, cold roast beef, and some excellent cheese that would do well to be eaten while traveling. If you will give me but a minute I will have everything ready as you pass my home on the way back to the western bluffs." Jessanne offered sweetly but more importantly her gesture was one of true concern and sympathy for my plight.

"I cannot tell you how much I appreciate your thoughtfulness Mrs. Gates. I shall stop by your front gate in a few minutes if that will allow enough time." I responded with a pleasant smile and song in my voice.

"That will provide ample time sir; all will be in readiness when you arrive." Jessanne said enticingly before turning on her heel and hurrying down the street in the direction of the Gates house.

To say I was anxious to take my leave of Buck Mills and fly to Jessanne Gates home was a gross understatement but I did not wish my landlord to sense the urgency I felt, less he become suspicious of my true feelings. I restrained my eagerness and allowed Mills to present a feeble explanation as to why the church leaders rushed out of town on such short notice but refused to assist the Honeyman's. I suffered through what seemed to be an endless amount of evidence on behalf of the community's leaders and all of their good Christian works until desire drove me to begrudgingly agree. It was then Buck Mills donated a piece of worn wagon canvass to serve as a coffin for the boy. We wrapped the boy in the rough material and tied him to my saddle once more. After a cool farewell and a promise to return to the Mills home before sunset, I departed with a new spring in my step and song in my heart even though I had a distasteful afternoon ahead of me.

I led my steed and its unseemly cargo down the street to the west, past the church house and the still empty park, to the lane Jessanne Gates' house bordered on. It was a difficult walk those two blocks, for I had just returned from a harrowing night and should have shown signs of fatigue, but I wished to run the distance for my heart was soaring at the thought of speaking to Jessanne alone. Alone yes, but proprietary demanded we meet outside of the house in plain view of every prying eye and gossip in the small village.

Mr. Mills had dominated so much of my time I feared Jessanne would be put off by my delayed arrival and not readily present herself. But I was delighted to see the beautiful young woman seated in a rocking chair on her front porch patiently awaiting my tardy appearance. As I neared, she rose gracefully and hurried to the edge of the street boldly rendering a warm wave of her petite hand.

"I must apologize for detaining you Mrs. Gates but Mr. Mills wished to speak further on the matter of last evenings events." I tried to explain, hoping she would understand but the wide smile on her youthful face told all there was to say on the matter.

"Oh sir, you have no need to ask forgiveness of me; it is truly an honor to be of service to such an exceptionally brave gentleman as yourself." She said shyly and at that moment I knew the woman was indeed feeling the same infatuation that was burning in my heart. We exchanged an intimate smile that made my blood race and Jessanne's face flush. It was an improper yet unavoidable moment fate had willed to happen. The sudden self-realization of her blushing embarrassed the young woman and she quickly averted her eyes from mine and tried to compliment me on finding little Ada Honeywell but it was a ruse. Jessanne's eyes again met mine and sparks jumped as explosively as if steel and flint were struck over an open powder keg.

"Oh, my." Jessanne muttered as our eyes remained entwined and our hearts raced well beyond the speed at which our brains could comprehend the implications of the moment. It was I who came to my senses first and suggested I take my leave under the guise of needing to hurry about the burial business and thankfully Jessanne responded in kind, handing over the food she had prepared for the long trek to the Missouri River bluffs.

"Thank you very much Mrs. Gates, a full stomach will make my feet lighter and my heart brighter." I said quickly without weighing the depth of my words.

"Please Captain, call me Jessanne, everyone in the area does." She had regained her composure and strove to make pleasant conversation.

"Do you think it proper for a stranger to address you, a married woman in such a familiar manner?" I asked hoping the answer would be yes, but at the same time providing her with an opportunity to recall an over eager suggestion.

"I insist sir, it is the name I feel most comfortable with, especially when being referred to by my closest friends." A knowing smile accentuated the words closest friends.

"Then you should use my first name James, when speaking of me."

"Thank you sir but I prefer Captain if you do not mind, it has a familiar ring to it of friendship and trust."

"Whatever you wish. If the name Captain is endearing to your ears then I hope you will always use that title whenever speaking or thinking of me. However, I very much like the title of My Lady and it seems quite fitting to your personality. It comes most naturally from my southern upbringing." I said convincingly.

"My Lady," Jessanne repeated, "it does have a certain flair to it, My Lady. Yes, I believe I shall feel quite comfortable being addressed with such a fine title."

"Then it's settled I will call you My Lady."

"And I shall consider it a great privilege to refer to you by your military title and will always think of you as such, no matter what rank you may attain or where you may travel." Jessanne confirmed.

"I would say the honor is entirely mine Mrs.... er, ah, I mean My Lady." I stammered out.

"I have a feeling we shall become fast friends Captain and will remain so no matter what life may bring." The woman's words were unusually forward but in truth we had both betrayed our true feelings in that moment when we first met at the dress shop.

"Yes, I will know we are still friends as long as you address me as Captain." I was proposing the forming of a secret bond between we two which would be reinforced by using the code words Captain and My Lady.

"Yes and I will expect you to use "My Lady" as long as you share my friendship." She had fallen in league with my desire to share a relationship much closer than mere acquaintance.

"Then it shall be My Lady from this time forth no matter the circumstance or worldly interferences."

She smiled brightly extending her small right hand to seal a pact which the world about us would consider scandalous if not adulterous.

"I would love to spend the remainder of this day in conversation with you but I fear I must tend to the business at hand." I said in my most sincere tone. "I hope we shall have the opportunity to speak further in the days ahead." The statement was more of a request for permission to see Jessanne again than a simple polite ending to our conversation.

"I am quite sure we shall find common grounds on which to have future discussions." She said promisingly.

"Then let me wish you a good day and again thank you for the food."

"You are quite welcome Captain and I will have you in my mind this afternoon as you go about your unsavory obligation. Remain ever vigilant and please take care of yourself this day." Jessanne's words were filled with warmth and affection and went directly to my heart.

"I will My Lady, and I hope you have a pleasant afternoon." I tipped my hat gallantly, took up Sergeant's bridle reins, smiled and walked away. I have never in my life departed more reluctantly from a place as I did at that glorious moment in time. Being separated from this beautiful angel tore at my heart and melted my brain into feebleness but move on I must or people would begin to talk.

I had traveled the one block distance to the path leading west and could not resist the temptation to look back over my left shoulder in the direction of Jessanne's house as I made the turn. To my surprise she remained standing on the edge of the street staring in my direction waiting for my backward glance. As my head turned in her direction Jessanne boldly raised her right hand far in the air and waved it vigorously in an effort to signal a fond farewell. I unthinking responded in kind hesitating for a moment to enjoy the warm glow her gesture had produced in my heart.

I walked along slowly at first; the impulse to turn about and retrace my steps to the Gates house was so overwhelming it required all my self-restraint to place one foot in front of the other. This is one moment when my strict military training served me in good stead and forced me to carry out the assignment at hand. My mind whirled in thought as I walked down the first long slippery hill. Every second of the conversation with Jessanne was replayed over and over in my head, being dissected down to minute fragments. The scenes at the Mills store came flooding back in vivid pictures and her words were endearing innuendos -- or were they? I questioned every word, every action, hoping to make some sense of the meeting and yet knowing it was all an exercise in futility for the lady was married; married and devoutly religious with no intentions of breaking her wedding vows or committing a sin against God's holy ordinance.

REVELATIONS

As I struggled up the steep mucky slope to the proposed burial site I had convinced myself the whole conversation was over eagerness on my part. It was an act of a generous God fearing Christian woman on her part. Yes, that must be what had transpired I told myself, a mere innocent act of kindness and charity from a young naïve woman who was not in complete agreement with her strict overbearing minister husband.

Once atop the barren bluff's crest I unloaded the deceased and unsaddled my weary mount so he might graze and rest unhindered for the trip back to town. The sun was just past its zenith by this time, so I too paused to rest and enjoy the food Jessanne had so generously prepared and to take in the glorious view of the wide flat Missouri River bottom the grassy pinnacle provided.

Although the spring day was warm and the air heavy with moisture after last night's storm, a cool breeze swept up the bluff refreshing my tired battered body and elevating my defeated spirit. The scene that unfolded below and to the west of the line of vertical bluffs was indeed awe inspiring. I wished for nothing more of this life than to share such an afternoon with Jessanne watching the sun move magically across this enchanting vista. But deep in my heart I knew it could never be, no matter how hard I might wish it. As for praying, only a fool would pray for a sin and expect the Lord to grant such a request.

Finishing the meal I began to dig through the heavy roots of the tall prairie grass and into the rich soil that made up these strange tall hills. One hard hour and a crude grave began to take shape that most would have considered appropriate for a Negro, but something drove me to provide the best burial possible for this lost youth. When the repository was completed I lined the hole with grass and lowered the departed child's blanket wrapped body into the waiting ground. I said a prayer over the body and hoped his mother would somehow know that her son had received a Christian burial.

Filling the grave with dirt was somehow harder, much more trying on my spirit than the more physical digging had been. I, a good southern boy, born to wealth and property should feel no more remorse in burying a Negro than a cur dog but this was not the case with this funeral. I knew deep in my heart this young man had met his fate in a futile attempt to escape people just like myself and the slavery to which we subjected him.

I stood at the foot of the new grave and said a prayer; for myself, for at that moment I realized this poor dead child never had the opportunity to sin against God but I most certainly had by being part of a society which would drive anyone to undertake such a desperate journey. My words flowed like water over a fall, fine educated words this poor dead youth probably could not comprehend. I stopped in mid-sentence for these beseeching words were falling on deaf ears, those of the deceased and God in heaven. It was then I asked the forgiveness of the Negro lying in a pauper's grave high atop a deserted windswept hill. While God may never pardon my transgression, it was my earnest desire that the departed boy forgive me for having even an indirect hand in his untimely demise.

It was at this point a sudden blast of wind roared unrestricted up the bluff from the valley below. The flexible long stemmed prairie grass bent nearly flat against the hills perpendicular sides. That shock wave of hot air struck me like a gun powder explosion. I was inundated with debris consisting of leaves, pieces of grass and a fine brown dust, but in a second or two the tempest had played itself out. I was left standing at the foot of the runaway's grave wondering if the passing gale had been more than an updraft. I wondered if the momentary blow had been caused by the angel Gabriel whisking unseen the dead Negro boy's soul to heaven; or had it been a sign to me from God himself to mend my sinful ways and to follow the newly found path of righteousness.

It was at that instant that I realized I had become one of those people; people known as abolitionists. These were the very same people I had shown so much distain over the years; the same people I had come to Mt. Zion to spy on. I had become one of them, an abolitionist. My heart had become light and my spirit soared from my body and a strange new sense of enlightenment filled my brain with a feeling of joy.

I drove the new shovel deep in the soil at the head of the grave to serve as the only source of recognition this poor unknown soul would ever have. It was a pitiful marker at best but I knew his maker was fully aware who rested in this small piece of soil overlooking the majestic Missouri River bottom. I would never pass this prominent point again without thinking of that unfortunate grave, so in my mind that huge stately bluff became the youths enduring monument for all eternity.

ESCORTING JESSANNE HOME

My return to Mt. Zion was less than triumphant; in fact it was witnessed only by a lone dog barking a warning of my approach for its master which he conveniently ignored. I stabled and fed my exhausted mount before pumping a bucket of cold well water in which to take an invigorating spit bath. The hour was well past midnight as I approached my private little cottage behind the Mills' main house. I paused to look around and it was then I spied a light still burning in the front window of Jessanne Gates' home. I stepped back a bit from the entryway slightly dumbstruck and stared intently at the small flickering flame. I dare not think what was in my heart; could it be Jessanne had allowed that singular beacon to glow through the night as a signal indicating I was in her thoughts or had the lady of the house merely overlooked it being extinguish at bedtime? It was too much to hope the former was the reason for wasting a valuable candle but still a false hope is better than no hope at all.

Wearily I stumbled through the cottage doorway and began to fumble about in the unfamiliar house for the candle which sat in the center of the small table. The head of the match produced what seemed an unusually loud roar as I drug it across the rough wooden tabletop before it exploded into a brilliant yellow flare. Sulfur smoke filled my nostrils as I applied the little wooden torch to the exposed wick atop of the tallow candle. The

73

wick gave out a sizzle and faint snap before bursting to life, driving the darkness from the tiny abode. I quickly shed my damp filthy clothing and placed them on the ground just outside the cottage door in hopes Mrs. Mills would find them in the morning and clean them for me. Just as I stood up, my eyes automatically turned to Jessanne's home across the park. That tiny beacon in her front window that had flared my imagination and caused my spirits to soar suddenly vanished. The Gates house fell into total darkness, its exterior corners forming a ghostly outline nearly indistinguishable in the moonless night.

Again my overworked tired brain ran through a series of scenarios as to the meaning of this sudden flame out. Did the lady of the house awake and realize the candle burned on unabated or had she stood a lone vigil through the night beside that solitary flame until my own light signaled all was well and she could retire in peace. The implications were enormous but if incorrect could lead to a devastating situation. I shortly found my own bed, but slept in fits and starts for dreams of a brilliant light turned off and on in my mind's eye as if someone was attempting to signal me from a dark distant shore.

The next morning dawned clear and hot with the little settlement of Mt. Zion coming to life with its usual punctuality. The men performed their morning chores while their wives and children readied the meager breakfast that all had become accustom to. Main Street took on its normal hustle and bustle of the everyday humdrum life, without a word or thought to what had transpired with Ada Honeywell or the death of the black youth. The entire population seemed content to ignore subjects which would have been exciting topics of gossips in any other town. Instead, they discussed the weather and Cyrus Ford's hog wandering off. I anticipated a round of questioning and perhaps a reprimand for my part in the affairs, but the subject was never spoken of even by the Mills family. I had given the town an ultimatum upon departing to search for little Ada Honeywell but no decision was forthcoming.

In surprise I went about the business of laying out a proper rifle range, examining the village green for use as a military camp and parade grounds as well as designing sanitary facilities. This village green lay directly across the street from the Gates home and I unabashedly admit to expending far too much time in my reconnaissance, however my time was spent in vain for Jessanne never appeared in the yard or on the street out front as I had hoped. All contacts with the locals during this tour about town generated polite, sometimes cool, responses to my warm greetings and it became quite obvious I had broken an unspoken code of absolute submission to the wishes of Reverend Gates and the church deacons. It became clear that if I intended to remain in this position I would have to walk a fine line between my principles and/or temper and the demands made by the leadership of the community, which in truth was the church.

Late in the afternoon Reverend Brown rode into town, questioned me briefly on what I had accomplished this day, and then nervously rode off again in the direction from which he had first appeared. Brown exuded a preoccupation that resulted in an extreme change in his character and ability to focus on the report of my activities. This was just the first of many such experiences I witnessed of the famous pseudo soldier's peculiar behavior; but I have neither the education nor training to judge the man's peccadilloes.

I shared a somber evening meal at the Mills home as per our agreement; again there was no reference to the prior night or for that matter if the search for Ada Honeywell had been successful. The food was as cold as the conversation but Mrs. Mills did let slip that because of the storms interruption the previous night, a service would be held this evening.

"You are welcome to attend if you so desire." The kindly woman offered, not wishing to hurt my feelings but not quite sure about extending an invitation.

"I am honored that you would ask me Mrs. Mills and yes, I would like to attend the meeting this evening. Oh, and I will endeavor to be on my best behavior for your sake if not for my own." I laughed and Mr. and Mrs. Mills smiled and nodded to one another hoping for the best.

The meal ended amiably and there was no feeling of urgency as was the case the evening before, which apparently was attributed to the absence of the Reverend Gates. These proceedings were officiated over by a deacon named Sounder Elliot who I had not met until that moment. Elliot was a large framed man with a voice like a croaking bull frog on a hot summer eve, but he was clearly a man of deep religious convictions and preached hell fire and brimstone for forty five minutes without taking a deep breath. At that point Elliott paused and requested Jessanne rise and lead the congregation in singing Rock of Ages.

Until now I had not spotted Jessanne in the congregation and did not wish to make my quest for her too obvious; so it was a great pleasure to watch her rise gracefully from the front pew and turn to face the assembly. Once in position Jessanne's flaming green eyes flashed across the faces seated before her until those piercing green orbs locked on my own and a sweet smile lit those beautiful features with a radiant glow. I felt my face redden as all eyes turned my way; but there was nothing to do but sit calmly and roast in the glares of the holy-er-than-thou stares.

Thankfully, the organist struck up the first notes and heads began to turn in the direction of the inspiring music and to enjoy the golden voice of the most perfect woman I had ever met. Jessanne kept her eyes on the hymnal in her hands throughout the remainder of the song and refrained from looking at me or anyone else in the small gathering. It was a great relief when the hymn was finished and Jessanne returned to her seat in the front pew and Deacon Elliot ended the meeting with a short prayer for the souls of all the church members, whether in attendance or busy in the field rendering service to the Lord.

Sounder Elliot, I never learned from what source his first name was derived, walked to the church door in order to thank all those who had attended the evening service. I watched out of the corner of my eye as Jessanne passed by the end of the pew the Mills' and I occupied, and prayed no one caught the quick glance she gave me while exiting the church. I lagged a bit behind the crowd not wishing to be exposed to any further open displays of familiarity on either Jessanne's or my part; however, my plan went awry as Mrs. Mills engaged Jessanne in a lengthy conversation just in front of the small church's steps. It was impossible to give my regards to the Deacon Elliot without bumping into the little group as they exchanged pleasantries. I tipped my wide brimmed hat and greeted the Reverend's wife with "Good evening Mrs. Gates."

"Good evening Captain." There was that title, the word she had promised to use when addressing me as her friend. "I am glad to see you safely returned from your expedition to the river bluffs." Only Jessanne Gates, of all the residence in Mt. Zion, had shown enough courage to make comment on the incident of the night before.

"Thank you for your concern; I am glad to be back." I said weighing each word carefully before speaking.

"I must admit I knew of your return last night, for I fell asleep while reading and awoke early this morning to see a light in your house." She said, looking deep in my eyes.

"I do believe I saw a light in your window as I entered my house early this morning." Again it seemed wise to play ignorant of any signal which might have been intended by the late night lights. But no matter how hard I tried, I could not force myself to break away from Jessanne's mesmerizing deep green eyes. There was a magnetism between us that kept our eyes focused on one another, each pair of orbs ravenously devouring the other's set. Without uttering a sound, our hearts exchanged thousands of words, thoughts, and deeds in split seconds; our eyes serving as the only source of contact.

"Jessanne," Mrs. Mills said, "Jessanne." She repeated with more volume. "Are you all right child?"

"Oh, yes." Jessanne whispered embarrassingly, coming to her wits. "I was lost in thought for a moment. I apologize I did not intend to ignore you."

"It's just that you looked a trifle faint for a moment, are you sure you are feeling all right?" Mrs. Mills continued to pry.

"It was nothing, just the heat." Jessanne agreed, hoping to find a way out of Mrs. Mills' keen observation.

"I think it best if someone sees you home my dear." Mrs. Mills insisted, turning to her husband who merely smiled. "Would you be so kind Captain Lang, as to escort our Jessanne home safely this evening?" The matronly lady asked sweetly, sure in her mind a refusal was unheard of. My heart leaped at Mrs. Mills' suggestion.

"I, aaah, - well certainly, if Mrs. Gates feels comfortable with the arrangement." I agreed unsure of what to say and completely at a loss for a convincing reason not to comply with her request.

"Who better than a big strong officer and gentleman to walk one of our favorite ladies home on a dark night?" Mrs. Mills said, reassuring both of us it was all quite proper because she had suggested it.

I turned my attention to Jessanne, not sure what expression her pretty youthful face might now display.

"I would greatly appreciate an escort home, if Captain Lang feels up to the walk." She accepted pleasantly but not showing any degree of eagerness.

"Good, I will feel much better knowing Jessanne has been escorted safely to her door and I do thank you sir for being so gallant." Mrs. Mills cooed.

"Then I shall say good evening and take my leave of you good folks so the Captain may fulfill his duty without consuming too much of his night." Jessanne said graciously to Mr. and Mrs. Mills.

"The privilege of walking you home is truly an honor, but if it is duty as you say, then I am delighted to answer the call." I said teasingly extending my right arm as was the accepted manner when escorting a proper lady. Jessanne wrapped her slender left arm about my right elbow and hugged it close to her breast.

"Thank you sir." she purred.

"Good night then." Mrs. Mills called after us as I led Jessanne away from the church down the grassy surface that lined the still muddy street.

We walked along slowly, carefully watching where each foot fell, hoping to avoid stepping on any irregular surface or slick spots which might produce an unwelcome mishap.

"I do greatly appreciate you taking the time to see me home." Jessanne said appreciatively once we were out of earshot of the church goers.

"I can think of nothing I would rather be doing at this very minute than walking arm in arm with you on a beautiful starlit night." I replied trying to convey my true feelings without being unduly forward.

"Yes, it is a wonderful night for a stroll." Jessanne agreed pulling my arm ever tighter to her breast. "I wish we could go on walking together forever." Her words just seemed to blurt out and if the moon had been full I am sure a deep red blush would have been visible on both of our faces.

"I . . . . I should not have said that, but you know what I mean." Her nervous voice betrayed the intention behind the slip of her tongue.

"I feel exactly the same way. I wish you and I could just travel on through the night and never look back at this town." I paused, waiting for either a sharp reprimand or a bashful word of agreement but the woman said nothing, then suddenly her head fell as silently as a snow flake on my shoulder. The move was no accident for it rested there unseen in the dark of night for several steps before Jessanne nestled her winsome face against my nervously heaving chest. We moved along at a snail's pace in this configuration until arriving at the corner of the next street where we had to turn south to reach the Gates house. We were now in a near total blackout for no houses sat on the northwest corner of the large village green but it was plain to see in the limited starlight the street lay quite deep in mud.

"I hate to see you soil the hem of your beautiful dress in such a quagmire." I commented unthinkingly.

"I doubt if it can be helped." Jessanne sighed resigned to cleaning the mess of staining mud and animal waste from the bottom of her long flowing dress.

"I may be out of order here and please say so if I am but I would willingly carry you across this offending mess. That is, if you trust my ability to do so in a discreet and gentlemanly fashion." I suggested knowing the whole idea was quite improper for a lady of such high standing in the community.

"Would you do that for me Captain?" She asked temptingly. "I am certain you would not take advantage of a lady in such an intimate moment, Sir." She paused, and then whispered almost childlike, "I think it very chivalrous of you sir knight and I do grant you permission to embrace my person in your arms for the purpose of overcoming the obstacle ahead."

Without a word I slipped my right arm behind the small of her back while my left swooped the petite woman's feet, full skirt and all into the air.

Jessanne automatically threw her arms about my neck, her head coming to rest on my right shoulder. I stood there so overcome with sheer delight that I was unable to move and I received no indication the lady was in any hurry to end the moment. It was only with great resolve that I stepped from the comparative safety of the grass into the sticky lick-dab that passed for a street in this frontier settlement. Jessanne spoke not a word in the crossing but clung tightly to me as I slipped and stumbled through the mud and mire which had contrived to bring about such an unheard of intimate situation.

I willingly admit to loitering slightly, as if studying the obstacles which lay between our position and the much firmer grass on the opposite corner; but this was the opportunity of a life time; one I would savior forever. On I trudged finally finding secure footing on the west side of the dark street and at the same time ending a truly magical moment I wished could have gone on forever. Once we had gained solid ground neither made a move to part from the embrace of the other, but instead we remained transfixed, as if our bodies were inseparably molded as one. We had surpassed the boundaries of propriety and were now pounding on the door of scandalous behavior which good common sense would have precluded more prudent people from continuing to commit.

My head spun like a top and I knew this could not go on and certainly not escalate beyond what seemed a point of no return. With all the strength I could muster I bent slowly from the waist to lower Jessanne's feet to the grassy path below. That initial movement induced the woman to increase her grip on my neck and I knew I must resolve this situation instantly or fall into a downward spiral we could never reconcile ourselves from. With both feet firmly on the drier ground, Jessanne released her arms from about my neck but kept her head against my chest as her tiny hands slid ever so slowly down my arms finally coming to rest with her fingers entwined in mine.

How long we lingered in that position with her head on my chest, bodies pressed together, and hands entwined I will never know. Fortunately for all, a dog disturbed by some unseen night prowler commenced to bark or we might very well have met the rising sun still in a forbidden embrace.

"Oh my," Jessanne whispered, "it is getting very late and Mrs. Mills will begin to wonder what has kept you."

"Yes, I fear I have imposed upon your time." I agreed as we moved a few inches apart, eyes connecting once more, hands still clasped firmly together. I swung Jessanne's hand around my arm in the same fashion as we had begun the journey from the church to the Gates home. She smiled sweetly then whispered, "Thank you Captain."

We walked on arm in arm, hand in hand in complete silence, a powerful unspoken current passing between our bodies drawing us together like the sun attracts the moon. I have never experienced such exhilaration, such desire to live, even during the heat of battle. The energy ebbed and flowed back and forth from my heart to hers as if my spirit had penetrated her body and in turn hers possessed mine. No word, no deed, no painting could convey what was taking place at that instant in time and no power in heaven or on earth could stop it.

Suddenly we were at the front door of the Gates home and Jessanne turned to look me in the face once again. "I pray sir you will not think me a wanton woman for my actions this night, but.... well, I simply had no control of either mind or body. It was as if someone unknown to me took procession of my heart and soul." She paused, still looking deep in my eyes then said, "I do pray Captain, you were not sent here to test my religious moral conviction and in the process purloined my soul."

"No My Lady, I am not an agent of the devil but I certainly feel his hot breath on the back of my neck. I think it best for both of us if I make my excuses and depart this village as quickly as possible." I made the offer in all seriousness fearing Jessanne would be delighted to see the last of me.

"Oh please Captain, do not take such a desperate measure, for you would be sorely missed. Your independence and strong will are a breath of fresh air in a community existing under the tyrannical

85

dominance of the church." Jessanne hesitated, tightening her grasp on my arm then added, "I am alone in my beliefs in this small town, as alone as a person on a deserted island. I pray you will remain with us for a while, for I would be truly lost without you to serve as my confidant and friend." She tenderly uttered these words with sincere conviction.

"Please promise you will remain my loyal friend and never leave Mt. Zion without my being consulted first."

"I promise when it comes time for me to take my leave of this village you will most certainly be well informed of the event." I said humorously and she accepted my prediction in that same vain.

"Shall I see you on the morrow?" She asked with a genuine concern in her voice.

"Yes, My Lady, I shall be about town all day, dutifully performing my military obligations." I made the same promise as I had before to the enchanting woman I would indeed be in the area but not that I would see her.

"Will you be working on the common across the street again?"Jessanne indicated by pointing at the large village green.

"Then you were watching me there today?" I teased.

"Why ………. Well yes, but only because of all the noise you were making." Jessanne laughed.

"As I remember the day, all I did was step off the parade field and camp ground."

"Is that what you were doing? You military men certainly do walk heavy for each step you made rattled the dishes in my cupboard." Jessanne joked. "I dread what will happen to my house when hundreds of troops are stomping about with only a narrow street for protection."

"I shall instruct this prospective army to march on its tip toes so as not to disturb any of the homes in the area." I promised in a stern voice.

"That is very considerate of you Captain; and while you are at it, please whisper your commands just in case I might sleep late one morning."

"I shall go you one better, My Lady, we shall use only hand signals during morning drills so all the civilians may sleep undisturbed."

"I have no knowledge of hand signals Captain, except this one." Jessanne said sweetly, taking my right hand in hers. "Thank you for seeing me home and for being so understanding of a lonely woman."

"I fear I understand you and you understand me perfectly My Lady, it's now a matter of where destiny will lead us." My meaning was sincere and my heart was laid bare with every word.

"Dame Destiny is often a fickle female who cares not for truth and happiness." Jessanne said tenderly squeezing my hand.

"Yes but there are no other avenues open than to place ourselves in the hands of God, or fate, or destiny, or whatever controls the lives of those who are powerless to change their future." I starred longingly into Jessanne's bright green eyes and feared we would fall unwillingly into a kiss, an act that would jeopardize our relationship forever. Quickly I turned away, stepped back and whispered, "Good night My Lady, sweet dreams be with you."

"Yes, good night Captain and may your dreams be filled with joy and happiness." Jessanne's meaning was clear as had been my own. I stepped back to a full arms length while our hands remained clasped firmly together as if they had a mind of their own. It was with the greatest difficulty the grip slackened and the hands slipped slowly apart until only the tips of our fingers refused to separate. Our eyes fell to the small patches of skin on the ends of our index fingers holding on for dear life to that magical connection between two lonely souls who had finally happened on perfection. When the friction of skin on skin finally yielded to the overwhelming power of the universe, the digits fell away as if the weight of the world had broken the bond. My eyes flashed to Jessanne's face to record her reactions and my heart wrenched to see a tear form in her eye and slowly trickle down her rose colored cheek.

"Until the morrow." I whispered before turning to hurry away less she see the moisture welling up in my own eyes.

THE EVIDENCE UNFOLDS

Time being of the essence, I chose a path that led directly across the complctely dark open common that divided the Gates house from my lodging at the Mills place on the corner. I normally possess a keen instinct for what transpires about my person but on this night my mind was befuddled by the beautiful Jessanne. I was torn by my feelings for the lady and thoughts of what was proper, when my senses suddenly recorded a slight movement just to the south of where I trod. At first I thought it was some animal that I had disturbed but the sounds indicated something larger than a rabbit or squirrel.

"Hello." I called, but the only response was the same dog barking Jessanne and I had heard earlier. "Hello." I called once more but no one spoke out or moved. Still I knew something was out there in the blackness watching my every move. I, having been cursed with an over curious nature, could not resist moving closer to where the sounds had originated with the idea of discovering the source of the noise. When I had completed several short cautious steps, an unexpected explosion of sound and fury which could only be compared to the startled eruption of a covey of quail breaking cover, shattered the security of the night. I froze in place allowing my senses to measure the activity and judge any threat to my safety. My hearing, being well schooled from years of hunting in the fields and forests quickly determined there were two animals present both in wild flight. One raced off due west, crossing the street and disappearing between the houses situated south of the Gates home. The second moved north, then angled back to the west after striking the muddy street bordering between the common and the church. The poor creature attempted to flee through the nearly impassible street, but gave up in vain and moved to the better footing of the grassy path Jessanne and I had just strolled upon only moments before.

I made no attempt to pursue either of the flushed creatures, not knowing for certain what they were, nor why they fled in such panic. I was suddenly filled with dread knowing that both creatures had disappeared in the direction of the Gates home. With Jessanne home alone I feared for her safety. The urge to run to her side was overpowering, but controlling my anguish, I struck a match in hopes of finding any sign the pair might have left in the soft rain soaked soil of the village common. There, to my astonishment, lay a small faded neck scarf folded and knotted into a poke. It resembled pouches I had seen the black slaves back home carry their few precious belongings in when forced to leave home for whatever reason. With the discovery of the scarf, my concern for My Lady faded. Before the match flame flickered completely out, I bent down to retrieve the mud spattered parcel for a closer examination of its contents. Without striking another match which might draw inquisitive villagers, I merely felt through the thin cloth in an effort to identify whatever had been secreted within.

One heavy object felt very much like a thin metal ring, while another I was certain was an oblong metal frame probably containing a tin type of some loved one. Another object felt soft and disintegrated rapidly under the pressure of my harsh examining fingers; this item I was sure would prove to be a morsel of tenderly preserved food. This was not the time or place to make a further examination so I concealed the poke under my jacket and hurried off to the Mills home. I spoke only briefly to the couple who were taking the night air on their back porch and excused myself as being extremely tired. I did not wish to chance their discovery of what I had found on the green or to be subjected to curious scrutiny of what transpired between Jessanne and me.

Once safely within the confines of my small cottage, I quickly struck a match to the wick of a candle, eager to open the abandoned possible pouch hoping to learn more of its owner. The four corners were secured by means of a common square knot that I untied after laying the paupers luggage on the table under the candles flickering light. Gently folding back the four corners of the bag revealed how astute my original assessment of the contents had been. There reflecting the light from the single candle flame laid a petite inexpensive ring. I lifted the thin metal hoop up and held it close to the flame with the thought of inspecting it for a name or initials, but no such markings were visible and whatever stone that may have long ago occupied the setting was now only a memory.

The ring gave off a silvery sheen but its weight declared its true makeup as pewter or some cheaper variety of metal. Laying the ring aside, the ornate metal picture frame caught my attention next; so much so that I could not wait to bring it into the candlelight and attempt to define whatever image was protected within. My heart sank as my eyes focused on the surprising scene persevered on the small square tin type. The image was of a well dressed Mulatto boy of about nine or ten, obviously laid out in death, awaiting burial. This was not a wholly unheard of practice among the wealthily white men of the south who had sired children by their slave mistress then found themselves endeared to this illegitimate off spring. Whoever this now deceased young man was, he must have been dearly loved by someone who cared enough to pay for this likeness and endure the scorn its making would produce. But he must have been very close to another for only the most valuable of processions would have found their way into so small of a travel bag.

The haunting picture was difficult to put aside and I stood for several minutes studying its contents and its significance to those who had loved the youth. But put it down I did, only to continue my search of the pouches few remaining contents. The soft item I originally predicted to be food was indeed a square of cornmeal cake baked from crudely milled grain which had not crushed the kernels completely into fine flour. Intermixed with the now crumbled meal cake were three small coins which were nearly lost except for one that glinted brightly in the candlelight. My fingers sifted carefully through the cornmeal and, to my great surprise, retrieved a five dollar gold piece, then a second, followed by a third. It did not seem possible that someone with such a dilapidated scarf serving as make-shift luggage would be in the procession of such a large sum of money.

I poured the combination of cornbread crumbs and dirt out of the scarf onto my table for one last minute examination hoping against hope it would produce the ring's missing stone. If the stone were present it would surely be of low value as was the ring itself; but the search was in vain for nothing other than crumbs, dirt and a couple of dead insects remained in the faded piece of red cloth.

I blew the crumbs off the table and unable to resist, gathered up the haunting picture for one more close scrutiny of the youth's cold somber features. I then unthinking, laid the frame on the red scarf and turned away to find a hiding place for these objects that if found in my procession would be very difficult to explain. Something..... Some realization stopped me in my tracks and I turned back to the table and lifted the scarf up by two corners so the candle's flame glowed through the thin fabric from behind. The yellow flame illuminated several lines which were crooked and several that ran straight but for the most part the lines were parallel to one another. It was in that moment I realized the faded red scarf was a make-shift map. The crooked lines were the main rivers, Mississippi, Missouri, and so forth while the straight lines indicated north-south roads. All the lines, both crooked and straight, led to one star shaped insignia which could only represent the North Star.

The North Star was the one sure beacon for fugitive slaves for they were told by song and folklore to keep moving in the direction of that one stationary light in the night sky which would lead them to the promise land and freedom.

My God, I thought, the people I had encountered in the village green were runaway slaves following the Underground Railroad. Fitting pieces of the puzzle together took little skill; the blacks in the park, the dead black boy on the bluff and the presence of John Brown. The evidence was clear. It was as my father had thought; this area was part of the hated abolitionist trail which induced slaves to hazard their life and limb for a chance to be free.

A myriad of questions whirled through my mind. Which of this hamlet's fine citizens knew of this operation? Did they intentionally give aid to the fugitives and knowingly break the federal fugitive slave law? But the most profound question to trouble my thoughts dealt with Jessanne Gates and if she was involved in this nefarious activity.

My head reeled and my heart ached at the very thought of Jessanne being involved in such a sorted affair. This was a very serious business with some very unsavory characters lurking in the wings on both side of the issue. There was nearly a full fledge war unfolding on the Missouri-Kansas border with more combatants joining the movements each day. For the sake of my own sanity and for her own safety, I had to ascertain to what extent, if any, Jessanne aided and abetted this sacrilege.

John Brown was well known for his radical beliefs and he not only had the run of the town but its clearly unanimous support. One could only surmise from the dead black youth on the bluff and the discovery of the pouch dropped by two fleeing people that Mt. Zion was indeed a station on the Underground Railway.

I knew I must not speak of this discovery to anyone but instead bide my time and wait for undeniable proof of the treachery and law breaking that surely was being conducted under the auspices of Reverend Gates and the Church itself. This could prove to be a very complicated subject, full of intrigue and danger, but whatever happened, I must protect Jessanne's reputation as well as her person.

I replaced all the items; ring, tintype, coins and all, back in the red scarf and tied the ends up just as they were when discovered on the village green. As for a hiding place, the cottage held little in the way of a safe secure depository. After considerable study a small hole was found in the uppermost beams supporting the building's ridge pole. It was in this nearly invisible nook where I secreted the unknown transient's belongings. I hoped if the package were found to deny any knowledge of it and insist another tenant had placed it there for safe keeping before I arrived in town.

I knew this was a thin ploy that could easily explode in my face but I could think of no other way to preserve such valuable evidence except to keep it close at hand. The effort to conceal these purloined goods brought about a hint of guilt for whoever dropped the scarf had lost what would amount to their whole life's savings not to mention personal keepsakes. Still I could not very well advertise for its owners nor could they come forward to make a legitimate claim.

No, there was no other choice but to follow this course; a course of treachery and deceit, one of lies and mistrust. I openly cursed my father for placing his son in such a dreadful position but I had made my bed and now I must lay in it.

BAKED GOODS

The night passed painfully without sleep or comfort for body or soul. Still I managed to be present for Mrs. Mills' six AM breakfast of eggs and bacon but fortunately very little conversation. Perhaps my demeanor was not normal or I may have given off some scent that all was not well but the couple kept their own counsel as did I throughout the quick meal. It was not until I had excused myself from the table and began to go about my duties that the thought came to me the Mills' silence may have been induced as word spread about my accidental encounter with the two people on the green. I say two people for I had only suspicions they were runaway black slaves.

I walked slowly across the green that morning sure every eye in the vicinity was on me; so I made a pretense of laying out the bivouac area while at the same time examining the ground for any further sign. There were of course, imprints of my heavy boots as well as several others which had foolishly trod upon my own from the night before. Whoever had made these tracks, and there were more than one set, had been on the green during the overnight hours. Perhaps the tracks were those of the conductor in search of the Underground Railroad passengers who I had startled into blind flight. I studied the boot prints with the idea of possibly recognizing them in the future, although, none of them displayed any distinctive marks. I fought a burning desire to investigate both the north and west street bordering the common. The two fleeing fugitives from the night before had crossed those muddy streets and would surely have left easily recognizable tracks. But many prying eyes observed my every movement that day and searching for tracks would be an absolute give-away of my interest. I also realized an unusual number of horses and horse drawn equipment plied those two avenues that day. Their objective was clear; they wished to obliterate any footprints before I could make a casual search.

I passed the better part of the morning dissecting the village green for future use by the yet-to-appear troops I was expected to train. I reluctantly stole an occasional glance at the Gates house but never saw a sign of Jessanne or for that matter, any indication of daily activity one would expect to see around an occupied home. One would normally see water being drawn from the well, windows being opened to allow a breeze to break the heat of the day, or clothing hung on the clothes line to dry or air out. As the noon hour neared and still no sign of life could be spotted around the Gates home, I became concerned for Jessanne's safety but I knew it would be unwise for a stranger to question the activity of another man's wife, especially a man as important in the community as the Reverend Joshua Gates. I bit my tongue and trudged wearily back to the Mills house for the noon meal wishing to broach the subject of Jessanne over the dinner table but resigning myself to keep quiet on the matter.

Mr. and Mrs. Mills were already at the table as I stepped through the rear kitchen door and was bid to take a chair just in time to say grace. The meal itself was one of a light nature compared to breakfast or supper but I came to realize that was Mrs. Mills' way during the heat of summer. The fair consisted of fresh bread, cold roast beef, early vegetables from the garden and plenty of butter and honey. The noon conversation was much more amicable than the earlier meal had been, for it mostly centered on the large amount of honey a man named Fisk had brought to the mercantile to trade for much needed goods.

As the meal ended, Mrs. Mills poured another round of hot coffee, which I stated I did not wish for on such a warm day. "Oh, but I am sure you will need another cup of coffee to wash down the big piece of chocolate cake that is to be your desert." Mrs. Mills said smiling as she removed a large chocolate frosted cake from the cupboard.

"Thank you, Ma'am," I replied. "Baking a cake on such a hot morning is very thoughtful of you."

"It would be indeed, if I had baked this cake, but I did not. This cake is a thank you from Jessanne Gates for escorting her last evening."

"Indeed?" Mr. Mills announced in surprise.

"Yes indeed, Jessanne dropped it by mid morning with the wish I convey her appreciation to you Captain, I believe that is how she put it." Mrs. Mills' words filled me with great relief knowing Jessanne was well and her reference to my rank of Captain indicated there were no morning-after regrets.

"That is a very generous gesture on Mrs. Gates' part; I must remember to thank her." Were the only words I could muster and manage to smile at the same time. "It looks delightful and I hope you will both join me in consuming this delicacy before it dries out."

"I thought you would never ask." Buck Mills laughed. "I'd never turn down a slice of cake Jessanne baked." The idea of a married woman going to so much trouble on my behalf was quickly forgotten as both of the Mills' wished to get a fair share of that beautiful chocolate cake.

After dinner I resumed my pretense of working on the village common but one troubling thought reoccurred throughout the long tiring hot afternoon: *How did Jessanne Gates manage to leave her home without my having seen her depart?*

The other irritating question that came to my mind concerned the baking of the chocolate cake. I had not observed even a faint trace of smoke coming from either of the dwellings two chimneys during the morning hours so how on earth did the woman manage to bake a cake for me?

These questions weighed heavily on my mind, still weary from the sleepless night before, so much so that at one point I convinced myself I had simply missed both the woman's departure and the cooking smoke. *That must be it.* I thought. I was so wrapped up in searching for more signs in the grass and at the same time appearing busy with my duties I did not notice all that took place about the Gates house. I could not account for these strange happenings in any other way; besides my heart often overcame any semblance of common sense at that time in my life. By the time supper rolled around the whole matter was settled and I enjoyed an inner peace knowing Jessanne had baked a cake especially for me and used the title of Captain when referring to me.

I met Mr. Mills at his front gate a few minutes past the six o'clock hour where we exchanged greetings and then hurriedly cleaned up for supper. Mrs. Mills had set a fine table for the evening meal and the couple emitted a casual air about their person. The church bell had not rung that evening and somehow I felt they knew there would not be a gathering this night. The dining proceeded at a leisurely pace with the last of Jessanne's delicious cake being consumed for our desert. As I savored those final crumbs of the light chocolate cake my now refreshed and rested brain recalled the doubts I had experienced earlier concerning Jessanne's activities but I was unwilling to present such questions to the Mills family. Still I knew I must find an answer if I were to ever have any peace of mind this night.

I praised Mrs. Mills' cooking and thanked her graciously before asking to be excused. I made up the cover story stating I wished to take my horse out to the tall grassland west of town to allow him to graze for an hour or so. This the couple readily accepted as it was a good reason to be out and about in the evening.

THE DEVIL'S DECIPLES

Shortly I rode slowly into the setting sun along the street that served as the boundary on the south side of the village green. At the corner of the common I wished with all my heart to turn my mount north and ride past the Gates home in hopes of catching a fleeting glimpse of Jessanne but after a moment's hesitation I continued on west as I knew I must.

The area east of the steep Missouri River bluffs consisted of large rolling mounds covered with deep green grass which reminded one of huge rolling waves on a storm tossed sea. These gentle hills were interspersed with small creeks and clear flowing streams outlined with several varieties of trees thriving on the plentiful moisture. The topography was so similar that one could easily become confused and travel up the wrong draw only to arrive at some unknown hilltop far from their chosen destination. A good sense of direction was a blessing and a necessity when traversing the unoccupied knolls that formed the great watershed which lay between the Missouri River and a second river bottom some fifteen miles to the east. This second bottom was created by a much smaller river named the Nishnabotna, whose shallow muddy channel ran in a southwesterly direction eventually joining the massive Missouri River very close to the Iowa-Missouri state line.

The Nishnabotna River was navigable only by small rafts and row boats, unlike the Missouri which could easily accommodate large steam powered commercial vessels; however both valleys were easily followed avenues for traffic moving through the sparsely settled land.

I rode to where the street faded into the open unfenced grasslands that spread west of town to the towering bluffs. Here I paused to reconnoiter the unsettled open windblown terrain. Although the trail to the bluffs lay only a half mile north of this position, the two areas differed greatly in makeup. The trail west followed an entirely different creek bed running due west before turning southwest leading to even larger tributaries until finally terminating at the Missouri River bottom. However this area was drained by a small creek which ran straight south for over a mile before feeding into a larger creek flowing due west. It was at this moment I realized the wide plateau on which Mt. Zion had been established was the divide of the two great water sheds. The waters from the west side of town found their way to the Missouri while any springs or rain falling on the east edge of town fell to the Nishnabotna River.

I unsaddled my horse and allowed him to graze and roll in the fresh grass as he willed, while I wandered down to the heavily tree lined creek originating near the houses on the west side of town. This particular waterway began life as a small spring that surfaced just near the small barn that sat behind the Gates house. The spring began as a trickle in a deep cut bank that could easily hide the movements of a man, especially if the person were short or walking in a crouched position. *Could it be Jessanne had used this low lying path when departing from home this morning on the way to deliver the chocolate cake at the Mills house?*

I stared intently, or more correctly one would say unconsciously, at the clear spring water rushing past the toe of my knee-high boots, as gravity caused it to tumble down the incline of the stream bed until this singular power of nature was at last satisfied the water could travel no further. In day dreaming of where this water's journey might end, a large white stone in the bottom of the normally rockless creek caught my eye. I stepped into the main stream and sank several inches into the soft muddy creek bottom suddenly changing the clean clear water into an ugly brown boiling mess. I kept my eye on the stone and managed to retrieve it in the midst of the riled up waters. Holding the stone up to catch the fading sunlight, I recognized it as being a handmade spear point some wandering Indian had the misfortune of losing somewhere in the immediate area. I had always been intrigued by such tools, as it represented great value to the original owner, considering the amount of time, effort and skill required to manufacture such an implement. I quickly pocketed the stone point to show others of the community knowing in the back of my mind few people shared my appreciation for such a piece of art.

The discovery of the Indian artifact peaked my interest enough that further searching of the creek bed seemed a reasonable move before the light faded. I moved slowly down stream away from town not wishing to be seen skulking about Jessanne's house at such a late hour. I carefully scrutinized the banks as well as the creek bed itself in hopes of finding similar Indian handiwork to no avail. But my eyes did make a rather startling discovery that made me wish whole heartedly I had never held an interest in Indians relics. There before me were the perfect imprints of two bare feet; strangely enough, both were of the left foot but of different sizes. I moved close and kneeled down to read all the myriad of information that muddy foot prints may disclose. The large print was very wide, and as long as my foot, which was considered extreme by most boot maker's standards. The second and much smaller print was narrow and did not sink as deep into the soft dark medium as the first. I had seen enough tracks of barefoot blacks on my father's estate to know these marks were produced by feet unaccustomed to wearing shoes.

As I kneeled there in deep study it occurred to me that these tracks were most assuredly left by the two people I had happened upon in the village green the night before. They had fled in this general direction and they would certainly have sought to make an unseen escape down this hidden creek bed. The tracks lent more credence to my belief that run-away slaves were being ushered through this area by members of the local population.

I rose, took a few more steps, and then bent down to inspect another almost indistinguishable footprint some distance from the creek. It was obvious this person was attempting to cover any sign of having trespassed along the narrow stream while following the ever more visible barefoot prints. This faint print was difficult to read but about two feet further on I spied a much clearer track where the perpetrator had made a misstep into softer ground.

I was shocked to discover this track was most definitely that of a woman's shoe, a small woman's shoe. *Could it be Jessanne had exited her home early this morning, traveled down this path for some legitimate reason and only by accident created tracks paralleling those of the two black fugitives? All three sets of tracks were leading away from town. But what reason could the Reverend's wife have for traveling alone down in the mud rather than taking the higher dryer ground, if say she were searching for a lost milch cow?* Whatever the reason I could not, nor would not approach her for an explanation. I admit, I could not ask Jessanne these questions, for deep in my heart I feared what the answer would be; an answer that would destroy my soul like a hungry wolf devours the body of a helpless rabbit.

I moved through the twilight on down the hill, having little trouble finding further examples of the bare foot prints but nothing indicated the shod woman had traveled any farther along this avenue of escape.

The sun was setting and the shadows grew longer by the minute. I knew it was time to find my horse and return to my lodging but that ingrained curiosity drove me onward. The old parable about the demise of the curious cat should have been my fate on many an occasion and in this particular instant I wish it had struck me down; for something, call it a sense or a gift, but an unknown power willed that I climb up the creek bank and creep over a grassy knoll bringing me to a clump of bushes overlooking a wide spot in the creek below. Even in the fading light I could easily make out the three individuals gathered against the far bank in an attempt to conceal their meeting.

Two blacks, one a very large young man attired in tattered shirt and pants was kneeling down beside the figure of a very small Negro female who lay prostrate on the brilliant green grass. The black female, also dressed very poorly, appeared ill as she lay very quiet and still as if the grim reaper was in the act of harvesting her weary soul.

The long shadow of the creek bank fell heavily over the third person who was kneeling down on the opposite side of the ill woman. The shadow made identification of this third person nearly impossible but I felt quite certain it was a small framed white woman. Much of this conclusion I derived from the fact that her dark silhouette appeared to be richly attired, at least more so than the two blacks. It was obvious both the black male and the white female were showing deep concern for the condition of the small black female. They were washing her face with a piece of cloth dampened in the creeks clear water and at the same time attempting to induce her to drink from a small metal cup. From my vantage point the ill woman showed little sign of life; her body, arms and head lay limp certainly not under the control of her faculties.

A discussion, perhaps a disagreement, was in process between the white woman and the black male but it was conducted in such low tones I was unable to hear anything being said. However, from the wild gesturing and head shaking it became clear the ill girl was the topic of conversation. As darkness set in, the disagreement became more animated and the black man displayed a more aggressive behavior as if demanding to have his way, whatever that might be. But in the end the male gently scooped his ill companion into his powerful arms and began to follow the small white woman up the creek in the direction of town.

I crouched low behind the bushes and waited for the three to wind their way discretely up the creek and disappear from my line of view. I did not wish to reveal my presence to them, even though I could have assisted in carrying the black woman, which in truth, the big black man handled easily. My intent was to follow the trio and try to ascertain where the ill woman would be deposited for the night. I suspected being of poor health someone in town would be prevailed upon to give the woman sanctuary from the night dampness and perhaps for an even longer period. I had to know who in this town would willingly defy the federal government by aiding a fugitive slave, for such an act could be punishable with severe consequences, both from official and nonofficial sources.

The afternoon winds which had whipped the long stemmed blue-green grass expired with the sunlight as if driven over the western horizon by the much more powerful shadows of night. That first calm dead silence of evening was a dangerous time for anyone wishing to move undetected over the lush verdant prairie, for the vegetation crackled with every footfall or hissed out a startling warning if accidentally brushed against by cloth or skin. In just moments the world of daylight creatures gave way to their nighttime counterparts and the blackness began to sing with the sound of untold numbers of insects suddenly rising up to claim their share of time to occupy the world. The nocturnal mammals, fox, coon, coyote and wolf left their daylight beddings to join the owl that swooped down from its tree branch and the bats that disserted some dark hidden sanctuary to move about in the protective freedom of the night.

This near invisibility and the covering sounds of the night encouraged the three to move along a bit more recklessly in an effort to find a place of safety as quickly as possible. They moved so fast and with complete disregard for any danger present about them that they passed within just feet of my horse Sergeant who lay quietly on the rich prairie grass enjoying his last moments of freedom.

I followed close behind, realizing the man and woman were very inept at the art of stealth-hunting and woods-craft for they blundered on as if taking a leisurely evening stroll. A combination of concern for the ill black female and a false sense of security that darkness instills in these uninitiated, caused both to dispel any commonly held fears of being sighted. I had learned long ago one may see best in the dark by not looking directly at the object of interest; in this case three rapidly moving bodies. It was quite easy to watch the white woman lead the way up the creek bed to the north, then make a sharp turn to the east. Without so much as pausing to reconnoiter the area, the woman marched straight up to the rear door of the small barn occupying the rear of the Reverend Joshua Gates property. Opening the small door, the white woman hurriedly ushered the large black man and his burden into the dark interior of the barn. In a few seconds a candle flickered to life, its faint yellow light escaping through a small side window, plus every knot hole and crack in the rough cut board walls.

I knew then the white woman inside the barn must indeed be Jessanne Gates. 'My Lady', I had called her. The realization of the seriousness of the situation struck me dumb-founded. I dropped to the ground mesmerized by the ghostly pale yellow lines of candlelight conveniently outlining the crude structure. The setting reminded me of a picture from the Bible I had once seen as a child of the stable in Bethlehem on the night of Christ's birth. It was a truly inspiring moment, one which filled me with doubt about my life and religious beliefs.

I must have kept vigil over that little barn for an hour or more and would have remained longer if the large black male had not slipped out the door to retrace his tracks back down to the creek. The fleeing man

113

passed within inches of where I sat but his fear and eagerness to escape prevented his ability to detect my presence. This was a foolish mistake on his part and a very dangerous practice in which to become accustomed. I was now sure that the black man was a runaway slave. I gave him very little chance of success if he continued to charge about so brashly and without contemplating his every move before it was made.

I remained in hiding for several minutes after the big black rushed by in anticipation of his return or that Jessanne might reappear at the barn door and discover my unauthorized trespassing. However, that old curiosity once more took command of my better judgment and I found myself creeping up on the yellow tinged portal serving as a window to the barn. It was a small diamond shaped affair consisting of one solid pane of poorly manufactured glass, so inferior in quality that numerous bubbles and distortions made peering through it nearly impossible. This type of window, though of faulty construction, was difficult to come by on the frontier and was installed only for the purpose of emitting light into the barn and not for admiring the view from without. All I could make out through the defective glass was several wooden boxes piled high along the opposite wall and one very long wooden box that was serving as a make-shift bed for the ill black female.

The window made recognizing the white woman impossible; besides, she worked crouched so low over her patient her face was turned down and away from my position. The barn was constructed of one by eight inch green cut boards which were nailed on vertically and allowed to dry in place. This caused great cracks to form between the boards as they cured in the heat of the sun. Some of these gaps were better than an inch wide and ran top to bottom of the building. I moved carefully along the west wall of the building, placing my eye to each crack, and then moving up and down in an attempt to peer around harness and tools hanging on the interior of the wall.

The visibility through some of the cracks appeared to be blocked by the same wooded boxes I had seen stacked against the inside of the east wall. I continued to silently move from board to board until I reached the corner of the barn, which would place me on the north side of the building and would greatly expose my movement to anyone on the street who might be passing the Gates house.

I cautiously scanned the area and decided the risk of being discovered was worth the information which might be gleaned from further investigation. Board by board I moved along the north wall and in each crack something hindered my view of whom and what was within this intriguing building. Finally I came upon a small knot hole which was unobstructed on the inside and there in the glow of the smoking candle flame I could clearly see the top of the white woman's head still bent over the patient who was lying on a long box. The woman's bonnet-less head was covered in flowing tresses of raven black hair with a part so wide down the middle one could easily view her shining white scalp and a wide red bow of ribbon was tied tight to keep the long coiled ringlets from falling in her face as she bent at her task.

I stood frozen in dreadful anticipation for untold minutes, eyes welded to the crown of the mysterious woman's head, praying for one glimpse of the face beneath; but knowing deep in my soul the revelation would shatter my heart like the shell of an egg dropped on a stone walk. I felt guilty, like a young school boy sneaking his first peak through a key hole at some distant female relative as she disrobed in another room. In your heart you knew you were breaking a sacred trust and you must avert your eyes but no matter how hard you tried no power on earth could turn your head or close your eyes.

Suddenly the woman's head flew straight up then turned slowly to look directly at the very knot hole I peered through as if some mysterious power had informed her of the prying eye from without.

I had not made a sound up to that point but when Jessanne's piercing green eyes fell on mine, I sucked in one long very audible breath that she undoubtedly heard. Her eyes remained fixed on my peep hole for what seemed an eternity then she shook her head knowingly and resumed her efforts to treat the ill woman.

I fell back in shock, my right hand clutching the corner of the barn in an attempt to stabilize my shaking knees, before slinking away like some despicable Peeping Tom caught in the act.

I staggered down the draw to the west, my brain in such turmoil that I had nearly forgotten about my horse still enjoying the rich grassland beyond. As I approached, the loyal animal moved in position to playfully push me with his nose, a trait not desirable in a war horse but one I had not been successful in breaking. I overlooked this minor defect for he was a fearless fighter of either man or beast when need be, and he knew how in combat, to shoulder an enemy horse off its feet.

The head butt managed to bring me back to my senses and to what might prove to be an unfavorable situation in which to be found. My first less than heroic instinct was to saddle up and ride as far away from this nest of vipers as possible and I was in fact preparing to do that very thing when I heard horses approaching from the south creek. If I had been in my normal frame of mind I would have recognized the signs my mount displayed, having sensed the movement long before me.

I waited until the two horsemen were only a few rods away before I hailed them with a friendly hello. Both riders reined in hard, startled by my undetected presence standing beside my horse in the dark of night.

"Who is there?" The lead man demanded sharply, reaching for a revolver in his wide leather belt. His voice carried the familiar distinct twang of the Alabama hill people.

"I am Captain James Lang." I replied firmly knowing it best to show no weakness in such encounters.

"What are you doing out here alone at night?" The same man asked gruffly.

"I have been pasturing my horse and about to return to town," came my stern reply, "and now sir, if you will be so kind as to answer those same questions for me."

I could hear a low mumble exchanged between the two men but no answer was forthcoming.

"Come now gentlemen; are you travelers in search of food and lodging? If so I might direct you to a place to fill your needs." My words were accommodating but not pleasant.

"Have you seen anyone wandering around on foot out here this evening?" The man demanded.

My initial fears appeared correct; the two men were slave chasers who had picked up the runaway's barefoot tracks in the creek mud. They had lost the tracks due to the darkness and now were following the creek in hopes of overtaking the fugitive.

"Good evening gentlemen, I hope you find your way for I have nothing more to say to you." I stated in my deepest military tone while swinging into the saddle.

"Halt, I have a weapon aimed at you!" The voice from the dark ordered.

"Do you have a good sense of hearing?" I asked flatly.

"Yes, mine is as good as anyone's, I reckon." The man replied.

"Good, then tell me if you recognize this sound." My voice was filled with humor as I slowly thumbed back the hammer of the huge Colt Walker revolver that I habitually carried in a holster on the pommel of my saddle.

The loud clacking sounds of the action being worked as the massive cylinder turned and the hammer notches clicked into full lock was an unmistakable sound to anyone familiar with firearms.

"It's a six shot 44 Walker if you boys are wondering." I announced defiantly.

A deadly silence engulfed the three of us before the lead man spoke once more. "Be about your business then sir," came the surly statement.

"And you yours." I called out in a most unfriendly way.

The two men turned their mounts about and rode hurriedly off to the west, leaving me to sit there alone on that vast dark prairie and ponder what had just happened.

I rode directly to the Mills home, stabled my mount and made an excuse for my tardiness saying my horse had been difficult to recapture. I had no intention of recounting what I had witnessed on the prairie west of town so I retired to the confines of my small cottage to prepare mentally for what the morrow would bring.

I slept little and rose early; my attire this day to include my Colt Walker in my waist belt. I shared a quick breakfast with the Mills couple then pretended to go about my business. As I anticipated, my work was soon interrupted by a young boy sent with an urgent summons requiring my presence at the Mills Mercantile. I thanked the youth and followed him the two blocks to Main Street where I could see several horses tied up in front of Mr. Mills store and a like number of men gathered in the shade of the buildings porch.

I walked confidently to the store, sure in my mind the two men I confronted on the prairie the night before would be directly involved in this impromptu meeting. Mr. Mills greeted me nervously as I stepped into the welcome shade of the stores front porch but no one else even acknowledged they knew who I was.

"This gentleman is Captain James Lang." Mr. Mills said cordially, trying to hide his fear.

"Yes, this is the man from last night!" The tall scruffy looking man with the Alabama accent snapped. His voice was easily recognizable from the conversation the night before. "What were you doing and where were you going last night when we met you west of town?" He demanded.

"I believe we had this discussion last night and unless you two identify yourselves this meeting will end as quickly as that one did." I said in a loud distinct voice.

"Now Captain, let us treat these gentlemen kindly." Buck Mills interceded.

"I give what I get and I will say nothing more until such time as I know who these men are and what their business is here in town."

"The only thing you need to know is that we are carrying papers that allows us to legally capture and return three runaway slaves. There is a large male, a teenage boy and a small female that are property of a gentleman in Missouri." The tall heavily armed man took a step in my direction with intent to intimidate me all the while staring me in the eye.

"Now we have established why you are here." I paused, my eyes boring into the tall man as I took a step in his direction bringing us only inches apart. "But you still have not provided your names." He had challenged me and now I had returned it in kind, the next move was up to him.

"Our names are of no importance but our search damn sure is!" The tall man raised his voice to a hurricane level.

"Well I don't care about your search, but you're right, without names you are of no importance. I will not carry on any further dialogue with you now or at any other time until I have your names." The power of my voice equaled the tall man's in furry and conviction.

"We can have the law here shortly to make you talk." The tall man said in a more subdued tone.

"You do whatever you like but I can tell you this; that lawman, whoever he may be, had better have a name and proper identification if he expects to question me." I roared, turning on my heel and stepping off the porch's board floor into the mud-hole pocked street.

"Please Captain." Mills called after me, but I refused to be dissuaded and continued to walk away. I could hear the tall man speaking in a near whisper to his companion. The second man was utterly filthy, of heavy build with long greasy hair and a mouth full of rotted teeth. It was clear the tall man was in control and provided most of the limited brain work; still he did seek his partner's approval before speaking again.

"Alright I will tell you our names if that will get you to speak up about the three runners. But I'll have you know I could legally make you talk if I wanted to." The tall man threatened.

I turned slowly to face the men on the porch, placed my right hand on the butt of the Colt Walker before snarling. "You can try anytime you wish." A dead silence fell over the group and the tall man snapped a quick look at his partner, then back at my hand resting on the big revolvers smooth wooden grips.

"Name is Hixon, Lyman Hixon, and this here is Ira Ketchum." The tall man blurted out.

"Now that is much better." I smiled a cocky little smile for I had held out and backed the two men down giving me a bit of an upper hand in any future dealings.

"That's enough foolishness. I only gave in 'cause I know those three are in this area and they would be long gone afore I could get any law back here." Hixon growled. "I say I know they're here 'cause we tracked 'em to the creek just where we ran into you last night. So I figure you seen 'em and just maybe you know their where-abouts."

I knew I must lie to the men for if I admitted anything, Jessanne and the whole town would be in grave danger. "No." I said flatly.

"But they was all up and down that creek bed. You must have seen 'em." Hixon insisted.

"No, as I said before, I never saw anyone while I was out with my horse. I have good eye sight but I never could see darkies on a dark night." The statement brought a nervous giggle from some of the towns citizens gathered on the Mills store porch.

"There was lots of sign; in fact there was hoof prints over the top of some of their tracks!" The tall man would not give up his attempt to gain confirmation that the blacks were in town.

"Lots of folks run horses out that way, could have been most anybody's animal; maybe even your own." I argued.

"Looked like someone helped 'em at one point but we couldn't make out all of the sign." Hixon kept chipping away.

"Well if anyone helped them, it certainly was not me." I stated flatly. "Maybe you just got on the wrong trail, easy enough to do around these parts." I challenged.

"No sir, they was out in that creek about the same time as you." Hixon reiterated.

"Well if there were anyone out on the creek when I was there, I did not see them. Say what you want; they are pretty cunning - just like wild animals." I suggested in language the two men would understand.

"I hear tell you found a dead nigger buck a couple days back." Hixon commented in a friendlier tone.

"Yes, that's true but he was not dead when I first found him on top of the river bluffs."

"Did you kill him?" Hixon demanded infuriated he might have lost the fee for capturing a runaway.

"No, lightning bolt." Was my only reply.

"What did this nigger look like?" Hixon growled.

"Maybe six feet tall, black hair, black skin, hell I don't know they all look the same to me." I hoped the description would throw the two men off their scent and they would move on. "Mr. Mills saw him; maybe he has a better eye for judging those fellas." I suggested hoping he would back me up as to the boy's size.

"Yes, yes, that sounds about right, six feet and strong, like he had been worked hard."

"Where is he buried at?" Hixon demanded.

"I buried him on top of the bluff that he died on."

"Then you're goin' to have to take us out there and dig him up again just in case he is the one we are carrying paper on."

"I am not taking you any place, especially to dig up some poor soul's grave." I said sternly.

"I don't know mister, but I think you are trying to skin us with this story of yours." Hixon growled threateningly.

"Mr. Hixon, I was born and raised in the south and I have unfortunately been exposed to scum like you and your partner all my life. As a soldier I have been in the business of killing most of my life. I have no qualms about killing either or both of you and if you just once more appear to question my integrity, I shall be forced to do just that! Do I make myself clear?"

"You can't go around threatenin' to kill someone." Hixon's voice was shaky and filled with stress.

"Oh, let me make this perfectly clear. That is not a threat, Mr. Hixon what I said is a bonafide promise."

"Are all the people in this town so unfriendly?" Hixon asked Mills.

"Why no sir, this is a very warm friendly community, I think you two just got off on the wrong foot is all." Mills said apologetically.

"Then why is this fella causin' me so much trouble?" Hixon questioned.

"You just do not understand, Mr. Hixon." I interjected. "I am not a resident of Mt. Zion but rather a mere wayfarer like yourselves. I am in search of an income opportunity; again like yourself, I hope for quick riches with little effort. Now then, your animals look rested and ready for the trail, so I heartily suggest the two of you be on your way."

"Are you ordering us out of town?" Hixon asked in disbelief.

"No, just a word to the wise, for I am certain you have other interests; let's say safer interests to pursue elsewhere." I offered pleasantly.

"Just who do you think you are, trying to run us out of town?" Hixon's voice reflected his fear and loathing of me and I knew I had the upper hand in this situation.

"A man of my profession has only three possessions; integrity, honor, and courage. You, Hixon have called into question all three." I added. "Once a man like myself loses any one of these three traits he can no longer function or earn a living. Its winner take all, live or die by what I represent, do you understand?" I fell silent for several seconds, my eyes boring intently into Hixon's face. "Well there it lays, either you two ride out of town now or my pride demands that I kill you both for your transgressions." I spoke these final words with all the hard edged bitterness I could muster.

"You are crazy!" Hixon yelled. "I have heard some strange stories about the crazy abolitionists in this town but I never thought I'd see it for myself." The tall man nodded to Ira Ketchum indicating it was time to be moving on. The two men hurriedly untied their mounts and jumped in the saddles as their excited horses sprang to action.

"Maybe someday I will catch you alone without your big Colt revolver and then we will see who is bull of the woods!" Hixon yelled over his shoulder as he fought to control his rearing horse.

"I will be looking to the day I meet the two of you without any witnesses." I warned as the two men raced down Main Street and out of town.

"I wish you had not treated those men so roughly." Buck Mills said painfully, his fear evident in both words and actions.

"What do you think I should have done with them sir, invite them to supper at your house?" I asked a bit angered at the disdain the gathered group of men, who had remained silent throughout the entire confrontations, was now subjecting me to. "I made my position quite clear at the first church meeting I attended that I live by my code and not one you or anyone else may hold up as a shining example of how

127

they wish life to be." I stated gruffly. "I make no apologies for my actions but I will warn you the citizens of this community are playing a very dangerous game which will ultimately cost human lives." With those words of doom I turned and walked back to the village common, my blood boiling for having been such a fool.

I had moved here to watch for abolitionist activities, I had found proof positive of such illegal acts, and now I find myself protecting these criminals at the risk of my own life. What a fool an infatuated heart can make of a grown man.

Still in a huff, I refused to eat the noon meal at Mrs. Mills' house, ignoring her repeated calls as if unable to hear her. Instead I made my way north across the western trail in the pretense of inspecting the location for the new rifle range.

The rifle range was a quiet place, giving a man the opportunity to think through the troubles of the day and I took complete advantage of the solitude. By mid afternoon I knew my course was set and, come hell or high water, it was the path I must take regardless of consequences.

As evening approached I began to walk north, then west not far off the western trail, hoping deep in my soul I would encounter Hixon and Ketchum alone in this sea of tall grass and put an end to either them or me. As for myself, at this point death was a very appealing alternative to the situation I now found myself in.

I, a product of slave holders, a son of the south and staunch supporter of the lifestyle that had given me all the advantages I now enjoyed; I had betrayed my heritage. I was in love with a married woman who was an unabashed abolitionist, hiding run-away slaves on her very own property. I had made enemies of two hard cases who would think nothing of taking mine or anyone else's life in order to destroy these illegal activities and the woman I loved so futility. What made matters even worse was the fact that the very people I defended against the two bounty hunters did not appreciate one bit my efforts.

SECRETS OF THE GATES BARN

I found myself standing alone atop a windswept grassy knoll about a mile west of Mt. Zion, mesmerized by the innocent glow of the settlement in the afternoons waning sunlight. The long stemmed blue grass tossed by the wind gave the buildings an image of ships riding on a rolling sea. That serene fantasy was shattered by the first strike of the church bell indicating it was six o'clock and all the faithful citizens would be expected to be present for the evening meeting in one hour.

While I had stubbornly refused to eat at noon I had no intention of boycotting supper but the mile walk to town would prevent my arriving at Mrs. Mills' table in time to partake of the evening meal before meeting time. I resigned myself to the fact this would be one of those days of hunger every soldier knows and must willingly endure.

With no reason to hurry, I started walking slowly toward town purposely intending to arrive too late for a punctual arrival at the evening meeting. I had already incurred the wrath of the church earlier that day so I saw no reason to make amends by attending the meeting, let alone arriving promptly.

At six o'clock the church bell had been struck six times and now sixty minutes later three loud evenly spaced tones rang from the tower and out across the surrounding hills to indicate the meeting had come to order. Those three distinct vibrating sounds caused an idea to form in my head; admittedly a devious idea but the chance of a life time. I was certain Jessanne would answer the call to church as a representative of her absent husband and in so doing leave her home and barn unsecured. This was a golden opportunity to search the barn and possibly her very house for evidence of the illegal activities I knew to be taking place.

It seemed prudent to act casual in approaching the Gates property from the west as if one were out for a late afternoon stroll; this also made scouting the area for prying eyes much easier. After a quick look about, I moved swiftly to the side door of the barn where Jessanne had disappeared with the slave girl the night before. This normally insignificant door might prove to be a porthole to another world or possibly the end of mine, but whatever it concealed, passage through it was irresistible. The door itself was fabricated from two large slabs of rough cut native lumber, with two smaller strips of the same wood held in place with wooden dowels to serve as bracing. Four pieces of whang leather nailed to the doorsill constituted the hinges which aided in swinging the heavy obstacle to its open position.

The good Reverend had put his trust in God and not in a lock, so gaining entry to the barn required nothing more than desire and an application of brute strength. Leaving the door slightly open to facilitate the sudden need to exit the structure, I studied the gloomy interior while my eyes adjusted from the brilliant exterior sun light that failed to penetrate the one small window in the west wall. The large wooden boxes I had spied through the cracks in the boards remained stacked just as I remember them. The long low crate still rested in the center of the dirt floor but, fortunately, no black body bedded upon it as before. The faint light hindered investigation; and lighting the small candle would certainly draw unwanted attention to my trespassing in the Gates barn.

I could distinguish white lettering hand painted on the wooden boxes which most certainly had been applied for the purpose of shipping cross country, most likely by steamboat. The large words were quite easily read: furniture, books, and glassware - handle with care. All were addressed to Reverend Joshua Gates, Mt. Zion, Fremont County Iowa. The small print proved to be the name of the shipper and obviously intended to be more difficult to interpret in any light. It read New England Christian Missionary and Bible Society. No town or state was listed as point of origin nor any individuals name as responsible in case of damage or loss.

The whole affair struck a strange cord in my mind, for here was a community lacking in nearly every sort of worldly goods and these luxuries were stored away in a barn. The houses were sparsely decorated and the church was lacking in Bibles and hymnals and yet here in the Reverend's barn were stacks of crates full of such goods. That old cursed cat curiosity, wishing to gamble one more of its lives came to the fore and I began to look about for some sturdy implement to pry open the lid of these boxes and explore their secreted contents.

A faint scuffling sound from the open doorway caused me to freeze in place with hopes the sound was a cat after a mouse or some such innocent activity. The door was at my back and I waited nervously for any further noise or movement which might reveal the source of the disturbance, yet when several seconds passed without a repeat of the sound, I relaxed certain I had not been discovered. Curiosity compelled me to turn then and look at the door. There in the orange glow of the setting sun I could make out only the black silhouette of a small female form.

"Captain." The words came forth calm and warm without a hint of surprise or alarm.

I could not speak, but instead raised my right hand in an attempt to block out the brilliant rays of the setting sun. I tried to visualize the face of the woman who had said my name, but it was an act of embarrassment for I knew full well the voice was none other than Jessanne Gates.

"I – I." My stuttering only made my shame more evident. Pitifully, Jessanne interrupt my babbling.

"I, sir, am greatly disappointed in you." She scolded sharply.

"Yes, yes, I know I must beg your forgiveness for taking such a liberty as to trespass on your property uninvited." I said sporting a silly grin.

"Oh your being here is not what disappoints me. I have been standing vigil over this barn since you peeked through that corner knot hole last night." She said calmly. "I knew a man of your caliber would not be satisfied until he had inspected the contents of these boxes."

"How on earth did you know I was watching through that hole?" I asked in all sincerity.

Jessanne's complexion suddenly matched the red glow of the setting sun and her eyes flashed first at me then at the barns dirt floor. "That is not important now but your being caught here is. You must leave before anyone else discovers you know of these boxes." She said urgently looking back over her shoulder.

"Oh, no it's too late," she whispered, "please crouch down in the corner and remain absolutely silent." Jessanne's words were pleading for my compliance, which I judged would be wise to follow. She hurried out of the partially opened door and I could hear her voice and a man's reply. The male voice was easily identifiable as that of Deacon Boyd, who's booming words rang loud and clear in my ears.

"Is she ready?" Deacon Boyd asked his voice slightly shaky.

"No she is still too ill to travel tonight, but the male is waiting for you just down the creek."

"Will he go on without her?" Boyd asked.

"Yes, I explained it was very dangerous for the woman to remain behind and doubly so if he were seen loitering about." Jessanne's words were so low I had to strain to understand what had been said.

"It's getting dark and I must go," Boyd tried to whisper, "you be very careful, there have been strangers prowling about town." He warned in a serious tone.

"You also sir, and may God be with you this night." Jessanne said in a low tone.

A few moments later Jessanne slid back through the partially opened barn door. "All clear." She whispered.

"I'm afraid to ask what that was all about." I said softly rising from my hiding place.

"You know very well what just took place. Deacon Boyd is a conductor on the Underground Railroad. It's his job to lead the runaways on to the next station; hopefully without being detected." Jessanne smiled slightly. "He was here to pick up the black girl you saw lying on this box last night. However, she is too ill with fever to move tonight so her brother will have to travel on alone. I moved her to the root cellar under the back of my house where I can take better care of her. I have a secret passage from the house to the cellar so I can go back and forth without being seen by anyone watching the house." Jessanne explained.

"Now if you will be so kind as to slide the lid of this long box to one side, I shall reveal unto you a great secret." As she directed, I grasped the lid on the box marked 'Bibles' by the rope handle. With the empty box's lid fully open Jessanne opened a trap door in the bottom. There just beneath was a hole in the barns dirt floor which led to who knows where.

"This opening leads to a tunnel which connects with my root cellar. By using these tunnels I can move unseen from my house to the root cellar thence to this barn; this way I can feed and water my charges without raising any suspicions.

"So that is how you managed to leave the house unseen by me from across the street and still deliver a cake to the Mills house." The surprise must have shown on my face for Jessanne laughed softly covering her mouth to stifle the sound.

"Yes Captain, and please remember that cake was intended for you." She smiled coyly.

"I never had the chance to thank you properly for such a delightful gift, so may I do so at this time."

"I meant the cake as a thank you for walking me home that night and for carrying me across the muddy street."

"That I assure you was my distinct pleasure, My Lady." I smiled graciously.

"How gallant Sir, and so I understand were your actions at the Mills store today when you braced those two slave chasers. They are a loathsome despicable breed of men." Jessanne spoke very much out of character with venom dripping from every word.

"I fear the rest of the town does not share your sentiment; in fact they rebuked me for my actions."

"Unfortunately some in our midst are cowards and fools; they are fair weather Christians who are devout when it is in their interest." She said scornfully.

"That may be true but I know the type of men who pursue slaves and they have no morals or scruples. Please be extremely careful in any dealings you might have with them." I warned pleadingly.

"We try to be as careful and professional as possible as I am sure you have figured out our bell signals by now."

"I realized the call to evening meetings were indeed signals but as to what end I have yet to ascertain." I hated to admit my ignorance but I hoped by doing so I would receive an explanation.

"The whole matter is very simple, when blacks are ready to move we call a meeting with six stokes of the bell and everyone knows they must be in attendance by seven o'clock when the bell is struck three more times to give the conductors an all clear. If any other number than three beats are rung, it is an indication to be very careful or not to move at all."

"I see, with everyone in church any person out and about would be considered a hazard to the conductor."

"Absolutely, and this way none of us are eye witness to the actual transaction, so we can not testify if the occasion of an arrest and trial should come to pass."

"That is cleaver of you people, but if you are apprehended with a fugitive slave in your procession the law will still bring charges and prosecute the guilty party." I argued with great conviction.

"That is very true Captain, but look about you, these wooden crates could conceivably get us all hung." Jessanne said with a sweep of her small graceful hand, to indicate she referred to the boxes lining the barn walls.

"The labels say Bibles, books, glass, and farm implements but that's not what they really contain. Those words are meant to fool the public. In truth the ones marked books hold two hundred Sharps rifles to arm settlers bound for Kansas; the china is ammunition for the rifles, the implements are metal pikes and knives which are to be distributed among the blacks when the prophesied uprising comes." She paused to catch her breath and for me to grasp the seriousness of the dubious honor which had just been bestowed on me.

"And this, friend Captain," Jessanne kicked the long wooden crate I had opened in the middle of the barns dirt floor, "this box we used as a bed for the ill black girl once contained a small brass canon, for what reason God only knows." Jessanne's words reflected a pain that came from deep inside.

I stood mute in utter disbelief. Two hundred rifles, pikes and a canon stored in one small barn, harbored there with only one intent; to initiate a black revolt. Revolt, a word when only whispered in the south brought shivers to ones spine. It was without question the white slave owner's greatest fear; insurrection, uprising, words that were never spoken of in polite society, not even in jest.

"My God, this barn is setting on a powder keg and there are sparks flying all about. If the wrong person learns of this, it will mean prison for many of the town's people." I shuddered at the thought of Jessanne standing trial and the humiliation of her being confined to a filthy jail cell. But worse yet was the picture of what the southern gentry would do to people with such brazen plans.

"Why did you tell me of this?" I demanded in shock, thinking how forthright and honest the woman had been about the whole affair.

"Because Captain, you are one of us now, no matter how much you may be offended at the thought."

"I – I, you think me an abolitionist?" My voice was sharp and it obviously hurt Jessanne's feelings.

"Yes Captain Lang. You sir are now part and parcel to our plot to free the slaves and at the same time redeem this country in the eyes of our Lord God."

"But I am of the south; the very idea of such actions is horrifying to me." I insisted, trying to make Jessanne understand the consequence of such a clandestine operation.

"Be that as it may, you set a course for complicity this very afternoon by humiliating Hixon. The name of Captain James Lang will now be synonymous with Mt. Zion and the fire storm to come." Jessanne said bluntly. "May I ask you a personal question Captain?" The young woman spoke haltingly, wishing to know the answer yet fearing to find the truth.

"Yes of course, I have no secrets from you."

"If in fact you did not wish to become entrapped in this little web of deceit, why did you not inform Hixon, or for that matter the officials about what you know?" She asked reluctantly.

"To be very frank, My Lady, it would place you in great jeopardy. I – ah, well I have an uncontrollable feeling for you and I could not allow anything bad to befall you." I stopped, knowing I had over-stepped the bounds of propriety once again but she had asked and I responded the only way I could -- truthfully.

"I feared that was the situation Captain, I have the exact same feeling for you, sir." She paused, brushed a tear from her eye and turned to look away from me.

I waited unspeaking until Jessanne had composed herself and found the will to speak. "But you know very well I am a married woman who could never renounce my marital vows." Again she was forced to dry the tears that began to stream down her beautiful face.

"Yes I know, what you say is true, but as long as my heart beats and my eyes weep they will do so for no one else but you My Lady." My words poured forth before I could stop them even though they should have remained unspoken. The impact of my words on Jessanne must have been devastating for she ran into my arms, her head pressing against my chest. She cried uncontrollably as a woman filled with despair would over the loss of a loved one.

"Please," I said raising her head so I could look her in the eyes, "I cannot bear to see you cry knowing it is my fault. I wish to always remember your beautiful smile and sweet harmonious voice." I whispered.

"It is not your fault Captain that I shed these tears. I cry because destiny has always played such cruel jokes on me. I have prayed for guidance and even divine intervention, but my words fall on deaf ears. I have even thought, down in my deepest innermost soul, about divorce and that is the only time the good Lord responded to my prayers and denounced me as wicked for even considering such a sinful act." Jessanne's head slipped from my hand and returned to its place on my chest before she spoke again.

"Why is life so unfair? Why would a truly loving God prevent two people from attaining happiness at the cost of so much displeasure by all concerned parties?" She whispered.

142

"I am not wise enough to give you an answer to that My Lady but the question troubles me also. Perhaps the answer will be revealed to us in the far off future when the desires of youth have burned out and wisdom that comes with age will allow us to accept God's master plan." I tried to be reassuring.

"I pray it is so sir, for I cannot bear to think we must endure a life of pain and loneliness for naught." She said tenderly.

We remained in this tender embrace for several minutes of unspeaking bliss; absolutely the happiest moments of my life. I was in a state of euphoria which I wanted to go on forever but deep inside I knew it must end. Neither she nor I moved, each refusing to separate, sure it would be the only time we would share the comfort of one another's arms. But the parting of ways did come abruptly with a scraping sound and the sudden brief movement of a shadow across the barn door opening.

"What was that?" Jessanne whispered, as I rushed to peer through the crack in the door.

"Perhaps it's the Deacon returning." I suggested hopefully.

"No, no he would never bring baggage through this part of town." Jessanne replied, joining me at the door to stare into the gathering darkness.

"We had better part." I suggested. "I will remain here until you are safely within your house."

Jessanne turned to me saying, "Captain Lang you are a wonderful man and I shall love you always." And with that she kissed my lips ever so tenderly for the briefest of moments, and then disappeared through the tunnel's opening in the wooden crate. I never had a chance to return her sentiment but I am sure though unspoken, the woman knew what was in my heart.

Once Jessanne was safely inside her home she lit a candle indicating all was well and I could go about normal business. Slipping out of the dark barn, I closed the door then moved north to the road before turning to walk casually along the street in front of the Gates house. The single candle moved from room to room paralleling my movements finally coming to rest in the front window. That one anemic flickering candle flame cast a perfect shadow on the window curtain of a slim young woman who had been cradled in my arms only moments before. I stopped to gaze longingly at the dark unmoving image and I wondered if she were in turn gazing at me standing in the middle of the nearly black street.

Begrudgingly, I turned and headed across the village common hoping to avoid the departing church goers and arrive at my lodging before Mr. and Mrs. Mills returned. Unfortunately, we met at their front gate and exchanged pleasantries and my apology for missing the evening services.

Mrs. Mills was more concerned that I had missed supper than my being absent from church and insisted on preparing a late meal to make amends. Food at that very minute was the last thing on my mind; for my stomach churned, my heart was nearly bursting, and my mind moved in a thousand directions all at the same time.

"No thank you, Ma'am." I declined politely. "I think a good night's rest is what is called for after the long journey I just completed." And what a journey it had been, from slave holder to abolitionist, to federal law breaker, to unrepentant sinner all in a matter of a few hours.

THE ABDUCTION

I found no comfort in my bed or solace in the small cottage for images and words of that night bedeviled my mind. The torment was incessant, all of course of my own making and without any avenue of escape. All I could do was wait for the sunrise and pray with it would dawn the remedy to this suffering.

The brightening of the eastern sky found me dressed and standing outside in the Mills back yard. I longed to watch the fiery birth of the new day but my eyes were drawn in the opposite direction to the Gates house, across the vacant village green. The first seconds of this day vibrated with a tension foretelling what an eventful day this particular twenty four hours would become.

The new sun crept higher in the eastern sky driving the shadows of darkness before it like the receding waters of a great flood. When the first rays of light edged down the front of Jessanne's white clapboard house the reflection was nothing short of blinding and in that moment of intense glare my eyes detected a slight movement just behind her barn. I shaded my eyes in an effort to identify what the commotion might be but the reflection of the sunlight was so intense it made observation impossible.

Then suddenly a horse and rider raced out from behind the house; it was quickly followed by a second horse and rider but this animal carried a second passenger. I immediately broke into a run for my first thoughts were that Jessanne, being home alone had been abducted by some unscrupulous characters opposed to her husband's political views. I raced across the street and into the edge of the village green and was nearing the center when I saw Jessanne bolt from her front door and head in my direction.

We met in the middle of the street, both breathless from physical exertion and extreme emotions.

"It's Hixon!" Jessanne blurted out. "He has taken the slave girl and is headed south with her!"

"Are you alright?" I asked more concerned about Jessanne than the black girl.

"Yes, I am fine but you must stop them!" She pleaded.

"I will do the best I can." I promised, turning to retrieve my horse.

Jessanne grasped my arm to prevent my rushing off and as I turned back to face her I recognized the grimace of a deeper fear on the normally beautiful face.

"Hixon knows about us, it was he that we heard outside the barn last night. He threatened to tell all if any attempt is made to hinder his ride south."

"What do you want me to do?" I asked in bewilderment.

"The girl's safety was my responsibility and she must come first." Jessanne's voice was filled with sincerity and true concern.

"Then I promise to do whatever is necessary to prevent Hixon from delivering the girl or damaging your reputation, My Lady." My words brought a tear to her eye and a smile to her lips.

"I place my fate in your hands, Captain. However I would rather be dishonored than have you hurt in any way."

"I am a soldier first and have no qualms about what I must do to rectify this situation."

"I pray that God be with you, Captain, for I know my heart will be." Jessanne said softly placing her hand gently on mine.

"Thank you, My Lady."

I moved back a step not wishing to appear too familiar with Jessanne to the crowd beginning to form about us. She attempted to answer the barrage of questions which were fired at her in rapid succession, and in doing so gave an admirable account of herself. I was amazed Jessanne was calm enough to report a story that did not implicate me or what Hixon had warned.

Some of the church elders demanded Reverend John Brown be brought forth to take charge in Reverend Gates' absence but they were quickly informed Brown was on an operation in Kansas. With the lack of leadership established, the group turned to me for guidance in deference to my military experience.

I quickly accepted the command with my first act being to organize a pursuit party and to break up this attention gathering crowd. I instructed any man who would ride with me to be ready in fifteen minutes and meet me at the Mills house. I then admonished everyone else to go about their usual business and not to discuss this matter any further.

I looked Jessanne in the face once more and smiled, which she returned most hopefully, and then I hurried to my lodging for my horse and gear. I hurriedly saddled, adding the heavy cavalry saber to rings on the left side of the saddle and my rifle into a scabbard on the right. I anticipated both weapons would be of indispensable service in the days that lay ahead.

The saber was of the finest hammered German steel, a graduation gift on completion of my term at Virginia Military Institute. The rifle was an elegant .50 caliber Kentucky style weapon with a cap-lock and double set triggers. It was known for its extreme accuracy when loaded properly and in the hands of a capable marksman. Of course, the big Walker Colt .44 revolver was ready in the holster on the saddles pommel and just for added precaution; a smaller Colt .36 caliber revolver rode snuggly in my pants belt. The multiple shot hand guns were for quick close-up defense work. With them a man could get off a number of rapid shots with mediocre accuracy. The rifle's single shot was reserved for slow fire long range shots of a more offensive nature. The saber, while a finely constructed weapon, could at times be unwieldy and injurious to the users own arm, so a wide thick bladed sheath knife of about eighteen inch length was carried on my belt as a close-quarter back up for last ditch defense in the event of lack of ammunition or if the gun powder should become damp. With this arsenal at the ready I felt fully prepared to undertake the chase and confrontation that certainly must take place in the next few days.

Leading my mount to the street, I waited impatiently for those who offered to join in pursuing the slave girl and the two low-lives who had abducted her. When the allotted fifteen minutes had expired and no one had reported; I swung into the saddle and turned west in hopes of picking up Hixon's trail behind Jessanne's house.

Moving along the street at a trot, two men on horseback intercepted me at the southwest corner of the village common. As we stopped to speak, two more mounted men raced up from behind me. The men introduced themselves in rapid fire fashion in consideration of the urgency of our task.

The men were nearly unknown to me so I had to trust the fact they were indeed in sympathy with the town's abolitionist leanings. The two men who approached the corner from the south were the Butler brothers, Tom and Everett. The two who caught up from behind were Angus Stuart and Albert Rowe.

151

We moved smartly up the street dismounting in front of the Gates house before walking carefully where I had spotted the two horses heading south. The tracks were plain enough, two horses, two men's boot prints and the signs of a brief scuffle as the ill girl weakly resisted the more powerful men. Their mounts were newly shod and unfortunately left little in the way of distinguishing marks in the soft ground. The men recognized the fact that a quick hot pursuit was our best chance of catching the culprits and recovering the girl.

"We must move fast and hope to catch these men before they can travel very far. But," I warned "in riding hard it will be easy to fall into an ambush so be ready and be alert to anything which might signal trouble ahead."

I, being driven by a personal cause and the four townsmen, by civic duty, hurried south from town. Enthusiasm and the thought of a quick capture drove the men forward, greatly restricting our ability to become familiar with the quarry's tracks. Hixon had chosen to flee down a well-worn game path that marked the ridge of the very same watershed Mt. Zion sat upon. A roughly three feet wide and four to eight inch deep trench had been excavated by the hooves of millions of animals as they passed along the narrow hilltop, producing a thoroughfare horsemen in a hurry would instinctively travel. This deeply worn rut extended approximately two miles before splitting southeast and southwest to make use of creeks that began at the crest of the ridge and flowed off to eventually join up with the main rivers. It was at this point we five were forced to halt the pursuit as Hixon's tracks became entangled with those of horses moving across the trail.

After several moments of attempting to decipher the tracks, a disagreement arose over which direction the desperados had proceeded. Angus Stuart and Albert Rowe believed the tracks led in a southwesterly direction which would eventually end at the Missouri River. The Butler Brothers on the other hand were equally certain the tracks had taken a southeastern course to the Nishnabotna River.

Stuart and Rowe argued that the route to the Missouri River and Nebraska City where sympathetic slave holders would give the two bounty hunters sanctuary was the obvious course of pursuit and they insisted on taking that singular fork in the trail.

Tom and Everett Butler were equally positive Hixon would wisely race south east striking the Nishnabotna River bottom that would join the Missouri river much farther south of Nebraska City, somewhere in the area of the ill defined state line with Missouri where the slave chasers would be legally safe from prosecution or our intervention. They argued the Nishnabotna River route would be safer for the two men forcibly removing a runaway slave girl because of the limited amount of traffic in that river bottom as compared to that of the Missouri River. Also, once Hixon had reached the confluence of the two rivers near the state line it would be possible to flee to Missouri, Nebraska, or Kansas which were only a few miles away.

The debate continued for several minutes before it was agreed that Stuart and Rowe would search to the southwest and then on as far as Nebraska City if no contact had been made before reaching the river ferry. The Butler brothers had vowed to take the southeastern creek and the Nishnabotna River trail and if they had not discovered the two villains by the time they arrived at the Missouri River they would cross over the river and proceed to Nebraska City, in case the other two were more fortunate and required help in rescuing the girl.

THE PURSUIT BEGINS

The decision to separate had both good and bad points; it weakened the pursuit party by half, making their numbers equal to the pursued, but at the same time both avenues of escape would be searched. I had remained neutral in the argument of which path to follow, but now I must decide and as I read the horse track, I felt quite positive the animal the slave girl rode had indeed traveled east. The Butler brother's theory, that Hixon's plan to take a less populated route which would provide optional safe destinations made sense. And there was nothing to say that Hixon would not proceed farther east toward the heart of the established slave states before moving south once again.

I threw my lot in with the Butler boys, choosing to take the eastern route and said goodbye to Stuart and Rowe who rode west. The parting was an amicable one, all differences aside; the men swore to do their best by the fugitive slave girl. We all knew the law was on Hixon's side even in the free state of Iowa but a good deal of pressure could be brought to bear on the pair if they could be apprehended before reaching Missouri or Kansas.

Tom Butler led the way, being more familiar with the country to the southeast of Mt. Zion; what's more, he also proved to be a competent tracker. Everett, the other Butler boy followed close behind his older brother, verbally acknowledging every sign and discussing each decision thoroughly before an action was taken. The brothers worked well as a team, moving quietly and carefully but still making good time in the difficult terrain.

The Butler Brothers were tall lanky men in their mid-twenties, possessing handsome clean shaven faces, which seemed to wear perpetual smiles. They rode gracefully and found little difficulty in moving about the brush, tree covered hills and boggy creek bottoms that the bounty hunters partially disguised trail led through. I followed along in an absent-minded state, giving Tom the command position while my thoughts were filled with images of Mt. Zion, steeling myself for what the confrontation with Hixon might bring. Tom topped a small rise with a fine view of the Nishnabotna River just below. He pointed silently to a set of tracks on the ground then turned his horse toward a tree lined creek. Only a mile or so farther on that creek emptied into a wide flood plain of tall grasses and small islands that supported a cottonwood tree here and there. Large numbers of graceful water fowl covered the open areas of the slow meandering river. A white tailed buck deer broke from cover to race at full speed into the protection of the hills farther upstream. It was a very calm idyllic scene that played out before us three overeager pursers.

Tom reached the creek mouth first, pausing to point out signs in the mud to Everett who turned facing me, nodding his head in agreement when a sudden explosion of smoke and flame erupted from the brush on the south side of the creek. Everett, whose back was to the shooter, was blown from his saddle landing face first in the mud while Tom's horse spun around in fear as the rider fought to remain astride, before also toppling to the ground.

I pulled the big Walker Colt from its saddle holster and raced forward in a foolish attempt to protect the brothers, only to become the target of a second volley of gunfire from the same point that struck down the Butlers. A bullet cut painfully into the outside of my left bicep while a second projectile impacted the lower left side of my rib cage, nearly throwing me to the ground. I clung to my saddle for dear life even though the original pain threw my brain into a state of shock; I knew my horse Sergeant would pull me from the fray.

The magnificent animal spun about on his rear legs and ran at full speed safely back up the creek not slowing down until reaching the safety of the knoll where we had first caught sight of the river bottom. Sergeant paused on top of the hill to blow, and then turned to look back the mile or so to where the attack had taken place. I swayed in the saddle nearly falling to the ground as I tried to clear my mind and vision enough to determine exactly what had transpired at the mouth of the small creek.

The painful wounds kept my head spinning, and yet, I managed some semblance of concentration on the ambush scene a mile below. Study as I might, I could not remember hearing any further gunshot or any movement about the row of bushes lining the south side of this unnamed creek. Both of the Butler brothers lay unmoving in the muddy bottom presenting a perfect picture of death that could, I fear, be true.

The thought of riding back to town without certain knowledge of the young men's fate produced a very unsavory flavor in my mouth. It was that bitter taste of fear like gall welling uncontrollably up the back of your throat. There was no doubt, try or die, I must ride down to where the brothers lay and meet the challenge of the cowardly attackers.

With a grimace of pain I inspected my Walker Colt, a cap was on every nipple, a ball in every chamber and the loading lever securely locked in place. A misfire or jammed cylinder was something which might prove deadly in the advance on the creek mouth.

I patted Sergeant on the neck and tried a few words of praise for his brave action but the attention I gave was short lived as breathing and moving dramatically increased the level of pain in my rib cage. It called into question what effectiveness I would have in attempting to reach, let alone aid the wounded Butler brothers.

How ridiculous, I thought to myself; *to argue such a point was an exercise in futility for a military man. I must ride to the brothers' aid as long as there was a breath left in my body, no matter how uncomfortable that normal function would be. It was just such moments as these the instructors in military school were speaking of when they described a soldier's loss of common sense while being driven into a foolish action by pure emotion.*

With the heavy Walker Colt in my right hand and the reins in my wounded left, I felt fortunate to be mounted on a fine cavalry horse like Sergeant, who was trained to respond to leg pressure. This trait came in very handy for a rider in the midst of a fight when both hands were filled with weapons, or the reins were dropped or cut and din of battle was far too loud to use voice commands.

"Forward." I whispered and received an instant response from the spirited animal who instinctively retraced the same route we used to flee the ambush only moments before. The magnificent animal's ears were erect and his nostrils flared open and closed in an effort to detect any source of danger that might lie ahead. The heavy scent of blood was on the breeze; both the horse and rider were able to easily detect its familiar odor from the many other pungent aromas of the muddy creek bottom.

The senses of an animal, nearly any animal, are normally far superior to that of a man. This gift is nature's way of compensating for what they lack in intelligence, putting man and animal on a more equal footing when the question of survival arises. Sergeant was no exception to the rule; his combined senses pinpointed the skulking bushwhacker long before my pain befuddled brain became suspicious of his location. The big powerful horse began to move forward and yet sideways at the same time in order to keep his head pointed in the direction of the hidden danger. Sergeant's breathing rate increased and odd noises began to roll up from deep inside the animals massive neck; sounds similar to those a stud horse would emit in challenging to fight another stud. I could feel Sergeant's muscles become tense and his normally smooth gait converted to short choppy steps which jarred and tormented my arm and ribs. It was this irregular pace that finally penetrated my foggy brain and alerted my body to heed the signs of danger this uncommonly fearless animal was displaying.

My eyes struggled to focus on the indicated spot in the brush much further up stream than where the original shooting had taken place; a place where the creek bed was considerably narrower. Suddenly as if a light penetrated the dense fog in my brain, I recognized the movements of a man in the process of standing up and at the same time shouldering a rifle.

A mystical power of unknown origin lifted up the heavy Walker Colt in my right hand and with blinding speed cocked the hammer, lined up the barrel and pulled the trigger. It felt like minutes passed before the black powder compressed under the big round 44 caliber ball detonated in a roaring display of smoke and fire. Sergeant's training showed through and he steadfastly held his place, not spooking about like many a lesser horse would have done in a similar situation. Through the haze of the burning gun powder I could see the man drop his weapon and tumble over backwards to the accompaniment of a high pitched scream.

Man and animal, like a well drilled team calmly stood our ground waiting for an indication of what action would be required next; attack or retreat, we would accept our fate like soldiers. Our wait was short, for the wounded man jumped to his feet and raced off down the creek, quickly disappearing into the tall grass of the river bottom.

A careful visual reconnoiter of the area found no other immediate danger and once again I praised and petted the battle wise animal for having saved my life twice in only a matter of minutes.

A slight touch of my right heel to Sergeant's side, a signal to move forward, was instantly obeyed without question or delay. The big horse's attention remained on sentinel duty, senses on edge, ready for a rapid response to any aggression, and yet, he managed to deliver me close between the fallen brothers without stepping on their extremities.

The very thought of dismounting produced a dreadful image in my mind, still it was essential the brothers be examined and given any aid that might ease their suffering. In preparation for what would surely prove to be an unpleasant experience, I placed the Walker Colt in the saddle holster and tied a loose knot in the end of Sergeant's bridle reins so they would remain about his neck. I tucked my wounded left arm and hand inside my coat then with my right hand grabbed a large tuft of Sergeant's long mane and slid quite ungainly from the English style saddle. Both feet hit the ground at the same time providing a solid footing but producing a sharp pain from my damaged ribs. The handful of Sergeant's mane gave some sense of balance as my head spun in a blinding whirl like a roulette wheel. Just as that famous gambling device eventually slows to a stop so did the misery inside my head and I thanked God for the relief. With the aid of my left stirrup, I cautiously knelt down beside Tom Butler who laid prostrate face-down in the mud. Blood from his head-wound rhythmically dripped off the end of his nose into a water puddle below.

At the touch of my hand on his shoulder Tom Butler groaned and moved slightly as if trying to resist help. "It's me, James Lang." I said reassuringly. "That bushwhacker is gone now."

Tom opened his eyes and looked up slowly at my face before trying to speak. "Is Everett alright?" He asked.

"How are you?" I asked, first things first.

"Hurting some." He answered attempting to rise to his hands and knees. "That fella must have had a scatter gun for I am shot in several places." Tom felt for the wound on the right side of his head then for a hole in his upper arm. "I reckon I will live though, but let's see to Everett." He insisted, crawling under Sergeant the two or three feet to where his brother laid, his back covered in blood.

"It appears your brother bore the brunt of the shotgun blast." I commented after working my way around the front of Sergeant's neck and joining Tom at Everett's side.

A quick examination indicated the large heavy buckshot had penetrated deeply into Everett's back, possibly damaging the spine or entering the lungs. "This man needs a doctor and in a hurry!" I pronounced looking about for the brother's horses. "Can you ride?" I asked.

"Our horses ran away but I reckon I could ride," came Tom's reply.

"I will recover your horses then you must get help for your brother." I insisted.

"It's a far piece back to Mt. Zion, Captain; I don't think we can make it." He argued. "But there is a small village about a mile east of the far river bank called Snow Hill. Maybe you could ride over there and fetch some help for us."

That was the first time Tom had really looked at me and it was only then he discovered that I too was wounded.

"But you are injured also; do you think you can ride?"

"I rode back down here from the knoll and I figure on riding after whoever it was that shot us." My words were harsh and filled with hate which brought a surprised look to Tom Butler's face.

"Continue on after what has happened here?...... in your condition? You must be a fool!" Tom declared with a shake of his still bleeding head.

"I will ride over to this town of Snow Hill and request help for the both of you, but no matter what, I will return as soon as possible." I promised, using my good right arm to pull myself erect and keep my balance while moving to Sergeant's left side in order to mount up.

Sergeant had not moved one step from the place where I had dismounted for he was on duty, sentry duty, still alert to any possible danger. I grabbed a handful of Sergeant's mane and released a long groan as I swung into the saddle, coming to rest with a distinct plop. The exertion produced the same spinning effect in my brain as dismounting had and I knew if Sergeant moved I would most surely fall to the creek mud below. But the faithful friend stood his ground, like a good soldier awaiting his orders.

"When you get to Snow Hill, ask for Mr. Stansbury." Tom suggested. "He is a friend of ours from back east and I am sure he will provide us help."

"Stansbury." I repeated as the tornado within my head slowed and the complaint from my wounds receded to a dull throb. "I will return one way or the other, remain here until then." I ordered, the old military training compensating for my pain-confused brain.

With the slightest urging Sergeant moved slowly forward picking his way through the tangle of brush and sticks at the mouth of the creek and then out into the tall grass of the river bottom. The river bed at this point was about two miles wide but circumnavigating deep water holes and mud bogs more than doubled the distance to reach the eastern bank of the Nishnabotna River. Once more on dry ground, I gave Sergeant a well deserved breather. During that short rest I discovered an eastbound trail that I followed on the assumption it would lead in the general direction of the village of Snow Hill.

I had lost all track of time in the confusion of the day, but the sun indicated it was early afternoon as Sergeant and I plodded up the faint trail to a small rise that served as a new cemetery. This was the first sign of civilization I had seen since departing the Butler brothers on the west side of the river. A faint scent of wood smoke pleasantly mingled with the sweet fragrance of wild roses which bloomed in abundance all around the few grave markers. The trees on the knoll provided a cooling shade from the sun's ever increasing temperature and I was enticed to dismount and rest my aching body. Still, duty and recalled promises kept us moving. The smoke and cemetery indicated Snow Hill or at least some human habitation must be close by where a weary man could rest.

The view from the far side of the cemetery knoll revealed a narrow wooded valley, shallow by comparison to those nearer the river but the thing which really set it apart from the others was the sight of a young woman leading a milch cow. They were heading away from my location, moving along at a hurried gait on the same path I rode upon. I wished to call out to the woman but was physically unable to do so, owing to my wounds; but mostly I hesitated fearing to frighten the lone female unnecessarily.

I watched as she tugged the wayward cow up the path to the top of the next rise and disappeared into the dense growth of trees beyond before I urged my steed to move forward. In just minutes we had crossed the lush narrow valley and were cresting the opposite rise where the woman and cow had vanished, not knowing they were under my observation. At this point we paused to make a quick evaluation of what lay ahead, a habit ingrained from years of hunting and military experience.

The grove of trees gave way to a grassy hilltop park that contained three large buildings and twice that number of smaller structures. There was no sign proclaiming it as Snow Hill but I presumed from its location this was indeed the settlement being sought. The woman and cow were nowhere to be seen; in fact the entire area seemed deserted, no people, no horses, not even a stray dog to rush forth barking a warning that an intruder was present.

At my signal, Sergeant began to walk the narrow path weaving through the trees to the clearing beyond; his senses on high alert once more for he recognized we were entering an unfamiliar dwelling place. All the settlement's buildings resembled homes, not a single business structure was to be seen but then I came here in search of assistance and not to purchase anything. Still I questioned if this was indeed Snow Hill or just a farm commune many of the Scandinavian immigrants were so fond of starting.

I gently reined back on Sergeant as we neared the centermost point of the irregularly laid out buildings, then took a full measure of each in its turn. The main construction was of frame lumber, indicating some affluence among the residents; yet rough cut wooden slabs and logs were employed in the lesser important out buildings.

After several minutes had passed in the appraisal of the community and without encountering any sign of life, I attempted to call out to summons any living creature in the area. The wound in my side greatly restricted the volume of the yell for it emitted as more of a low whisper than a cry for assistance. I considered firing my revolver in the air but worried at what type of response one might receive from the group of unseen strangers. Finally, I directed Sergeant to walk next to a sidewall of the nearest house so I might strike a blow to the exterior wall; thus drawing attention from those inside. I made a fist with my good right hand and delivered a hammer blow to the wall that sounded as hollow as a ripe watermelon but to my great dismay it produced no immediate response. A second and possibly harder strike on the very same spot on the sidewall was quickly meet with a loud "What the hell?" before someone raced out the front door and into the yard.

A tall muscular middle aged man turned the corner of the house then froze in place when I came into view.

"Who are you?" he demanded in a harsh voice.

"I am Captain James Lang, sir. I must apologize for the disturbance but I am on an errand of mercy."

"What is this errand?" The man asked in the same hard voice.

"I am in search of a man named Stansbury of Snow Hill sir; I would greatly appreciate any guidance you could possibly give me."

"I am Cyrus Stansbury and this is Snow Hill." The man replied, a surprised expression flashing across his bearded face.

"Do you know Tom and Everett Butler of Mt. Zion?" I asked in my most pleasant voice.

Midway through the question the young woman I had seen leading the milch cow raced up from behind the house coming to a stop directly beside me, not quite near enough to touch.

"Who did you say you are again?" The man asked.

I repeated my name and that of the Butler brothers but still Stansbury avoided answering the question.

The young woman who had remained quiet but who had done a proper job of looking me over suddenly blurted out. "Father this man is injured; there is blood all over his arm and waist."

"It is not for myself that I come in search of you sir, the Butler brothers have been ambushed and are in grave need of medical treatment. Tom Butler sent me here to find help saying you were a friend of his."

"Please Father." The girl pleaded. "Help me get this man off his horse so we can try to treat his wounds." The young woman extended her hand to take Sergeant's bridle to guide him around front of the house but the ever wary animal reared his head violently and bared his teeth refusing to allow her to touch either him or me.

"I must apologize for my mounts actions, Miss. He is very protective and can be somewhat of a rogue where good manners are concerned."

The young woman, startled by Sergeant's actions, stepped back several paces. "I only wished to get you around to the front of the house so you could dismount and sit in the shade of the porch while I look at your injuries."

"Thank you Miss, I will ride around to the front and once Sergeant realizes you are a friend he will be on his best behavior."

Sergeant stood firm seemingly anticipating a very ungainly dismount which proved to be just that, a very unique half slide, half falling maneuver that would have been comical in a less desperate situation. Once the world stopped spinning and I had moved away from Sergeant, the young woman rushed in to assist me to the front porch. Cyrus Stansbury however, held back

169

until I was well situated on the rough sawed splintery boards of the porch floor before moving or speaking.

"Let the man be, Victoria Rose!" He ordered. "His wounds will wait until we know more about his business here!" This time Stansbury's demand was made in a strict parental tone.

The young woman, however, failed to obey her father's gruff instructions saying, "The man is bleeding Father, whether friend or foe we cannot allow him to expire here in Snow Hill for lack of treatment."

Cyrus Stansbury dismissed his daughter's disobedience with a loud clearing of his throat before turning his wrath on me. "Now as to these brothers you say have been shot, what am I suppose to do about it?" Stansbury snarled as if trying to disavow any knowledge of the Butler brothers.

"I fear I have made a grievous err in coming here. I was informed Snow Hill was a good Christian settlement and a real man could be found here. This has been a waste of time that may well cost the lives of two good men, but then cowards and fools are a common lot in this area." I roared, my famous anger coming into play. I pushed Victoria Rose's small gentle hands from where she tended my stomach wound and struggled to rise to my feet.

"I must be on my way." I growled from the pain in my wounds and the anguish in my heart that Cyrus Stansbury would refuse aid to a man who called him a friend.

"This man is in need of help and we in good consciousness cannot turn him away!" Victoria Rose snapped.

"But we know nothing of this individual. He could be a slave hunter or federal law man setting a trap for abolitionists or their cohorts."

"I believe him Father; no one would go to the extreme of inflicting such wounds just to trick us." Victoria Rose argued, pulling on my arm in an attempt to set me on the porch floor once more.

"Well," Stansbury grumbled while vigorously rubbing his bearded chin with his large right hand as if in deep thought, "that's good thinking but I still don't trust the man. Go on and tend his wounds while I discuss this with Mr. Cook."

"You may all go to blazes!" I roared, doubling over in pain from the effort. "I will be on my way and while you are holding this discussion I will be in search of a real man!" These last few words, though clear and audible, were much weaker than before as I struggle to Sergeant and began to mount.

Once settled in the saddle I tipped my hat to the young woman saying. "Good day Victoria Rose and to you Cyrus Stansbury, may God be with you and all the residents of Snow Hill for the devil is already dwelling here." With that I turned Sergeant's head around and we rode briskly back along the trail we had entered the settlement by.

It was with a heavy heart I followed the dirt track back to the edge of the river bank, for I had failed in my mission to bring aid back to the suffering Butler brothers. It was not within my power to force Stansbury to comply with my wishes and might have proven fool-hearted to try. Still, I must find someone to render aid to the brothers and return to the pursuit of Hixon and his party.

VICTORIA ROSE

The combination of pain and shock by the denial of assistance from the citizens of Snow Hill made retracing the wandering course across the river bottom difficult. My mind was so consumed by my reception at Snow Hill and the pain in my body that I made several false turns which expended even more valuable time. In desperation, I paused briefly atop a small island in hopes of regaining my bearings, when my ear detected the sound of a team and wagon splashing through the shallow water to our rear. Suddenly a team of small black mules broke through the tall grass just a few rods downstream from my position.

"Captain Lang!" A female voice called out. "Where are you?"

"Here, just upstream Miss Stansbury." I called back directing Sergeant to move in her direction.

"Thank God I found you sir, I feared you had gotten lost or passed out and fallen off your horse." Victoria Rose called warmly as I approached her small spring wagon.

Victoria Rose Stansbury was an attractive, slight built, young woman with naturally curly, flaming red hair which she kept cut short exposing a slightly freckled face. A bright blue bonnet whose ribbons were tied about her slender neck hung down her back and contrasted sharply with the faded long yellow dress covering the full length of her arms and legs.

"I have come to help you and the Butler brothers in any way I can." Victoria Rose promised in a sincere dedicated voice which I judged to be genuine.

"Bless you Miss, for those boys do certainly deserve deliverance from their discomfort."

Miss Stansbury cracked a buggy whip over the heads of the mules causing the team to immediately and simultaneously lean into their harness and begin dragging the spring wagon through the murky river water. She gave every indication of knowing where to go so I fell in just behind the rig as it navigated the treacherous parts of the river bed, finally emerging on the west bank just above the creek mouth where the ambush had taken place.

"Tom Butler." The young woman called out loud and clear. "Where are you?"

"Here, I am here in the creek bottom next to Brother Everett," came a faint reply.

As directed, the team pulled the light wagon over a small rise rather than going around it by way of the soft mud at the creeks mouth. Once on top the dry mound Victoria Rose halted the team and unconsciously tied off the long reins before springing from the wagon seat and running to Tom Butler's side.

"Tom, how bad are you hurt?" She snapped, taking his bleeding head in her hands to inspect the obvious wound. Even my slow wits picked up on the fact that an air of familiarity passed between these two young people.

"I will be alright, but I'm afraid Everett is seriously injured." Tom exclaimed, trying to direct the woman's attention to his unmoving brother.

Victoria Rose honored Tom's request and bent to attend Everett Butler's profusely bleeding back. She tore away his hole-riddled blue cotton work shirt before racing to the back of the spring wagon to retrieve water, bandages and tools needed to treat the men's wounds.

I found an appealing spot and once again preformed a less than graceful dismount before allowing Sergeant to roam free to drink and eat as he might wish, while I too rested. The resulting movement and discomfort was beginning to take a toll on my strength, not to mention my frame of mind.

Tom Butler explained the facts that led up to the ambush to Victoria Rose while she spent time removing buckshot from Everett Butler's back with the final pronouncement: "he will live" and no serious or permanent damage had been done. She then turned her medical skills on treating Tom's head wound and trying to make both men as comfortable as possible. With that accomplished the strong-willed young woman rose, wiped her hand on a piece of white cotton cloth and announced: "Now sir, it is your turn." It was more of an order than an inquiry or offer of assistance.

"I will be just fine after I rest a bit." I argued.

"You, Captain will do as I say, because I will not have you getting sick later and condemning me for not seeing to your wounds!" The fiery redhead scolded in no uncertain terms.

"You best give in to her Captain, 'cause everyone knows whatever Victoria Rose sets her mind to is going to happen one way or the other." Tom Butler laughed before grimacing in pain.

"It's my way of apologizing to you Captain for my father's refusal to help. You must understand we have been hounded by slave hunters of late. They have beaten one of our citizens who they accused of being part of the Underground Railway and have made death threats to others." Victoria Rose said as she readied to care for my wounds. "Now just lay still while I have a look at these holes in your hide. I swear, if it weren't for babies being born and you men getting hurt all the time I'd have nothing to do except housework." She exclaimed light heartedly.

"Take it you are not partial to housework Miss?"

"Would you be? ...... Dusting and washing and cooking and hauling water all day? That's not my idea of a good life, or for that matter, any kind of a life." Her words faded away as she inserted a knitting needle in the hole in my upper left arm and began to probe about for the offending piece of lead.

I managed to hold my tongue throughout the procedure until the lone projectile was extracted from my arm. Victoria Rose held the piece of buck shot up high between her bloody thumb and forefinger like a trophy saying: "Now that did not hurt a bit, did it?" The young redhead said teasingly. With that over, my stomach wound became the next project for Miss Stansbury's ambitious hands to explore at will. She knew full well no real man would yell or even so much as flinch from the pain tending a wound might inflict, no matter how rough or inept the practitioner might be.

"You are very lucky Captain Lang; the lead merely struck your lower rib then skipped out the other side. But it did break the rib, so I figure the pain will be severe for a while, but nothing a hard old army officer like you can't handle." A strange haunting laugh roared from the young woman's lips and she smiled as if the whole matter were quite comical. "I will bind you up a bit but you had best have the Doctor Rutledge look at these ribs as soon as you get back to Mt. Zion." She warned.

"I am not going back to Mt. Zion, Miss; I must be on Hixon's trail as soon as possible. But I would be indebted to you even more if you would see the Butlers back to their home for me."

"But you have no business going on alone, especially in the shape you are in, Sir." Victoria Rose insisted.

"I have no choice Miss; I must stay on the trail while it is fresh and before Hixon reaches the safety of the state line."

"Then I will see the brothers home Captain, but I must state I believe you are committing suicide if you attempt to rescue a fugitive slave from that bunch of cut throats!"

"The Captain won't exactly be alone." Tom Butler interjected into the conversation.

"And just who, Thomas Butler, do you think is going along with this crazy man? It certainly will not be you!" Victoria Rose's words rolled out hot and fast as she made it crystal clear who was in charge of decisions between the two youngsters.

"No, no, not me, I meant the Captain's horse. Why, he pointed that back shooter out of the bushes better than any hound I've ever seen." Tom attempted to laugh at the thought of the bushwhacker being exposed by a horse.

"Yes that's quite true, Sergeant is a very intelligent animal and he is a loyal and capable ally in any fight." I agreed.

"That might be all well and good if you were in fighting condition but these wounds will slow you down a great deal." Victoria Rose continued trying to dissuade me from continuing the chase.

"Thank you for your concern and for tending to my wounds Miss Stansbury but I have made promises that I must keep and an obligation to see this matter through to the bitter end," I reaffirmed. "Now, if you are ready to depart, I will assist in loading these young men into your wagon."

"Yes, I am ready to go but I do so under protest Sir. However, my heart and my prayers go with you on this daring yet foolish quest." Victoria Rose knelt close and quickly kissed my cheek. "That is for good luck and may God be with you Captain Lang."

"Thank you Miss Stansbury for you are truly an angel of mercy. I pray God be with you and your patients on the trip to Mt. Zion." I said with as much of a smile as I could conjure up, for we had no idea where Hixon might be at this very moment and another encounter with him could prove fatal for all.

Victoria Rose gathered up her medical equipment, placed it under the buggy seat, and then moved the rig down to the creek as near as possible to where the Butler brothers still lay. Tom supported his brother on one side while I lifted on the other and Victoria Rose wrestled his feet until we managed to load Everett Butler into the back of the spring wagon. With our help Tom climbed in beside his brother, situated himself in such a way as to prevent Everett's wounded back from being abused by the bouncing of the wagon over the rough terrain on the route to town.

I gave Victoria Rose a hand up as she mounted the spring wagon, saw that the long leather reins were straight, then offered her the single shot pistol Everett Butler had carried in his belt.

"Keep this close at hand." I suggested. "One never knows who you might encounter on these back trails."

"Thank you sir, I shall." Victoria Rose smiled warmly. "I must say Captain, I have found our brief meeting unusual; one might even say pleasant under different circumstances."

"Yes, Miss Victoria Rose Stansbury, the feeling is mutual. If we should never meet again I will always remember you and be indebted to you for treating my wounds." I said politely with a partial tip of my hat.

"Please be careful Captain Lang and any time that you are near Snow Hill I shall expect you to stop for a visit and a meal."

"It would be my pleasure to call on you Miss Stansbury, thank you for your kindness."

Victoria Rose smiled warmly at me; her pretty freckled face had a continual expression of bedevilment that, even in great discomfort, forced a chuckle to well up in my throat. Then without further conversation she cracked the buggy whip over the head of the mule team and the whole affair lunged forward. I watched until the small wagon and its passengers disappeared over the hill to the west before saying a silent prayer for their safe arrival at Mt. Zion.

THE CHASE RESUMES

A soft whistle brought Sergeant to my side and working together I struggled to a solid place in the polished saddle seat. The pain seemed a bit less now that the lead had been removed from my arm and a bandage tied tightly about the broken ribs; still, I was in a sorry state of repair for a soldier in hot pursuit of two, desperate would-be killers.

Sergeant and I started by picking up the trail of blood left by the fleeing bushwhacker as he limped to where a horse had been hidden. This had been an impromptu and poorly planned attack; but it nearly succeeded and would have if I had not lagged behind daydreaming about Jessanne. The hoof prints of the shooter's horse looked very much like one of those we had followed out of Mt. Zion, at least as viewed from the seat of my saddle, for I had no inclination to dismount for a closer examination. The tracks led away from the ambush site and that was good enough for me. I had to intercept Hixon in hopes of freeing the girl and at the same time silence any rumors about Jessanne Gates, if possible. But, I also wished to find the man who had unleashed the murderous attack on the Butlers and me. One might term it unfinished business but I felt certain following this one would culminate in a confrontation with the whole rotten crew.

The shooter's tracks took a southerly course and within a mile had rejoined a well worn path that skirted the base of the hills where they met the Nishnabotna River bottom. This trace was used heavily by foot and animal traffic but only lightly used by wagons due to its narrow rough route. Fortunately, a large heavy wagon with wide steel rimmed wheels had passed by shortly before the shooter entered the trail. I had feared confusing the shooters tracks among the others in the soft dirt of the rudimentary roadway, but for some reason his horse had chosen to walk in the print the wide wagon wheel had cut. Perhaps the wound I had inflicted on the bushwhacker diverted his attention from where his horse walked or perhaps he just did not think to hide his tracks. Whatever the case, it was surely a boon to me. Occasionally, I would spy a large drop of blood next to the wagon wheel track which confirmed this was indeed the man I sought, the one with which I had a score to settle.

Knowing the back-shooter was just in front of me with a serious wound and very likely in desperate straits, I took extra measures of safety at every point on the trail where this devil might attempt a repeat attack. These precautions markedly delayed my advance but another wound would eliminate me from the chase entirely, something I could ill afford at this time.

As I carefully skirted around a small stand of cottonwood trees that grew right down to the river bank, I spotted a place where the damp soil had been widely disturbed. Riding closer it was obvious from the sign that someone had waited in this area for the shooter to appear. The soil was extremely churned up by horse's hooves, men's boots, and a pair of bare feet. An altercation of some type had ensued here between the barefoot person and one pair of boots, probably before the second pair of boots arrived. Suddenly, there it was, several large drops of blood beside the second set of boot prints. Now I knew that I was correct, the shooter was Ira Ketchum, Hixon's cohort and a partner in the slave girl's abduction.

My aching body longed to rest, but I appeased it with slight adjustments in seating position, which provided brief periods of relief, but not the lasting peace that laying flat on the ground would render. A thirst like none I had ever experienced came over me, consuming my willpower, driving me to drain the small canteen which hung by leather thongs from my military style saddles pommel. I realized that no amount of liquid would slacken this desire for drink, but with an empty canteen I must now find fresh water. Sergeant was well served by the muddy water of the shallow river, yet experience told me not to imbibe from the same source animals can tolerate. The rest would have to wait for my thirst would propel me onward in hopes of locating either Hixon or a source of fresh water.

A hawk soared down low overhead and cried as if in pain and I felt sympathy for his plight for a good high pitched scream seemed the only viable relief from this torment. I could not retreat, nor rest, nor partake of the murky water at Sergeant's feet. Continuing to march was the only alternative and a poor alternative it was. I urged my partner forward past the cottonwood tree grove and back on the trace bordering the rivers southwesterly flow, holding high hopes of encountering a wayfarer with fresh water or a farmer who was generous with his well.

I was becoming distinctly sloppy in my riding and relied more and more on my trusted mount's common sense and ability to overcome obstacles in our path. My mind wandered from matters of security, to thoughts of home, Mt. Zion and Jessanne, to ridiculous visions of waterfalls and bath tubs overflowing wastefully on a dirt floor.

Sergeant's sudden halt jarred me back to my senses, but for the life of me I could not ascertain where I was or why the animal had paused. The sun reflected blindingly off the pool of standing brackish river water just to our front, but there to my right side was a small clear stream of water pouring from a crack in a ridge of white limestone rock; pure clean water, the blessings of the Gods. It poured forth freely, bouncing off several large rocks before winding its way to the river below. Whether through instinct or uncommon intelligence, Sergeant had known I was in poor condition and required water and rest. Without any guidance the horse moved close to the spring's origin at the rock ridge where two tall cottonwood trees shaded the entire miniature oasis from the intense heat of the late afternoon sun.

One long groan accompanied my feeble dismount that terminated with me lying on a large flat limestone rock at the very edge of the sweet spring water's babbling course. I rolled over to lay face down in the cold, clear water and drank wisely and slowly before turning onto my back once more. That intoxicating water tasted sweeter than any wine or concoction of man's creation I have ever experienced before or after that day.

I remained on that hard rock bed for the remainder of that evening and night, partaking of the cool water to quench my thirst and to slacken the heat of my fever-ravaged body. I understood now how wise Victoria Rose had been in her warning of the possible reaction from the wounds I had received earlier. I found solace in the thought that perhaps the wound I had inflicted on the bushwhacker was at this very moment dealing him just as much discomfort. I worried, however, that the Butler brothers were in the same situation but felt sure Victoria Rose would have found a way to ease such discomfort.

Sleep came in short deep spurts; the stone bed beside the spring was not conducive to a solid nights rest, yet the ability to readily indulge in a cool drink more than made up for the discomfort. The coming of the morning sun was heralded in by the cry of a large eagle that over-nighted on a dead limb in the cotton wood tree just over my head. The bird woke, preened its feathers for a few minutes, and then dropped from the towering perch as if struck dead. After falling a few feet, the majestic animal unfolded its massive wings and spread its tail before emitting a piercing scream and soared out over the river bottom in search of breakfast.

The unmistakable cry of the eagle startled the world awake and other birds took up the celebration of life at the beginning of another fine summer day. The cry also served as revelry for Sergeant and me to be up and on our way no matter what. The loyal animal had remained saddled through the night yet he still managed to rest and find forage among the tall green grass prospering all about the watershed drainage.

I found the night's immobility had brought on a great stiffness in all my joints and muscles especially those associated with the wounds from the previous day. A great deal of effort was required just to sit upright. Fortunately, Sergeant responded to my call and approached close enough that I might grasp the saddle stirrup with my good right hand. I pulled with all my strength and have no doubt my scream of pain at least equaled the call of the early rising eagle. Thankfully no human ears were present to suffer the inhumane sound. Sergeant's ears however did stand at attention but the faithful animal remained unmoving, allowing me to self-inflict whatever torment was required to gain my footing.

I managed to fill the empty canteen and mount up without any further utterances, at least none that would shock the senses. I felt a reluctance to depart the protection and comfort of the secluded sanctuary, but duty called. I looked all about for any signs then rode slowly back to the river trail and a continuation of our pursuit. It was only then I realized Sergeant had followed the trace to an opening in the high barren bluffs where the Nishnabotna River and the much larger Missouri River waters became one mighty mass of moving copious amounts of liquefied dirt.

We had traveled many miles during my near unconscious state the day before and I feared we had now lost the trail of our illusive quarry. Just as the water flow dramatically increased at the confluence of the two rivers, so did the number of hoof prints where the two trails merged. The tracks moved every which way and I spent a lot of time riding in slow circles, eyes straining to pick out any indication of what direction Hixon might have chosen to travel. It would be a matter of luck more than skill, to decipher the mix of horse, mule, oxen and human tracks masking the trail I desired to take on this bright summer morning.

I widened the circles moving farther and farther from the muddy intersection, up and down the main north-south river road and west on a somewhat lesser used trail that crossed the Missouri bottom. This western route was little more than a horse path, for it passed through head high grass and slender willow trees. These willows marked the small islands among the many dozens of small riverbeds making up the normal course of the famed Missouri River's bottom. Unless it is at flood stage, and then the entire bottom would be under water. This western trail was nearly identical to the one to the north I followed from Nebraska City to Mt. Zion, twisting and turning through nearly impenetrable walls of green plants and muddy bogs.

Logic suggested Hixon would turn south at the crossroad for the Missouri state line which lay only a few miles in that direction; while the western route would just lead him deeper into abolitionist territory. Besides, the western trail would be more difficult to travel and would deliver the party to southeastern Nebraska and doubtful security. Still, on the western trail fewer travelers would be encountered and its heavy overgrowth provided plentiful concealment in case an altercation should ensue, I argued with myself. This theory grew stronger by the moment driving me to ride further west, paying close attention to the tall blades of grass for any sign of blood from Ketchum's wounds.

The grasses of the Missouri bottom grew so high that one would eventually lose sight of the towering bluffs lining both sides of the river, making estimates of distance traveled quite difficult. But roughly a mile into this swirling sea of vegetation one single broken blade of grass caught my eye. Close inspection of the damaged plant stem revealed three dark spots that were the telltale remains of once red bloody finger prints which were now dried to blackened stains.

Hixon had chosen the more obscure river bottom trail in hopes of reaching the Nebraska bank then turn south for the race to Kansas and safety with the border ruffians who roamed there. True elation coursed through my body for I now knew which direction the two scoundrels had fled. The trail across the Missouri River bottom would be a strenuous undertaking for a person in my condition and the dense foliage would provide Hixon prime opportunity to repeat a surprise attack on any pursuers. All things considered, continuing the chase was not an intelligent decision and yet there seemed no alternative but to pray for celestial intervention and ride on as quickly as possible.

Crossing the Missouri River bottom west to east proved much more difficult than my earlier west to east trip on the trail from Nebraska City. This one being less used and narrower, the tall grasses blocked the breezes while containing the heat from the rapidly rising sun. The dense undergrowth harbored swarms of insects that attacked out of nowhere biting and stinging at will. At times the air was black with these pests that not only drew blood but invaded our nostrils and crawled inside our ears.

Sergeant was particularly vulnerable to this savage onslaught, his tail swished side to side the entire ride, his head was in constant motion in an effort to shake free of the tiny creatures that droned in his ears, flew up his nose, and crashed into his eyes. When the invaders became too numerous, my companion would increase his regular gate in an attempt to outrun the ever-present tormenters. But no matter how infuriating the assault became the pitiful animal never lost self-control, giving in to kicking or bucking wildly as I have witnessed some animals and even humans do.

As for me, my fever had returned; combined with a lack of food and rest brought on a weakness that made resisting the hoards of winged assailants impossible. I struggled to remain alert and in the saddle while delegating all authority to Sergeant's good judgment as to course and speed. The crossing seemed an endless journey of heat, insects, cutting grass and the incessant smell of rotted plants and dead fish.

Just when I felt I could not tolerate the agony any longer, I felt Sergeant sprint up a steep muddy bank and we broke into the glorious clear air of Nebraska. The ever-loyal animal moved a few rods farther inland to avoid the droning insects and odorous air before stopping to rest. Trying to dismount, I almost fell from the saddle ending in a grand sprawl on the short green grass of the hillside. Sergeant chose to move a short distance away to rest from the trials of the river bottom ride. I had been blessed to have been mounted on such an intelligent faithful animal at one of the most trying times of my life. There was no way to repay the valiant animal for his efforts, but as I lay there too weak to move, I praised God in Heaven for our deliverance from the pestilence of the river bottom and asked for renewed strength to continue our pursuit of another plague, Lyman Hixon.

BAILEY'S CROSSING

These precious moments of rest and peaceful contemplation came to an abrupt end with the sudden appearance of a large barking dog followed close behind by a small boy with fishing pole in hand.

"Brutus!" The boy reprimanded the wolf-like canine. "Stop Brutus! Heal boy!" The youth shouted, finally coming alongside the huge snarling beast which had paused just a few feet from where I lay. Brutus demonstrated all the warning signs of an enraged animal protecting its young and had me thoroughly convinced any show of aggression toward the boy would be met with a counter attack of claws and fangs. This was not a time for fool-hearted bravery, so I lay still in hopes Brutus would eventually recognize I posed no threat to the youth and calm down of his own accord. The boy stroked the big dogs head and spoke reassuring words that slowly took effect on the animal's demeanor; the barking ceased and the threatening white fangs disappeared behind the grey whiskered lips but the penetrating yellow eyes never strayed from mine. The commotion had Sergeant on the high alert, he knowing little respect for dogs and wolves.

"I'm sorry about Brutus, mister; he is a bit on the grouchy side today." The boy apologized in a nasally high pitched voice. "My name is Timothy Bailey and you already know this here is my friend Brutus."

"Yes, Brutus is a very impressive animal." I replied. "I am Captain James Lang and that is my horse Sergeant."

"Are you hurt, Mister?" Timothy asked, looking at my bloody bandages in wide eyed wonder.

"Yes Timothy, I have been shot in the arm and stomach and I am very weak from fever and hunger. Do you live near here?" I asked in a warm cordial tone hoping the youth would offer to help me.

"Yes sir, my folks run the ferry a couple miles upstream from here. Did you just cross the river?" The boy asked in disbelief.

"Yes, we arrived here just before you and Brutus."

"No wonder you look so bad, seeings how you must have swam the river to get here."

"I have been out of my head so if we did indeed swim the river it was Sergeant who did the work for I have absolutely no recollection of it."

"You must be sick if you crossed the main channel of the Missouri River and don't remember it." Timothy's jaw dropped at the thought of such a happening. "My maw is pretty good at healing up the sick; maybe I should take you to her." The boy suggested in a questioning fashion.

"I would greatly appreciate any help your parents might provide. In fact I would be more than willing to pay for some food and a place to rest."

"Let me catch your horse and we will be on our way." Timothy announced starting for Sergeant.

"No son, Sergeant has a similar disposition as Brutus; he is very leery of strangers. I will call him over and then I can get mounted up. Sergeant, come." I called weakly and the animal responded to orders as any well drilled soldier would, trotting up close enough so I could get a hold of the stirrup and climb on board.

Timothy and Brutus led the way north along the Missouri River bank, both moving at a steady lope Sergeant found quite easy to equal. I on the other hand, found the pace viciously jarring to my ribs. Cursing through clenched teeth, I managed to stay in the saddle until reaching the Bailey ferry. Brutus sprinted ahead, barking every step of the way spreading the news of our arrival to the little cluster of buildings sitting on a rock ledge just above the crossing site. A large woman attired in a faded blue work dress stopped hanging up her wash and turned, then shaded her eyes trying to make out what the ruckus was all about. On the ferry boat a tall muscular man abandoned the large catfish he was in the process of cleaning and hurried to meet the excited boy and dog.

The woman, man, boy and dog came together midpoint between the river bank and rock ledge talking and gesturing in my direction. I had slowed Sergeant to a walk once the settlement came into sight in an effort to look the place over before riding into a possibly undesirable situation. Sergeant walked wearily to where the Bailey family gathered. Brutus still in an aggressive mood barked and moved about the family nervously. The man called the dog to his side and commanded that he set down beside his leg and remain silent. To my amazement Brutus complied fully with his every wish. The incessant barking had become very annoying and it was a blessing when the man put a stop to the animals repeated vocalizing.

"Good day." The big man said, extending his large rough hand in a warm greeting. "I am Samuel Bailey and this is my wife Lucy. I see you have already met Timothy and Brutus." The huge man laughed.

"Yes Mr. Bailey, I have had the honor of meeting your son. I am Captain James Lang. Your son thought perhaps you could provide me with some food and a place to rest."

"Yes certainly Captain. And the boy says you are injured as well. My Lucy is quite handy with treating wounds. She would be more than happy to dress your wounds if you like." The ferryman offered with unusual politeness.

"Thank you folks, that would be a blessing indeed."

Flashing a warm smile he wrapped his massive arms around my torso and all but carried me from the saddle to his house where Mrs. Bailey took charge of my care. She bathed my wounds and bound them with clean dressings and spoon fed me a thick soup that had a pleasing taste of rabbit. This was washed down by a strong hot tea which opened up my head and caused my eyes to water.

"There, sir." Lucy said caringly. "I have treated your wounds with a salve of my own making. It will ease the discomfort and speed the healing. I will send a tin of this ointment with you when you leave and it should be applied once a day for best results." She instructed in a low tone. "The tea, as you probably noted is also a special blend that will renew your strength and help you to sleep. I will send some of it along as well; try to drink a cup every night before you go to sleep."

"Thank you Mrs. Bailey, I don't know how to repay you folks for you kindness."

"Please call me Lucy; everyone does and as for our kindness, it is our religious belief to help our fellow man in any way possible. It pleases me greatly when I have the opportunity to assist those in need. No one leaves the Bailey place hungry or ill sir, and we see a great many of both pass through our ferry. Now you will sleep deeply, a result of the tea and the food. You will be a new man by morning." Lucy promised with a bashful smile.

"But I must attend to my horse." I insisted weakly, the tea beginning to take effect.

"Timothy will take proper care of your horse sir; in fact I would imagine he has finished by now."

"Beg your pardon Ma'am but Sergeant has a mean streak especially where strangers are concerned." I warned.

"Timothy was blessed with the love of animals and they all seem to sense his affection and respond in kind. Now you stop worrying and get some rest, you will not wake again before breakfast and I promise not to let you miss it." Lucy said with a gentle pat of her hand on mine.

Lucy Bailey knew of what she spoke, for it was indeed sunrise before I had any conscious thoughts, and that was the smell of the turbid river carried on the breeze through an open window at the head of my bed. Timothy half fell through the kitchen door, his thin small body struggling with a large wooden bucket full of water from the spring behind the house.

"Breakfast is nearly ready." Lucy announced looking directly at me to determine if I had come out of the long nights sleep. "Good morning Captain Lang, how did you sleep?"

"Quite well thank you." I answered a bit groggily.

"Good, then you should be ready for a hearty breakfast." Lucy smiled.

"Yes'm."

"Do you feel well enough to join the family at the table?" She asked knowing I would wish to do so.

"Yes, I would enjoy that very much."

"Timothy, will you call your father to breakfast while I help Captain Lang to the table?"

The boy raced out of the door and Lucy's strong hands lifted me up and placed my weak body on the split log bench that served as seating around the small homemade table. Lucy's nearness while helping me to the breakfast table was the first time I had a chance to study the large woman's facial features with a clear mind. Her hair, red in color was pulled back into a braid; her skin was white in areas where the sun had not burned it to a saddle-leather brown. The woman's green eyes snapped and flashed with a zest for living. But it was her pretty freckled face that could be read like a map of Ireland which betrayed her true heritage and strength to persevere through such a difficult existence.

Timothy and Samuel hurried through the small doorway and quickly found seats across the table from me.

Perhaps it was the long nights rest after drinking Lucy's special tea or the lingering effects of the tea, but it was at that moment I realized how huge and homely Samuel Bailey appeared up close. His massive thick hands were in direct proportion to the tree trunk-like arms they grew from. While Bailey's physic was impressive it was the man's face that was truly unforgettable. His brow protruded far out over his eyes and he had a heavy growth of long black hair which stood out every which way. Samuel's eyes were dark and deep set on either side of a wide flat nose that hung down over a mouth which was far too small, giving it a puckered look.

"Good morning Captain, how are you feeling this morning?" The man asked with as wide of a smile as his tiny mouth would permit.

"Much better sir, thanks to you and your good family." I answered trying not to stare at the man's unusual features.

"Good morning sir." Timothy said.

"Good morning to you Timothy." I said smiling at the boy. "I understand I have you to thank for taking care of Sergeant for me. I hope he was a good soldier for you." I added.

"He was a bit standoffish at first but I reckon he got hungry and thirsty enough to let me close enough to unsaddle." Timothy admitted sheepishly.

"Why do you keep such a difficult creature, Mr. Lang?" Mrs. Bailey inquired.

"Sergeant is a real campaigner; been through many battles, fears no one or no thing and at the same time cares for no one or no thing. In a battle he attacks any man or beast that gets within his reach, unfortunately that could be friend as well as foe. The army didn't want him any longer so I bought him and the old boy has never let me down, no matter what the situation might be." I explained to the family as they settled about the table.

"Can you whistle Timothy?" I asked with a smile.

"Yes sir, I can whistle several different tunes good enough so you know what they are."

"Then I will tell you a secret about Sergeant that I have never told another living soul."

The lad's eyes grew wide with anticipation as he exchanged glances with his parents.

"If you will whistle a military tune when getting near Sergeant he will calm right down. But as I said I have never revealed this to anyone else to prevent their taking advantage of the information."

"I will try that this very morning if you will allow me to care for Sergeant again." Timothy said excitedly.

"Yes indeed, I was counting on you to feed and water him and I insist on paying you for doing my chores." The offer of payment came as a surprise and brought a wide smile from the youth.

Lucy Bailey must have been up all night preparing breakfast, as the menu and table were over crowded with food. She had prepared bacon, eggs, biscuits and gravy, a big bowl of grits and strong black coffee. I partook sparingly of each dish while I watched in amazement at the copious quantities Samuel Bailey consumed without batting an eye.

"Why did you swim the river instead of taking the ferry?" Timothy asked between mouths full of food.

"Timothy!" His mother scolded. "You know it's not polite to ask strangers their business."

"Yes'm." the boy apologized sheepishly starring at his plate.

"That's alright Mrs. Bailey." I reassured her no offense was taken by the boy's curiosity. I had no indication of where these folks stood on the slavery issue, even though we said grace before eating and Lucy professed to be religious. I had known a good many of my southern neighbors who attended church regularly and still owned slaves. In fact many a minister had house servants or stable boys to do the menial labor about their homes. Still I did not wish to dishonor the Bailey's generosity by keeping such a serious matter secret from them.

"I feel I must confide in you good people." I began to explain. "I and four other men from Mt. Zion, Iowa were in pursuit of two men who had captured a runaway slave girl and are trying to reach the safety of their friends in Kansas. Two of the men took the trail to Nebraska City while I and two others followed the trail to the Nishnabotna River where we were ambushed. All three of us were wounded; the other two turned back to home but I felt compelled to continue on. I did manage to shoot one attacker before he ran off to join his companion. Sergeant and I followed their tracks to the mouth of the Nishnabotna River then across the wide flood plain. As I said before, if we did swim across the Missouri River I have no recollection of it." I paused and looked at Samuel and Lucy's faces for any indication of their feelings on the matter. "I think it only fair that you know my situation before anyone happens by who might not agree with my mission. If you are offended by what I am trying to do, I shall depart immediately." I promised taking a sip of coffee.

"You do know that these men you pursue have the law on their side?" Lucy asked with a blank expression on her face.

"Oh yes, certainly, but there is more to it than a simple runaway slave; some of which I dare not declare at this time, but the two men I pursue are mean evil scum of the worst order and I cannot abide them to travel alone with this young female, black though she may be."

"Well Captain, you certainly have opened a kettle of worms, for we abhor slavery and at the same time must run our business that is often used to transport slave owners and their property across the river." Lucy Bailey said with a shake of her head.

"We praise you for such a hazardous undertakin' and bid you stay as long as you wish in our humble home but we cannot afford to break the law to protect you if matters should come to a head. But we pray that God be with you."

"Thank you and I would never presume to ask you to break the law nor endanger your lives or property on my behalf. If any trouble should arise I will take full responsibility."

"It is plain that you are a gentleman of the south yourself, Captain Lang so it is difficult to understand why you are so bent on retrieving this slave girl." Lucy Bailey stated straight out not making any pretense of minding her own business.

"You are a very astute judge of people Mrs. Bailey." I replied with a smile I hoped would ease the lady's concern a bit. "I am indeed a son of the privileged south and not long ago would have looked the other way over the matter. I would have been disgusted at the whole affair for I have known a number of these trashy slave chasers but I would not have interfered with their business." I explained. "However this is a matter of honor and a solemn promise to some good people that I would do all within my power to save this particular girl or die in the attempt." I explained.

"This girl must be very special for a body to pay chasers to travel this far to retrieve her and for you people to take such a chance to prevent their succeeding." Lucy said flatly.

"I cannot say, for I have only seen the girl from a distance and in truth never have spoken to her. I have no idea who the owner might be or where they lived. As I said it all hinges on a matter of honor."

"I believe you sir; I just wanted to make certain that you were not after the runaway girl for your own monetary gain." Lucy smiled at me then shot a quick look at her husband Samuel for a consensual nod of the head before beginning to speak once more. "I will be so bold as to inform you that no one meeting those three descriptions have used our ferry or passed this way in the last 48 hours." Lucy went on.

"You see Captain, we are abolitionists at heart but we must be very careful about our movements and who we may take into our confidence. I feel you are an honest God fearing man and that what you say is true. We will do anything we can to assist you in this rescue attempt but you must use extreme care from here on south for the area is in a near state of war. The free soilers and the southern sympathizers shoot and kill one another nearly every day. Keep your own council when possible, for either side will exact a heavy toll from you if they suspect you are in league with the other side."

"I will remember that, and thank you for the advice. I hope to be on my way later today and with any luck overtake Hixon and Ketchum before they can cross over into Kansas."

"But they have a big lead on you now." Samuel commented speaking for the first time since taking his seat at the breakfast table.

"Yes but one of them, Ketchum I believe, is wounded and traveling with the girl riding double will slow them down some." I argued. "Besides they probably feel safe that no one is following them after the three of us were wounded in the backwoods ambush."

"You too sir, are wounded and in no shape to travel, let alone fight with anyone." Lucy's words were those of a physician to patient.

"Yes but time is of the essence, I must move on. But if your offer to help still holds I do have a favor to ask of you." I directed my words to Lucy who seemed to be the head of the Bailey family where decisions on matters of a serious nature were concerned.

"We will do what we can, Captain."

"Could you find a way to get word to the two men from Mt. Zion who took the west trail? I suppose they are in Nebraska City by now. It is very likely that they would come to my aid on the ride south."

"I am sure we can manage to send word to these men if they are still in town." Lucy agreed.

"The men's names are Albert Rowe and Angus Stuart but I fear I cannot describe them very well nor say where they might be in town." I warned earnestly. "I can tell you both are big men with short cropped beards and they will not be in a drinking establishment. Whatever happens, do not take chances or expose yourself to this murderous mob." I warned.

"Good then, Timothy and I will drive into town this morning and make inquires about these men. If we should find them we will tell them exactly what you have told us." Lucy smiled knowing her son always enjoys a trip to the bustling river port Nebraska City had become.

"Can Brutus go along?" Timothy asked excitedly.

"Not this time, we may have to speak to many different people and enter several stores and Brutus is not too well mannered around some of those folks." The boy's face reflected his dejection at having to leave his dog at home. "Besides, your father will need Brutus to help around the ferry with you gone."

"Timothy smiled at his father and asked, "Is that true pa, will Brutus help you?"

"Sure, he can guard the house if I have to ferry someone over the river." Samuel responded trying to give the boy good reason to leave the big dog at home.

"I will testify that I would not disturb this house if I found Brutus standing guard duty." I stated with a straight face.

"Then I reckon he best stay at home this time." The youth agreed.

"Well now, if you are going to be in all those stores in town, a fella needs some jingle in his pocket, so tell me Timothy what is my bill for tending to Sergeant?" I asked, reaching for my long dark coat that hung on the bedpost just behind me.

"I cannot take your money Captain." Timothy said with disappointment in his voice.

"That's true sir, the boy did very little and besides you are our guest." Lucy declined for she son.

"No, this young man performed a chore for me that few others could and I greatly appreciate it. Since you will not set a price I will have to guess and hope not to offend you." I said setting a bright shinny half dollar on the table in front of the boy.

207

"Oh sir, I cannot take that kind of money from you just for caring for your horse." The boy said wide eyed staring at the coin before him.

"You can and will; that's an order from a Captain, and I expect to have my orders followed to the letter." I lowered my voice to an official sounding roar but winked and smiled the whole time so Timothy would realize it was all in fun." The boy's eyes flashed from the coin to his mothers face for permission to accept the payment. She only stared back at first before breaking into a wide grin to signify her approval.

"Thank you very much sir, I have never had more than a penny to spend before."

"Well I passed through Nebraska City a while back and some of those stores had some really delicious looking candy in them." I teased the boy. "But you spend that however you see fit because you earned every penny stabling old Sergeant."

"Now to the matter of what I owe you folks." I began by raising my hand to stop Lucy's impending protest. "I have a new double eagle in my pocket." I said reaching back inside my coat's interior pocket and removing a small leather pouch. I untied the leather draw string and fished out the big $20.00 gold piece. "If this is not sufficient payment, please say so Mrs. Bailey."

"My word sir, you are far too free with your money! I could never justify taking money from you, let alone such a large amount." Lucy refused.

"I know – build your house by the side of the road and be a friend to man is a wonderful proverb, however it still takes money to feed and clothe a family. In my book your care, medicine and food are worth a great deal more and someday I hope to repay you in full." I promised the family. "Now take that money and my thanks for all you have done." I insisted while retying the knot in the leather pouch string.

With breakfast over Timothy hurried out to feed and water Sergeant, whistling all the way. This allowed Lucy an opportunity to tend to my wounds one more time before I departed. She pronounced the injuries much improved and healing should be complete without any after effects.

I gathered my belongs, expressed my sincere thanks to Lucy Bailey again before dragging my sore body outside to find Sergeant saddled and ready to travel. It was a beautiful morning and I envied Lucy and Timothy's leisurely trip to town; my trip would be anything but enjoyable no matter how it ended. I patted Sergeant softly before pulling myself onto his back and adjusting all the accruements that hung from the small saddle.

Samuel Bailey extended his huge right hand saying: "I wish you all the luck in the world and hope you can save that poor girl from those scum." I carefully shook his hand and offered my gratitude for the good wishes.

Young Timothy stretched his small thin hand as high as possible causing me to bend over, a bit painfully, to shake his hand but felt the discomfort worth the honor.

Lucy Bailey was at her family's side by that time with a canvass bag filled with medicine, bandages, and food which she tied on behind my saddle.

"May God go with you Captain Lang." She said with a warm smile. "We shall pray for your safety and your success. If you pass this way again consider our home your home; you are welcome at anytime."

I smiled, tipped my hat and replied: "That is a great honor and I will never forget you folks; may the good Lord bless you."

"He already has." Lucy responded pleasantly wrapping her arms about her husband and son. "Please be careful and, like I said, keep your own council when traveling south of here."

"I shall do just that Mrs. Bailey." I nodded my head and turned Sergeant to the southern trail calling back, "Thank you again." I could still hear Brutus steadily barking as I rode over the small rise a quarter mile or so south of the ferry crossing.

Pausing there for a moment I could see the Bailey family standing just where I had left them, I raised my hat high in one last salute. The three Baileys waved back in unison and a strange feeling of loneliness passed through my heart. I had known these people for only a few hours and yet my sense of loss at the separation was greater than when I departed from my own home for the first time.

DEATH ON THE RIVER

I kicked Sergeant into a trot in order to make the break faster and hopefully less painful for myself if for no one else. As the ferry crossing disappeared from view I could not free my mind of the Bailey's and the boy; Timothy who found me on the river bank and led me home. Samuel..... Silent Samuel, the herculean ferry boat operator, who never questioned my intentions or motives; only inquiring if I were comfortable. Then there was Lucy, an original angel dropped to the center of sin on earth, whose mere touch eased discomfort, and whose smile automatically elevated ones spirits no matter how difficult the situation. A little voice deep within told me she was much more than the plain uneducated frontier woman she portrayed.

Bailey's Ferry was the most intriguing aspect of the whole situation. True, it was located on a perfect piece of real estate along the river but, unlike the Nebraska City version, it served a nearly unused trail at a dying settlement. One might attribute this to a grievous error of judgment or false hope for the areas growth. The only real conclusion I could develop dealt with the Underground Railway's ability to move combatants and equipment into Kansas and runaways into Iowa without being observed.

I rode along in silence finally concluding I should take Lucy Bailey's advice and keep my own council just as she was doing. I pledged then and there not to ever forget the Baileys, but at the same time not to ever speak of them again.

The river-road south toward Kansas skirted the base of the hills, and at times, moved inland for a few rods to avoid deep water or some other obstacle. It was on these departures from the river that I most anticipated a repeat ambush. My senses were on edge and I kept my belt pistol close at hand. Occasionally, a rabbit would bolt across the trail or scamper noisily through the underbrush and shatter my nerves completely. I keenly observed Sergeant's response to each new sound for I felt he was my first line of defense.

By mid day the tracks on the river road became more numerous and of a newer vintage than those near Bailey's Ferry, which indicated to me that I was nearing civilization. I paused beside the ever widening road, while Sergeant drank and rested, I stepped down to more closely study the maze of confusing tracks. It would prove impossible to sort out a particular set of hoof prints even if they were of a distinctive nature, which Hixon's were not. All I could do now would be to continue to ride south in hopes of seeing or hearing of the odd trio's movements.

As we rested, I ate a few bites of the food Lucy Bailey had sent along, all the while enjoying the idyllic scenery. The Missouri River ran open and free here; its muddy waters all but touching the base of the nearly vertical grassy bluffs. Song birds filled the large old oak trees while hawks soared in huge lazy circles high above the hill tops. Squirrels chattered and raced up and down the tree limbs in an effort to drive the human intruder from their tiny domain.

Farther down the river two men rowed a small wooden boat toward an island in mid stream, presumably in an attempt to catch some of the huge catfish that made the turbulent waters their home. This was as beautiful a place as I had ever visited, calm, quiet, and peaceful. Or at least so I thought, for as I watched the men in the boat, shots exploded from the west river bank causing the man at the oars to spring erect, clutch his chest and then fall face first into the water. A second volley struck the other man who was attempting to pull his wounded partner back into the boat. The second man froze in place for a moment, as the projectiles took their deadly effect on his body, and then he slowly slumped over sideways disappearing into the bottom of the boat.

I instinctively pulled my belt revolver, spinning in a circle to look for any unseen threats, then immediately returned my eyes to the site where the gun shots rang out, then to the boat that now floated gently along with the current. It all came as such a rude awaking! One minute I was enjoying a quiet moment in the Garden of Eden, watching two men leisurely rowing a boat, and suddenly some unseen son's of Satin had disrupted the whole scene. Now two men had been shot, most likely killed with no obvious rhyme or reason for such violence.

I watched intently expecting the ambushers to follow up the initial attack by pursuing the drifting boat to make certain of the fatalness of their endeavor, or at least, to fire more shots into the visible floating body. But nothing further happened; in fact, there were no sounds of horses racing away, no shouts of success, only dead silence spread through the woods. I knew from the multiple gun shots and amount of blue powder smoke hanging over the river that several shooters had been involved; and they were not amateurs at this business, for they did nothing to give themselves away once the deadly deed was completed.

I led Sergeant off the main trail finding concealment in a small stand of trees, while nervously waiting riders to pass by. I fully expected either the shooters to come up the trail from the south riding wildly in an effort to flee the scene of the crime or horsemen to come from the north to investigate the incident.

Minutes passed - fifteen, twenty, thirty, and then a full hour and not a single sound, not a movement from any direction. Wild life in the area returned to their normal activities; birds sang and squirrel chattered. The row boat drifted peacefully down river until it became entangled in the limbs of a large tree half buried in river water and sand.

The whole matter was quite unsettling to me in that my position, at the time of the attack, was no more than one quarter mile from where the two men launched their boat. The shooters must have departed during the elapsed time but even at this close proximity I heard nothing. Surely someone else would have heard the unusually high number of gun shots and become curious.

Now over an hour later, I still stood revolver in hand; my whole body in readiness to respond to any threat but none was forth coming. The lack of activity provided ample time to consider my options. I could not return north and following the river road south would surely bring me in contact with the unseen killers. I had no other choice but to move west; farther from the river and hope to circle undiscovered around the perpetrators of the killings.

Mounting Sergeant had become less difficult, although the rib wound was still painful. With Lucy's treatment, my left arm had improved greatly allowing near full range of movement. Once in the saddle, we moved westward through the trees and brush avoiding the trail completely for fear of encountering groups of armed men on the scout for trouble. And trouble was something I wished to avoid unless it involved Hixon and Ketchum.

Riding west across country proved more difficult for we encountered many small but deep-walled ravines and thick underbrush which slowed progress appreciably. The country was also ideally suited for surprise attacks, warranting a double precaution to prevent such dire happenings. My wounded left arm had improved enough to handle Sergeant's bridle reins, freeing my right hand for the duty of carrying my belt revolver at the ready. This might seem like a minor improvement but having my gun hand free was very reassuring while traveling through such rough country.

About three miles west of the river road I gave Sergeant his head to find the best path to descend another sharp gulley; while I kept my senses alert to any danger. The slightest of breezes was moving up the draw from its outlet toward the hilltop and with it came the faintest hint of wood smoke. I reined in turning Sergeant into the faint breeze and inhaled deeply questioning my senses, but by the second sniff I was convinced there was indeed a fire burning very nearby.

FOOD AND A FIRE

The afternoon was waning and I desired to find shelter for the night if it could be accomplished safely; if not, it would mean a night of no fire and camping alone. I decided to ride to the ridge on the opposite side of the draw, then proceed down it, in hopes of seeing the source of the smoke before my presence was discovered. This ridge was barren of cover, feeling the need to shield our approach; I rode into the next ravine west and carefully traced its route to the bottom. Once out on the small ravine bank, we turned back east; riding as close as possible to the base of the hills in case we might be required to take cover very quickly.

I could hear the lowing of unhappy oxen before gaining sight of a camp, and as an aware Sergeant carried me around a blind corner we were suddenly in the midst of a wagon train encampment. There approximately ten high sided freight wagons parked in a circle while the oxen which pulled them were near the creek drinking and grazing on the well irrigated vegetation that grew there.

"Hello!" Came a booming voice from behind one of the huge wooden wagons.

"Hello." I responded in a polite yet firm voice.

"Ride on in stranger." The hefty voice came from a mountain of a man who stepped around the front of a wagon; large bore Hawkins rifle cradled in his massive arms.

"Thank you sir," I replied cautiously, "I was riding by and smelled smoke, so I came by to investigate; didn't mean to disturb."

"You're not disturbing mister; we just made camp for the night and were fixing up some grub, maybe you'd like to join us." The big man offered in a warm pleasant tone.

"I would not want to intrude on your meal sir."

"We are always looking for company and there is plenty of beans and coffee to go around." The big man said encouragingly.

"I thank you kindly sir; I could certainly use a cup of coffee." I replied riding in close to the wagon where the big man stood. I stepped down from the saddle but allowed Sergeant to roam free to drink and forage on his own.

"Don't you tie up your animal or at least hobble him?" The man asked surprised at my actions.

"No, Sergeant would never wander off and he is too mean for anyone to steal. In fact, I will warn you fellas right now it's best not to approach him for any reason.

"I will tell the rest of the men about your mount mister." The big man shook his head in disbelieve then put forth his massive right hand saying: "I am Reese Sawyer, wagon boss on this train."

I took the wagon bosses enormous right hand in mine before speaking. "I am James Lang, at your service sir." I purposely withheld my army title not wishing to make a long explanation of my recent activities.

"Very glad to meet you Mr. Lang, but you look a little worse for wear." Sawyer said now having the opportunity to eye me up close. "Is your arm injured?" He asked visually inspecting the bloody ragged tear in my upper coat sleeve.

"Just a minor scratch, I have been hurt worse peeling an apple." I laughed trying to divert the man's attention away from my wounds before he got up the nerve to ask how I became injured. "I believe you said something about having some coffee."

The sun was struggling to slide beyond the western hills and the fading daylight made it difficult for Reese Sawyer to see the wound on my abdomen. He gestured to a small wooden keg sitting on end near the cook fire. "Have a seat Mr. Lang, and I'll pour you a cup of hot black coffee."

I accepted Sawyers offer, taking a seat on the keg but it rolled a bit, throwing me in a backward direction. I instinctively lurched forward to regain my balance. That reflex action tore at my injured ribs and I unconsciously groaned and grabbed my side.

"Are you alright?" Sawyer asked while trying to prevent my falling over backwards.

"Oh yes, just a cracked rib." I said adjusting the keg so it would not move before attempting to sit down again.

"Sounds to me like you had your share of troubles of late."

"Yes sir, not been one of my better weeks." I laughed.

Sawyer threw some larger pieces of wood on the fire then called his men to supper. They hurried to the fireside famished from a hard day on the trail, showing not the least bit of interest in my presence. Only the food in the cook-pot held their attention as each of the five men gathered up a tin plate in preparation to assault the bubbling cauldron.

"Boys, this is James Lang." Reese Sawyer announced in a loud firm voice that demanded respect, And he got results, for each man paused in mid-stride to turn and look in my direction, giving out a nod of the head or a grunt in acknowledgement. "You'll have to excuse these boys; they ain't much for talking when the feed bag is on." Sawyer apologized.

"I know the feeling myself Mr. Sawyer." I said pleasantly.

"Let me fill you a plate Mr. Lang." Sawyer offered, stepping in front of the other men and grabbing up a metal plate, which he filled to the brim with some sort of dark stew. "I said we had beans but this here is my favorite meal, Mr. Lang. I hope your fond of possum stew, they may be stupid critters but they taste mighty good. In fact I was brung up on possum stew; well, sometimes it was whatever we could catch but this here is my favorite."

Sawyer towered over me setting on the keg when he handed me the plate of stew and cup of coffee. He retrieved a large wooden spoon and wiped it clean on the tail of his filthy sweat stained shirt before offering it to me. "Eat up mister." He encouraged.

To tell the truth, the steaming pile of food smelled awful and tasted even worse but I was in no condition to insult this good natured giant of a man. So, I smilingly ate every bite of the enormous pile of so-called stew. The coffee was hot and strong; and it played a valued role in consuming the vile meal, for I took a drink of the fiery liquid with each and every mouthful of the cook's special.

Reese Sawyer introduced each man of the crew as they took a turn ladling out a heaping portion of the famous stew. "That fella is Pete Newman from New York; the next is Adam Cox, he hails from Texas; the tall lanky man is Ashford Dunlop and he calls Arkansas home." Sawyer continued to name his crew as I ingested the meal with a false smile and a nod of the head, as if I were admiring his cooking. "These last two are the Tompkins brothers, Herb and Allen, there's not a place in this country that would claim either one of 'em." The big man laughed, slapping his thigh to emphasize the point.

"Nice to meet you men." I managed to choke out between bites of stew and sips of hot coffee. But my greeting met with a silent response as each of the bull whackers found a private place to ravenously devour their boss's favorite meal.

"You got a bit of a drawl to your voice Mr. Lang, just where do you hail from and what are you doing in these parts?" Reese Sawyer inquired just before shoveling a large spoonful of the dark smelly concoction into his large mouth, which was hidden behind a long scraggily beard and mustache. The question caught me off guard, for it was not common practice to ask a perfect stranger their origin or business; but there it was like a big shinny black eye that everyone stares at and the entire crew now looked to me for a reply.

"I was born in South Carolina but Father moved us to Georgia when I was about ten." I explained.

"Slave owners huh." Sawyer stated rather than asked.

"Yes, my parents had field hands as well as house servants." I agreed not wishing to hide any more than necessary.

"Uh-huh." Sawyer muttered without making comment one way or the other on a topic which usually drew hot words and heated debates from most people.

"Now if I'm out of line you just say so, but I gotta ask how you came about those wounds?" Reese Sawyer smiled very self confident I would not refuse to answer. It became quite apparent this big man made his own rules and lived by them irregardless of what others might think.

"I hope you will forgive my prying but I use to be a lawman down in Texas and asking questions has become a habit." He apologized before I had time to answer his question, but the apology provided enough time for me to think up a story other than the truth.

"I don't mind a person asking questions Mr. Sawyer, I have nothing to hide." I began, delaying for a little more time to think up a plausible tale. "I got in a card game in a little country roadhouse outside of Kanesville, Iowa and I caught the dealer cheating. I called him on it, then one thing led to another and he pulled out a big old double barrel scattergun and proceeds to cut loose. The first blast missed me but the second one clipped my arm and side knocking me to the ground. I thought the action over and done with, but the dealer pulled out a Colt and began blazing away. I guess calling him a cheat really made him mad. Well, after he fired a couple times, I drew my revolver and put a lead ball in his mid-section; that pretty much cooled his temper down. The owner of the roadhouse explained how this fella I shot was a brother to the local law and it would be best if I were not there when he arrived. I mounted up and rode south until I came to the ferry and thought it smart to get out of the state; so I crossed into Nebraska and headed south again."

"Did this man die?" Sawyer asked in a serious tone.

"I have no idea, I was warned not to wait around and I didn't. I figured being shot up once was bad enough and that maybe I belonged in the south again."

223

"Are you a gambler by trade?" The big man asked, a touch of disdain in his voice.

"No, I thought it was a friendly game and a way to pass some time on a long trip."

"Might I ask just why are you scouting about this part of the country anyway?" Sawyer asked.

"Oh, the whole thing was a foolish idea; Father had sent me to look the country over and maybe make some business connections where he could market his crops at a higher price or buy new land."

All is fair, as people say; so I turned the tables on Sawyer and began to ask him questions. "Now it's my turn, where are you fells bound for?" I asked attentively, wondering how the inquiries would set with the wagon boss.

"We picked up a load of goods in St. Joe that is bound for Ft. Laramie. It seems this stuff was to be boated to Nebraska City, but got put off in St. Joe by mistake; so we made a deal to move it north to the Platte River road and then west to the fort." Sawyer explained matter-of-factly.

"Have you traveled that route before?" I asked, hoping to keep the discussion focused on anything but me.

"I have freighted all the way to Oregon once and down the Santa Fe Trail three times and of course a lot of these short trips like this one." The wagon master said with a hint of pride in his voice.

"I have always wanted to make that Oregon trip myself but I hear it's a hard trail for man or beast." My words were intended to draw a story or two from the big man and he fell right into the trap, relating tales of daring do on the Oregon Trail for the next several minutes. Sawyer spoke of Indian raids, wild animals, and lack of food and water. The narration contained descriptive tales of the many ways one could perish while attempting to cross half a continent of wasteland and mountains. Sawyer was an accomplished story teller and would answer each of my questions with a lengthy and often humorous antidote of life on the road. I truly began to like the man and felt a twinge of guilt for the lies I had told; but it was not the time or place to have a heartfelt cleansing of the soul.

Reese Sawyer and I talked through supper and several hours beyond, until the other men drifted off to their bed rolls and the last of the coffee was consumed. I was offered a place by the fire for the night and breakfast in the morning if I so desired, which I of course quickly accepted. My only reservation in accepting Sawyer's hospitality revolved around the breakfast menu. I prayed it would not be left over possum stew from our dinners repast. I called Sergeant in to the fire light and managed to remove his saddle and my gear before releasing the animal to find a bed for the night.

I passed the night as comfortably as one could under such conditions, sleeping on hard ground, with injuries which nagged painfully with every movement. The fire drove away the night chill and the promise of hot coffee and breakfast in the morning was enticements that kept me in the freighters camp.

The sunrise broke over a camp already up and preparing for another hot dusty day on the long trail to supply the western forts. Reese Sawyer shouted out commands to his bull whackers while at the same time stoked up the camp fire and fixed a hurried breakfast. I fully expected the meal to be a repeat of the previous night's supper but Sawyer managed to produce some potatoes for frying and some greasy sow belly which tasted heavenly compared to his famous possum stew.

"I'm sure sorry the men ate up all my stew last night so now we will have to make do with some pork and 'taters." Sawyer apologized with deep sincerity. "I wish I could offer you a better breakfast Mr. Lang but that's life on the trail."

"Oh, that's fine sir, I have become partial to pork since coming to Iowa; in fact, I think that is all these people eat." I said with a groan trying to rise from my blankets and join in the morning activities.

"Well, I ain't never had a taste for it myself." Sawyer grunted. "I reckon it's all what a fella gets use to. I bought these taters and sow belly off a farmer down by the Kansas line but I had hoped to live off of game for most of the trip. I never thought to tell you last night we have a man out hunting and scouting right now. I never know when to expect him to come riding in with a deer or big fish or a story of what's happened ahead of us. His name is Enoch Van Sickel, small quiet kid but he is a real hunter and woodsman; just thought I'd mention him in case you happen to run into him in your travels." He explained, rising from the cook fire.

"Well, sorry as it may be Mr. Lang, here is a plate full of breakfast and a cup of coffee for you." The big man apologized.

"Come and get it boys." Sawyer bellowed to his teamsters who were just finishing hitching the teams of oxen to the large freight wagons. Once again the stampede was on as each of the five men raced to be first to fill their plate with whatever Reese Sawyer served up to slake their appetites.

With all the plates filled and only the sound of the men eating, Reese raised his massive hand needlessly calling for silence. "I think I hear a horse coming this way and he is in a big hurry." The wagon boss announced rising to his feet and setting down his plate in anticipation of meeting the approaching rider.

"Speak of the devil!" Sawyer shouted out. "Wouldn't you know, just when a meal is ready Enoch would show up." Reese Sawyer announced as a horse and rider cleared the southern horizon.

The rider lay low over the neck of the big black horse, which was running for all he was worth, covering the open creek bottom in a matter of seconds. The pair slid to a stop just a few feet from the cook fire; their dust catching up and blowing on by as the small rider's feet hit the ground.

"You must really be hungry." Reese Sawyer called out to Enoch Van Sickel. "Come on and grab a plate and I'll cut up some more taters."

"Sounds great but your cooking is not why I was in such a hurry." Enoch replied emptying the last dregs of food from the huge black skillet. "Been a big killin' over on the river." The youth stated matter of factly while stuffing a piece of greasy pork in his mouth.

"Anybody we know?" Sawyer asked, not too surprised at the news.

"One man was named Whitlock and the other was a Hunt. Don't think I ever heard of them." Van Sickel gruffed out between bites of food.

"I knew a Hunt once; did you get any first name?" Sawyer asked dumping the potato slices in the frying pan's hot grease. The mixing of the cold wet potatoes with the hot grease made a violent reaction that splattered Sawyers hand causing him to vent a long string of colorful profanity. The big man placed the filthy burned fingers in his mouth in an attempt to ease the pain before cramming the hand in a can of semi liquid rancid smelling animal fat kept on hand to grease the skillet.

"What started this ruckus?" Sawyer managed to ask between curses and examinations of the burned hand.

"Ain't no one talking, but it looks like the same old thing--niggers." Enoch replied, helping himself to the potatoes still cooking in the hot grease.

228

"These two fellas was in a boat on the river when a bunch of jay birds on the bank opened fire, killin' them both."

"Who did the shooting?"

"Don't know, like I said, weren't many folks brave enough to speak on it, at least to me." The scout volleyed the hot potato slice from one hand to the other in an attempt to cool the pilfered morsel.

"Had you heard about this, Mr. Lang?" Sawyer demanded then paused realizing he had not introduced me to the young scout. "Oh, Enoch Van Sickel this is James Lang. He passed the night with us; he's on his way south."

Enoch, more interested in food than introductions, made a passing glance in my direction then merely nodded his small shaggy blonde head in acknowledgement.

"Pleased to meet you." I made a point of speaking politely to the young man, that way I hoped Sawyer would forget the question he had asked of me. Then in an attempt to change the subject, I rose and took the wagon bosses burned hand in mine to examine it more closely. "I think that should be wrapped up to keep the dirt out." I commented as if I knew something of medicine.

"You really think so?"

"Oh yes, don't want that to get infection do you?" I asked in a stern voice.

229

"What sorta business you in Mr. Lang?" Enoch Van Sickel shot the question at me in a very nonchalant way while pouring another cup of coffee.

"Business." I repeated. "I'm on an inspection tour for my father and some of his business associates. As I told Mr. Sawyer, they are interested in possible investments in this growing area. Why do you ask?" I questioned.

"Just curious." Enoch's expression changed to a peculiar little smile. "I understand some preacher named John Brown was part of the shooters on the river yesterday; and with those fancy clothes and the way you talk educated and all you just might be him."

"Let me assure you that I am anything but a minister." I responded with a quick chuckle, praying they would not question if I knew John Brown.

"You say they think some Bible thumper killed those two men on the river?" Sawyer asked in amazement. "Don't sound like a very religious preacher to me." He growled.

"They say he's a nigger lover." Enoch spit the words out bitterly. "They say his religion allows him to kill white men to free a nigger. What the hell is this world coming to when one white man would kill another white man over some stinking nigger?" Enoch Van Sickel said very adamantly.

"I'm not surprised; what with all the trouble those folks down in Kansas have been causing one another." Reese Sawyer said with a shake of his shaggy head. "I'll warn you Mr. Lang to be mighty cautious from here on south, not everyone is as easy going as we are." Sawyer spoke earnestly as I wrapped his burned hand in a piece of old flour sack.

"I will be careful; thank you for the advice. And speaking of going south I had best be on my way as I am sure you men need to be moving along." I caught up Sergeant, thanked the wagon crew for their generosity and hurried out of camp before any more discussion of John Brown or the shooting could entrap me. I certainly did not wish the young scout to discover I had associated with Reverend Brown and that I was at this very moment on a quest to rescue a runaway slave girl.

SURPRISE AT THE CROSSROADS

I guided Sergeant down the same trail south Enoch Van Sickel had just raced in on to spread the word of the shooting. I had a disquieting feeling of being watched until I crossed a small ridge blocking us from view of the freighters camp.

I knew John Brown had departed from Mt. Zion for Kansas before Hixon stole away with the slave girl and it appeared we were now in the same general area, although on separate missions. It seemed prudent that I avoid all contact with the easily recognizable Reverend, unfortunately, for I could definitely use his help. But John Brown gave me the impression of being a loose cannon, considering the circumstance I would be operating under. That attitude could prove fool-hearty, if not fatal in this area. However, the truth of the matter was questions might arise if Brown were to suspect the truth of my intentions toward Hixon and Ketchum. I now must be extremely vigil to prevent accidentally blundering into either slave hunter Hixon, or abolitionist Brown, both dangerous men but on the opposite end of the philosophy of life. I suddenly realized that both sides of this border war were my enemy. I could not count on help from anyone.

The ride south brought me into more and more contact with civilization; houses being built, land being cleared and at least a pretext of planting crops was evident. This activity indicated I was near the territory line of Kansas; for many of the people were not true settlers but were homesteaders in name only. They came from both sides of the slavery issue, finding citizenship within the territory of Kansas with the intent of swinging the political power and statehood in the direction their loyalties lay. The area was a powder keg and the sparks which could set off the explosion were flying fast and furious every day. The killing on the river yesterday would call for retaliation by the opposite party which would in turn call for more retribution. So, on and on it would go with no acceptable end in sight.

The rolling green hills of northeastern Kansas provided an interesting ride which might have been quite enjoyable under different circumstances but I had to limit my sightseeing, due to the business at hand. I remained alert for signs of movement and, at the same time, endeavored to be as invisible as possible.

Late afternoon from the top of a small rise, I spied a tiny crossroad settlement, which seemed quiet enough to chance investigating. I entered town from the north, riding slowly and suspiciously down what served as the main, and actually only, street in the little cluster of buildings. I counted five houses, a general store, a saloon, and blacksmith shop; a very typical frontier outpost. I reined in my mount in front of the store wishing to buy supplies and inquire about possible lodging for the night.

A quick glance around the village from the shade of the general store's covered front porch rendered the typical inactivity of a wide spot in the road late on a hot afternoon. The only visible forms of life were a large draft horse grazing in the pasture across the road and a large, brown, battle-scarred dog that lay in the shade of an old cottonwood tree. The king canine of this one-dog town took his title seriously by watching every move I made. This place I thought could easily be confused with a dozen other such villages I had passed through in my travels along the western edge of civilization.

The entrance to the store, a large double door, stood open to allow easy egress but no great rush of customers were in evidence. The building's interior was dark and smelled of spices and old tobacco smoke. Three elderly men sat around a small gaming table, each trying to out yell the other two. It seems the subject of conversation had produced a heated debate in the little group. Each old man was so intent on proving their point, they did not notice my entry.

"I tell you it was Brown that killed those men!" The largest of the trio bellowed shaking his knurled fist to emphasize his emotion.

"What makes you so damn sure?" The smaller and older appearing man demanded.

"Cause my son Edward saw Brown ride by our house the morning of the shooting, that's why!"

"How would your son know John Brown?" The third man asked in a hot tempered tone.

"Edward heard Brown preach at a church up in Iowa awhile back." The first man replied in a know-it-all tone.

"Excuse me gentlemen." I broke in. "But who is the proprietor of this establishment?" I asked, startling the three old men.

"Just what is it you want mister?" The small older man growled out.

"I had hoped to purchase some provisions and inquire about lodging for the night." I said in a firm voice.

The small feeble man rose from the table and slowly made his way behind a short wooden counter cluttered with animal pelts, piles of clothing, dried meat, and who knows what else.

"What will it be mister?" The frail old man demanded impatiently.

"I'd like a half pound of coffee, a little salt, some salt pork, and some cheese if you have any." I answered in an authoritative manner.

The old man shuffled about finding the few items I had requested and placed them on the counter directly in front of where I stood. When he had filled the order, the old gentleman looked me square in the eye and said. "That'll be three dollars and fifty cents."

The shocked expression on my face must have been a dead giveaway as to my thoughts, for the old man began to mumble something about the high cost of freight and how good coffee was hard to come by. I said nothing of what I was thinking but merely counted out the money in silence and placed it on the counter beside the small pile of goods. With my money visible the old man placed my purchase in an old flour sack.

"Now can you direct a person to a room for the night?" I asked in as pleasant of a voice as possible.

"Ain't no rooms to be had in these parts mister, everybody's afeared to have strangers in their homes at night." The store keeper replied with a broad smile as he raked my money off the counter top.

"Too many of those damn abolitionists running around here for a body to feel safe." The big man at the table announced. "They just shot and killed two men on the river yesterday for no reason. Just wanted to kill somebody I reckon."

"Which side might you be on mister?" The store owner asked boldly.

"I am just passing through sir; I have no interest in politics." I replied curtly, but my accent should have given a clue.

"You might try the big house on the corner." The third elderly man offered in a calm voice. "They let folks stay in their barn now and then, if you ain't no abolitionist that is."

"Thank you gentlemen. It has been a pleasure doing business with you." I laughed and shook my head turning for the door, provisions in hand.

"You wouldn't have laughed at me ten years ago." The large man snapped in a harsh heated warning.

I smiled and said "Good evening gentlemen," then exited the store, not wishing to start trouble or to attract any more attention to myself than necessary.

I tied the store bought goods on Sergeant's saddle. Then, with weary steps, led him across the dusty street to a large, two story white frame house that sat on what one might term, the corner of the street. I say corner because the north-south road ran down the west side of the house's yard while the less prominent east-west trail ran along the south edge of the property. I was amazed to see a home of such proportion in such a remote settlement, for it truly rivaled some of the stately houses in the much more populated St. Joseph or Nebraska City. Whoever lives here must be a person of means. The question was, why a person with wealth would decide to build in this minor mud hole?

A quick reconnaissance of the neat clean yard showed no trace of dogs which might take disfavor of my trespassing on their domain. Suddenly I remembered the large black dog that had been so intent on tracking my movements before entering the store; but a glance indicated he still lay in the dense shade of the cottonwood tree as before. Thus encouraged, I approached the front door of the impressive home and using the large brass knocker, rapped smartly to attract whoever dwelled within.

Several minutes passed and I repeated the exercise of striking the brightly polished brass knocker against the door plate, a bit more enthusiastically than the previous time, only to have the door open in mid-blow. An aged, white headed, Negro man dressed in a fine suit of clothes smiled politely and asked if he might be of service.

"I wish to speak to the master of the house." I replied cordially.

"One moment please, sir." The black man bowed slightly before disappearing down a long narrow hallway.

Several minutes passed before the black servant returned. Following close on his heels was a small, frail, middle-aged, white man clad in an expensive dressing gown.

"I am so sorry to disturb you sir," I apologized, "I was told to inquire here about lodging for the night."

"Who might you be sir?" The pasty faced man asked in a raspy voice; a fine linen handkerchief always at his mouth.

"I beg your pardon, I am James Lang." I replied courteously.

"My name is Franklin Tompkins and this is my man, Ames." He coughed mid way through the introduction. "I must reluctantly refuse you the hospitality of my home; however, you and your horse may make full use of the barn. I know it is a poor substitute for a bed but my wife and I have both been ill and would feel uncomfortable with a stranger in the house. I hope you understand sir."

"Of course Mr. Tompkins, the barn will serve admirably for a night's shelter," I replied graciously, for in truth, if there was illness in the house, and Tompkins did indeed appear to be ill, I would have preferred to sleep in the barn.

"Fine, my man Ames will show you the way. Now, if you will be so kind as to excuse me, I shall retire to my bed."

"May I reimburse you for your kindness Mr. Tompkins?" I asked in gesture of politeness which I felt sure would be declined.

"That will not be necessary sir, just make yourself to home."

"I shall and thank you very much."

"You are welcome; and now I must bid you good day sir." Mr. Tompkins grabbed the edge of the door as he displayed all the signs of one on the verge of passing out, and the black servant Ames rushed to support his ill master. The two men turned to struggle up the dimly lit hall, one old and ill the other old and feeble. With a shake of my head I closed the front door on the pitiful scene.

I returned to my mount, which patiently waited at the roadside. Gathering up his reins, we walked slowly around the house to wait at the barn door for Mr.

Tompkin's servant. When Ames did not materialize, I unsaddled Sergeant and let him drink from the wooden trough that sat beside the barn. I worked the long wooden pump handle with my good right arm to replace water the thirsty animal had consumed, which in most parts was considered good manners at the time. I sat on the edge of the water trough to rest and catch my breath, while watching the rear entrance to the Tompkins' house for the servant, Ames to appear and escort us into the barn.

When the rear door finally opened, the old black man stepped gingerly onto the ground as if he were unsure of his footing, then proceeded at a slow painful pace in my direction.

"I beg your pardon sir, but I had to do for Master Tompkins afore I could come show you the barn." Ames was a bit breathless due to the short walk from the house to the barn and it was reflected in his speech.

"I understand." I replied in an aloof manner, for it was my upbringing not to be too familiar with servants such as Ames.

"This way sir." Ames instructed as he shuffled to the large barn door and attempted to swing it open. His efforts resulted in the heavy door opening only a crack, not nearly wide enough for Sergeant to pass through. Without a word, I put my right shoulder to the task and managed to move the unwieldy door far enough to allow easy entry by the three of us.

241

"Thank you sir." Ames sputtered out, holding his heaving chest as if in pain. I waited for the old colored man to recover his breath but he still staggered as he entered the musty world of the barn's odorous interior. He leaned against one of the roof support posts, trembling from exertion and lack of air; a strange rattling sound accompanied each of his short inhalations, followed by a wheezing noise on each exhale.

"Are you alright?" I asked fearing the man might very well collapse on me at any second. Ames nodded his head, wearily holding up one hand to indicate this reaction was quite normal, and he would recover in a few seconds.

"Yes sir; thank you for asking." Ames' voice was weak as he attempted to smile at my unusual concern for a black man. Finally, the old man regained his composure and pointed to a wooden door saying. "There are oats in the granary and plenty of hay in the loft. The master has brushes and curry combs over on the south wall and shoeing tools, if you need them. Now, if you will come this way sir, I will show you to the tack room." The old man gestured with a wave of his boney black arm, at the same time he pushed away from his leaning post and started around the granary. Ames lifted the wooden latch on the narrow door leading to the tack room saying, as he opened the door, "There is an old cot in here that you may use." But he stopped in mid sentence, jumping backward in freight, crashing directly into me.

"What is the matter?" I demanded firmly.

"I --- I am sorry sir but there is someone in the cot already." Ames skinny old body was once again trembling but this time it was from fear. "I don't know who it is, ain't suppose to be nobody in there." He babbled out, obliviously reluctant to enter the tack room.

I moved past the timid old servant and entered the room, striking a match on the open door in the passing. There indeed was a fully clothed man laid out on the cot; and I knew the instant the match flickered to life it was Ira Ketchum, Hixon's partner in crime.

I grasped the man by his shoulder in an effort to wake him but I knew from the first touch of the cold rigid muscle that he was dead. I bent near his chest, listening for a heart beat or an indication of life but the signs were all negative. I called to Ames that the man was dead but was careful not to mention I knew who he was.

"I'll fetch Master Tompkins." Ames whispered, turning to hurry from the presence of the dead body, which inspired the old servant to move at a greater speed than before its discovery.

A small, very battered, lantern hung on the wall above the tack room cot and I managed to light it without striking a second match. It would be only minutes before all hell would break loose and I wished to search Ketchum's body for any items which might divulge the true nature of my presence at this man's death bed. But it quickly became clear someone had previously conducted this ritual, for even the dirt and lint had been turned out of the deceased's pockets.

The smoky lantern flame threw out an anemic light but it was healthy enough to reveal a large blood stain on Ketchum's dirty white shirt. The blood was discolored and dried, indicating the wound was old; probably the one I gave him at the creek ambush in Iowa. I speculated that Ketchum had finally succumbed to the bullet wound and Hixon had abandoned his old partner in this drab dusty tack room. A dreary place to expire, and yet, it seemed quite fitting for a man of such a low nature as Ira Ketchum. The only bright spot in this unfortunate incident was at least one mouth had been silenced and would not spread filth about Jessanne and myself.

Suddenly, I heard loud voices outside the barn and I knew it was the beginning of hours of repeated questioning by the locals, who will surely try to blame the whole affair on me or John Brown. The fact that Ames had been present when the body was discovered would carry little weight, for the word of a black man, especially one so old and frail, would quickly be discredited.

Fortunately, the small village had few inhabitants, yet, the inquisition went on and on, but I held to my story. Where had I come from? Why was I in the Tompkins barn? How well did I know the deceased? Since there was no official law in the area, both helped and hindered the investigation; for everyone thought it their duty to question me but no one was willing to take any action against me. Finally, in desperation and great irritation, I announced I was going to depart and if any man among them had different ideas he best prepare for a fight.

Darkness had long since fallen as I resaddled and loaded my belongings in preparation to flee this disgusting little settlement. I had reaped one benefit from this infuriating delay in that Sergeant had been fed and rested; however, I had not. Thus, we traveled south a couple of miles and set up a cold camp just off the main trail. I thought it best not to light a fire just in case the villagers came looking for me with more questions; this resulted in a supper of cheese and water, and a bed on the hard ground.

HIXON STRIKES AGAIN

I woke well before sunrise, stiff and sore from sleeping on the ground and chilled from lack of fire or sufficient blankets. At least, I thought those were the reasons for my waking but I quickly realized it was the sound of pounding hooves on the main trail. It was easy to determine several horses were moving at a rapid pace in a southwardly direction. I lay still until the pounding sound diminished, then I rose and quickly broke camp, making every effort to put as much distance as possible between those riders and myself. I had no knowledge of who the riders were, nor where they were hurrying to but it seemed wise to avoid finding the answers.

Still that little devil curiosity dwelling within my heart yearned to pursue the thundering horses and spy on their activities. But duty, like a band of iron, held me to the task at hand before any fool-hardy chase could take place. Without any unnecessary sound, Sergeant and I moved west away from the trail, intending to make a large, cross country semicircle, eventually coming back to the road south.

Traveling without the benefit of hot food or proper rest was beginning to take its toll on my body and I dozed in the saddle from time to time; confident my trusted mount would proceed in the direction we were headed. I was shocked awake from one such nap by the realization that Sergeant had stopped moving in the gentle rocking motion, which was his normal gate. My eyes open on the scene of a small log cabin in a green grassy valley below the sharp ridge we stood on. My old war horse was wise enough not to walk into a strange place without my command; for we knew not who was friend and who was foe in this land. For that matter, I no longer knew which side of this confrontation I belonged to; except that I always managed to be on the wrong side of those I came in contact with. Sergeant deserved a pat on the neck and a word of praise for having more sense than most humans for not walking blindly into a possibly dangerous situation.

I watched the cabin closely in hopes of determining who the occupants were and their strength; but all that was visible from this vantage point were two skinny draft horses and white smoke rising from the stone chimney. We moved cautiously up the ridge to the north, where we could see part of the west side of the log structure, the well and outhouse.

I could avoid the cabin altogether but I craved food and fresh water; not to mention having my wounds attended to once again. A command decision was called for and it was apparent Sergeant was not willing to take on such a heavy responsibility.

The decision made, it seemed best to circle around until we could approach the cabin from the front; so no mistakes were made as to our intention. I hailed the cabin from thirty rods away then began to ride in slowly, repeating my call in a loud voice. Not a sign of reaction, no dog barked, nor could I see any movement at the window or door. At a distance of about ten yards from the cabin, I waited uneasily for some sign of life but to my surprise none was forth coming.

I wished to dismount but feared it would be considered a breach of etiquette by the occupant; so I remained seated not allowing Sergeant to move about.

"Hello in the cabin!" I called out in the loudest voice my injured ribs would permit.

A loud crash from within the cabin walls told me someone was indeed home and they had just given themselves away. Seconds later the door opened a crack and a faint voice called out: "What is it you want?"

"I need food and rest and water for my mount and myself." I replied. "I mean you no harm and I am willing to pay."

"Are you a free soiler or a states' rights man?" The voice demanded.

"Neither one, I am but a simple pilgrim passing through this troubled land in need of refreshment." I said in a calm even tone.

"Just one minute." The voice behind the door declared in a higher pitch than before.

The unseen person closed the partially open door and did not return for several moments, then only to crack open the door once more and call out: "You may water yourself and your horse at the well if you wish but then be on your way."

"Thank you very much." I replied politely dismounting and leading Sergeant to the well. I used my good right arm to turn the crank handle of the windlass, pulling the bucket full of water to the top of the wooden well housing. A loop of rope was used to tie off the handle to prevent the bucket from plunging back down the opening, while one pulled it over the side. I poured the water into a small wooden trough at the base of the well housing, using my right hand in order to prevent reinjuring my wounded left arm.

"Are you injured sir?" The strange little voice called from the cabin's side window.

"Yes, I have a slight injury in my upper left arm. Do you know anything about medicine?" I asked hesitantly.

"No sir, I was in hopes that you might." The meek voice replied dejectedly.

"Why do you ask?"

Voices could be heard in a muffled discussion from within the tiny cabin but no answer was forth coming.

"Do you need help?" I called out. "Is someone in need of help?"

The sound of Sergeant slurping up water was the only sound to be heard in the entire farmstead. I raised my voice to full volume then called out once more "May I be of assistance?" The sharp pain in my side reminded me that my ribs were still unhealed.

"I don't know mister, I just don't know." The small voice trembled with uncertainty.

"You have nothing to fear from me, I will do whatever possible, if you wish."

"I, well we....... Aaah, we have a wounded man in here and I have no idea what to do for him." The mournful response struck a chord in my heart and I knew that I must convince the cabin's occupants to permit me to help.

"I have a scatter gun pointed at you sir, and I will let you in only if you will leave your weapons outside." My number one rule of survival has to do with never surrendering my weapons. The very idea went against the grain.

I paused to contemplate the demand, for this could very easily be a trap set by Hixon. I had never heard the slave girl speak; so this mysterious spokesman could very well be her. On the other hand Hixon would not have waited this long to spring the trap, as Sergeant and I had been well within gunshot range for some time.

"All right." I replied hesitantly removing my belt knife and revolver before hanging them on my saddle. "Please be careful with that shot gun." I called out edging cautiously to the front door, my right arm in the air and my left still hanging at my side.

The thick, rough cut planks of the cabin's front door made an ominous shield between those within and those without. A close inspection revealed two lead rifle balls

251

imbedded deep in its splintery surface. The barrier swung open slowly, producing a metallic squeak, indicating the owners had enough money to buy metal hinges rather than using leather straps, which was quite common on the frontier. A foul smell poured through the opening, assaulting the nose, and turned my normally strong stomach; but I dare not move. The cabins interior was dark and hazy enough that I could only make out the general outline of a small person aiming a large double barrel shot gun at my mid section.

"Get in here and close that door!" The frail unauthorative voice demanded as if speaking to a child.

I stepped through the entrance, setting foot on a hard packed dirt floor that felt uneven and irregular, as if the ground had not been leveled during the cabins construction. Once inside, I immediately closed the heavy wooden door then turned back to face the lethal shot gun and its owner.

"Stand easy mister." The metal on the double barrels of the threatening weapon caught a glint of light through the side window; and I thought how enormous the muzzle openings looked when held at eye level only inches from my face. "I wouldn't hesitate to shoot you if I have to." The little voice warned.

"That will not be necessary. I came to help, not to hurt." I argued. "Now who needs medical help?"

"Over there on the bed; it's my husband." The slight built woman's tiny voice lowered in sadness.

I moved to the side of the small, handmade wooden framed bed where a short thin man lay covered to the chin with a white sheet soaked red with blood. The lighting was so poor that I could distinguish little else about the man.

"I must have more light!" I demanded firmly.

"I have been afraid to light the lamp since Christopher was attacked." The woman replied, nervousness in her soft feminine voice.

"I must have more light if I am to help. Besides not having a light will not hide this cabin from the outside world."

Surprisingly, the woman complied with my request. Striking a match on the table top, she ignited the wick of a stubby candle and carried it close to the bed.

"Thank you, ma'am." I said pleasantly trying to win the woman's confidence.

The glow from the single little flame revealed to me for the first time the personage who held sway over my life with that feared shot gun. She was a small-framed woman, more of a girl really, in her late teens with light hair and a sweet innocent face, which should have been laughing at a party joke and not wielding a scatter gun while bemoaning the fate of a wounded husband.

"I am James Lang. Your husband is Christopher and what is your name?" I asked politely.

"I am Beebe Stuvant; we are from Massachusetts originally. Christopher is a minister of the Episcopal Church back home."

"I am pleased to meet you folks; I just wish it were under more pleasant circumstances." I replied in a calm reassuring tone.

"Do you think you can be of help?" Beebe asked, her eyes filling with tears of concern.

"Hold the candle closer while you tell me how this all came about." I instructed hoping to divert her attention.

The man on the bed was the Reverend Christopher Stuvant, age late twenties, slight of build with light brown hair and a fair complexion. His injury proved to be a knife wound that ran diagonally across the lower abdomen and appeared very deep. The man was fortunately unconscious, due I am sure, to the pain he experienced from such a massive incision in this particular area of the body. I held the candle close and gently inspected the wound, having my fears confirmed that the bowels had indeed been severed, which accounted in part for the putrid odor in the small cabin. I knew from past experiences, even if the bleeding could be stemmed, infection would surely inflict a slow miserable death on the man.

I continued tending Reverend Stuvant's wound while his youthful wife related the tale of how the injuries were incurred. It seems a man traveling in the company of a young black girl had stopped by the night before. They, like I was in search of a meal and a nights lodging. The

Stuvants had reluctantly complied with the request but the Reverend would not abide the two sleeping together, no matter how vehemently the white man protested. One thing led to another until the Reverend Christopher Stuvant demanded to know the extent of the relationship between the two travelers. The white man, who never divulged his name, became quite irate and without warning pulled out a belt-knife and cut the Reverend across the stomach. The man laughed; and then cursed the minister for the interference before dragging the black girl outside to their waiting horses.

When Mrs. Stuvant finished the narration she was in deep distress, nearly unable to speak or control her emotions. I had listened intently, realizing this unnamed white man must be Hixon and the slave girl I hoped to rescue. However, I kept my own council just as Lucy Bailey had warned at the ferry crossing.

"Do you have any more bandages?" I asked the distraught Mrs. Stuvant still with the thought in mind of distracting her from the grief that now possessed her body and soul.

"I will find some sir," she replied "will Christopher be all right, can you help him?" She asked softly, the answer written across her pretty young face.

"Please find some more bandages." I insisted, for it was the only way I could answer her without giving false hope or telling the truth.

Thankfully, leaning the shotgun against the cabin's exterior wall, Mrs. Stuvant rushed blindly to the opposite side of the one room cabin and yanked an oil cloth from the top of a large trunk. She tore the lid open and began throwing clothing every which way from its interior. She fought franticly with dress after dress, as if finding the correct one could mean the difference between the life and death for her husband. Suddenly the young woman froze in place before slowly extending her slender hand deep inside the bowels of the trunk and gently removed a beautiful white wedding gown.

Lovingly, she cradled the garment to her bosom, as if it were a cherished new born babe. Mrs. Stuvant rocked to and fro for several moments and it was apparent her mind was either reliving the past or dreaming of some impossible future event. Slowly the young woman rose and, still hugging the white gown, walked to the side of the bed where her dying husband lay.

"Here, use this." She said delicately extending the dress out to me.

"Oh please, ma'am not your wedding dress." I protested most fervently.

"This dress was my mothers and mine and would have been my daughters; but if it will save Christopher's life I will gladly make bandages of it."

I shook my head and said directly, "Sacrificing your wedding dress will not save your husband's life. Nothing on earth will do that Mrs. Stuvant." Those were some of the most difficult words I have ever had the misfortune to utter to another human being.

All the color drained from Mrs. Stuvant's face. She collapsed to the dirt floor in a heap that consisted of a tiny unconscious woman, a lacy white wedding gown and the end of a beautiful dream. Two bright young idealists had abandoned the safety of hearth and home to venture into an unknown land, to help erase the stain of sin that hung over their country. Now, one lay near death and the other passed out on the floor devastated in the realization the master plan had gone awry without serving any good purpose.

I allowed the woman to remain on the floor, for there was nowhere else in the tiny cabin to place her limp body and turned my attention to the wounded man. The Reverend Christopher Stuvant's heartbeat weakened rapidly and in only moments it stuttered to a stop, beat once more and then ceased its struggle against death for all eternity. It all seemed an enormous waste, a clash of wills between two groups of people identical in nearly every aspect, except, this one deadly difference, slavery.

How many deaths, how much suffering had this disagreement cost? I asked myself, for I did not know then the very fires of hell this nation would pass through before the matter would be settled.

A feeling of disgust filled my heart as I wrapped the small deceased figure in the bloody sheet that would now serve as his death shroud. It did not seem a fitting funeral attire for the man but I saw nothing else in the cabin that might be more suitable.

I decided to wake Mrs. Stuvant for her input on the disposition of her husband's remains, which required some effort and several minutes of work to accomplish. I lifted the distraught woman to her feet and as her eyes fell on her dead husband's body, she turned away in revulsion. Mrs. Stuvant, her back to the deathbed, sobbed long and hard into the once so highly prized wedding gown, which would never clad another exuberant bride as she exchanged the vows of life.

"What are your wishes for Mr. Stuvant's body?" I asked as respectfully as possible.

The woman continued to cry her heart out and refused to answer or even hear my pleading to make a decision.

I turned from the Reverend Christopher Stuvant's deathbed and hurried out the door in order to escape all the pent up emotion and offensive odor of the tiny dwelling. The fresh air smelled sweet and clean and the discomfort in my heart slackened a bit, not being in the immediate presence of the grieving widow. I and the grim reaper were old acquaintances, but this particular instance left me hollow and indeed stunned by the senselessness of the act. Worst of all, I found myself at a loss to console the grieving young widow.

Looking about for something to take my mind off the situation I discovered Sergeant standing quietly near the water well, the grass grew a bit greener there making the grazing more enjoyable. The stillness of the morning had a strange beauty to it that was in marked contrast with the sorrow of death that hung heavily over the cabin. The contaminated air drove me away from the cabin door a few more paces to a point where the small valley could be easily viewed. The area was the head of a water shed which fed a major creek some mile of so south of the cabin. The stream was lined with many large cottonwood trees; some of which had filled out with large heavy branches that had attained extreme heights. These trees grew quickly and produced a poor quality wood which burned fast and was unsuitable for use as building material, however often times it was all that fell to hand in this remote area.

In doing my therapeutic survey of the land I discovered the smoke from a small camp fire drifting up through the cottonwoods about two miles down the creek. I studied the tree line for several minutes, and especially the area of the campfire, for any sign of life but it was too far for the naked eye to perceive any movement. I called Sergeant over to where I stood and retrieved my three-piece collapsing eye glass from its holster on the saddle. I had great hopes the glass would improve my intelligence of the camp fire scene. Using only one hand, I struggled to slide the glistening brass tubes back and forth one inside the other until the trees near the camp came into clear focus through the small round eye piece.

The camp was situated nearly due south. The morning sun reflected off the brilliant green grass and thoroughly illuminated the light brown bark of the stately cottonwood trees. The smoke from the campfire rose white and lazy in the calm morning air; eventually disappearing in the overhanging leaves high above the ground. Two hobbled horses grazed together in the tall grass some distance from the camp; so if one would take all this into consideration it presented a very tranquil scene. Still the spy glass tells all, if enough patience can be applied and so it was with this situation. In short order, a small black figure, obliviously a female, rose above the grass and moved to the fire then away again.

I raced to the cabin and all but drug the stunned Mrs. Stuvant into the yard demanding she look through the glass at the camp near the creek.

"Please see if you can identify any of the people or possibly the horses in that camp." I insisted holding the spy glass out to the young woman. But the distraught woman was beyond interest in someone's camp, she was unable to connect the people there with the murder of her husband.

"Thank you anyway ma'am, and please forgive me." I said softly, removing the precious glass from her hands before leading the dazed widow back inside her home.

"I don't know who is down there but the land belongs to a Mr. Willard, a slave owner and a despicable man of low reputation." Mrs. Stuvant warned in a more lucid moment.

THE QUARRY COMES TO GROUND

I closed the cabin door securely then hurried to catch Sergeant, making as little sound as possible. Mounting up, I glanced at the cabin reluctant to abandon Mrs. Stuvant in her time of need but my military training left no doubt in my mind that it had to be. I believed I had caught Hixon off guard, sleeping late with his mount out of reach, I could ask for nothing better from a tactical stand point.

There were however; some unknowns in the situation. First, this man Willard, the land owner; could he be in Hixon's camp? If so, would he back up any resistance the desperate man might make? Second, making an unseen approach to the camp could prove difficult, unless a man could use the large cottonwood trees as a screen. Still, this was not the time to lose ones head; for the whole thing could be a trap. The approach to Indian Creek camp would be difficult even if the cottonwoods were employed to their maximum screening effect. Still I pondered who this man Willard was and what part he might play in the fight Hixon was sure to put up. The number of men in camp and their dispositions would remain unknown until I had committed myself to action. These variables were considerable, and yet, acceptable in light of the urgency of intercepting Hixon before he reached the protection of southern states.

I inspected both revolvers and my fine Kentucky rifle wishing I had time to pull the old rounds and reload new ones as was my practice before such risky encounters. But time was of the essence if I intended to catch Hixon in such a vulnerable position; a situation that was not likely to happen again. I was certain the next hour or so would prove to be the undoing of one or the other of us; and perhaps, if all went poorly the end of all three parties involved in the action. A soldier must accept the possibility of his death and certainly that of others, for it is part of life under arms. However, when the prospect is this close at hand, one does stop to ponder the necessity of it. Death, and the reason for it, must weigh out evenly on the balance scale in the brain in order to offer up ones most valuable of all processions, life. Merely freeing the slave girl did not swing the scale far enough to make this a just cause, but protecting Jessanne's name and reputation tipped the balance beam completely out of level in our favor. This was a matter of honor, which must be settled at all cost and at any hazard. I steeled myself to the thought that my prime objective was to prevent Hixon from relating his dirty gossip or tales of innuendos to others who might use the information to damage the citizens of Mt. Zion, and most especially, Jessanne.

I rode slowly away from the Stuvant's cabin, my heart heavy with grief for the young widow, who mourned so uncontrollably inside. The proper thing for a gentleman to do would have been to console the widow and give the dead a decent burial; instead, I rode selfishly onward trying to put the image from my mind.

Sergeant sensed the severity of the situation at hand and reverted to his warrior posture, muscles tense, head held high and alert; he was definitely ready for a fight. I too put on a war face and knew it was imperative to be in the correct frame of mind and spirit. A willing body combined with an alert mind is necessary to meet any call to action.

We turned west hoping to reach Indian Creek and its line of cottonwood trees without being discovered by those in Hixon's camp. This would be the easier part of the stalk for the tall grass and trees provided concealment from the prying eyes of the prey downstream. We covered the half mile or so to the creek bank quickly and without incident; pausing there momentarily to visually reconnoiter the entire area, not wishing to be surprised by those in league with Hixon. It was then I discovered a number of black field hands toiling industriously just across the creek from Hixon's camp. This, of course, was a red flag warning, for wherever there were black laborers, there would normally be found a white overseer not far away. The odds were that any man working slaves would be in sympathy with Hixon's cause and in fact throw in with him in a time of trouble.

Glassing the camp once more indicated only two horses were present there and none could be seen near the blacks. It was possible, but highly unlikely; the white overseer was on foot, visiting the Hixon camp this very minute.

Someone once said "He who hesitates is lost." My mother always alleged, "The sooner the break, the sooner it heals." I personally have been inclined to be a little less aggressive but the plan was now in motion and I must see it through.

I urged Sergeant forward, left hand on the reins, right hand clutching the huge 44 caliber Walker Colt. My attention was riveted on the camp fire, while Sergeant silently wound his way through the trees and brush to a point approximately seventy five yards from where the white smoke rose from the top of the tall prairie grass. The vegetation was so tall around the camp that I could not see anybody from this location but from here on in it would be my only form of cover. We rested there for a moment, taking enough time to look over the surroundings for any source of trouble or impedance which might prevent easy approach to or escape from the quarry.

I experienced a tinge of guilt as my faithful war horse moved with the uncanny stealth of a wild cat stalking its prey, a talent I regrettably had never quite mastered. We closed breathlessly to within fifty yards with no sign of alarm in the camp, which caused me to wonder if we were riding into a well prepared trap. Ten more yards and one of Hixon's horses nickered nervously having caught our scent even though the air was quite calm. Sergeant instinctively stopped as the tall grass directly in front of us suddenly began to sway; gently at first before an explosion of movement and noise that left no doubt Hixon had finally discovered our presence. Whatever was in motion stayed low and out of sight; traveling directly away from our position but producing a telling wake as it sped towards the creek bank.

At the creek bank the fleeing creature stopped before turning up stream, then turning down stream, only to come back to its original position and pause once more. It became very obvious Hixon had been caught completely unprepared and had failed one of the first tenets of war, a safe avenue of escape.

All this rapid movement was an abortive attempt to gain the protection of the cottonwood trees, but had actually driven the desperate villain to more open ground. The creek bank was open mud, which would require much time, effort and exposure to cross, not counting the creek itself. The grass up and down stream was short and would not provide sufficient cover to allow unseen movement. In essence, my prey had trapped himself in one small clump of foliage. Hixon's flight through the undergrowth had landed him a bit over fifty yards from our position with nowhere to turn.

I rose up in the stirrups scanning the area for the slave girl but she remained out of view, concealed somewhere in the lush vegetation that thrived in the well irrigated soil along the small creek. My eyes probed every nook and cranny of the camp site in hopes of determining the girl's location, not wishing to accidentally harm her if gun fire erupted.

I was caught off guard by the sudden call from Hixon's hiding place. "Who goes there?" He called in a harsh voice.

"James Lang." I replied firmly.

"What is your business here?" Hixon demanded.

"I have come to seek the release of the slave girl." Was my simple answer.

"That will never happen; the girl is property of one Col. Jackson Woodside of Jamaica Point, Missouri." At that Hixon paused as if waiting for my response. "I have legal papers on her and the law is on my side." He continued to nervously argue his case. "Now be about your business and move away from this camp."

I stood my ground and remained silent not wishing to make a foolish move until I knew the position of the slave girl.

"This is private property that I have permission to camp on but you, on the other hand are trespassing, so I order you to depart before I call the law." Hixon warned, but still refused to let himself be seen.

Again I remained silent still seated in Sergeant's saddle, revolver in hand but unwilling to start any action.

"If you refuse to leave I will have you arrested for the murder of Ira Ketchum." Hixon snarled in defiance.

266

"Ketchum was shot in self defense after he ambushed and shot me and two other men, I would not call that murder." I called back in a strong angry voice. "Now you produce the girl or I shall be forced to fire on your position." I announced in no uncertain terms.

That statement must have struck a nerve with the hidden henchman for the report of a pistol being fired in my direction was his angry counterpoint in our debate. The projectile whizzed close by my head but to my great fortune the trapped man's aim had been in error. Knowing that firing on me had given away his exact position, the desperate man jumped from cover, dragging the black slave girl into the open ground. A typical coward, the man crouched behind the cover of the small girl's body as he prepared to fire a second shot at me. Still mounted, I watched in wonder as the hammer of Hixon's revolver fell on the priming cap, the results being a mild report of the cap only as the black powder charge in the cylinder chamber failed to ignite.

In the brief moment the bushwhacking scoundrel took to inspect the misfired weapon, I slid down from Sergeant's back while pulling my rifle from its scabbard. Before I could move around Sergeant's rump and deploy the heavy firearm, Hixon attempted once more to discharge his revolver in my direction. The third primer detonated under the heavy blow of the revolver's hammer and the main charge did indeed fire followed by a chain fire of the other three remaining loaded chambers. This massive and unnerving explosion was often the result of the loader's carelessness in sealing the mouth of the loaded

267

chambers with grease. All four of the pistol balls missed their mark and the shooter, in shock and disgust, dropped the now empty weapon to the muddy ground at his feet.

"You have the luck of the devil himself!" Hixon bellowed, now holding the black girl by the hair of her head directly in front of his body. "But then you must be the spawn of Satin to cause me so much trouble."

"Any trouble you have is of your own making." I declared trying to hold the heavy barreled rifle at the ready with my wounded left arm. "Now let the girl go and we can talk this matter over as gentlemen." I called to the obviously agitated man.

"I can't do that. I am well within the law in returning this slave to her master. Col. Woodside will have the authorities on you sir, if you continue to interfere with his business." Hixon warned, also uttering a profane oath concerning my parentage.

"If the Col. is from Missouri, what are you doing with her in Kansas?" I asked, trying to distract the desperate man's mind from formulating any attempts to escape.

"What fools you abolitionists are," my opponent laughed, "you do know what is going on down here don't you? It is a war sir, a war to see if Kansas shall enter the union slave or free and the Col. is here to make certain that the States Rights men win this war. He allowed this winch and two men to escape knowing they would flee north making contact with the

Underground Railroad and my job was to follow them and discover what low scum would aid them. The information will go to the law and those I expose will be prosecuted in federal courts."

"And just whom do you have on this list of desperate characters?" I asked again, making small talk hoping for a clear shot at Hixon.

"Well, you sir are at the very top of the list; you and your friends at Mt Zion, and those at the Bailey ferry and of course the Reverend Brown himself, oh, and the pompous Reverend Gates and his pretty strumpet wife that you have such a warm friendship with."

That last statement brought my blood to a boiling point and I knew without question what must be done. Although my heart ached and my brain screamed for action, I managed to continue a verbal discussion on a moderate level.

"What makes you think the law will believe your accusations." I asked, edging a step nearer to Hixon and his terrified hostage.

"That has already been discussed. Those that the law fails to prosecute; the Col. and his men will exact a measure of punishment from." The idea brought a smile to Hixon's face; he relished the thought of raiding into the north.

I fully realized the Missouri-Kansas border was in a true state of war. In fact that was my reason for being in this area, but I had never suspected any such plan was afoot to trap abolitionists who aided runaway slaves. The information Hixon had so foolishly shared with me about the trap had signed his death warrant; but then I suspected all along that would be the ultimate outcome of our meeting. No matter what happened, if it cost my life, or the slave girl's life, I could not allow Hixon to present his list of names to this Col. Woodside.

I moved slightly to my left in an effort to see more of my advisory's face to acquire a better target for a quick head shot. Hixon's right hand flashed to the top of his knee high, black leather boots where he retrieved a long thin bladed knife from inside the boot that he quickly brought to bear on the slave girl's slender black throat.

"If you move again I will slit this wench's throat!" He roared, signs of fear and anger hanging on every word.

"What would your Colonel say if you returned with a corpse?" I asked quickly, hoping to prevent the girl's death.

"I would tell him you did the foul deed and that would set him hard on your trail for certain." Hixon mused thinking he had out-smarted me. "In fact, that is a fine idea; you see the Colonial is rather picky about the condition of his property when it's returned, especially the females. He has this peculiar notion that we should not soil these runaway wenches; reckon he wants it all for himself. Fact is, the ground was kinda cold last night and this little wench kept my bed warm, real nice and warm, ain't that right?" Hixon laughed, pressing the sharp edge of the knife to the hysterical girl's throat.

A strange feeling welled up in my body, like hot water boiling and scalding the inside of my blood vessels. I suddenly realized I was experiencing true pity for the helpless tortured Negro girl. The folks back home would be shocked a man of my upbringing and military background could share the fear and pain of this simple female darky.

"If you kill the girl I will not hesitate to shoot you down like a mad dog!" I bellowed, leveling the rifle muzzle at Hixon's head.

"They will hang you for murder of a white man!" Hixon snarled back, his attention was divided between my movements and holding the hostage girl upright as she was very near fainting. This diversion prevented Hixon from noticing the black field hands working just across the creek had overheard the fight and were now moving in behind him.

"If you want this nigger gal to live then you best be out of my sight by the time I count to ten!" Hixon demanded without hesitation, thinking he had the upper hand.

"Alright just give me a chance to catch up my mount, and then I will ride out of here." I agreed still looking for an opening to get off a shot. "Sergeant." I called and the animal hurried to my position stopping crossways between me and Hixon. I laid the rifle across

Sergeant's rump and started to mount up when the girl let out a blood curdling scream.

"You are a liar! You have men sneaking up behind me!" Hixon called out, a mixture of excitement and fear in his voice. I could see a fine trickle of brilliant red blood begin to well up on the girls ebony throat as Hixon began to make a slow excruciatingly painful diagonal cut across her neck.

The girl's screams continued to fill the air as I rolled the heavy rifle barrel upright using Sergeant's rump as a convenient resting place. In a split second I cocked the hammer back, sighted and pulled the trigger on the extremely accurate firearm. I had aimed for the middle of Hixon forehead but the large soft lead ball struck low on the bridge of the nose before sliding off and entering the head through his left eye.

Hixon and the girl fell to the ground in one large tangled heap of thrashing arms and legs.

The error in shot placement had been mine alone and not due to any movement on Sergeant's part. I had in my hurry and excitement bypassed the set trigger on the fine rifle, instead going immediately to the main trigger with its much harder pull. Still the shot had accomplished the desired end; that is preventing Hixon from cutting the slave girl's throat. Leaving the now empty single shot rifle laying on Sergeant's back and drawing the big Colt revolver I rushed to the pile of withering, groaning flesh and to my despair affirmed that Hixon was still alive.

The girl's screams continued unabated as she fought to free herself from the clutches of her kidnapper, while he flopped about in pain like a fish out of water. Drawing near, it was obvious the man was seriously wounded but his fate was unclear. It is one thing to shoot a man in defense of another person or even to kill for a principal, but here lay before me a man of my own wounding, one incapacitated and in great pain. If this were an animal injured either by accident or intent, ending its life would be the humane thing to do but this was a man, an evil man it's true, but a man none the less.

I pulled the still hysterical girl a safe distance away from where her tormenter writhed about in agony before carefully cocking back the hammer of the big Walker Colt. I paused a moment in a combination of thought and prayer, before bringing the revolvers muzzle to bear on the man's bloody head in preparation to deliver the coupe de grase.

"Mass'r." A deep Negro voice called out from somewhere behind me.

"Please Mass'r." The voice repeated in a pleading manner.

This was an interruption I had not anticipated, nor for that matter wished to recognize now that I was ready to fulfill my oath to Jessanne and myself. But the heavily Negro-accented words boomed in my ears once more and this time from very nearby.

"What is it?" I demanded without looking up at the speaker.

"You don't have to trouble yo'self none with this trash Mass'r, we un's will see it's taked care of for you." The voice was deep and soothing and offered an escape from my dilemma.

"What do you mean?" I asked, finally raising my eyes to look at the man who possessed this powerful voice.

Four sweaty black men dressed in rags and carrying axes and hoes stood before me like a committee of delegates currying favors from a politician. One large black man, tattered hat in hand stared me straight in the eye while the others refused to be so bold, looking down at the ground in the expected submissive manner.

"It's this way, Mass'r. We knowed what that man did to this little girl and well, I figure it's my place to seek retribution like the Bible say." The big man said with a serious expression on his wide round face.

"But it could go bad for you men if your owner or any white men discover you took a hand in this affair." I argued, trying to talk sense to these extremely angry men.

"We knows Mass'r, we un's will cleans up here if you take the girl to a safe place." A questioning look flashed over the big, black sweaty face and that was followed by a wide, white-toothed grin.

It was a difficult decision. I had no desire to be saddled with a fugitive slave, and at the same time, I felt obligated to be certain of Hixon's demise; still the big muscular Negro made good sense. With a sigh of relief I lowered the hammer of the heavy Walker Colt after swinging its muzzle in a safe direction. This was no time for an accidental shooting. The big slave and another man rushed in to take custody of Hixon while the other two blacks assisted the still crying girl to her feet. One of those two scurried off to round up the saddle horses.

The big black attempted to calmly explain to the distraught girl that she must go with me; but his words were wasted on her confused and troubled mind. The large slave tried once more in a soft soothing voice to penetrate the young female's hysterical brain that he was doing the best for her but it was to no avail. Finally, in desperation the big man grabbed the girl by her upper arms lifting her off her feet and shook her like a rag doll.

"Now you hears me child and you hears me good!" He roared in her face. "Me and my boys is takin' awful chances on yo' account and this here white gentleman just risk his life to save ya'. Now you stop that bawlin' an' git agoin' or else we all runs off and leaves you all alone here to fin for yo'self! It could be freedom for ya' gal, freedom!" The big man pleaded exposing his own burning desire to flee north out of bondage.

Slowly the black girl began to see the reasoning in what she was being asked to do and nodded her head between deep rattling sobs.

A wide white-toothed smile spread across the big man's face. His massive, muscled biceps rippled beneath his sweaty black skin as he gently lifted the girl onto the back of Hixon's horse, saying firmly, "now child go along with this man and don't be a-causin' him no trouble." He said in a kind fatherly way.

As he spoke the other three blacks were carrying the still groaning Hixon across the open mud in the direction of the creek. I felt fairly certain what would happen next and when the big black suggest it was time to depart I jumped at the opportunity.

"Its time you gets gone." He paused to smile slightly before continuing on. "Thank you Mass'r and I pray the Lord be with ya'. I knows that St. Peter hisself will be a-holdin' the gate to heaven open for you Mass'r." The big black man praised and promised at the same time.

I extended my right hand to the man only to see a look of shock and surprise spread over his massive features. I pushed my hand even closer and his eyes met mine with a questioning look which brought a smile to my face for the first time in days. "I am not sure if this will get me into heaven or send me to hell, but whichever I expect to shake your hand now and when we meet again in the hereafter." I said in my most friendly voice.

The big man's right hand hesitantly engulfed mine as he shook it warmly with a wide grin and a nod of his massive head. "Thank you sir, it's an honor to deal with a true gentleman. I will pray for you every night." He added pumping my hand earnestly to emphasize the point. I noticed the man's language had suddenly lost its field hand phrasing.

"And I will do the same for you and your men." I replied realizing what had just taken place in my life. It was truly the first time I had ever made a friend of a black person let alone promised to pray for his safety.

We parted hands and I gathered up Sergeant, placing my highly valued rifle in its scabbard before quickly mounting up. The big man handed me the reins to Hixon's horse to which I nodded and smiled; and he replied in kind. It was in silence we parted company; sure in our minds we would never meet again in this world.

However years later I did indeed encounter him working in a hotel in Omaha and the reunion was shared with some great joy. He had a family then, a house and decent clothing which was a great source of pride to the ex-slave. I was pleased to break social customs and accept the invitation to dinner his handsome wife so cordially extended to me. We never spoke of our meeting at the creek, or for that matter, how we come to meet; even though I could feel his family was very curious. It was his place alone to decide what his family should know about the incident; but it was quite obvious to all present that evening that we had now shared two very unique experiences.

Any soldier will confirm that the act of taking another humans life can produce an unshatterable bond between even the most diverse men.

TWO WORLDS IN CHAOS

With the fugitive girl mounted on Hixon's horse, I retraced my steps north, intent on stopping at the Stuvant cabin with another offer of assistance to the new widow. Common sense dictated we could not tarry long in this territory or we all could face incarceration or worse; but making the offer was the proper thing to do. Besides, I wanted Mrs. Stuvant to know her husband's murder had been avenged and the slave girl rescued.

We circled from the creek bank below the cabin to the top of the hill in order to gain a higher vantage point. Here I could again employ the spy glass to its best advantage. The girl rode in a silent daze, never making a sound or protesting the convoluted route to the cabin. I allowed the horses to rest from the climb while I scanned the entire area with naked eyes before closely scrutinizing the Stuvant homestead with the powerful brass eye glass. The time was nearing the noon hour but everything below appeared the same as it had early that morning. The team of horses remained tied in the same place, the chickens were still locked in their small hen house from the night before and the milch cow bellowed at the back fence wishing to be milked. The only remarkable difference was the lack of smoke boiling up from the chimney's top cap.

The scene was almost too calm after what had just taken place downstream, but who can argue with good fortune. With no threat in sight I chose to approach the cabin from the north side, for it contained no windows for an unseen assailant to use as a firing port. Once at the cabin, we cautiously rode to the door and I called to Mrs. Stuvant that I had returned and would like to enter.

"You may enter if you wish." She replied in a faint voice from somewhere inside the structure.

I dismounted and then helped the slave girl to the ground before opening the door, only to be struck by the same overwhelming odor as earlier that day. Mrs. Stuvant sat quietly moving to and fro in her small rocking chair, her eyes on the dying embers in the fire place. I am sure her mind was miles from the sorrow and pain filling this small Kansas log cabin.

"Mrs. Stuvant." I began softly as I removed my hat. "The man who killed your husband has been dealt with. He will never bother anyone else." I informed her, but my words did not sink in as I had expected. "We must bury your husband now Mrs. Stuvant, then I must be on my way." Still the woman did not show any recognition of my words. "You may go with us if you please but you must make up your mind by the time I have dug your husband's grave." I said in a stern tone hoping to see a spark of response in the young widow, but none was forth coming. I stepped out and closed the door behind me in order to allow the woman some privacy with her deceased husband for the short time it would take to dig the man's final resting place.

I fed and watered the animals and at the same time scanned the small property for the best location for the Reverend Stuvant's internment. The buildings sat on the creek flat, a poor choice for either home or grave but there was a small treeless grassy knoll at the foot of the hills which would serve proudly as a proper cemetery. The selection of the grave site may have been easy but the knoll proved to be rocky soil which made one-armed digging slow and arduous; still, in due time, an opening of the proper size was completed.

The last spade of dirt was reluctantly thrown on the pile for I knew informing the grieving widow all was prepared for her husband's funeral would prove difficult. I remember thinking how unlucky I had been to have two mentally distraught women to deal with; but such fate has been my lot in life. I walked wearily to the cabin while donning coat and hat before delivering a soft wrap on the closed door.

"It's James Lang, Mrs. Stuvant; I have prepared the grave for your husband's burial." It was with halting voice I announced the completion of the unsavory task.

"You may enter, sir." The young woman called from within the small cabin.

I swung the door open slowly and, removing my hat, stepped inside trying to show as much respect for the deceased as possible under the circumstances. There to my great surprise I discovered the Reverend Stuvant bathed, dressed in his Sunday best and laid out on top of a clean white sheet. Mrs. Stuvant was also in her best black dress, that a minister's wife would keep on hand for just such an occasion.

"We are in complete readiness Mr. Lang." The woman said in a pleasant collected manner.

"Good, I have dug a grave on the small knoll near the hills. I hope this meets with your wishes." I said, realizing I was a bit late in asking her thoughts on the matter.

"Thank you sir, I am sure it will do nicely." She paused then added. "The Reverend Stuvant was a modest man, never one for fanfare or material display."

"With your permission, Madame, I will wrap the shroud about him now and proceed to the grave." The woman consented with a mere nod of the head before she turned and passed through the door.

The slave girl and I carried the body outside and up the slope to the freshly dug grave and carefully laid it on the ground beside the hole. Mrs. Stuvant followed, head down, close on our heels to the top of the knoll, solemnly taking her place at the foot of the grave. I opened the white sheet to expose the good youthful face of the Reverend Stuvant for the world to view one last time.

I was pleased to see the black slave girl take a place on the side of the grave opposite the dirt pile, head down and respectful in demeanor. I was astounded with her manners and that she chose to join in the service.

"Mrs. Stuvant is there anything I or we can do to make this easier for you?" I asked in a soft voice from my place at the head of the grave.

"Would you be so kind as to read from my Bible?" She replied producing as small black leather bound Bible from under her folded arms.

"Certainly." I agreed, moving around the edge of the grave to accept the Good Book from her out stretched hand.

"Is there anything in particular you wish me to read?"

She requested two versus which I cannot recall at this late date, but I am quite certain they were her husband's favorites. The thing I do remember though was what happened when the widow and I began to sing "Rock of Ages" and the slave girl joined in. The tiny black girl's voice was like an angel, powerful, yet somehow passionate and so moving that Mrs. Stuvant and I both ceased singing in order to listen to this amazingly talented child. I swear I can hear that girl to this day as she warbled like a wild song bird each note and word performed to perfection.

Mrs. Stuvant was so taken aback she requested the girl sing a second song, one of the late husband's favorite hymns. But neither the child nor I knew the words of that particular song, so the girl offered to sing

283

"Swing Low Sweet Chariot." Mrs. Stuvant was pleased for it was the tune her husband always sang while at work or anytime he felt in good spirits.

The service was short and simple and somehow settling to Mrs. Stuvant; perhaps it was the assurance that her beloved husband had some semblance of a Christian burial. Whatever happened while I was digging the grave must have been a Biblical transformation for the once distraught widow threw the first spade of dirt on her husband's body after I had awkwardly wrestled the deceased man into the ground. The two contrasting females stood to one side and struck up a very unusual conversation as I refilled the grave and patted the rocky soil down flat.

"Was your man a preacher?" The girl asked in a low near whisper.

"Yes," came the widow's simple reply.

"Then he will likely go to heaven, right?" The girl asked curiously.

"Of that I am quite certain."

The two remained silent for a moment before the slave girl spoke again.

"I always thought I would go to heaven someday." The girl's somber words carried a hint of dejection.

"If you are a good Christian and follow God's teaching you will go to heaven." Mrs. Stuvant reassured the girl.

"No Ma'am, not after what that Hixon man do to me last night. God ain't about to let a sinner like me into his home. My mammy done told me so." The slave girl dropped her head into her hands and began to sob uncontrollably.

Mrs. Stuvant placed her arm around the girl's shoulders and pulled her close. "I am sure whatever took place last night was done against your will child. God will not punish you for a sin someone else committed. And I can assure you that Hixon will be held accountable for what he did to you and for killing my husband when judgment day comes. You will go to heaven child to compensate for all the hell you have endured while here on earth, of that I am certain." Mrs. Stuvant promised.

"Do you really think so Ma'am?" The slave girl asked drying her eyes on her ragged skirt tail.

"I do indeed child, I do indeed."

In that brief exchange a true friendship was born, between an uneducated young slave girl, who needed love and guidance and a kind hearted, young, religious widow, who had love and guidance to give. The relationship was a God-sent to me for the two completely different women bonded to form one solid independent person. The trip north might prove to be less burdensome than I had anticipated.

With the funeral service completed for the departed Reverend, Mrs. Stuvant bowed her head and said one final silent prayer for the man who she had chosen to spend her life with. It had proven to be a short marriage of just over one year before fate or foolishness intervened ending one life and destroying another.

Shortly the young widow whispered "Amen", raised her tear-stained face, looked each of us in the eye and said, "Thank you both for your kindness and support. I could never have done this on my own."

"I am indeed sorry we haven't a cross to mark the Reverend's last resting place." I apologized.

"Thank you sir but the good Lord knows exactly where my husband rests. Come resurrection day, God will visit this very spot and raise the good Reverend from this rocky grave, marker or no." With that said Mrs. Stuvant took the slave girl by the hand and headed down the slope toward her log cabin.

I remained standing at the head of the grave, shovel in hand, taking in the sad scene below. The two women coming from distant and now shattered worlds, the tiny cabin built with love and high expectations and the small creek just beyond. My heart ached for all those suffering in pain and the firm belief it would become exceedingly worse before the misery ended. I shouldered the spade and, with a sinking heart, followed the women to the cabin; fearful Mrs. Stuvant would wish to remain in Kansas or even worse refuse to decide her next move. Whatever the outcome, the slave girl and I must be moving on shortly or suffer the wrath of Hixon's compatriots.

"Mrs. Stuvant." I began in a soft yet sincere tone. "You are welcome to accompany us north if you desire but we have little time to waste." I feared the thought of being uprooted and leaving her husband's grave behind would be more than the young widow could handle; but it was a matter of fact she needed to understand.

"Yes Mr. Lang, I appreciate your position and if you would be so kind as to hitch up my team I will gather my belongings; so we can depart immediately. I was stunned by the woman's words but thought it best to do as the widow suggested before she had a change of heart.

In short order the team of work horses were hitched to the small spring wagon and Mrs. Stuvant's baggage placed securely in the back. The young widow made one final survey of the cabin's interior then backed out of the door, pausing to take one last look at the home that was to be, but now was gone.

"Do you have a match sir?" She asked in a soft faint voice.

I handed her a match; she struck it on the rough cut door frame, and then cupped her hand about the newborn flame until it reached maturity. She hesitated for only a second before tossing the small flaming torch onto the hard packed dirt floor. It was only then I realized the woman had been pouring lamp oil on the cabin's interior as she backed out the door.

The hot match landed in the middle of the oil and with a whoosh the fire spread across the floor to the bed and then to the wooden walls. In only minutes the entire structure was engulfed in bright red and yellow flames while a plume of dense white smoke rose high in the air before dissipating.

"Are you quite sure this is what you want Ma'am?" I asked in shock at the woman's eccentric endeavors.

"Yes, it was our home; we built it together and I do not wish anyone else to live here, most especially any of those loathsome murdering Missourians." With that said the young woman turned and walked to her spring wagon ready to make her departure from a life lost to violence and tyranny.

"What of the well and out buildings?" I asked in bewilderment.

"It would not be Christian to deprive Satan himself from a drink of water and the shed is of no importance." Mrs. Stuvant added gathering up the teams reins in her gloved hands.

"You would be more comfortable riding beside me in the seat." The kind hearted young widow declared while gesturing to the slave girl to join her in the wagon. "By the way what is your name child?" She asked in a warm friendly voice.

"My mammy always called me Jamaica 'cause I was born on the Jamaica Point Plantation in Missouri." The girl muttered sheepishly, embarrassed at being asked her name and the unbelievable offer to ride in the wagon seat beside a white woman.

"That is a beautiful name; your mother must have loved you very much to give you such a flattering name." Mrs. Stuvant praised beckoning the girl into the wagon.

The black girl resisted a bit at first but Mrs. Stuvant's warm winning smile won out in the end with Jamaica cautiously climbing into the wagon and taking a place on the wooden seat.

As the team pulled away from the hotly burning cabin the two females struck up a conversation of such importance neither looked back as the flame engulfed roof collapsed with a roar and a shower of flying embers.

Sergeant and I rode on ahead of the wagon to inspect the trail and to encourage the women to hurry along. The country being quite open, we would be at a great disadvantage if put upon by border ruffians; so I was continually on the scout for any source of cover we could flee to in case of an attack. It was necessary to keep a vigil in all directions; although, common sense said if trouble came it would be from the south where smoke from the still smoldering cabin could be seen for miles.

It was my intention to push hard all day in hopes of reaching the Bailey's ferry with at least enough light remaining to allow a safe crossing of the river. The women seemed to understand and complied with my every instruction, moving along trails that were less negotiable for a team and wagon than a horse. Our efforts were well rewarded as we arrived at the Bailey's ferry just as the sun melted into an orange ball of fire where it collided with the western horizon.

FIGHT AT THE FERRY

"Brutus." Timothy Bailey called out as his huge dog rushed to meet us barking in a full strong voice to herald our appearance. The boy was close behind, followed by his parents, who extend a warm welcome to all three of us weary travelers. They offered food and drink and a place to rest for the night, if we so desired. However, concern for everyone's lives forced me to decline the generous hospitality in order to gain the relative safety of Iowa's muddy bank just across the wide Missouri River. Mrs. Bailey hurriedly explained that their trip to Nebraska City to locate Stuart and Rowe had been a failure.

The experienced Bailey clan understood fully; and as Mr. Bailey guided Mrs. Stuvant's team and wagon onto the ferry Mrs. Bailey and the boy scurried around in an effort to provide victuals for we three to share during the crossing.

I lingered by the Bailey's house to render payment and a special word of appreciation for everything these fine folks had done for me; when three men on horseback raced in, out of the gathering gloom. Sergeant and I spun about to face the men as they slid their mounts to a dusty stop in front of the Bailey's doorway.

"Who are you sir and what is your business here?" The smallest of the three demanded in a harsh voice.

"Who might be asking?" I countered, keeping Sergeant in the narrow opening which led to the ferry.

"I will ask the questions here!" The same man announced gruffly, his tone raising an octave in aggravation.

"I refuse to provide any information until you identify yourself and your men." I stated firmly holding my ground in the hopes Mr. Bailey would cast off his ferry and convey the women to Iowa and safety.

"Out of the way sir, I must inspect the party that just boarded the ferry." The small man ordered in a manner indicative of one accustom to giving orders.

I did not speak but held my position which was nearly perfect to defend the entryway if the three horsemen chose to advance. Sergeant's ears were erect and I could feel his muscles become taught with the anticipation of the fight to come.

"Hold that ferry!" The man called out at the top of his lungs. "Halt or we shall be forced to fire on you!" Came the next command and the three began to ready their weapons for action. However, they were overconfident and extremely slow, for in the time it took to utter those words I had brought both of my revolvers to bear on the offenders.

"That could prove to be a fatal mistake!" I shouted out to their great surprise. "Now if you gentlemen will be so good as to lower your weapons and explain this breach of manners, we may yet settle this without drawing blood." I warned, never taking my eyes or weapons off of the three men.

"You are aiding a murderer and fugitive slave to escape on that ferryboat sir; and if you do not step aside this instant, I will see you are prosecuted to the fullest extent of the law."

"Are you a dully sworn law man?" I demanded in a harsh voice.

"No but in times like these we must all do our part to uphold the law." The small man snarled bitterly.

"Well that may be true but you are barking up the wrong tree here. I saw that wagon before it loaded and it contained only a single young white female; didn't look very dangerous nor black to me." I offered in a humorous vein but the man was not up to joking on this day.

"Either move out of our way or you shall pay with either your freedom or your life!" Came the terse rebuttal to my jesting.

"I refuse to submit to any of the three options. I will not move nor forfeit my liberty or my life; but you have my permission to enforce your words if you are man enough." I threw out a clear unavoidable challenge to either fight or back down; so this would be the moment of truth. There are but a few seconds in the course of a normal man's life when he must decide to risk all, for whatever reason, and gamble with his very existence. For me, those few seconds out of all the millions I have lived were truly the most exhilarating and rewarding I had ever experienced.

The small man's eyes grew large and his face flushed with uncontrollable anger; all the signs were there, obviously he would chose to fight.

"You have defied me for the last time sir!" The small man bellowed, his right hand streaking for a revolver on his belt.

Sergeant, sensing the urgency of the man's voice lunged forward striking his horse and knocking it off balance. This threw the small man backwards requiring the use of both hands to remain mounted. The other two men drew weapons at the same instant; the one to my right fought to bring a long barreled shot gun into play while the man to my left tugged at the butt of a revolver snagged in his waist belt.

I instinctively fired the big Walker Colt in my right hand, dead center at the shot gun wielder's chest at a distance of about fifteen feet. The loud explosion and resulting powder smoke clearly demoralized all three men. I could tell by the expression on his face, the heavily charged .44 caliber ball impacting his chest did more than frighten him. I quickly leveled the smaller .36 caliber revolver in my left hand on the man, who in mad desperation, had managed to free his weapon from the resistive belt; but was now fighting to gain control of the errant weapon. It may seem unfair of me but I did not wait for the man to overcome his clumsiness; but instead fired a round into his chest as well.

As the smoke cleared, I realized Sergeant was thrashing about a bit erratically and I feared he had been injured in the collision with the other horse. I soon discovered he had the small man by a shoulder flailing him about like a wet rag. Sergeant's teeth had penetrated the man's coat and from the high pitched level of the man's screams it was clear he was doing great damage to the contents within.

I glanced at the two men I had shot; the first was on the ground, hands on his bloody chest but without any sign of movement or more importantly without any threat to my person. The second man sagged over in his saddle trying to remain on board but Sergeant's violent actions spooked the wounded man's horse out from under his control. I watched as he fell in a heap on the ground only to be stomped on by his own fear-crazed mount.

The fight had lasted less time than the verbal exchange that proceeded. I had survived once more as a direct result of Sergeant's instinct and aggressiveness. His spinning and thrashing about ended shortly after the small man's screams subsided and he let the limp body fall to the ground as if it were of no consequence now. Sergeant spit and sputtered a couple of times then stepped away from the tangle of bodies and the thick odor of warm blood and gun smoke.

Mrs. Bailey and the boy ran from the cabin to the scene of the deadly encounter kneeling to inspect each body for signs of life. I dismounted and moved quickly to remove the weapons from the three men in case one might recover enough to attempt to inflict wounds on those now offering assistance.

"This one is dead." Mrs. Bailey announced, rising from the man shot with the 44 caliber Colt. "And is this one." She declared after searching for a heart beat in the man shot with the smaller 36 caliber Colt. Mrs. Bailey then moved to the disheveled bloody mess Sergeant had made of the small man who had done all the talking. "This man is also dead." She reported with a shake of her head. "I would never have believed this if I had not seen it for myself but your horse broke this man's neck."

"That is truly amazing." Mr. Bailey agreed running from the ferry to where the three dead men lay. "I witnessed the whole thing from the ferry and I have never seen a horse attack a man so savagely. When you warned us not to get too close to that animal, I had no idea just how serious you were."

"I must apologize for what has happened here tonight, I fear I have placed you good people in real jeopardy. I would never have brought this trouble on you if I could have avoided it." My words were useless if we were caught and I knew we must cover our tracks as soon as possible.

"Do you know who this is?" Bailey asked in a serious tone as he neared the mangled man. "This is Hunter Whitlock, a very rich and powerful man."

"No, I have never heard of the man but it is clear we must dispose of these bodies very quickly or face the consequences." I warned, hoping the Bailey's would assist in the work ahead.

"Yes." Mrs. Bailey agreed without any thought or debate on the subject. "We must weight down the bodies and dump them in the river as you make your ferry crossing. With any luck it will be several days before they are found. I will have Timothy take the three horses north to Nebraska City, leave them there, then he can float back down river. That way their horse's tracks may be followed away from here and by floating back down river the boy will not leave any tracks to lead to us."

"Do you think you can do that lad?" I asked the boy with a smile.

"Yes sir." He replied smartly.

"You will have to leave Brutus here so anyone trailing these mounts will not find dog prints alongside the horse hooves. Also, you must be careful not to be seen especially when you abandon the horses." I instructed Timothy in my usual military manner to which the boy put on a stern face and replied. "You can count on me sir."

"I am quite sure I can, it's just my military background that makes me give everyone orders whether they need them or not." I smiled patting Timothy on the shoulder.

The boy tied up his faithful dog Brutus then pulled his skinny frame into the saddle of Hunter Whitlock's still nervous horse. "I have to leave now if I'm going to reach town and float back before sunrise." Timothy announced confidently.

"You be careful." I warned the boy warmly. "I cannot afford to lose a good soldier like you at this time." I then saluted the boy and he sat bolt upright and returned my gesture in a proper military fashion.

Mrs. Bailey hugged her son's leg and instructed him not to take chances. "If for some reason you are not able to reach Nebraska City unseen tie the animals up near the river and head home." She instructed her son in a firm yet loving tone.

"Yes mother." The boy agreed then turned the horse to head up stream on what I am sure was a great adventure in his life.

I gathered up Sergeant and the food Mrs. Bailey had prepared for us, then closely examined the area of the shooting for any weapons or personal belongings the three deceased men might have dropped. With everything policed up and dirt kicked over the bloody ground I hurried to join the others on the ferry, for the sooner we cast off, the better.

Mrs. Bailey bestowed upon me a warm embrace and thanked me for what I had done by facing the three men before they could find Jamaica hiding on the ferry. I in turn apologized to her once more for having delivered the problem on their door step to begin with. But she did not see the situation in that light; feeling we were all performing God's work in helping the two women to safety.

"Please feel free to stop by our home anytime sir, the door is always open to you." She offered in a polite yet earnest tone.

"Thank you Madame and if I can ever be of service to you and yours please feel free to call on me." I replied.

Fortunately, Mrs. Stuvant and Jamaica had remained with the wagon on the ferry during the violent altercation with the three men. Samuel Bailey and I carried the dead bodies to the river bank where they were weighted down with pieces of chain and small stones which lay close at hand. The remains were quite unceremoniously thrown on the downstream side of the ferry's deck to allow for a rapid disposal once we were midstream. This procedure to my surprise offended Mrs. Stuvant's female and religious sensibility and completely unnerved the black slave girl Jamaica to the point of tears. Mrs. Bailey on the other hand aided the process as adequately as any soldier in a combat situation. I must say I admired the whole Bailey family immensely for having the courage of their convictions and for working as a team through the dark times in life.

As the last faint glow of sunlight disappeared behind the western range of bluffs my attention fell on one of the finest women I had ever known and I admitted to a bit of envy at the ferryman's good fortune to be mated for life with such a truly gifted person.

The massive Samuel Bailey strained against the rope that would guide his flat bottomed ferry across the wide swift waters of the mighty Missouri River. Once underway, the river's powerful current would be employed to propel the craft, while Samuel would use a large tiller board to hold us in position. This source of power was slower than other ferries but it was cheaper and often more reliable than those that bragged of steam or animal driven conveyances. I watched in awe as the big man pulled the heavy craft from its mooring out into the main stream of rushing water before hurrying to wrestle the long tiller handle.

"You will have to roll the bodies over board by yourself." Samuel called to me. "I must stay on the tiller to keep us into the current or we might capsize." He warned in a knowing voice.

"You just tell me when to throw them over and I will do the rest." I promised before moving to the front of the ferry to inquire as to how the ladies were withstanding the crossing.

"How are you feeling Mrs. Stuvant?" I asked of the young widow.

"I shall endure anything I must Mr. Lang," she responded gamely, "but I am indeed sorry that you had to kill those men on my account." She sighed; the words reflected her true concern for my feelings.

"That might have happened even if you or the girl were not present, Mrs. Stuvant. Those men and I are of a different breed, a different belief if you will. We would probably have clashed irregardless, for I detest a bully and a swaggering one at that."

"But sir, what of your soul, do you not fear such actions will put your immortal soul in jeopardy?" She asked in a very worried tone.

"I fear Madame that those three are just a repeat of others I have dispatched before. You see I was a Captain in the army during the Mexican War and now provide my skills to those who are in need of such services. I have been exposed to similar situations many times before; so you might say the destiny of my soul is preordained by the circumstances of my chosen career." I explained as calmly as possible to the naive young woman.

"Do you enjoy the taking of life sir?" She asked in all seriousness.

"No Mrs. Stuvant, I endeavor to avoid any form of violence. However, it is part of the path I have taken and I do not shy away from nor apologize for the actions I am forced to take on behalf of others or myself when endangered."

"I understand, or at least I think I understand, but it is all quite foreign to my upbringing. However, with your permission, I shall pray for you and hope God also understands your position." She said with a warm smile.

"That would be very kind of you Mrs. Stuvant and I thank you for pleading my case with the Almighty." I said with a tip of my hat and moved away to inspect the horses and make ready to jettison the bodies when Samuel gave the signal.

The Missouri River was now under full darkness as the ferry, with its illicit cargo, moved ever onward through the muddy waters. I crouched beside the dead men's remains and, when the nearly invisible Samuel Bailey whispered the order, I slid the first body over the side into the murky water, careful not to make a telltale splash. Crawling to the second, then the third corpse, the process was repeated until all the evidence of the earlier confrontation was committed to the river's turbulent depths. The fate of the three men now lay with the whims of the currents; for they alone would determine if the bodies were destine for recovery or for burial in one of the many quickly shifting sand bars. In a moment of selfishness, I hoped one of the famous river snags or a big whirlpool would delay the bodies being discovered long enough to give us a good head start on anyone seeking revenge.

"It is done." I whispered to the women and Samuel once the morbid cargo had been placed over the ferry's side. Sound travels easily across water and I knew full well many men lived and worked upon this sprawling waterway and I did not wish them to be privy to what my compatriots knew.

Samuel kept the ferry into the current. In short order we were approaching the Iowa bank and what we hoped would be relative safety from any pursuit. As we neared the muddy bank, Samuel tied off the tiller handle and once again grasped the heavy rope to pull us hard aground.

Ferryman Bailey opened the front gate of his boat and quickly unloaded the team and wagon along with the two females, before I and Sergeant jumped over the strip of mud marking the edge of the river bank.

The big man was naturally eager to return to his home and unprotected wife waiting bravely on the Nebraska side of the river. In silence I offered Samuel several gold coins but he merely waved his massive hand no. We shook hands in silence; no conversation was needed between two men of like minds and hearts. He pulled the ferry away from the bank as I hurried the team and wagon away from the debarkation point; anxious to put as much distance as possible between ourselves and the river.

RETURN TO MT. ZION

We traveled through the pitch black night across the wide Missouri flood plain by employing dead reckoning. Once we reached the bluffs we relied on Sergeant's superior night vision, until stumbling onto the main north-south road that led to Mr. Zion. The road was rutted making a rough passage for the women in the wagon. Its ridged wooden-spoke wheels struck every unseen obstacle with a jarring force preventing more than a moment's sleep between impacts. I cat-napped in the saddle as faithful Sergeant trudged ever onward in a valiant effort to reach the safety of Mt. Zion before the mornings light would reveal our illegal movements.

The first faint streaks of yellow were invading the black eastern sky and I had no idea of our exact location, other than being on the road south of Mt. Zion, when the distant crow of a barnyard rooster fell on our ears. That familiar call was welcome music to my soul for I knew we were very close to a farm; and that meant very close to finding sanctuary for we three fugitives. As the light from the rising sun increased, I recognized a faint trail that veered off to the northwest from the main road. It would lead to the creek whose headwater started very near the Reverend Joshua Gates' barn. If we hurried, and luck was with us, it might be possible to reach the protection of that structure without being observed by any of the early rising town's citizens.

The sun had not broken the eastern horizon as we neared the west side of the barn still cloaked in dark shadows of the surrounding trees. I carefully scanned the area for any movement but detected only one small dog, who barked once, and then scurried off to safety. The light from candle flames could be seen in a few of the windows; and I heard the door to a privy close indicating someone was moving about outside at this early morning hour.

In an effort to hide the unfamiliar team and wagon, I dismounted and opened the door to the Gates' barn then backed the wagon inside before unhitching the team. I helped Mrs. Stuvant and Jamaica out of the wagon and settled them in the barn with a word of warning to remain silent until I returned. I led the exhausted team of horses into the grassy wash just outside of town, knowing in their condition they would not wander very far during the day.

I then rode Sergeant around to the street and approached the Gates home at the front door, in the proper manner of someone who was making a casual call. It was my intention to make everything appear as normal as possible to any citizen who might notice my activity about town in this early morning hour.

I tapped lightly at the Reverend Gates' front door then stepped back to wait for a response. After a minute and with no sign of life from within I rapped a bit harder on the plain hard wood door. A rustle of activity came from within before the Reverend called out, "who is there?"

"Captain Lang." I replied in a low voice not wishing all the neighbors to hear our exchange of words.

"What is it Captain?" The sleepy minister demanded in a harsh tone.

"Important business, sir." I replied in as calm and collected way as possible.

With that said, Gates turned the key in the lock and opened the door a crack, peering out with just one eye, as if he did not believe who was there. Once assured that it was safe and his eyes adjusted to the morning light, he opened the door wide, a look of disgust on his stone featured face.

"Now what is so important that you would disturb an honest man at this hour of the morning?" He demanded with a snarl.

"May I step inside sir; I would rather the whole town not know the contents of this conversation." I asked, hoping he would admit me into the entry way, and, deep down inside, I hoped to catch a fleeting glimpse of Jessanne.

"If you must sir, but please be brief for my wife is not well."

I removed my hat, wiped my boots then moved through the front door to a small entryway that opened into a large parlor. He wore a long red dressing gown over a floor length white cotton night shirt. Jessanne, Mrs. Gates, remained unseen in the kitchen directly behind the partially opened door dividing the two rooms.

"Now I ask you once again sir, what is this urgent matter that brings you to my home at such an early hour?" The minister demanded, realizing my attention had been drawn to Mrs. Gates in the other room.

I stammered for a second, and then gathering my wits. I began to tell the tale of the chase, rescue and how the two women happened to become hidden in his barn. As I spoke, a very strange expression spread across the religious leaders face; one which could only be described as indescribable. I would say he wore the look of a man caught in a very embarrassing situation; and yet, there was a combination of fear and anger mingled in the ever changing facial features.

"Why in God's name did you bring them to my home if they are wanted by those kill-crazy Kansans?" Reverend Gates shouted nervously waving his hands in the air.

"Well sir, the girl was abducted from this very property and the widow, Mrs. Stuvant has nowhere else to turn for assistance at this time."

"I had no hand in any fugitive white or black hiding on my property; so you just go out there and move them elsewhere and do it in damn short order!" The Reverend bellowed.

"I cannot do that; at least not until night fall." I responded.

The Reverend Gates' use of profanity caught me off guard and silence was the only response I could come up with at first. Then a better rebuttal came to me. "You say you had no knowledge of anyone hiding on your land; but you cannot deny the fact that crates of fire arms and even a cannon have been secreted in your barn for quite some time now." I said brazenly, as a look of horror engulfed the Reverend's pasty white face.

"Where did you ever hear such fabrications?" He snorted. "That tyrant John Brown is in league with the devil and runs about the country spreading these foolish ideas in hopes of glorifying his own illicit actives!" Gates declared in a futile attempt to prove his innocence.

"You are less than a convincing liar Reverend Gates." I quipped. "I have had the liberty of viewing the weapons myself. In fact they were there this very morning as I backed Mrs. Stuvant wagon inside."

"And what other liberties have you taken in my barn, sir?" The irate minister shouted in a threatening tone loud enough for his wife to hear.

"None, sir!" I snapped back instantly. "However, I take your insinuation as a black mark on my name and reputation. If you are challenging me to meet you on the field of honor then I am at your disposal at a moment's notice." I said in a firm no-nonsense voice, my anger rising with every word the man uttered.

"No, I.... aaah,... errr,.. no." The good Reverend stammered meekly. "I did not mean to imply any

309

improprieties on your part sir. Please do not misunderstand me. I was speaking in regards to using my barn for illegal activities." A nervous pleading was obvious in his voice and I felt ashamed for the man.

"We will overlook that point at this moment but I do expect you to be a good Christian and provide food and water for your guests in the barn. I will do my best to escort them elsewhere this night after they have had the day to rest."

Gates stood mute, unwilling or unable to argue with me over the disposition of the women. "Does that meet with your approval?" I asked in a more relaxed tone.

"Yes, we shall see they are fed and rested if you insist." Gates agreed begrudgingly.

"Yes I do insist, sir." I replied tersely unsure of his reasoning but certain I did not trust a man of such weak character.

"Now if you will be so kind sir, my wife and I wish to make ready for the day ahead." This was Gates' way of telling me to get out of his house.

"Good day to you." I said, stepping through the door he had just opened in an effort to hurry me along. It was clear to me the Reverend Joshua Gates and I would never be fast friends. In fact I decided not to place myself in a position where the good minister's assistance would prevent my undoing.

SECURING PASSAGE ON THE RAILROAD

The prior night's ride began to show in my step as I walked away from the Gates home to the ever patiently waiting Sergeant, who stood head erect at the edge of the street. Although, the strong spirited animal refused to show his fatigue, I knew full well how diminished his strength must be and decided to lead rather than ride around the common to our lodging.

Once at the Mills house, I fed and stabled my loyal friend for a day's rest suspecting his services would be required again that night. Mr. and Mrs. Mills provided a warm reception and a bountiful breakfast, in addition to a thousand questions about the ride to Kansas. I wisely refrained from reporting the demise of Hixon and Ketchum, not to mention the three men at the Bailey ferry. In fact, I never revealed my warm association with the Bailey family, fearing for their safety. I in turn, inquired as to the condition of the men who had initially accompanied me; especially the Butler Brothers, who were wounded in my presence. I was pleased to learn they had returned home safely and the brother's wounds were healing nicely. Mrs. Mills reported both men were anxious to attend the big church meeting and supper scheduled for the following night.

"I am sure they will be delighted to see you." Mrs. Mills said cheerfully. "That is if you are up to attending yourself."

"May I inquire as to the condition of your own wounds?" Buck Mills asked in a concerned tone.

"I am fine sir, nothing a good night's rest will not cure." I replied, wishing I had the time to indulge myself so but I had only that day to make arrangements for the disposition of Mrs. Stuvant and Jamaica. It would not be easy for an outsider to make connection with one of the conductors on the Underground Railway in order to move the slave girl tonight. I had given my word as a gentleman, that the two women would be out of Reverend Gates' barn tonight and I fully intended to see it done, sleep or not.

Wearily and perhaps foolishly, I informed Mr. and Mrs. Mills of my dilemma concerning the two women and my promise to Gates. I knew I must confide in someone in the town in order to make contact with the proper people and, since I knew them best I felt sure where their sympathy lay. I could read their faces like an open book that said fear and mistrust. It was time to be very careful of what was said and to choose each word wisely, less I might lose all chance of gaining their invaluable assistance in solving my problem.

"I am not asking you to betray any confidences nor for a face to face with anyone. Rather, I hoped you might speak on these two women's behalf, but only if you do not endanger yourself." I said in a serious

312

fashion, for I truly did not wish to place those kind folks in jeopardy for my benefit.

The middle aged couple silently exchanged glances before Mrs. Mills cleared her throat, and then looked at Mr. Mills once more for his consent before speaking. "I might possibly know of a family who would be willing to take in the widow woman if you swear that her late husband was a minister and that she is a true believer in Jesus."

"I firmly believe that the deceased man was a Reverend and that the widow is a very religious woman and an ardent abolitionist." I declared with all the sincerity my weary body could muster.

"Then I will place the matter before these people this very morning." Mrs. Mills promised with a tentative smile.

"Thank you. I know this is very difficult for you but it is the proper thing to do for a good Christian lady down on her luck." I praised, hoping to reaffirm in Mrs. Mills' mind that finding Mrs. Stuvant adequate lodging was indeed the right thing to do.

"Now, about the girl." Buck Mills said with a shake of his head. "That is a cat of a different color."

"But the girl was here just days ago ready to continue on along the railway. How have things changed?" I asked a bit bewildered.

"The fact that she was found here and forcibly removed is the difference; no one will be eager to touch such a recognizable and sought-after person as that little black gal," Buck replied as he ran his fingers through his hair, "allowing her to remain in our presence will serve no good."

"We must think of some plan to move the girl." Mrs. Mills declared softly, an expression of deep thought on her face. The room fell silent for a long moment, each person mulling over ideas for the fugitive slave girl's movement out of town.

"I will do it myself." I offered, disgusted that no one in the group had enough courage to see through what they had started.

"An honorable suggestion sir, however you do not know the route or the contacts or alternates in case you would encounter trouble. No, that is not a workable plan." Mr. Mills stated unequivocally, holding up his hand to signify he did not wish to discuss it further.

"There is old Sutter." Buck Mills said hesitantly after some minutes of deep thought.

"Oh sir, you do not mean to suggest sending Alva Sutter on such a mission?" Mrs. Mills asked in a scolding tone that implied that Alva Sutter was not a man of good repute.

"Yes my dear, for I can think of none other who might consider such a dangerous assignment."

314

"I do not believe I have met this Mr. Sutter." My words were a question rather than a statement and Mr. Mills instantly picked up on that fact.

"Well no, I doubt it. You see Mr. Sutter is something of a recluse in our little community."

"The word outcast is much more appropriate." Mrs. Mills added sourly.

"Is there a problem with this man?" I asked in a concerned tone.

"No, not really." Buck Mills replied hesitantly. "Alva Sutter is cut from a different bolt of cloth is all. He lives alone on a small farm east of town and is rarely seen by any of us. We have been forced to use his place as an emergency stop on a few occasions and he knows the route and stops to the east."

"Then I do not see your reluctance to use him in this time of need." I said flatly. "Is this man Sutter of a different religion or disagree with your stance on slavery?"

"Oh no sir. Quite the contrary, Mr. Sutter is an ardent abolitionist and a staunch supporter of our church but,.... well......" Mrs. Mills attempted to explain then stopped short glancing at her husband for guidance.

"The truth of the matter is Alva Sutter is, well deformed. The man is huge in stature, with absolutely

315

the most homely face I have ever seen." Buck Mills stated humbly.

"Yes." Mrs. Mills agreed quickly. "He has a long heavy beard and a massive nose and his head is an irregular shape." The woman pronounced in a hearty condemnation. "Alva Sutter."

"Where might I find this Mr. Sutter?" I asked, a bit amazed at these professed religious zealots who would shun a person for no other reason other than his physical appearance.

"Please sir, allow me to make all the arrangements. Mr. Sutter can be, shall we say, ill mannered when meeting strangers." Buck Mills argued. "Besides, I am sure no one will attempt to move the slave girl until tomorrow night under the cover of our church meeting."

"Yes, that is the standard way of doing things." Mrs. Mills confirmed with a wide smile. "You must be sure to attend the meeting Captain Lang, there will be a dinner afterward that you will surely enjoy."

"I fear it is more important than that, Captain, and it may concern you." Buck's words were spoken in all seriousness obviously aimed at gaining my attention. "There seems to be some trouble brewing within the congregation as to our mission here in southwest Iowa."

"I gather Reverend Brown is part of the difficulties." I said.

"I would rather not speak out of turn but I have been informed that the whole matter will come to a head at the meeting. The council may wish to hear from you and it will give you an undeniable alibi at the same time."

"Alibi sir?" I questioned the man unsure of what he meant.

"Yes indeed, we have higher attendance at night when the bell rings than for Sunday morning services. Most people find it very convenient to be in church when the bell rings, so no one can accuse them of being a conductor on the railroad."

"Oh, I see." I muttered embarrassingly, not considering a person might be asked to prove their whereabouts at any given time.

"I will defer the entire matter to you good folks. I am confident in your knowledge of the correct protocol for such business." I consented, becoming extremely weary from the trip to Kansas.

"We will see that everything is taken care of to your satisfaction." Buck promised, rising from the breakfast table to don his hat and coat for the walk to his store.

"I am certain you will sir; and I thank you both for your efforts on my behalf."

"No thanks needed, sir." He replied. "After all this is an affair of our own making and you have done more to remedy the situation than one could expect of a stranger. Now, I must bid you both a good morning and suggest, sir, that you stop by the store later for a progress report."

"I shall do that very thing, sir, and good day to you." I said pleasantly, too tired to rise from my chair as was proper when Mills exited the door. I turned my attention to Mrs. Mills with a question I feared would shock the matronly woman with its boldness.

"Please do not misunderstand, nor read more into this than there is, but I would very much like to speak to Mrs. Gates without the benefit of the Reverend Gates interrupting. I fear the man has taken an understandable dislike for me; most likely due to the differences in our ways of life. I am reluctant to inquire about such delicate information of you, but is there any way that a discrete word with Mrs. Gates might be possible?" I asked in a shy embarrassed voice; my eyes diverted away from those of my landlady. When I looked up, I saw a sly fleeting smile cross her round aged face.

"I know exactly what you are referring to; the man is a bit of a fop at times." Mrs. Mills grinned. "I am sure that any discourse between you and Jessanne Gates is purely based on innocent friendship and concern. And yes, there is a way that you might have a legitimate word with the woman, if you will do me a favor at the same time."

"Certainly, how may I be of service to you Madame?" I asked eagerly.

"We provide food and lodging as part of the ministers pay; and I am in the process of baking bread and other goods which will need delivering later this morning. You rest for a couple of hours until all is in readiness then I will call on you to make the delivery." She hesitated, smiled then added, "The good Reverend is in his office at the church from nine until eleven each morning where he receives callers and writes his sermons. I believe the baked goods will be out of the oven and into a basket by half passed nine." Mrs. Mills said with a wink, and then turned to her cooking without another word.

To say I was shocked at the woman's candor is truly an understatement; but my heart leapt at the unexpected opportunity to visit Jessanne unencumbered by the presence of her disagreeable husband.

I adjourned to my quarters for a short rest and a quick bath with the understanding Mrs. Mills would summons me when the appointed hour arrived; but my heightened anticipation prevented sleep regardless of my physical exhaustion. I rehearsed what I would say and tried to predict Jessanne's response. It soon became obvious this was an impossible exercise, and the only real preparation I could make was to be honest, understanding and kind to the beautiful young woman, no matter what positions she may now take.

My eyes prowled about the room in search of some item to take my mind off of the subject at hand, however they always seemed to seek out the west window which looked out across the common to Jessanne's house. Time and time again, I forced my eyes to settle on another object but, as if under some hypnotic power, my vision returned to the same small window and the house across the way. In futile despair, I turned to face the opening so that all my senses could partake of the home, so near, yet so far away and the only place in this world my heart longed to be.

Suddenly, the front door of the Gates' house opened and a man dressed in a black suit stepped forth, placed a top hat on his head, then hurried down the path and across the road to the grassy common. I sprang upright in excitement knowing Mrs. Mills would soon be summoning me to make the long awaited delivery.

I washed my face, combed my hair and made myself as presentable as possible under the circumstances; but the reflection I saw in my small mirror was far from that of an army officer. The image before me was more in keeping with that of a bedraggled bum, looking for a kind word and a hand out. A sharp rap at my quarter's door jarred me from my primping, for I knew it was opportunity knocking or at least it was Mrs. Mills, which in this case was one in the same.

"Yes." I replied quickly not wishing to give the lady the chance to change her mind.

"I have the baked goods ready Captain, if you are up to the task." She announced in a cordial almost teasing voice.

I rushed out the door to greet Mrs. Mills and assured her I was indeed anxious to make the delivery to the Gates house. She held out a large wicker basket with a high arching handle and baked goods piled nearly to its zenith. The sweet aroma of fresh baked bread was nearly over powering but this was business and there would be no sampling of the delicacies, for my head and heart lay elsewhere this morning.

I thanked Mrs. Mills and hurried out the yard gate, making a bee line for the Gates home on the opposite side of the large empty common. I was half way across the open grassy park before I realized my gait was unusually quick and perhaps appeared in a bit of a rush to reach my destination. I slowed my cadence slightly and endeavored to look less intent about securing my objective; but the effort was quite difficult.

Upon reaching the street on the west side of the common, I encountered a man and wife, who I recognized from church, driving a small wagon toward the south. They paused for a moment of cordial conversation about the weather and crops which was the normal polite topic of exchange by residents of the area. I held up my end of the discussion quite adequately; but in my desire for them to move on, failed to initiate any new subjects of interest that would prolong their stay.

When the lady of the wagon questioned my basket of baked goods, I explained I was merely running an errand for Mrs. Mills, my landlady. The couple accepted this without further question, then excused themselves and drove off down the wide dirt street. I tipped my hat as the couple departed, then glanced at the Gates home in time to see Jessanne step away from the window in her front parlor, vanishing into the house's shadowy interior.

Taking a deep breath, I crossed the street and moved uneasily up the walk to the Gates' front door unsure if Jessanne would respond to my knocking. But to my hearts delight, respond she did with a wide and a bit embarrassed smile.

"Good morning Captain." Jessanne's words were like music to my ears. With obvious emphases on the word Captain, I knew at that point I remained in the magnetic woman's good graces.

"Good morning, My Lady." I beamed, so delighted to speak to Jessanne that I could do little else. "I have a basket of goods that Mrs. Mills asked me to deliver to you." I smiled again as did she, easily recognizing the ruse involved in the errand.

"Why thank you Captain, it is very kind of you to walk all the way over here just so I can have fresh bread this day."

"It is my pleasure but in truth I wished to have a word with you in private." I said earnestly. "The problem that developed a few days ago has been completely resolved. There is no reason for you to be concerned that the subject will ever come to light again." I promised with great sincerity.

"Thank you sir. I feared that it would not end so but I feared more for your safety. I was devastated when the Butler brothers returned so severely wounded and telling that you had also been injured and had continued on alone. I was beside myself; and you were in my prayers and my thoughts every hour of the day. I was so relieved when you came to our door this morning and I could see for myself that you were indeed well. I guess God answers even a sinner's prayers if they pray hard enough." Jessanne said softly, dropping her eyes down and away from mine.

"You are no sinner. It is I who took advantage of the situation and I ask for your forgiveness." My words were intended to ease Jessanne's feelings of guilt but her response took me by surprise.

"That is very gallant but not entirely true Captain; I was a willing accomplice." She paused to look deep into my eyes then added, "In truth my heart has not changed one bit since that day in the barn." She whispered, a tear glistening in her beautiful eyes.

I stood dumb struck before Jessanne for I had no reasonable reply to her statement. The woman had just declared her love for me, and yet being married, there was no future for me in her life.

"I do not know what to say to you. I, of course, am of like sentiments; in fact, you have become a burning obsession in my life. I live for nothing else but to be in your presence and to hear your voice." I managed to choke out the words, as if their saying would save my

323

very life. I longed to touch Jessanne's delicate hand and take her in my arms; but we were standing at her front door exposed to the eyes of the whole world.

"I am at a loss for words myself; I only know what my heart says over and over. You are my hero, my champion and savior of my reputation not to mention my life. It is not mere hero-worship or the foolish infatuation of a young and lonely heart. This overwhelming sensation; this powerful driving force, is real emotion. I fear what I am experiencing is beyond anything I have ever known or hope to know. I fear my desire for you has even diminished my fear of God and the disposition of my everlasting soul." Jessanne blurted out in a confessional speech which rocked me back on my heels like a fist to the jaw.

I stared deep into Jessanne's eyes for a long minute, fighting the desire to embrace the beautiful woman, and yet at the same time, thoughts of elopement, sin, lies, and deceptions whirled in my mind's eye. There was no shinning light, no blaring perfect solution on how to handle the situation at hand. I had never been one to woo women during my travels; so I was quite unaccustomed to the ways of a scalawag. This was such a new experience for both parties that silence prevailed, except for the emotions stirring in our eyes.

Finally, in anguish I asked, "What shall we do?" It was a foolish question to put forth, for Jessanne was in just as deep a quandary as I.

She smiled warmly and shook her head gently from side to side. "I have not a clue Captain, for I am lost in a whirlpool of fear and disgust at my weakness which seems to be pulling me under and yet, I am soaring on high with the eagles. You evoke such an emotion in me; the feeling is like a powerful drug that cannot be denied by a mortal woman."

Again we fell silent for a long moment before Jessanne spoke again, "I hope Captain, that you do not think ill of me for speaking so boldly to you; but I have not the will to resist." She said hesitantly, a tinge of fear in her sweet voice.

"I could never think of you as being less than perfect. I am the one who has spoken out of turn and brought disarray to your life; for that I am truly sorry." I paused then hesitantly reiterated that all was safe where her reputation was concerned.

"I think it best if I retreat to my lodging to study fates foul tricks and ponder a course of action to circumvent this dire situation."

"I shall be of the same mind, my Captain, and hope a solution to our trials will quickly avail itself." Jessanne said softly, extending her hand to caress mine in the most sensuous moment I have ever experienced. The heat that melted our hands into one could only be equaled by the best blacksmith's fiery forge; for try as I might, I could not break the bond between us.

"I must take my leave of you, My Lady." I finally whispered hoarsely. I stepped back a few inches with one foot and then the other, until we were separated by the length of our outstretched arms but our hands remained locked as one. I gathered every ounce of strength in my body to step backwards once more, causing Jessanne's small hand to slip through mine until only our fingertips remained in firm contact for a long moment.

"Good day My Lady." I whispered, pulling my fingertips from hers in a futile attempt to depart. Breaking that physical connection sent a cold chill up my spine and left a ball of ice in my middle, which continued to grow as I stood gazing into Jessanne's bright green, tear filled eyes. I managed to tip my hat and step back in one short stride before turning to hurry down the path to the street. I dared not look back, not for an instant, knowing it would only increase the pain both of us were experiencing at that powerful moment. I stumbled onto the grassy common in a daze, unsure of where I was going and caring even less, for at that very instant I could have walked unconsciously into a burning building or off a steep cliff.

ALVA SUTTER

I finally became aware of my surroundings as I tripped on the wooden steps leading to the porch of Mr. Mills' mercantile. I had walked two blocks in a blind state; unaware of whom I might have met or what route I had followed to arrive at this point. I shook my head to clear the haze just as Buck Mills called from his doorway in recognition of my approach.

"You are just in time." He said with a sly smile. "I have good news for you."

I stumbled up the porch steps conscious of what Mills had said and yet oblivious as to his meaning. What good news could anyone have for me at this point in time?

"I have just spoken to Alva Sutter." He said in a very hushed tone looking about to make certain no one was within ear shot.

"Oh yes." I responded quickly, finally coming to my senses. "What are his thoughts on the matter?" I asked dryly, fearing I would expose my consternation; but Buck Mills was too proud of his morning's accomplishments to notice my plight.

"He will return in a few moments and I would like you to speak to the man, if you have the time." Mills suggested with a wink of his eye.

"Yes certainly, I think it best that I meet this man to whom I must entrust these women." I agreed not knowing how else to answer.

"Fine, in fact I see him crossing the street now." Mills indicated with a nod of his head toward the door.

Alva Sutter was not as I had expected him to appear, judging from what little information I had gleaned from Mrs. Mills earlier that morning. Sutter was long of limb, heavily muscled with a mop of long black hair pulled back and tied behind his head. His beard, long, thick and dark appeared to be combed and groomed as well as could be expected. His clothes were of home spun dark material, both shirt and pants, and he carried a large brimmed black hat. Sutter walked with a proud determined carriage; and one would have to say he was indeed an imposing figure. As the man neared the mercantile's front porch and his face became better defined, it was easy to see the beard-shrouded mass of misbegotten features. I now understood what Mrs. Mills was unable to politely convey in her description and why people might shun the man. Alva Sutter had a wide unfurrowed forehead, made more obvious because his hair was pulled back tight. A mass of barren flesh sat squarely atop a huge nose that erupted from his thick beard and bushy eye brows. Each nostril was a large black hole, which allowed one to peer straight into what seemed bottomless pits. No trace of a mouth could be identified in the tangle of beard overgrowing whatever lips the man possessed. All of this would have been enough disfigurement for one's face; but Alva Sutter was cursed with large black eyes which were aimed in two different directions at the same time. I was aghast at the man's facial features but steeled myself to the idea I would not let superficial impairments sway my judgment of this creature of God.

"Mr. Sutter." Mills called out as the mysterious man entered the front of the mercantile. Buck Mills motioned for Sutter to come to the rear of the building where we three gathered around a small table kept there for loafing, eating, and informal meetings such as this.

"Mr. Sutter, this is Captain Lang." Mills said in introduction. "I believe you two have something of a common interest." The store keeper continued trying to make all parties involved more comfortable.

"I am pleased to meet you sir." I smiled and extended my right hand to greet the man.

"Thank you Captain, this is an honor." Sutter's voice was a deep rich base with a musical flare. "You see we have more in common than Mr. Mills knows, for we have met before" he hesitated then added "of sorts."

"I don't understand sir; surely I would remember encountering you in the past." I questioned not his truthfulness but rather both our memories.

"I did not always appear as I do now sir, my face was altered by an accident. I was a Sergeant in the war with Mexico, however not in your company. I was wounded when an accidental spark ignited a keg of gun powder. What you see now is the results of an inept drunken army Doctor. I would not have even survived if not for that very Doctor's male slave, one Bleeker by name. The man, now dead, saved my life and, as dismal as my life may seem to others, I owe that black man a great unsettled debt. This is why I serve as I do; one more payment on an account, which shall never be marked paid in full."

"I never knew that Mr. Sutter." Mills declared in astonishment. "Why have you not spoken of this before?"

"To what end sir? I mention it now only because I shared bloody ground with the Captain a long time ago. We are, as I like to think, brothers of battle."

"Yes sir, we are indeed as you say brothers and I feel privileged to meet you once again Sgt. Sutter." I thrust forth my right hand and this time shook Sutter's huge hand with real gusto and pride.

"It's just Alva Sutter now sir," he paused, "or the monster, or the ghoul, or any one of the other nicknames people have hung on me." He said with true pain in his voice.

"I do not think anyone in Mt. Zion has made any such referrals about you Mr. Sutter." Mills tried to smooth Sutter's ruffled feathers but the expression on the big man's face indicated the attempt was futile.

"Say what they will sir, in my mind you are a friend and compatriot, which we all owe a great debt." I said in praise of the man.

"No sir, I have neither self-pity nor true sense of loss for we both witnessed those who were not so fortunate as I." Sutter said with a shake of his massive head.

"That is quite true but I still must admire you for your strength and dedication to the memory of a depart slave."

"Thank you sir. That is very kind. But perhaps we should get down to matters of the present before someone comes in and becomes suspicious of our clandestine plans."

"Yes," Mills agreed, "you gentlemen may sit here and I shall keep watch from the porch while you conclude your business." The store keeper gestured for us to have a seat then he quickly adjourned out the front door.

"I understand you have some goods to be transferred?" Sutter's statement was really a question.

"Yes sir, but this shipment is a bit unusual I fear."

"How so Captain?" He asked with a puzzled look.

"I have two females for you this time. How should I put this?" I paused to consider a delicate way to describe the situation. "You might say we have two distinctly different breeds."

"Oh I see, one black and one white. Well, they are all God's children." The man said openly.

"Yes, the black one is young and small, the white one young and recently widowed," I said, "I understand the community leaders prefer both be transported elsewhere."

"Should I expect trouble from pursuers?" Sutter asked unconcerned.

"It is possible but doubtful; much of that group has been dealt with for the time being. As for the women, they are amiable and should give no trouble. I do worry about both of them. They have had a very trying time the last few days."

"I shall do my best by them both." Sutter promised in his rich deep voice.

"I am sure you will; it's just that I wish the elders would allow the widow to rest here for a few days."

"I fear this group has lost the courage of its convictions, sir. They have learned to fear their own shadows and matters worsen daily." Alva confided, looking me straight in the eyes.

"I understand their concern; but surely they took such a possibility into consideration before undertaking such a hazardous movement?" I asked of Sutter.

"Oh they spoke of the matter; but religious zeal and lack of experience with desperate people who are willing to do whatever is required to promote their cause blinded them to the truth. Many of the raiders who roam about are of very low character and wish only to benefit from these troubled times. Those who struggle to spread the power of slavery through legal avenues are willing to bend the laws to accomplish the desired results. In both groups we are feared and hated, for we also bend the laws and commit depredation in the name of our cause. Only one side can prevail, there can be no middle ground, no compromise; this is a battle for all or nothing. They know if we succeed it will put an end to slavery and destroy their way of life and the world built on the suffering of others. The leaders of the south have come to realize they have nothing to lose. They must win, by hook or by crook and will continue to escalate the violence until one side or the other becomes the dominate power."

Alva Sutter paused then and I thought I could detect a blush through the heavy growth of beard but I said nothing, allowing the man to speak further or remain silent as he so chose. "I beg your pardon sir; I have not talked so much in years, but I must warn you to look to yourself. I believe the tide is turning among the elders, especially Reverend Gates; it could mean rough times for you and John Brown." Sutter warned with a knowing tone, perhaps he had been privy to the leaders' discussions.

"Thank you for your candor Mr. Sutter. I shall look to myself as you say and how ever this adventure ends, I shall always consider it an honor to have met you again sir."

I think the man blushed once more as a barely detectable smile caused the thick beard around his mouth to move as he said, "The honor is entirely mine Captain; but I do wish that you will address me by my given name, Alva. You see the town's people; those who do speak to me are very formal and very stingy with their conversation. This has been the longest verbal exchange I have had since arriving in Mt. Zion nearly two years ago; and I must say I have thoroughly enjoyed it." Sutter said, beginning to rise from his seat to leave.

"I too have enjoyed our talk and, if you like, we can continue or perhaps resume at some time in the future." I suggested in all sincerity.

"I do not wish to burden you further, sir, but I greatly appreciate the offer." Sutter's eyes lit up and it was clear a smile lay hidden beneath his bushy beard.

"I consider it a promise, Alva. We shall sit in the shade somewhere and exchange stories of the army and names of comrades, who were mutual friends." I am sure the man thought I was merely showing pity for his situation but I truthfully looked forward to having such a discussion with another veteran.

Once Sutter had reached his feet, I too stood up and we exchanged a hearty handshake across the small table, where I felt certain I had found a new friend. "Good day to you, sir, and good luck." I said in a positive tone, to which Sutter replied, "The same to you, sir, and may God go with you." I felt his words were more than a mere salutation, more like a dire prophecy.

We walked together in silence to the front door of Mills Mercantile, then onto the porch, where Sutter uttered a quick goodbye to the store's owner, without pausing in the process. The man walked to a nearby heavy wagon with a span of large draft horse hitched to it, climbed aboard and drove directly out of town.

"Ain't much of a talker is he." Mr. Mills declared with a shake of his head.

"No, but I would imagine he has good reason to keep his own council." I offered in the man's defense. "Tell me how Sutter came to settle in Mt. Zion." I asked Buck Mills, as his presence in this small, out-of-the-way village peaked my curiosity.

"I can't really say. He just came into town one day with a deed to a piece of land east of here and took up living there. Is there some question in your mind about the man?" Mills asked as if eager to find a flaw in Alva Sutter.

"No, I believe he is just what he claims to be, a good, honest, God-fearing man, who has vowed to fight to free the oppressed. I would trust him with my life." I replied before stepping off the stores front porch and moving slowly down the street.

TRIALS WITH THE PASSENGERS

As I walked away from the Mills store, the midday sun reflected off of the rutted, hard packed dirt street sending up dancing heat waves distorting houses setting farther down the road. The combined elements of heat, exhaustion and thoughts of Jessanne were beginning to take their toll on my mental state. Of the three, I had control over only one, the lack of sleep. I walked slowly toward the Mills' house; hoping a few hours of rest would bring relief to all three problems but such was not to be. As I turned the corner leaving Main Street I encountered Reverend Gates moving in a brisk stride coming from the opposite direction.

"I have been in search of you, sir." Gates declared bitterly and I wondered if the man had somehow learned of my feelings for his wife.

"How may I be of service?" I asked with a polite, yet cool smile.

Gates moved close before speaking, as if divulging a secret. "That woman you saddled me with is ill and wishes to have words with you." The Reverend growled as if it were my fault the woman was ill.

"I shall go to her at once." I replied, not wishing to aggravate the man further.

"You had better see to it she is off my property by sunrise." Gates said flatly in a harsh tone.

"That is not possible; I just made arrangements for a guide to move both women out of town tomorrow night during the church meeting." I explained in a positive reassuring way.

"Is that the best you can do?" Gates demanded through a scowl.

"It is, for no one else is willing to act as escort; however, they will be gone by the time church is over tomorrow night." I promised in good faith, hoping the man would yield to the fact that nothing else could be done.

"Alright then, but if anyone is in my barn on sunrise the next morning they will be reported to the officials. Do I make myself clear?" The Reverend Joshua Gates snarled with non-Christian sentiment.

"I understand you better than you may think, Reverend." I said in an accusing way with a look which matched what was in my mind.

"Well be that as it may, I demand you see to those women at once! My wife is with them now, and I fear she may become contaminated with illness and spread it to me! I abhor sickness and those that carry it; so it goes without saying I avoid contact with such people at all cost!" The good Reverend announced with a chill in his voice.

"I thought men of the cloth were dedicated to treating the sick and feeble." I snapped back in disbelief.

"Not I, for those less fortunate were made that way at God's direction. I believe sick people are being punished by God almighty for their sins and I certainly do not intend to interfere with the work of the Lord!"

"Tell me Reverend, how do you justify babies, who have not sinned at all but die of illness?" I ask in disgust.

"That is simple. The child either has a black soul or is paying the penalty of the parents for their indiscretions." He answered smugly.

"Yes sir, Reverend, I know you better than you think." I said coldly, fatigue supplanting my better judgment. My eyes stared into his as my temper raged unabated deep within my chest. With that I walked briskly away from the church leader who had never stood very tall in my eyes and in the last few seconds had plunged into complete obscurity.

I muttered to myself as I stomped along the south side of the town common in a futile attempt to control my fiery temper before I had to confront Jessanne and the women in the barn. I did not wish them to detect any hostility in my demeanor, which would require more thespian skills than I possessed.

The last few yards of the walk to the barn were the most difficult for I longed to see Jessanne again but alone; not in the presence of a slave girl and an ill woman. I paused, straightened my coat and hat so as to look my best, inhaled deeply and promised to leave the outside world outside. I rapped softly on the west door not wishing to intrude on the women if they happen to be indisposed or if Mrs. Stuvant were resting.

In only seconds Jessanne answered my knock by asking softly. "Who is there?"

"Captain Lang." I replied in a low secretive voice.

"Captain?" Jessanne replied softly in a questioning tone, as she slowly swung open the barn door.

"Reverend Gates informs me that Mrs. Stuvant is ill and wishes to speak to me."

"Oh." Jessanne replied a bit disappointed with my reason for coming to the barn. "Yes, Mrs. Stuvant does have a fever and chills but I do not think it serious; however I do not recommend that she be out and about until we know for sure." Jessanne whispered softly.

"I agree, but we have made arrangements with a conductor to guide both of the women out of here tomorrow night." I informed her with a smile. "Besides your husband demands that they be moved to avoid you're becoming ill."

"I am quite sure Reverend Gates is more concerned that he may become ill than I." Jessanne said with a frown.

I smiled; glad the women could see through her husband's selfishness. "May I visit with Mrs. Stuvant for moment?"

"Yes surely; she is resting in the back of her wagon." Jessanne turned to lead the way to the rear of the small barn.

"Captain Lang," Mrs. Stuvant said in surprise, "I am indeed glad to see you again but I wish you had not come for fear you will contract my fever."

"I could not stay away, for I take personal responsibility for you being in this situation." I replied while gently placing my hand on the woman's forehead to gauge the degree of fever she suffered. "Not bad." I stated, removing my hand from the lady's head. "But we must be safe and keep you down as long as possible. We have made connections to move you and Jamaica tomorrow night."

I looked at Jessanne and then added, "Mrs. Gates is needed at her home; so if you do not object I will stay with you for a while."

"Certainly. I do not wish to be a burden to anyone, plus it will give us an opportunity to become better acquainted." Mrs. Stuvant suggested in a proper manner.

"I gather that is what Reverend Gates wants." Jessanne smirked at the idea that she had pressing matters at home.

"Thank you Mrs. Gates." Mrs. Stuvant said softly offering a weak smile in payment for her hostess' efforts. "I will be in good hands with Captain Lang here to care for me."

"If you are sure, I will retire to the house but if there is anything you need be sure to summons me at once." Jessanne instructed the ill woman.

"I am positive we will be just fine. After all, Captain Lang is my knight in shining armor." The young widow smiled weakly.

"Then I will say good day to you." Jessanne's voice was full of sweetness and caring. "And good day to you Captain." This final salutation carried a different inflection and was accompanied by a wide smile and a familiar touch of her hand on mine.

"Good day to you My Lady." I smiled and looked longingly into Jessanne's eyes with the thought that Mrs. Stuvant was too ill to notice our warm exchange.

Jessanne's departure from the barn diminished the spirit of the situation; but to save face and meet my obligation, I would remain with the ill woman no matter how weary I became.

"And how are you feeling today, Mrs. Stuvant?" I inquired in a warm hopefully uplifting voice.

"Just fine sir, thanks to you." The widow replied with an obvious lie.

"And how has our runaway faired today?"

"The poor child is suffering the very fires of hell, Captain." Mrs. Stuvant began dejectedly. "I do not wish to betray a trust but she has confided in me her life story. I tell you only because you are a God-fearing Christian and a true gentleman. That and the fact you might be able to ease her suffering." The widow explained.

"I will do anything I can." I replied wondering just how much deeper I could be pulled into this quagmire.

"Well, it seems Jamaica's mother Jewel was a very pretty young woman and was selected as a house servant for a family near Jamaica Point, Missouri. Being young and attractive the poor woman became, against her will, the concubine of her master. This liaison produced a male child, who died very young. When the master's wife died, Jewel became a permanent replacement and three more off spring were sired; a male named Hannibal, Jamaica, and a younger boy called Carthage; all named after Missouri towns. All three, like their mother, were given easier work and more privileges than the other slaves. But as the master became older his white children, who resented Jewel and her off-spring, began to usurp his power. Eventually, all four were made field hands and were physically punished at every opportunity. In desperation, Jewel forced her three children to flee to the north. She gave each a five dollar gold piece that accounted for her life savings, a tintype of their deceased older brother and her favorite ring. I don't fully understand the situation but somehow the younger boy, Carthage, became separated from

Hannibal and Jamaica. Also, the pouch containing all her mother's worldly possessions became lost somewhere here in Mt. Zion. Jamaica is completely distraught at the loss of her younger brother and those belongings. I thought it might be possible for you to learn the where-abouts of the boy and the pouch." Mrs. Stuvant asked softly.

"Did Jamaica mention her father's name?" I asked stalling for time to think through the story.

"Yes, Col. Jackson Woodside of Jamaica Point, Missouri. Why do you ask?" Mrs. Stuvant replied.

"Colonel Woodside is the name of the man who set Hixon and Ketchum on Jamaica's trail. Carthage, the younger brother, sounds like the Negro boy I buried on top of the Missouri River bluffs a few days ago. As to the lost articles, I believe I know where they are." I stated without any explanation.

"That is wonderful Captain. I just knew I had confided in the right man." The woman declared then hesitated a moment obviously trying to think with a fever racked brain.

"I fear Jamaica will be devastated at the news of her brother's death; but on the other hand, the return of her family heirlooms will surely ease the pain." Mrs. Stuvant assured me.

Jamaica had, throughout our conversation, remained concealed in the rear corner of the barn exhausted physically and mentally from the ordeal she had experienced while a captive of Hixon and Ketchum. The girl was in such a poor state of mind that she was of no use in attending to Mrs. Stuvant and certainly could not be entrusted with her sole care.

With that matter settled, I gave Mrs. Stuvant a detailed description and my favorable appraisal of Alva Sutter. This seemed only fair in light of the fact that the young widow's life would soon be entrusted to the complete stranger. She had no reservation saying she put complete trust in my opinion.

We then passed the daylight hours in delightful conversation, most of which dealt with her past and home life as a young girl in New England. She was well educated and had a wide range of interests, some of which were truly amazing to a southern male like myself, who had been reared around a completely different type of woman. The widow had a thorough knowledge of the bible, something I had expected being the widow of a minister; but I was pleased to find she had her own opinions concerning some of the more controversial passages which seemed to stir people to argument.

I was shocked to find the woman held a deep interest in firearms and most things mechanical, of which we spoke at length. Mrs. Stuvant was an apt student of my knowledge of ordnance, asking many questions as to the function and reason for varying designs. We spoke of science and mathematics until the sun began to set, and as typical of such ailments, Mrs. Stuvant's fever began to rise. I applied more damp clothes to the lady's forehead and kept her covered, as was the thinking of the time, even though the barn was uncomfortably warm. The addition of the Stuvant wagon in the barn prevented easy access to the tunnel allowing passage from the Gates house, thus Jessanne waited until darkness before returning to the barn with our supper.

My Lady and I shared a great joy at this reunion knowing it was at the cowardly Reverend Gates' behest; however, finding the sharp increase in our patient's temperature caused deep concern in our hostess. Jessanne called me aside after a quick examination of Mrs. Stuvant and said "I fear her condition has worsened and we may be forced to call on Dr. Rutledge for assistance."

"Is there a problem with calling him? "I asked a bit surprised.

"Rumors are running rampant about Kansas raiders headed this way and I believe the good Doctor to be a sunshine patriot. I have not known him long enough to be certain where his loyalties lay." Jessanne explained in a low voice to prevent Mrs. Stuvant overhearing.

"I see. Well, I have some very good fever medicine in my gear at the Mills house if you are able to watch over our patient until I can retrieve it." I said, offering to go after the treatment with the hope of making the night pass easier for all of us.

"I shall remain here if you make haste, for I must return to the house shortly as the Reverend becomes increasingly nervous someone will discover our guest's presence."

"I will return just as quickly as possible." I promised, hurrying through the barn's west door. Now enveloped in the dark of night, I ran across the empty common, firm in the knowledge that few, if any could detect my rapid movements across the grassy square as they would if I had followed the perimeter street. I successfully avoided the Mills' front and kitchen doors to prevent being delayed by an endless round of questions as to my activities or if I thought raiders were a threat to the community.

Once safely within my quarters, I dare not light a candle for fear my presence be known; so I was forced to fumble about in the dark. I quickly climbed to the building's rafters and retrieved Jamaica's lost poke from its hiding place. I then searched blindly through my gear until the small cork-stopper heavy glass bottle came into hand. Clutching the vial close to my body, I jubilantly retraced my route to the Gates barn and the women who waited within.

I must admit, the thought of encountering Jessanne once again did quicken my steps and lighten my exhausted legs to a pace beyond normal. I would endure most anything to share even the briefest moment with this beguiling female whose love would always burn deep within my heart.

On reaching the back edge of the Gates property, I paused to recoup my breath, straighten my attire and be certain no one was about to witness my entry into the barn. A little caution now could prevent a great deal of explanation later, if word were to get out that clandestine meetings were being held in the Reverend's barn. I slipped silently into the dark wooden structure, looked about once more then quickly closed the heavy door.

The scene within remained unchanged, Jessanne was at the rear of the wagon busily nursing Mrs. Stuvant and Jamaica remained concealed in the far corner, too fearful to join the other ladies in my absence. I suddenly had doubts if Alva Sutter would have any passengers on his train scheduled for departure the following night. But that was twenty four hours away, the immediate business was to medicate Mrs. Stuvant and see Jessanne returned safely to her home before Reverend Gates became even more disgruntled with the situation.

I have always carried a monogrammed collapsible silver cup on my person since childhood, which I removed from my coat pocket and half filled with water before adding an estimated teaspoon full of the white powder from the small bottle.

"What is that concoction?" Jessanne whispered, watching the medicine preparation.

"It is reportedly made from the bark of a tree and it is reputed to ease pain and fever. I come by it first in the war with Mexico. It was very costly and I use it sparingly, for I have failed to find the powder available in the north." I explained to the fullest extent of my knowledge.

"Have you ever taken this potion yourself?" The lovely Jessanne questioned just out of ear shot of Mrs. Stuvant.

"Oh yes, I have used it on several occasions when I have a reoccurrence of my own fevers." I replied quickly. "I cannot report that it was a cure but I did enjoy relief from the symptoms of the fever." I added, so Jessanne would not expect a miraculous overnight transformation of Mrs. Stuvant.

Jessanne held our patients head up while I endeavored to administer the liquid to the weakened woman. "I believe she will feel better soon and you should be off to home." I instructed grudgingly.

"Do you wish me to leave so soon?" Jessanne asked, disappointment clearly affecting her demeanor.

"Absolutely not, I wish you could stay on forever; but in the effort to keep peace in the community, I think it best if you return home. Also, it would go better for the Gates family if you are not present here, if we are discovered by those who wish to derail this railway." I hoped she would understand my heart was torn between spending as much time as possible with the woman I loved and, at the same time, keeping her out of any hazards which could arise from my faulty judgment.

"What if I do not choose to leave Captain?" Jessanne asked coyly.

I smiled and shook my head slightly, "I wish it could be so My Lady, but for the sake of all concerned it must be; life is seldom what we want it to be." I whispered out the words I did not wish to speak, and yet knew she must leave the barn's sanctuary within the next few minutes if tranquility were to reign over Mt. Zion and the Gates home.

"Yes, yes, I know you are correct and at the same time incorrect. I must depart but it is against my innermost desire. Will you walk me home Captain?" She asked sweetly looking deep into my eyes.

"I will watch you from the corner of the barn to be sure you are safely home, however I feel it best not to be seen at your side this late in the evening." I suggested, not wishing to give Joshua Gates any more fuel to fire his burning suspicions.

"Perhaps you are correct." Jessanne sighed in an intimate voice that tore at my heart and soul.

"If you are ready My Lady, I will escort you to the corner of the barn." I suggested, holding out my arm for her. Jessanne smiled and embraced my forearm, pulling it close to her bosom in a tender and loving gesture that came across clear and plain to me.

With my heart beating wildly, we moved swiftly through the barn door then along the rough board wall until we reached the corner where we had agreed to part.

The barnyard was completely enveloped in pitch blackness. So concealing was the night, we could visualize one another's face only when in very close proximity and then only with the greatest of effort. Perhaps it was our excuse for remaining within touching distance and, in fact, we were in direct body contact for the walk from the barn's door to its corner. Just as we had moved as one to the departure point, neither one could or would willingly break their hold on the other.

We embraced there in the darkness for what seemed only seconds but in all actuality proved to be several long silent minutes. I was so enamored with the woman, that I could not resist her charm and she appeared to be equally mesmerized. The warmth and softness of Jessanne's body against mine was euphoric and the scent of her hair stimulated me so that I forgot myself completely. Then in the blackness, Jessanne pulled my head down to hers and quietly kissed my lips. This moment of magic ended with the rude creaking of the back door of the Gates house, obviously a worried husband in search of his wife absent from her place at hearth and home.

Without a word, Jessanne slipped from my arms before vanishing into the darkness between the house and barn. From where I stood cloaked in the black shadow of the barn, that short walk was a dark abyss, which had just swallowed the only woman I had ever loved. Jessanne's journey to the house was a long moment of torment I feared would never end; but the familiar creaking door closing was a sign she was indeed safe within the confines of her home. I stared at that same rear door for several moments wishing to know what was happening within and feeling like a coward for allowing her to go. I remained so until the single candle flame fluttered out and total darkness took possession of the community. Only then could I turn away, my heart filled with pain and sorrow, my life ebbing through the very pores of my soul.

The barn's interior was all too familiar and exceedingly lonely as I slipped through the rear door. The situation was unchanged. Jamaica still barricaded in the rear, Mrs. Stuvant still lying quietly on the bed of her wagon, I standing lost and alone; all three of us suffering the fires of the damned trapped in our own little worlds. *"How,"* I asked myself *"could life become so trying in such a short time?"*

Admittedly, my trials were for the most part of my own making but still God or fate or some such power had led the three of us to our present predicament and now we must pay the piper.

This day had proved very tiring and, at the same time, exhilarating; but now I faced a long night of nursing Mrs. Stuvant and soothing Jamaica's tattered nerves. In truth, there was little to do for either woman, as my white powder medicine had indeed lowered Mrs. Stuvant's fever and allowed healing sleep to take hold. The young black girl, exhausted from her ordeal with

Hixon, had followed suit and now lay in deep slumber still secluded in the shadowy reaches of the barn. I found waking Jamaica to deliver bad news of her brother impossible; so I placed the red scarf poke near her head. I felt honor bound to return the girl's belongings but had little desire for the numerous questions that were sure to follow.

TERROR IN MT. ZION

With the other residents of the premises asleep and the barn's interior quiet and dark, I soon nodded off to a land of dreams where Jessanne and I strolled through brilliantly lit green grassy meadows that were bordered by beautiful blue and yellow flowers. We laughed and talked and danced and embraced, delighted with one another's company in the expectation that this euphoric state would go on forever. But life is seldom as we wish it to be and a sudden knocking at the barn door brought that realization to full fruition.

I struggled to regain my conscious self by rubbing my face and attempting to rise to my feet; my dream of life with Jessanne now shattered beyond redemption. A second, louder knock, validated that my senses were not playing tricks on my weary brain. I stumbled to the door, and struggled with its simple latch. Without the presence of mind to inquire who was there, I threw the door back to find Reverend Gates, his arm raised to strike the heavy wooden door once more. His face was livid with rage as he stormed into the barn angrily closing the door behind him. My first brain-fogged thoughts were Jessanne had given in to a moment of guilt and exposed our relationship to the pious minister.

"This is all of your doing Captain!" The Reverend bellowed while waving his arms in the air and pacing to and fro across the barns hard packed dirt floor.

"Please Reverend, lower your voice and show some respect for the females present, both of whom are ill." I asked in a low polite voice.

"I do not care one wit how they feel! It's their fault we are in such a precarious predicament in the first place!" The clergyman continued to rant and pace. "I have not forgotten your part in all of this either." Gates added in a red faced display of anger.

Suddenly, the barn door swung open then closed as Alva Sutter stepped in, only to have the door handle pulled from his hand and swing open once more. This time the three church deacon's Mr. Vest, Mr. Kimball and Mr. Boyd in the company of Jessanne hurried through the opening.

"I warned you this would happen!" Reverend Gates scolded at the top of his voice, his right hand waving in the air to emphasize his emotion.

"Yes, yes." Alva Sutter replied motioning for the clergyman to lower his volume. "I could hear you from the front of your house."

"It is my barn and I will talk as loud as I like!" Gates screamed in Sutter's face.

"That's true and it is also your life and that of your good wife who you place in jeopardy, not to mention the safety of these other people by such childish actions." Alva Sutter warned in a calm, yet forceful tone.

"Will someone be so kind as to explain what is so pressing to bring you all together in this barn so late at night?" I asked, now fairly certain whatever the dilemma, it did not concern my feelings for the Reverend's wife.

Sutter cleared his throat while his eyes remained hard on the highly agitated minister. "A freight wagon from Nebraska City pulled in a couple of hours ago reporting a group of men, most likely Missouri regulators, are camped at the mouth of Coon Creek. The teamster knew some of the men and they confided in him that they were here to strike a blow against the Underground Railroad and the abolitionist who ran it."

"I see, and you think they were speaking of Mt. Zion?" I asked numbly.

"Absolutely! Who else do you think they mean?" Gates' temper flared once more in a heated verbal response.

"It could be most anyone or just bravadoes talk around a campfire." Alva Sutter replied.

"No, no they mean to raid and plunder this town just because Captain Lang was foolish enough to bring these outcast females among us!" Gates' tirades began to show the mark of fear for his own safety more than a true concern for the community or church.

"That is unfair of you to lay the blame for this at the Captain's feet." Sutter argued in my defense. "We were in this work long before he came into our midst and, as far as I can see, he has done his utmost to protect the operation." The three deacons nodded their heads in agreement with Alva Sutter's words, but it did little to cool the Reverend's fire. Jessanne did not speak but the expression on her face said it all as she turned away from the debate to examine Mrs. Stuvant.

"Did this driver say how many men were in this party?" I asked, trying to assess the situation and at the same time allow everyone to calm down a bit.

"Yes, the driver said he counted twelve well mounted heavily armed men but there could have been more in hiding or still in transit." Sutter reported in a calm military manner.

"Twelve." I repeated. "That is a sizeable number and I would expect no more than twenty if indeed reinforcements are what they are waiting for."

"What do you recommend we do, Captain?" Mr. Vest asked in a meek tone.

"One of the first rules of war is to select the most advantageous battlefield possible and, if that fails, avoid the worst possible battlefield. The best sight for a confrontation would be to hold the high ground around their campsite at the mouth of the creek. The worst choice would be on the streets of Mt. Zion, where we would be on the defensive protecting the women and children."

"Then you think we should attack the raiders in their camp?" Mr. Vest said in disbelief.

"I think catching them off guard with a reasonable show of force could in all likelihood defuse this powder keg before it can be ignited." I suggested in hopes the town's men would form a militia and move against the raiders.

"No, absolutely not!" Reverend Gates thundered. "I will not permit our men to take on such a hazardous campaign." Gates declared as if he were the town's commandant. "Besides, if the men rode off who would protect those of us who remained in town?" He asked with obvious fear in his words, while declaring his intention of staying in Mt. Zion.

"That is a chance we would have to take if we wish to intercept the raiders before they can reach town." I argued firmly.

"Again, I say no. I forbid such a foolish move." The shaking Reverend ordered defiantly.

"Then I shall go tonight and attempt to reconnoiter the group camped at the mouth of Coon Creek." I announced boldly, moved by the spirit of my now hot blood.

"But what can you hope to do alone Captain?" Jessanne asked from an unseen position, standing directly behind me. Her words were filled with emotion that I fear the other men did sense.

"It is none of your business Mrs. Gates." The Reverend snarled at his beautiful wife. "Besides, I have not given Captain Lang permission to waste time in an effort to confirm what we already know."

"I do not need your consent Reverend. I am, if nothing else, my own man." I protested in no uncertain terms.

"I would like very much to accompany you sir; that is, if you wish me to do so?" Alva Sutter asked in a low dignified voice reflecting the man's spirit and courage.

"I can think of no one I would rather have at my side sir; but be warned, the ride could end with the forfeiture of your very life." I wanted Sutter to know I intended to make every effort to oppose the raiders moving on Mt. Zion.

"My life is of little value Captain; it is doubtful anyone in this community would notice my absence." Sutter stated sadly.

"I would Mr. Sutter." Jessanne spoke up in defiance of the hard glare Reverend Gates shot her way.

"That is very kind of you to say Mrs. Gates and I thank you for it; but come what may I will cast my lot with Captain Lang's wishes." Sutter said with some gathering pride, realizing none of the other men were courageous enough to ride to the creek, let alone defy Joshua Gates.

"If anyone else is willing to ride with us, I will retrieve my mount and meet you in front of the church." I informed the group; but I knew there would be no takers, for as I spoke, their eyes fell to the barn's dirt floor betraying the collective fear of the Reverend Joshua Gates. I turned in disgust and bolted through the barn door without further conversation; my anger plainly displayed across my redden face.

I have little compassion for men who refuse to defend themselves in a time of crisis; especially men who migrated west, families in tow, to an uncivilized land with the intent of making great changes; only to turn coward at the first mention of trouble. I hurried through the dark of night across the town common to the Mills home to retrieve Sergeant from the barn; all the while my temper burned with the cowardice of the church leaders. Fair or not, my resentment focused on the Reverend Gates, who proposed to forbid my going to the mouth of Coon Creek to confront these feared border ruffians.

COON CREEK MASSACRE

Alva Sutter and one other man, Wilburn Whitlock, were waiting in front of the small frame church, mounted, armed and ready to depart. The darkness prevented my getting a proper look at Whitlock's face as Sutter introduced us. Even in the blackness, I could sense the man's nervousness and had serious doubts about his value on this type of venture. Still three against twelve would have far better odds of success than just the two; so I said nothing and inquired if this was all that would be going.

"Yes," Sutter replied in a stern voice, "no one else will challenge Reverend Gates' decree. In fact, Whitlock is here only because Gates ordered him to ride along to prevent or at least report if we do anything rash."

"Very true, and I might add, it is only under protest that I am here at all." Whitlock's shaky words lent even more credence to my original feeling he was not a man for the night's work which lay ahead.

"Do I understand that you are not here of your own free will?" I repeated in a harsh tone which came with my years of military experience.

"No, no sir." The voice from the unseen man turned suddenly squeaky and I realize this Wilburn Whitlock was a mere boy.

"How old are you and how much experience have you had at this sort of thing?" I growled out.

"Fifteen, 'er sixteen sir and I never, well, I never been in anything like this before." The lad exclaimed excitedly.

"This night's work is not about deflowering some poor maiden Mr. Whitlock. I have no need of a chaperone." I snapped; my ire increasing by the minute due the Reverend Gates' interference.

"Did Reverend Gates, or anyone else, explain to you the chances of returning alive from this ride are decidedly slim, and being injured is all but guaranteed?" I asked. "I need only men who will ask no quarter and give no quarter Whitlock; men who have nothing to regret if they must forfeit their life." I lowered my voice to a near whisper and leaned near to the youth before asking. "Are you ready to die this night?" I heard the boy swallow hard then squirm around in his saddle nervously before replying.

"No sir; but if I do not follow Reverend Gates' orders and accompany you, I will be severely reprimanded and become the laughing stock of the entire community." Whitlock's timid answer made sense in a childish way; so I offered a suggestion to help him save face with the Reverend and the citizens of Mt. Zion.

"I have no intention of allowing you to accompany this meager expedition; but if you wish to do your duty then follow us out of town for a couple of miles then stop and wait for daylight before returning to town. When Gates asks what happened, tell the truth, that we got separated in the dark, if either of us returns to town we will uphold your story."

"Well I don't know. It's kind of like lying ain't it?" The youth asked, unsure of what to do.

"You will be separated from us one way or another son, either lost or dead. Now, I know which one I would choose if it were my decision to make." I explained in a fatherly way hoping he would take the meaning of what I said to heart. "Now, you decide as we ride out of town for we have no more time to waste." I half snarled before turning Sergeants head and hurried out of town.

The combination of physical and mental exhaustion contributed to the bitter feeling in my heart as the three of us rode south following the faint wagon road. The route, crude at best, proved difficult to discern from the surrounding countryside, while hurrying through the black of night with my mind and heart wishing to be elsewhere. At the first creek crossing Wilburn Whitlock fell away to my great surprise; finally someone was taking my advice. His departure raised my spirits and eased my anger a bit; but I still resented the church's position and Gates' attempt to control my actions.

Shortly, we cut into Coon Creek and, without a word, turned west downstream toward the Missouri

River bottom; knowing we must catch the raiders in camp before they had saddled their mounts and were prepared to move. The creek itself was small and muddy with a very narrow bottom which forced us to ride single file; and at times, the trees and brush obstructed the path so much we were diverted higher up the side hill. These restrictions were impossible to foresee in the dark and delayed our advance so much that Sutter and I lost a great deal of time; making our arrival at the raider's camp much nearer sunrise than we had planned.

Our first indication the camp was close was the scent of burning wood in the air; just moments before spotting the red glow of the dying campfire embers. The detectable smoke worked in our favor, for we knew any breeze would not carry our scent to the horses, and they might alert the raiders.

Alva and I dismounted and stalked silently through the brush to a point where the entire camp movement and sounds were well exposed to our eyes and ears. Two men sat near the fire and one stood guard near where the mounts were picketed on the opposite side of the camp. We counted nine shadowy forms stretched out on the ground in a small circle around the fire, each deep in a state of slumber. We were relieved to find the correct camp and exactly as the freight wagon driver had described it. Being in the wrong location could prove a grievous error.

With little fanfare, the world was born once more; this particular delivery, like so many millions before it, passes nearly unnoticed by those of us standing midwife duty. Alva and I realize this could be our last time to witness such a stirring event, took note of even the smallest of wonders unfolding before our fated eyes. The eastern sky slid from dark to light and the colors bled slowly from shade to shade; all of which were a wake-up call to the furred and feathered beasts of the field.

Just as the animals began to stir, so did the twelve closely scrutinized men after a nights rest at the camp on Coon Creek. No one showed indication of nervousness from being watched, not a one looked about their surroundings for signs of trouble, and seemingly took for granted all was well on this new morning. This was a foolish error for members of a raiding party in what one should consider unfriendly territory. Having passed a quiet night, they had lulled themselves into a false sense of security.

The two men seated beside the fire added fuel to the small flame as man after man rose from the night's bedding to join those near the fire; making an effort to chase away the chill of dawn. A tall man made coffee in a large pot and hung it over the now roaring blaze while another passed around a flour sack containing biscuits and dried meat. Their preliminary conversation was muffled by food and drink as was the sole topic of the exchange, but soon a tall man began to describe the plan for the day ahead.

The party was scheduled to depart in an hour, moving unseen to a point close to Mt. Zion where they would rest the mounts and reconnoiter the area on foot. They hoped to find blacks being hidden by the town's folks to offer as evidence of wrong doing; but regardless of the findings, at ten o'clock the attack on the community would commence. The tall man instructed that a more thorough search of the buildings would take place, and any man who stood against the procedures would be shot. The twelve men were all in unanimous agreement of the proposed plan until someone questioned how the women should be treated if they attempted to interfere with the search and seizure of any Negroes who might be found. The tall man insisted no woman or minor child would be molested in any way; but several of the other men protested vehemently. They argued that a woman could be just as dangerous to the success of the mission as any man and must be dealt with in the same degree of force. The heated bickering over this point provided a good opening for Sutter and me to move back out of earshot, where we could make our own plans for the upcoming day's activities.

We moved low and slow until reaching the horses before either of us spoke. "I hope you have a plan Captain Lang." Sutter said in a low voice. "Because it appears the teamster was correct as to the number of men and their intent."

"Yes, the situation could not be much worse; but I do have an idea of how to limit the effectiveness of these marauders."

"What is it, and how may I assist you sir?" Sutter asked with a questioning look in his eyes, for they were about the only thing visible beneath his large black hat and above the dense growth of beard.

"As I see matters, we must reduce the number of effective fighters to the point the remainder will have to rethink their strategy and possibly give up on the scheme altogether. Sorta take the wind out of their sails, one might say."

"That sounds reasonable but how do just the two of us accomplish such a weighty task?" He asked flatly. "I do not mind the expenditure of my life, if it will truly spare Mt. Zion."

"It is my thought not to take a chance with your life for you are needed at the barn this night. At what range can you be certain of striking a man with your firearms?" I asked with a warm smile.

"Two hundred yards consistently with the rifle and about fifty with my Colt revolver." Sutter replied in a confident tone.

"Good, take up a position at a hundred yards. My rifle will match yours; although, it needs a fine sight, and carries a set trigger that requires one to merely breathe on it to release the hammer. Now, if you keep both rifles and your hand gun while taking up a position near where we were earlier, I will circle around on Sergeant to a location favorable for the launch of an attack. Give me fifteen minutes then you fire on your choice of targets among the raiders. That will be my signal to ride through the camp shooting as many of the party as possible." I explained the plan in full detail; so my compatriot would see the advantage of him firing first from ambush, so as to distract the raiders; until I moved close enough to do a proper job of my horseback attack. Alva Sutter slowly moved his head from side to side as his eyes fell to the ground sheepishly.

"Is there a problem?" I asked in surprise at the man's obvious reluctance.

"Yes sir." Sutter answered ashamedly. "I do not think I can shoot down a man in cold blood, not even these low scoundrels."

"I know it can be very difficult; but this way you will have a stationary target and we will be assured of at least one man being removed from the threat." I argued. But I could see it was to no avail; so I changed plans and offered a second idea.

"All right." I said softly, patting Sutter on the shoulder to signify I understood his plight. "I will open the dance myself. I will move as close to the group as possible then charge, both revolvers blazing away. The sudden explosion of gunfire may stun them for a second, giving you a chance to dispatch a target of opportunity. Can you fire proficiently on these men if the shooting has already begun?" I questioned not the man's loyalty but rather his sensibility.

"Yes certainly, if they have fired upon you then I will do my part; and I promise two men will fall moving or not." Alva Sutter said in a firm voice raising his eyes to meet mine.

"I am sure you will Mr. Sutter." I smiled once more to ease his tensions. "However, if I am brought down before passing completely through the camp, then you hold your fire and return to town as quickly and safely as you can." I instructed Sutter in no uncertain terms.

"But what of you sir?" He asked in dismay.

"You will not be able to aid me; and your firing will only jeopardize your life and do nothing to prevent the raid. You can do more good by carrying the word of the raiders back to Mt. Zion."

"Yes I see; that does make good sense." Sutter agreed.

"Now, if my first attack is successful and after you have fired both rifles; I will make a second pass through the raider's camp with hopes of striking down at least six men with the twelve shots in my Colts. The second charge should take their interest off of you and allow you to depart without pursuit. If I survive the second little canter, I will move off to the west giving any remaining raiders someone to hound. In any case, you must be back at the barn by night fall to fulfill my bargain with Gates to have both women vacate his property this day."

"But surely even Reverend Gates will not hold you to that promise under these conditions." Sutter said in surprise.

"I believe the Reverend is a frightened man looking to place blame anywhere he can. I want you to promise me you will move the women out of his barn tonight; if not sooner irregardless of what transpires here on Coon Creek." I said, holding out my hand for Alva Sutter to shake in a gesture of commitment to uphold his word.

Taking my hand in his, the disfigured man smiled, as much as his tormented face would allow and replied, "I promise sir. I will see the females out of town one way or the other this very evening."

"Good sir, I knew I could rely on you." We stood for a long moment in the new light of morning, unspeaking but both knowing something should be said.

I finally broke the silence offering my hand once more. "Good luck to you, Mr. Sutter," I said hesitating before adding, "May I call you my friend, Alva?"

"Indeed you may Captain, for I have no other who will address me in that once familiar term. It does my heart good to think of someone doing so once more. You honor me with that one simple word, sir." I could see Alva Sutter was sincere in his comments and somewhat emotional in his reply.

"It is I, who should feel honored to have a man of your caliber willing to accompany me on such a fool hearty errand. Especially, in light of the fact that your church elders forbid it."

We shook hands once more and Alva Sutter wished me good luck as I readied Sergeant and examined the charges in both revolvers. I handed over my prized hunting rifle and once again expressed a warning about the lightness of the trigger on that particular weapon.

"I shall remember sir. And just to let you know I will fire my rifle first but not until you have passed through the camp; then I will follow up with a shot from your rifle. You should recognize its report and it will be your signal to make your second strike on the raiders." Sutter informed me in a respectful way.

"That is a sound idea, Alva and you be sure to be mounted and on your way by the time the powder smoke from my rifle begins to clear. No looking back, just get safely back to Mt. Zion." I urged the big bearded man to comply with my instructions.

"I will be gone before you discharge your last shot sir." He agreed then paused, looked me straight in the eye and asked earnestly. "Is there any one you wish me to notify?"

I smiled weakly then answered politely. "No friend, it would be much too difficult to explain the predicament I now find myself in." With that I chuckled softly, and I am sure poor Alva Sutter had not an inkling of what I found humorous in this deadly situation. I suddenly had an image of my father's face if he were to be informed I had been killed in defense of a band of hated abolitionist. "But thank you for making the offer just the same." I added with a straight face.

"Now if we are ready I think it best to strike while our targets are distracted." I said swinging onto

Sergeant's back and riding away without further ado. I glanced back to see Sutter gather up both rifles and begin to move forward to his ambush position.

Sergeant and I moved with great stealth, using all the wood's skills we could muster; with the intent of reaching a point where the hills jutted out into the Missouri River bottom just a few rods straight north of the position where the raiders held their war council. I hoped by using the hill as a screen, I could suddenly materialize and, in so doing, startle the twelve men into a state of panic. I crouched low over Sergeant's neck, peeked through some tall weeds, and when none of the raiders were looking our way, moved swiftly into place. The plan worked so well, I had time to turn Sergeant's head toward the camp, draw both revolvers and place the braided leather reins in my teeth. Seconds later the tall man, who had been issuing orders, spotted me and called out a nervous challenge.

"Who goes there?" He demanded as all hell broke loose in the camp; every man scurrying to retrieve his weapons.

"Death!" I bellowed and gave Sergeant his head. That was the signal for him to charge straight into the teeth of the enemy.

The raiders were caught completely unaware. They ran about pointing at me and running into one another producing a mixture of warning shouts and cries of pain.

Sergeant's uncanny ability to recognize the possibility of combat came to the fore once more; and with the spirit of a true warrior; the animal erupted into a wide open sprint toward the raider's camp. His sudden explosion caught me a bit off guard and I could have become easily dismounted; except the highly intelligent animal felt my movement and quickly compensated for my lack of horsemanship.

I did not wait for the raiders to fire first; instead I leveled my Walker Colt at the man standing sentry duty as he came into the line of fire. I chose the guard because he was closest and already up and armed. Even if I missed, just being shot at might make him think twice about taking aim at my back after passing his position. But as good luck would have it, the big .44 caliber lead ball caught the sentry squarely in the chest, driving him off his feet. From the shocked expression on the young man's face, I would say he was as surprised as I that the bullet had found its mark.

Sergeant raced on, unconcerned with the fluke of accuracy, as I turned my attention to the eleven threatening men dead ahead, who were doing their best to welcome my arrival with a volley of white hot lead. One tall older man tried to bring the men into a line of skirmish, so all weapons would come to bear on me at one time. However, an obvious lack of discipline and training prevailed for they scrambled about uncontrollably.

My thinking was to use six shots on the first ride through the camp. Thus, allowing Sutter to fire as I turned; and, because there would be no time to reload I would save the six remaining rounds for the second pass; that is, if all went as planned.

Sergeant covered the ground at an unexpectedly fast pace and we were nearly in the raider's midst when I chose my second target from the mob of men. It was of course, the tall thin older man who stood his ground in a professional manner, saber raised in preparation to give the command to fire. I leveled the smaller Colt in my left hand at the man's chest but hesitated momentarily, certain this tall man had prior military training and like myself, here to lead a group of untrained boys to perform a man's task. His reprieve was short lived. As he stared me square in the eye, the hammer fell on the primer cap and the black powder in the .36 caliber chamber exploded with a roar. The cloud of blue smoke between us obscured my view, but I knew deep down inside the target had been struck a decisive blow.

At that point, one young man dropped his weapon and ran full tilt for the rearing wild eyed horses picketed near where the dead sentry lay. Another boy to my right turned excitedly to face my charge, fumbling with the hammer on his ancient well worn military rifle. I was reluctant to fire on the youth; but it appeared he was nearing success with the faulty lock and was about to shoulder the firearm. I raised the Walker Colt and fired at a very close range. The resulting impact knocked the slender young man off his feet to an unmoving position flat on his back.

Foolishly, my eyes remained on the dead youth too long and it was with great surprise that I felt the sudden impact of horse and man, for Sergeant had picked his own target and succeeded in running the man down, slowing for a brief second to be sure all four of his flaying hooves struck home before moving on.

We now had a count of four combatants down, one fleeing the fight with seven still standing. I picked out a man to my left, as we neared the far perimeter of the camp grounds. This man was very large framed, heavily muscled, dressed in a black suit much like a preacher, and armed with a long double barrel shot gun. Long barrel firearms are appropriate for the game field but can prove very unwieldy on the field of valor, and so it was in this case. As I raced nearer, the black attired man struggled to cock both hammers on the great double barreled weapon before bringing the massive hunk of wood and steel to his shoulder. I knew of all the weapons on the field this was the one I would least like to be molested by. I hesitated not a second; snapping off a shot with the .36 caliber in my left hand, which caught the big man high in the left shoulder. This was a painful but not necessarily incapacitating wound to a man of this size. I feared he might still find the will to fire the double load of buck shot into me at point blank range. I brought the already cocked, heavy Walker Colt across Sergeant's neck and fired a desperation shot which miraculously impacted dead center of the big man's forehead. He died instantly; the shot gun falling harmlessly to the ground beside its owner.

377

Sergeant and I had now cleared the camp for the first time and we began to slow as I heard Sutter's rifle report from high on the hill above the bloody battle ground. Sergeant wheeled in time for me to see another man collapse on the lush green grass kicking in one last death spasm. It was then that the familiar report of my own rifle filled the air and a second man succumbed to Alva Sutter's capable accuracy. The man had delivered as promised, two shots, two targets down; that's all I could ask for and more than I had expected.

The count now stood at seven dispatched, one running and four effectives still on the field of battle. The tactic had worked beautifully as all eyes in the camp were now directed to the hillside high above and the unseen shooter who lurked there. It was time to start my second run among those who gathered in fear beside the camp fire, uncertain of what would happen next or how they should respond.

Sergeant pawed at the green sod beneath his feet in anticipation of the return attack while I hurriedly assessed the four men, who seemingly had forgotten my presence, staring fixated at the hill position that Alva Sutter had hopefully abandoned by now. I quickly assessed the gathered enemy for obvious strengths or weaknesses, but found only four thunder-struck bewildered boys. The seconds were ticking by; it was time to drive home the attack once again but deep inside I felt a twinge of pity for the men I was about to shoot down.

Sergeant streaked forward on command. This time I took a deeper seat in the saddle and leaned over the animal's muscular neck to avoid the near disaster of the first charge. Nearing the still distracted men, I released a mighty yell that could only be described as a cross between what became the famous rebel yell of the late Civil War and the war cry of the Plains Indians that I had confronted in the west. The war cry was an unplanned, spur of the moment warning to the opposition they were again under the gun. All the while I hoped they would turn and run. I had decided if they broke and ran I would not pursue but would fire shots over their head as an inducement to keep moving. But it was not to be. My yell brought one man to his senses and he turned, firing a revolver in my direction, the ball fortunately flying wide of its mark. Sergeant and I made a much larger target than a man on foot, and I feared a lucky shot would put an abrupt end to our so far successful maneuvers. I responded to the errant firing by pointing the muzzle of the massive Walker Colt at the shooter and discharging the weapon. The ball produced a heavy blow to the chest and the eighth man went down without further resistance. The man standing just to the right of the last downed man dropped his weapon and threw both hands in the air to signal that he surrendered. Just as suddenly, the others followed suit in a last ditch bid to save their own lives.

Sergeant and I raced past the defeated little army and hurried on to the north until reaching the spot where we had originated the assault on the invader's camp only minutes before. At that point we halted, watching every move the group made as they carefully gathered up their mounts and loaded the dead on the animals. They were very cautious not to make contact with any of the scattered firearms, allowing the weapons to lie where they had fallen.

Once loaded, one of the men called to ask permission to leave the field and return home without any further conflict. My only reply was a nod of the head and a wave of the big Walker Colt revolver in the direction of the trail west. I watched in silence as the little caravan with dead men draped over their saddles, began the long journey home to waiting loved ones. The scene gave me pause to think on how devastated their home folks would be, but my mind countered with the knowledge this party of men had crossed into Iowa with the intent to inflict the same destruction on the citizens of Mt. Zion.·My only fear was this minor skirmish might fuel the fire of hatred and escalate the fighting further.

EXCOMMUNICATED

The sun had cleared the steep eastern bluffs which bordered the wide Missouri River bottom, illuminating the pitiful parade of the dead and wounded raiders, who were disappearing into the tall grasses that covered much of its broad flood plain. The survivors wore the shocked dazed expression that comes with sudden defeat, and the loss of pride and feeling of shame that goes with it. Only minutes before these same men were bragging about what punishment they would mete out to the hated Mt. Zion abolitionists, and now those words would be recalled as foolish pride. Combat is a fickle master, and if one is to follow that discipline long enough, one will eventually experience the bitter sting of defeat.

I rode part way up one of the steep barren bluffs to watch until the raiders vanished out of my sight. I then moved to Alva Sutter's ambush site and worked for the better part of an hour to erase his trail north then I rode off to the southeast. It was my thinking to leave a long confusing circumvented trail through the hills and bottoms to the east before turning back north. My intent was to be in Mt. Zion by sunset, for it had been several days since my last true meal and a long night's rest sounded even more enticing than the food.

Sergeant moved easily through the steep hills and out onto the muddy river bottom as we made trails then turned and rode back a mile or so on the same tracks.

We found places to cross creeks, which would leave few, if any, tracks that could be followed by only very well trained eyes. The remainder of the day was passed laying down such a false trail that I hoped any pursuers would give up or at least be uncertain as to which direction I had traveled.

The time was quickly slipping by and the sun had dropped close to the western hills as I approached the outskirts of Mt. Zion. The ride had been a long tiring one for me while Sergeant seemed to relish the whole affair from the fight on, trotting into town, head held high as if we had been on a leisurely outing in the country. Mills Mercantile was closed by the time we passed by, as were the other businesses up and down Main Street. It was only then I recalled the church meeting scheduled for the evening and that Alva Sutter would be busy conducting passengers on the railway out of town.

The ringing gong of the big church bell calling the faithful home caught me completely off guard, for I was in such a fatigued and groggy state after several days of travel and excitement. The second time the clapper struck the bell's heavy metal side, I came to my senses and knew I must forgo the pleasure of food and rest in order to attend what I feared would prove to be a defining moment in the course of my life and that of Mt. Zion's as well.

I turned Sergeant off Main Street in the direction of the church and was surprised to see a large number of horses and wagons tied up around the small white chapel. It was just as I feared; people had gotten word of the current events and had come from far and wide to be witness to a bit of history.

I dismounted, hung my weapons from Sergeant's saddle, and allowed him to roam free. I dusted off my coat, hat and pants and hurried to the front door of the church. Slipping quietly inside the standing room only building, I paused to look over the congregation hoping to spot Jessanne's beautiful smiling face. I would have been better served to have had my attention on the strangers in the crowd rather than on another man's wife; but a foolish heart has its own mind and mine is no exception. Out of the corner of my eye I detected movement in a pew to the right side of the isle, three rows back from the A-men pew. The movement was Mrs. Mills beckoning me to come forward and join her and Mr. Mills in a spot they had saved just in case I returned in time for the services.

"We are so glad to see you safely home Captain." Mrs. Mills whispered so as not to disturb the other parishioners, who were whispering among themselves.

"Thank you." I said wearily, trying to smile pleasantly.

"Sure are a lot of folks here tonight." Mr. Mills leaned across his wife to whisper to me. "I can't for the life of me figure why."

"I fear I am part of the reason." I whispered back. "In any case we shall know soon enough; I see Reverend Gates." I said nodding my head towards the pulpit.

The exalted minister rose to his feet, straightened his robes and strutted to the podium, Bible in hand. I knew before he opened his mouth that this meeting would be a far cry from any I had attended before.

"Let us pray." The Reverend intoned before muttering hurriedly the *Lords Prayer*; then closed with "A-men."

"Tonight we shall dispense with the usual formalities and move quickly to serious business that has come to my attention. Dreadful allegations have, just this day fallen on my ears that Captain Brown and his subordinates have committed heinous crimes in the name of the church while conducting raids in the Kansas Territory." With that, Reverend Gates paused to look around at the gathering, his eyes finally falling on a spot at the end of the front pew where I realized Jessanne sat quietly, head down.

"The accusations reported to me concern seizure of personnel property, burning of homes and the murder of several innocent men." Once more he paused for effect while trying to gauge the response of the congregation.

Gates cleared his throat then began again. "Speaking as head of this church, I must make it very clear that we do not now or ever have condoned the use of force as a means to an end. There is no cause that justifies such outrageous behavior, certainly not in the name of God or the religion we profess to spread to the heathens who occupy this vast empty land." Raising his hand to emphasize his power, Gates continued. "We have also just received word that several travelers camped on Coon Creek were brutally attacked this very morning with as many as twelve men killed or wounded by unknown assailants. The reports coming to us say the travelers were in search of land to settle on, when a much larger group of men rode down on their camp and began firing. These unarmed travelers were unable to defend themselves and so fell easy prey to the killers. I tell this not just as news, but because one of the travelers who was attacked this morning is among us this night, for he believes the killers are from Mt. Zion. This man feels certain he can identify the murderer of his companions if given the opportunity to do so. I have requested this eye witness to the slaying to walk through this gathering and attempt to identify any individuals involved in this despicable act." Gates said with fire in his voice and a smirk on his face.

A murmur rolled through the assemblage, not in protest but rather in surprise that Gates would make such statements and then allow some unknown person, with no verifiable credentials to make such serious accusations. The murmuring was in addition to all the twisting and turning as all eyes searched the crowd for this mysterious ambush survivor.

"Please rise sir and do your duty." Gates insisted, motioning with his right hand for the man to stand up and identify his assailant. Slowly, a slim built young man rose from his seat beside Jessanne and turned nervously to face the parishioners; his face transformed from pale white to bright red in an instant.

"Now take your time young man and look every man squarely in the face; we want a positive identification of these cowards." Gates' instructions were intimidating to the youth and I believe the boy took the matter very seriously.

"Yes sir." The young man replied softly. It was then I recognized him as the one who asked for permission to take the bodies and withdraw from the field of battle.

Slowly, and with a bit of fear the youthful accuser walked along the front pew examining one male face after another; each one of which turned their eyes away nervously not wishing to be mistakenly identified. The process was lengthy and nerve wracking for both the men and their wives, who shared the fear of being held up to serious charges, not to mention the ridicule and scorn of their friends and neighbors. People fidgeted about and looked in silent dread at one another and pleadingly to Reverend Gates hoping he would put an end to this torment.

Finally, the youth came to Buck Mills, but quickly passed by the older man, and then it became my turn to come under the boy's burning scrutiny. I made up my mind I would not squirm but would stare the boy down for I felt positive he would easily recognize me and there was nothing to be lost but my own pride.

When our eyes met the boy recoiled back a step as if he had just spotted a deadly serpent with poisonous fangs about to strike him. I never blinked, but kept a stern gaze on the boy's face until he turned away and moved eagerly to the next man.

"Did you recognize someone?" Gates asked, knowing in his own mind I was indeed the guilty party, but was

386

unable to make such an accusation without giving away his own part in this conspiracy.

The youth merely shook his head and moved along more quickly than before, and it was obvious to all present the search was over. I had intimidated my accuser so thoroughly that he refused to declare my existence when asked by Gates to do so. Reverend Gates dismounted from the pulpit and took the young raider by the hand in order to guide him back in front of my pew. "Now son there is no reason to be reluctant for we are all God-fearing people here." Gates said in his most reassuring and inspiring tone.

"I am not afraid sir. I just don't see the men here." The youth replied sheepishly.

"How can you come before us telling a tale of murder and mayhem then refuse to point out the perpetrator who killed your friends in such a cowardly manner?" Gates began to lose his patience with the distraught youth.

"I never said they were cowards, in fact just the opposite." The youth argued meekly.

"Now son, I am going to ask you one more time if you recognize the men who attacked your camp. If you continue to protect these despicable assassins I shall be forced to send word to your people that you failed them due to you own cowardice." Gates bellowed while shaking the boy by the shoulders and when that appeared to fail, the pious minister slapped the youth violently across the face.

"That will do sir!" I yelled, jumping to my feet. "You leave this boy alone or I shall be forced to physically intervene." I said in a lower and calmer voice as I regained my composure.

"Why are you defending this yellow dog?" Gates snarled at me as I stepped into the isle and proceeded to where the boy stood dazed and bleeding. I grasped the stunned boy and lowered him to the seat beside Jessanne. She removed a white handkerchief from the wrist cuff of her long sleeved dress and began to tenderly wipe the blood from the corner of his mouth.

"Why?" I roared, turning to face the irate minister. "Why you ask? Because you brought him before us, then treat him this way after telling of the ordeal he suffered earlier this day. I believe the young man has suffered enough for one day; and I doubt he is a coward, for he managed to survive what so many of his party did not."

"I, as head of the church, cannot accept your defense; I must get at the truth. If there is a killer among us, I must do my duty and cast him from the flock. Now speak boy or else!" Gates demanded, stepping close to the boy to further intimidate him.

"I – I can't sir." The boy said hiding his eyes in his hands.

I stepped close to the youth, kneeled in front of him and said in a soft calm way. "Go ahead and identify your suspect young man. I promise no harm or disgrace will befall you for telling the truth."

388

The boy dropped his hands and looked me straight in the eyes for a long breathless second before speaking. "Are you sure that is what you want, sir?"

"Yes, make your accusation. Rise and point out those you feel are responsible for the attack on your camp this morning." I insisted gently helping the skinny boy to his feet.

The boy stood shaking beside me, his eyes scanning the entire congregation before mustering the courage to speak. "I – well sir, I feel quite certain that the man I saw attack our camp this morning was......" The youth paused with a shake of his head as his eyes fell to the floor.

"Go ahead." I said in a positive fatherly voice. "I know you can do it."

The boy straightened up took a deep breath and tried to look brave. "I believe sir, the attacker of our camp was you." The boy's voice trailed off and he stepped back as if in fear of retaliation.

"There that wasn't so hard, was it?" I asked my accuser.

"No sir, thank you for your kindness in helping me." The boy replied taking his seat beside Jessanne who immediately returned to administering to his wounds.

"Is this true?" Reverend Gates demanded in a wild voice waving his arms for added theatrics.

"I was there at the camp on Coon Creek this morning." I admitted.

389

"Then you murdered all of these men in cold blood." Once again the Reverend used his public speaking experience to inflame the congregation.

"I would hardly call it murder. These men were well armed Missouri raiders intent on attacking Mt. Zion. They were given warning before the action began so they had time to defend themselves." I argued, beginning to plead my case to the citizens of Mt. Zion.

"How do you know these men were going to strike this village?" Gates asked, as if surprised at the idea.

"I was close enough to overhear their conversation around the breakfast fire. They even argued what degree of force would be allowed against the females if they resisted the invasion."

"Who else heard this conversation?" Gates asked, raising his voice to a high pitch again. "Do you have anyone who will verify these accusations sir?"

With Alva Sutter serving as Railway Conductor that night, I had no one to corroborate my statements, but even if he had been present, I would never have allowed his testimony. "No, I was the only person to overhear the discussion." I stated.

"Do you expect this gathering to take your word, the word of a stranger and confessed murderer that these honest citizens were going to attack our town for no apparent reason?" Gates was now in rare form twisting my words to fit his agenda.

"I never confessed to anything. I merely admitted to being at the Coon Creek camp this morning." I growled beginning to lose my temper.

"We shall let the law decide that point later Captain; but it will go easier on you if you give up the others, who were involved in this heinous crime." The sly Gates lowered the volume of his voice, feeling he had won the case and certain in the knowledge that I could not tell the truth of the matter without endangering many other lives including Jessanne's.

"There was but one other man and I refuse to divulge his identity if this is a sample of the treatment he can expect." I thundered out. Gates was fully aware that only I and Alva Sutter broke his decree and moved against the raiders.

"Do you sir; expect this gathering to believe you and one other man were able to murder twelve well armed men?" Gates' voice flared having found another point to persecute me on.

"It was not murder. It was a fair fight. In fact it was I who was out numbered. The reason for my success was due entirely to the surprise and my opponents' lack of experience. If I had used such tactics on a well disciplined military unit the results would have proved quite different." I blurted out having confessed my guilt.

"I am not a complete fool, Captain. I do not believe you and one other individual could wreak such havoc on twelve good men." Gates declared extending his hand to the youth still seated beside Jessanne.

"Rise young man and place your right hand on this Bible; so that we may know you speak the truth."

With a great reluctance the boy gained his feet and followed Gates' command.

"State your name so that everyone will know who you are." The Reverend ordered.

"I-I am Jackson Willet, sir, of Lone Jack, Missouri." The youth replied in a weak haltering voice.

"Do you believe in Jesus Christ our savior?" Reverend Gates asked in a firm harsh voice.

"Yes sir I do." Willet responded throwing out his chest proudly.

"Then you know you must tell the truth after swearing on the Bible."

"Yes sir."

"Were you at the camp in question on Coon Creek when it was attacked this morning?" Gates asked in a mild even temper.

"Yes Sir."

"Did you see Captain Lang at the camp?"

"Yes sir."

"Did the Captain fire on you and your companions?"

"Yes sir."

"How many men attacked your camp?" Came Gates' next question.

"Well sir, I never saw any other than Captain Lang but he was in plain sight when someone on the bluff fired on us."

"Just exactly where was Captain Lang when the hidden man fired on you?" Gates questioned sternly.

"The Captain had just ridden directly through our camp shooting several men with his revolvers, then turned to make a second charge when the two rifle shots from above dropped two more of us." Willet admitted in a somber voice.

"Then you are corroborating the Captain's story that there were just two men in the attacking party?" Gates' face flushed and his voice grew hot with anger as the boy's testimony damaged his case.

"But you were fired on without warning, is that not so?" Gates insisted, his actions meant to intimidate the young witness.

"Not exactly, sir. Captain Lang suddenly appeared in the river bottom; and when our leader, Major Lowery challenged him as to 'who goes there?' the reply was merely one roaring word --- 'Death'!" Willet exclaimed, still feeling the chill of the word.

"What did Captain Lang do then?" Gates continued his interrogation of the young man.

"He gave forth a horrifying yell, and then charged our camp firing on the sentry before shooting Major Lowery as he attempted to get us into a line of battle."

"Why do you think Captain Lang attacked your camp?" Gates asked in a solemn tone.

"I do not know sir," came the youths reply.

Not wishing to further intimidate the young survivor, I remained at some distance.

"You swore on the Bible to tell the truth now, Jackson Willet. Why were you men in Iowa to begin with?" I asked, joining in the questioning.

"Why, we were merely looking for a couple of runaway slaves, which is our legal right." Willet replied.

"Tell us where you intended to search for these runaways!" I demanded.

"I believe the Major was headed for this village, having heard there were abolitionists living here." Willet said sheepishly.

"Now tell us what your conversation was about just before I rode into your camp." I demanded of the youth.

"I am unable to remember." Willet's eyes fell to the floor for he knew he had lied after swearing on the Bible.

"I remember. It was how the raiders would deal with anyone harboring slaves; and especially the treatment that would be metered out to any women found in the presence of slaves. Is that not true?" I demanded in a firm loud voice.

"Yes sir." Willet mumbled out ashamed to admit to such a despicable conversation.

"Still that is no excuse for the type of violence you inflicted on these men." Gates argued, trying to make me look as bad as possible. "How many men did you slay this morning in the name of Mt. Zion and the church?"

"I did not stop to count who lived and who died. Jackson Willet here loaded the bodies and departed without asking if I would aid the wounded." I replied.

"Were there any wounded or did all men die?" Gates inquired of the distraught raider.

"No sir, everyone who was shot died before we reached the main river channel." Willet explained.

"Let us pray for these poor departed souls salvation." Gates exclaimed raising both hands above his head.

I stood silently as the minister used his so-called prayer for the dead as a vehicle to condemn my actions and promote the innocence of the Missouri raiders. Gates raved on until finally ending with an "Ah-men", still pretending to be praying for the dead.

"Now Captain Lang, I shall give you the floor so that you may defend yourself of the accusation lodged against you at this time?" The Reverend Joshua Gates knew full well I could not elaborate further on the reasons for my actions without giving names and revealing the operations of the Underground Railroad. It was a gamble on his part but a pretty safe bet for he knew of my feelings for Jessanne, and felt certain nothing could induce me to expose her to the world as a criminal.

"I cannot and will not speak further on the facts of my life in Mt. Zion, for we have one Missouri border raider in Jackson Willet present and I recognize two more such men seated in the rear of the church. I feel it would be a betrayal to myself and those that support my actions to give information to these men in the form of a defense." I argued in vain, for Gates had me where he wanted me and there was no honorable way out of the situation.

"All right then Captain, would you be so good as to tell those congregated here this night of the two men you murdered on Indian Creek in Kansas last week?" Gates asked, the words poured smoothly from his mouth for he felt the exhilaration of over confidence in the knowledge that he had won the first round.

"Your use of the word murdered needs to be defined, sir. I do not consider the act of slaying a person in self-defense, or in an act of war as being murder. One man wounded me from ambush and the other, in a senseless act, murdered a minister just a short time before I encountered him."

"Then it had nothing to do with stealing a young slave girl from them?" Gates demanded in a high handed tone.

"I refuse to speak further in front of these Missourians, Reverend. If you wish to dismiss this meeting and convene a board of the church elders, I will justify my every action." I hoped some of the elders would come forward and accept my offer but they all lacked the backbone to defy The Reverend Joshua Gates.

"There is no need to burden the church elders by calling a board meeting when I can give you the verdict right now!" Gates gloated, a smug smile on his pale face. "We have no choice but to order you to leave this settlement at the earliest possible moment!" He then turned from me to address his followers in an effort to justify his usurping the powers of the church board.

"This is a religious community, founded to advance the word of God among the heathen natives and reintroduce Jesus Christ to our white brethren who have lost their way in this wilderness. We cannot permit men like Captain Lang to commit acts of violence while hiding in our midst and under our protection. Men of such low mentality will bring only pain and heartache, all the while professing to be followers of Jesus and that they are acting in concert with God himself. We must cast these serpents from our homes and our church or we shall fall victim to their sinful ways!" Gates' voice rose to a highly emotional level. It was quite obvious the man was an experienced speaker, who knew how to influence a crowd to do his bidding.

Pausing, Gates turned to Jackson Willet and said in a soft consoling voice. "Please, Mr. Willet be assured that Captain Lang is not a representative of Mt. Zion or this church. The man is no longer welcome in this community and will be departing shortly. I hope you will relay this to your people. Please convince your friends that we here have no designs on your slaves or other property, and that we welcome their visits to verify this at any time." Gates' words were as slick as any peddler or snake oil salesman had ever mouthed and it appeared that Jackson Willet was buying the fake bill of goods.

"I will deliver the message for you sir." Willet tried to smile, but Gates' earlier treatment still burned in the youth's memory.

I was still standing in front of the congregation when Gates announced his verdict and delivered the ultimatum for my expulsion from Mt. Zion. I raised my hand to indicate that I wished to speak; then stole a glance at Jessanne. She, in turn, quickly averting her eyes from mine, seemed not to see me standing immediately in front of her pew.

"Please allow me to speak for a moment, even though I have no intentions of expanding on the accusations laid at my feet. I must remind the good citizens of Mt. Zion that I did prevent a mob of dedicated, undisciplined, angry men from riding into this community. While I may be guilty of taking lives, I did so only in defense of and to protect you people. This is not what I came here to do, and yet, that is the larger part of the work I have been engaged in since arriving in southwest Iowa. Those of you who sit in judgment of me should consider why it was necessary for such measures to be employed in the first place. Willet and the other men were on their way to Mt. Zion in search of run-away slaves. Ask yourselves why that happened. These Missouri raiders were not headed for any other settlement or village, but for Mt. Zion. There must have been a reason for these men to take up arms and invade a neighboring state. I would think it more than mere hearsay that made this village and you people a target for such a raid. Now you have banished me from Mt. Zion and I shall obey your wishes and depart without further ado. I now realize that no one present here tonight will step forward to speak on my behalf, but study on this after I am gone. I know the slave-holding south, as I was raised in that life, and I must warn you that they are not stupid, unthinking louts, who can be trifled with. They have good reason to believe your interests here are contradictory to their own. Mark my words well, for if the guilty parties in this area continue to brazenly flaunt abolitionist views and activities in front of these individuals, there will be further bloodshed and this time I will not be on hand to defend you nor to take the blame." I paused to scan the faces in the crowd only to see most turn away from my gaze in guilt. Even Jessanne kept her eyes riveted to the floor at her feet. Her complete rejection of me was the most painful part of the whole inquisition.

"Now I will take my leave of you good people and bid a heart-felt goodbye to those I have grown to love and respect. And pray that God be with you throughout all the black days that are surely ahead."

I paused to gaze around one last time. My eyes settled on Jessanne in the wild hope that my words would endear her to me once more, but alas, it was not to be. The beautiful young woman remained unresponsive, eyes downward, as if in a trance that my mere words could not break. I turned and slowly walked down the isle of the little white chapel for the last time in my life. Another piece of my heart cracked and fell away with each and every foot fall that echoed through the silent edifice.

"Lord God give this sinner the strength to reach the exit without shedding a tear or turning to look back at all those who betrayed me so." I whispered. Once outside the door, I collapsed to the ground in what I can only describe as the most desperate pain ever inflicted on my person; yet my body was not wounded only my heart and soul were dying.

I lay prostrate on the rich green grass; the fires of hell rampaging at will through my body. The agony I experienced was as real as any pain I have ever endured and it continued unabated, even as the sounds of the church meeting echoed all around me.

Sergeant, my loyal mount, sensed the torment I was passing through and hurried to my side. The powerful animal nickered and stomped at my side; finally placing his muzzle against my torso, pushing and prodding until I was forced to either gain my feet or be wallered to death. Fortunately, for the sake of my ego, the unrelenting horse goaded me to an upright position before any of the congregation exited the church to find me in such an undignified position. I have never before or since known such profound loss and paralyzing despair, with absolutely no idea what would follow. Sergeant, as if ashamed of my weakness, pressed his massive head against my back and pushed me away from the church yard down the street in the direction of the Mills house. After a few good solid nudges from behind, a light came through the fog in my head; and I knew I must resume control and prepare to depart Mt. Zion before the church meeting was dismissed.

At the Mills house, I threw my belongings together and swung into Sergeant's saddle just as the chapel door opened and the congregation filed out. We hurried off into the dark of night down Main Street and out onto the open prairie beyond. Once outside the town proper, I turned Sergeant to skirt around to the west side of Mt. Zion where we paused a hundred yards out on the dark prairie to gaze longingly at the Gates' barn. It was there, only days before, I had held Jessanne lovingly in my arms and we had kissed so tenderly that I thought surely the world must end. In fact, the world did, for all intent and purpose, end for me that night as I sat alone in the empty darkness and watched the light in the house where Jessanne lived. My heart ached to be there beside her for the remainder of my time.

I spent the night at that very point watching the back of the Gates' home with tear filled eyes and a broken heart; hoping for one last sight of the woman that I loved. The morning air grew chilly as the break of dawn drew near, and I knew I should ride away before someone recognized me sitting alone, like an abandoned hound in search of a home. But I could not force myself to do the proper thing; mount up and ride out of Jessanne's life.

Finally, the sun cracked the eastern horizon; its warming rays struck my face driving the teeth chattering chill away. Still, I stood my ground and waited like a foolish child hoping for a piece of candy. Just moments after the sun cleared the eastern hill, the rear door of the Gates' house opened and Jessanne appeared heading for the well, wooden water bucket in hand. Half way to the well Jessanne spied me standing alone beside Sergeant. The initial shock of seeing me standing so close brought her to an abrupt halt; but just as quickly, her eyes fell to her feet and she moved swiftly to the well and filled the water bucket. I expected her to look up at least out of curiosity, but she quickly turned and hurried to the house without ever looking back. My heart had soared on high like Icarus of old; only to crash to the ground like he when My Lady refused to cast her eyes in my direction for even the briefest part of a second. I stood in deep despair, the morning light growing stronger by the second, and I knew then that I must mount and ride away to suffer alone for the remainder of my life.

I paused in my departure atop the same hill where I first viewed Mt. Zion. I watched quietly as the sun rose higher, illuminating the well-kept group of houses and the gleaming white glow of the chapel's steeple. The beautiful view tore at my heart as a wild beast intent on my destruction; only a beast would have mercifully ended my torment while this torture would go on forever.

With the sun nearing its zenith, I mustered the strength to turn Sergeant's head to the west, never turning to look back again but forever asking the question --- *why*? I would never find the answer though I searched for it everywhere. I have sought the solution in drink and war, in health and illness. I have inquired of the rich and the poor, the literate and the illiterate to no avail. This quest has become my one true companion for the remainder of my life. Though I have traveled far and wide in this country and abroad, the '*why*' has never been revealed to me. Why God had sentenced me to a life of misery, that I should forsake all other women, wandering alone from place to place in search of an honorable end to my plight, I shall never know.

I have, in the intervening years, passed unnoticed through Mt. Zion like a moth to the flame on several occasions; never pausing for long. It was my wish only to discern the fate of those I had called friend and to inspect the growth and progress of this once crude little hamlet, now a proper town. I felt like a father viewing his child from afar. In these visits I never once saw or attempted to contact Jessanne Gates, for she had made her feelings abundantly clear that morning as she drew water from the well. Still, I listened to the gossip around the blacksmith shop or the barber's chair to learn how life had treated the town's minister.

There is one consolation that I learned on these quick trips through Mt. Zion. I discovered that Alva Sutter did move the two women from the Gates' barn that night. The female slave girl was handed off to another conductor on the Underground Railroad; however, Mrs. Stuvant fell ill and was unable to travel.

Alva Sutter hid the young widow on his farm and successfully nursed her back to good health. It seems they became fast friends and soon married. I know now that she was a true Christian lady, who could see the pure heart rather than the disfigured face of a good man. I always hoped I would find the same good fortune; but I never encountered another as full of the Christian spirit as Mrs. Stuvant.

EXTINGUISHED CANDLE

"Now I lay in this abandoned dirt hut dying an inch at a time; the fires of hell welling up to consume me for my sins of loving another man's wife. If I were able, by some miraculous act, to roll back time and have the opportunity to relive those days in order to prevent a life of anguish ending in a gruesome death, I would not change one minute, not one second. As difficult as it may be to understand my reasoning, I will attempt to explain. In those few precious days I enjoyed the only true love I have ever had the privilege of sharing with a woman. True, it was just a few days of sharing, and only minutes of bliss; still I would not trade one second for a place in heaven, or to escape the pains of purgatory."

The aging cavalier lay back on the filthy bed; his body burning up with fever, his mind exhausted from relating the story of his downfall. The priest, weary from lack of sleep could not resist the desire to close his eyes when Captain James Lang ceased the narration. Both men had endured a long difficult night, and now as the first rays of sun streaked across the eastern sky and the smoky candle flame flickered low; Captain Lang's prediction that he would not live to see another sunrise was coming true.

The dying was painful, and the manner in which it was being played out was demeaning, but the worst part for Captain Lang to accept was the fact that he would never see Jessanne's beautiful face or hear her sparkling voice again in this world. But the real pain derived from knowing she would never be informed of his demise or how and when it occurred. Jessanne would never know to say a prayer or light a candle on his behalf. Captain James Lang would remain only a faint memory to the woman he had loved and remained faithful to throughout these long lonely years; a memory without an end, a question without an answer. Captain Lang suffered in the fires of hell, fearing he could not deliver one final farewell to Jessanne; whether she was receptive to the message was not reverent to his fevered brain.

"Please Father," Lang whispered, "please send a letter to Mt. Zion and inform them of my demise. You need not compromise your religious beliefs or damage anyone's reputation by merely announcing that I have succumbed to my wounds." The old soldier's voice tapered off from exertion and a sense of desperation.

The priest sat quietly watching the dying man, all the while studying the details of the story just related to him. It was, he felt, a tale of bravery and cowardice, love and deceit, pain and sorrow; but most of all it recounted life's unjust treatment of an honest God fearing man.

"I have studied on your request Captain, and I have decided to write a letter to your friends in Mt. Zion and inform them of your plight and you wish to send them a final farewell. I will not, however, divulge anything of your feelings for Reverend Gates' wife or comment about any of your military activities. I shall relate your pleasant memories of the town and its citizens after all these years, and that you wish to have had such a place to have called home. Will that do?" The weary priest inquired.

"Oh yes, thank you Father, I merely wish those who were my friends to be aware that I have passed on. I have no desire to generate trouble or ill feelings, for I would have nothing to gain from inciting discontent as I near the end of my life."

"Good then Captain, you may consider the matter closed and your wish fulfilled. And I might add it will be my sincere pleasure to do so. I hope that such a message will not disturb your friends."

"I think not Father, most will have forgotten me and the rest will be surprised I did not meet such an end long before. It is for those few who might care that I ask this favor of you."

"I pray my words console their grieving." Father Francis said in a warm and modest way, partially to console Captain Lang.

"I doubt if anyone in Mt. Zion will be distraught by my passing Father. The family of my youth has long since disowned me for my actions in Iowa and for serving in the Union Army during the war. The intervening years I have spent as a hopeless vagabond, always in search of Eldorado, but it was not to be. I never took root again. I found no place or person who could woo me into staying longer than necessary to complete the work at hand. I have been like a land bird lost at sea, with no safe harbor to rest; I have been forced to just keep going and going. Now, I have landed for the last time, in a place certainly not of my choosing but then one unattended shallow grave is as good as any other. In truth, it makes me sad to know that no one will visit my grave or even know who is interred beneath the hard packed soil. I guess this is just one more punishment suffered upon me for my sins, a punishment that shall extend to the end of time."

"I shall visit you my son." The old priest promised.

"That will not be necessary, Father; just take my horse and give him a good home, for he is a fine animal. Of course, he can never equal old Sergeant for intelligence and fighting spirit, but a fine animal none the less."

"May I inquire as to what happened to your horse Sergeant?" Father Francis asked.

"Sergeant met his end at a little battle just outside of Appomattox Courthouse the day before Lee surrendered. I was astride the great horse, and he was in the thick of the fighting enjoying every minute of battle when a cannonball struck him full in the head. He died instantly; collapsing beneath me, never feeling anything, a true warrior's death and the only way I would have wished for him to go. Strange, how a human will pray for a quick demise of a beloved animal, even to the extent of destroying the beast to prevent its suffering, while we will do everything under heaven to keep a human alive and suffering."

"That is because animals do not have a soul as do humans, and we fight to preserve that soul on earth as long as possible." Father Francis proclaimed, in a knowing religious way.

"I believe Sergeant had a soul, you may not agree, but he was far more than a mere horse in my mind. Sergeant was my only friend through those long lonely years, from Mt. Zion to his death at Appomattox so long ago. Sadly, I have had no other friend since that dreadful day in '65. I have wept openly only twice in my adult life; the day of Sergeant's death and the day I rode out of Mt. Zion heartbroken, betrayed and disgraced."

James Lang shakily raised up on one elbow to make his point but fell back to a prone position, his eyes closing, overcome by the strain of such a minor movement. The candle's flame flickered again almost being extinguished by the liquid wax held in a little crater about the blackened wick. The rising sun provided enough light that the old priest bent close to blow out the struggling flame but paused, remembering his failing patient had somehow linked his fate with that of the nearly defunct candles flame.

"Let me give you a little wine to increase your strength so I may hear your confession." The priest offered in his normal soft gentle voice.

James Lang opened his eyes before responding. "No Father, no wine, no confession. I have no right to receive salvation or reason to believe my soul will go to heaven. I have been a sinner my entire life; fighting other peoples fights, taking the lives of their enemies for monetary gain. Worst of all, I have loved another man's wife for the greater part of that time........ Sins; too many sins." Lang mumbled, closing his eyes with a slight groan.

"Please Captain, if I hear your confession I can absolve you of all your sins and you will surely go to heaven." Father Francis pleaded, realizing the end was very near and wishing to offer whatever comfort and consolation was within his power.

"No thank you, Father. I do not wish to demean your ability, but I doubt if even Christ himself could pray me into God's good graces." Lang said softly, flashing a very weak smile.

"You have never been out of God's good graces, my son." The old priest spoke reassuringly. "God loves you Captain James Lang and has never given up on your redemption."

Lang lay quiet except for his breathing which had become extremely labored and audible as each inhalation and exhalation required great effort. "May we consider what I have already related as my confession Father? I fear the end is very near and it will have to suffice."

"If you wish, Captain and if so may I now give you the last rights?"

"Yes Father, if you wish to do so," Lang agreed, "but please do not send me to heaven for I am positive Jessanne will be there someday and I do not desire to spend eternity loving her from afar as I have suffered that torment long enough."

"I can only promise salvation and that you will dwell in God's house, I have no power over who you will share heaven with." The old priest declared, not knowing how to reply to such a remark.

"Perhaps you can put in a good word for me to be with Sergeant in the hereafter, for he was the only friend I knew here on earth."

"I will make the suggestion on your behalf Captain." The old priest smiled, again not sure how to respond to such an unusual request. "Now you rest Captain and I will perform the last rights so God will anticipate your arrival and prepare a place at his side."

"Thank you Father for writing the letter, for I can now truly die in peace. I was convinced I would pass to the grave in the same way that I have passed my life, alone and lonely, but your presence has made these final hours more tolerable. May God bless you Father for all your good works."

"God has already blessed me my son, and having discovered you here, at this point in your life, is truly one of his blessings." Father Francis said warmly.

With those words the old priest began to repeat in Latin the words of the last rights which he had preformed so many times before. Somewhere in the middle of the service, the softest breeze passed through the open window and extinguished, without resistance, the weakened candle flame and so too did the life and soul of Captain James Lang departed this world. It had been a harsh cold unreceptive world of pain and loneliness, made better by the existence of Captain James Lang.

The End

Gary J. Pool was born July 18, 1946 to a poor southwest Iowa farm family. His family consisted of his father Ben, who was a World War II veteran and a man of few words; his mother Helen an insatiable reader and conversationalist; and an older sister Gloria.

Being raised on a dead-end dirt road very near the Missouri River, Gary spent countless hours hunting and fishing and became an avid outdoorsman. The author's father spent his life trying to raise his only son to survive being a soldier in a war, which he somehow knew was coming. This training fell in line with Gary's choice to serve in the United States Army. A tour of Vietnam in Army Bomb Disposal provided the wealth of factual antidotes for his first book, Xuc May.

The Captain and the Candles is a fictionalized account of the Underground Railroad and a small religious abolitionist town that foolishly becomes involved in the 1850's Kansas Border Wars.